D0529470

THE BROOKLYN NINE

THE BROOKLYN NINE

A Novel in Nine Innings

by *Alan Gratz*

Dial Books

DIAL BOOKS
A member of Penguin Group (USA) Inc.
Published by The Penguin Group
Penguin Group (USA) Inc., 375 Hudson Street, New York, NY 10014, U.S.A.

Penguin Group (Canada), 90 Eglinton Avenue East, Suite 700, Toronto, Ontario, Canada
M4P 2Y3 (a division of Pearson Penguin Canada Inc.) • Penguin Books Ltd, 80 Strand,
London WC2R 0RL, England • Penguin Ireland, 25 St. Stephen's Green, Dublin 2, Ireland
(a division of Penguin Books Ltd) • Penguin Group (Australia), 250 Camberwell Road,
Camberwell, Victoria 3124, Australia (a division of Pearson Australia Group Pty Ltd) •
Penguin Books India Pvt Ltd, 11 Community Centre, Panchsheel Park, New Delhi - 110
017, India • Penguin Group (NZ), 67 Apollo Drive, Rosedale, North Shore 0632, New
Zealand (a division of Pearson New Zealand Ltd) • Penguin Books (South Africa) (Pty)
Ltd, 24 Sturdee Avenue, Rosebank, Johannesburg 2196, South Africa • Penguin Books Ltd,
Registered Offices: 80 Strand, London WC2R 0RL, England

The publisher does not have any control over and does not assume any
responsibility for author or third-party websites or their content.

Designed by Nancy R. Leo-Kelly
Text set in Adobe Garamond
Printed in the U.S.A.
3 5 7 9 10 8 6 4 2

Library of Congress Cataloging-in-Publication Data
Gratz, Alan, date.
The Brooklyn nine : a novel in nine innings / by Alan Gratz.
p.   cm.
Summary: Follows the fortunes of a German immigrant family through
nine generations, beginning in 1845, as they experience
American life and play baseball.
ISBN 978-0-8037-3224-7
[1. Baseball—History—Fiction. 2. United StatesvHistory—Fiction.] I.Title.
PZ7.G77224Br 2009   [Fic]—dc22   2008021263

For Mom and Dad, finally

THE BROOKLYN NINE

First Inning: Play Ball

Manhattan, New York, 1845

1

Nine months ago, Felix Schneider was the fastest boy in Bremen, Germany. Now he was the fastest boy in Manhattan, New York. He was so fast, in fact, the ship that had brought him to America arrived a day early.

Now he stood on first base, waiting to run.

"Put the poreen just about here, ya rawney Dutchman!" the Striker called. English was difficult enough for Felix to understand, and almost unintelligible when spoken by the Irish. But the "Dutchman" at Feeder—another German boy like Felix—didn't need to understand Cormac's words to know where he wanted him to throw the ball. He lobbed it toward the plate and the Irish boy slapped the ball to the right side beyond first base.

Felix ran full out. His legs churned in the soft mud, but his shoes gave him traction, propelling him toward second base. He was a racehorse, a locomotive. The world was a blur when he ran, and he could feel his blood thumping through his veins like the steam pistons pounding out a rhythm on the fast ferry to Staten Island. Felix flew past the parcel that stood for second base and dug for third.

"Soak him!" one of the boys called. Felix glanced over his shoulder just in time to see an English boy hurl the baseball at him. He danced out of the way and the ball sailed past him, missing his vest by less than an inch. Felix laughed and charged on to third, turning on the cap there and heading for home.

"Soak the bloody devil!" one of the other Irish boys cried. The ball came at Felix again, but this time the throw was well wide. He pounced on the rock at home plate with both feet and celebrated the point.

"Ace!" Felix cried. "Ace, ace, ace!"

"No it weren't," called one of the buckwheats, a boy just back from the Ohio territory. "You missed second base!"

Felix ran straight to second base to argue, and was met there by the boys on both teams.

"You're out, ya plonker!" said one of the Irish boys.

"The heck I was!" said Felix. He stepped forward to challenge him, and the boy laughed.

"You sure you want to get them fancy ones and twos there muddy, Dutchman?"

He was on again about Felix's shoes, which were better than everyone else's. Felix's father, a cobbler, had made them for him—sturdy brown leather lace-ups with good thick heels. They were the only thing he still had to remind him of his family back in Bremen.

The boys looked down at Felix's shoes. That's when they all saw Felix's footprints in the wet earth. He'd missed second base by a foot.

"Three out, all out," the buckwheat said.

Felix snatched the ball from the boy's hand and plunked him hard in the shoulder with it.

"Run!" Felix cried.

The lot became a battlefield as both teams went back and forth, tagging each other and dashing for home to see who would earn the right to bat next. Felix had just ducked out of the way of a ball aimed for his head when someone grabbed him by the ear and stood him up.

"Felix Schneider!" his uncle Albert yelled.

The game of tag ground to an abrupt halt and the boys shirked away as Felix's uncle laid into him.

"I knew you would be here, you worthless boy! You should have been back an hour ago! Where is the parcel you were sent to deliver?"

Felix glanced meekly at second base.

"You've buried it in the mud!?" Felix's uncle cuffed him. "If you've ruined those pieces, it'll mean both our jobs! My family will be out on the streets, and you will never earn passage for yours. Is this why you stowed away aboard that ship? To come to America and play games?"

"N-no sir."

Uncle Albert dragged Felix over to the parcel.

"Pick it up. Pick it up!"

"I didn't step on it, see? I missed the bag—"

His uncle struck him again, and Felix said nothing more. With his speed he knew he still had plenty of time to deliver the fabric pieces, and time enough to go to the Neumans', pick up their finished suits, and get them to Lord & Taylor by the close of business too. He also knew his uncle wouldn't want to hear it.

"Now go. Go!" Uncle Albert told him. "If you were my son, I'd whip you!"

And if I were your son, thought Felix as he dashed off with the parcel, *I'd run away to California.*

Felix ran to where the Neumans lived on East Eighth Street off Avenue B, in the heart of "Kleindeutschland," Little Germany. Their tenement stood in the shadow of a fancier building facing the street on the same lot. The Neumans lived on the fourth floor, two brothers and their families squeezed into a one-family flat with three rooms and no windows. Felix hated visiting there. It made him think of those preachers who stood on street corners throughout Kleindeutschland yelling warnings of damnation and hell. As much as he disliked his uncle, Felix knew that but for Uncle Albert's job as a cutter, their own Kleindeutschland flat would look like this. Or worse.

One of the Neuman boys, not much older than Felix, met him at the door. Felix only knew him from deliveries and pickups—he'd never seen any of the Neuman boys playing on Little Germany's streets or empty lots.

"Guten tag," the boy said.

"Good morning," said Felix. He held out the parcel. "I've got your new pieces."

The boy let Felix into the room. It was hot and dark, and Neumans young and old sweated as they sewed cut pieces of cloth into suits around the dim light of four flickering candles. Herr Neuman, the family "foreman," came forward to take the package from Felix.

"Danke schön," Herr Neuman said.

"You're welcome," Felix said. *"Bitte."*

Herr Neuman set the parcel on a table and opened it, counting out the pieces. He nodded to let Felix know everything was in order.

"Do you have anything for me to take back?" Felix asked. *"Haben Sie noch etwas fertig?"*

Herr Neuman held up a finger and went into another room. Felix waved to one or two of the women who looked up at him with weak smiles. Felix knew this wasn't what they had expected when they'd come to America. It wasn't what any of them had expected. Felix's own father had talked of New York as a promised land, where everyone had good jobs and plenty to eat. "Manhattan is a city of three hundred thousand," he'd said, "and half of those are men who will need a good pair of shoes." Herr Neuman, a skilled tailor, had probably said the same thing to his family about the men in Manhattan needing suits.

What neither of them knew, of course, what none of the

9

tailors and cobblers and haberdashers had known, was that those hundred and fifty thousand men needed only five men to sell them suits and shoes: Mr. A. T. Stewart, Messrs. Lord and Taylor, and the brothers Brooks. The five of them owned the three largest clothing stores in New York, massive, three- and four-story buildings Felix had gotten lost in more than once. Each had separate departments for men, women, and children, an army of clerks and fitters, and tables and tables of clothes, each outfit made not by a single tailor but by teams of men and women paid a fraction of what the suit cost. Felix, his uncle Albert, the Neumans, they were all just cogs in the great department store machine. Uncle Albert did nothing now but cut cloth all day, but he was better off than the Neumans, who sewed collars by candlelight sixteen hours a day, seven days a week. If they worked quickly, the Neumans might make twenty dollars a week sewing suits. Uncle Albert earned that by himself as a cutter.

Herr Neuman returned with a package of finished suits tied up with a string, and Felix left quickly, telling them he had to hurry the parcel back to Lord & Taylor but really just wanting to get away from there.

Felix ran past Tompkins Square Park to the Bowery, leaving Kleindeutschland and its crowded tenements and beer halls in his wake, but when he hit Broadway he slowed. This was Felix's favorite part of the city. Here the pigs being driven to market strutted down the sidewalk alongside flashy American women wearing their big, brightly colored dresses and ribbons. Gentlemen in serious gray suits hurried by with pocket watches in hand while b'hoys with curled mustaches and red shirts and black silk ties mocked them from painters' scaffolding and butcher shop doorways. Newsboys and street preachers shouted over each other on the corners. Buildings were torn down and rebuilt faster than Felix could keep up with them, and shootouts sometimes erupted in the streets. This wasn't the New York of the Germans or the Irish or the English, it was the New York of *Americans*, and Felix tucked his package under his arm and fell into step with the bustle of the young city.

Uncle Albert had warned him not to dawdle on the way, so he hurried along—fully intending to do his dawdling on the way back. At Lord & Taylor Felix delivered his package and picked up another, then made his way farther north on Broadway, adopting the American swagger of the lords, ladies, and swine. Felix found it easy to lose himself in Broadway's foot traffic, to be swept up by the rush and hurry of Manhattan, to hear the clatter of iron horseshoes on cobblestones and the catcalls and insults of the city's famously rude cabbies like a lullaby. On Broadway Felix was not a poor German Jew from Bremen walking the streets of a strange metropolis. Here, he was a *New Yorker*.

Felix made his way up Broadway to Madison Square, then down East Twenty-seventh Street to the corner of Fourth Avenue, where the New York Knickerbockers played baseball. He had found them by accident one day, following an oddly dressed man wearing blue woolen pantaloons, a white flannel shirt, and a straw hat, and now he went by the lot every time he ventured this far north in case a game was under way.

Felix had been overjoyed to discover grown men playing at the same game he and his friends played—only it wasn't *exactly* the same game. The Knickerbockers played three-out, all-out, but with more gentlemanly rules. For one thing, they didn't chase each other in between innings to see which team would bat next. For another, they didn't "soak" runners, but instead tried to deliver the ball to the next base before the runner could advance.

A game was under way when Felix arrived, and he joined three other spectators on a bank nearby, using the parcel with the cut cloth pieces as a seat cushion. The Striker at bat called for his pitch and smacked it to the outer field, where it was caught on the bounce.

"Hand out!" the Feeder cried, and the Striker tipped his cap and jogged merrily back to the sidelines.

Felix would have given all the sauerkraut in Kleindeutschland to be out there on the field with them. A new Striker took his place, and Felix imagined himself standing there in the blue and white uniform of the Knickerbockers, ready to deliver a base hit for his team.

The Striker bounced the first feed wide of first base, but didn't run.

"Foul ball," the Feeder called, and the Striker returned home to bat again.

This is new, Felix thought, and he watched as the Feeder pitched again and again until the Striker was able to hit the ball in the field between first and third base. Letting "foul balls" go would certainly save a lot of chasing, Felix realized, and let the fielding team concentrate its defenders in front of the batter, instead of all around him. There was still a catcher, he noted, but mainly to receive the pitches the Striker chose not to hit.

This was less and less the three-out, all-out Felix knew, but he liked it.

The next Striker put a well-placed ball in between two of the outlying fielders and scampered toward second. The ball was thrown back in quickly, and appeared to reach second base at the same time as the runner. Neither team could tell whether the Striker was out or not, and the top-hatted judge at the table beyond third base admitted he hadn't a clue. The judge came forward to examine the evidence, then threw his hands up in exasperation.

"Let us ask the young squire with the very nice shoes," one of the Knickerbockers said. With a start, Felix realized the player was talking about him. The judge and three of the players came over to where he sat.

"I—I think the ball beat the Striker," Felix told them.

"There we have it then," said the Feeder.

"Agreed," said the man in the top hat. "Umpire's decision: hand out."

13

"Three-out, all-out," the Feeder said, smiling. The Striker tipped his cap and jogged out onto the field to take his position at a base, but the Feeder remained on the sidelines and extended his hand. Felix shook it.

"Alexander Cartwright," the Feeder said. "And on behalf of the New York Knickerbocker Volunteer Fire Fighting Brigade, I'd like to thank you for your honest and impartial observation. I've seen you here before, haven't I?"

Felix didn't answer. He was transfixed by something over Cartwright's shoulder, a towering plume of smoke billowing up from the rooftops of the city to the south of them.

Manhattan was on fire.

2

Church bells pealed across the city, and Cartwright and the rest of the volunteer fire brigade abandoned their game and raced the few blocks to their station to ready their wagon. Felix followed behind, watching the smoke thicken. The smell of it was already heavy in the air, the way Aunt Jenell's stove smelled when first lit each morning. At the firehouse the ballplayers were quickly joined by other men who stripped off their suit coats and collars and ties and changed into the colorful blue jerseys of the Knickerbocker Volunteer Fire Fighting Brigade before taking their places around the engine. The brigade had no horse, so the cart would have to be guided by hand.

"I'm fast," Felix told Cartwright. "I can help you push."

Cartwright considered Felix's offer, and looked like he might say no. In the distance, a bigger, deeper bell started to sound over the church bells.

"If they're ringing the bell at City Hall, it's a big one. You're probably safer with us than without," Cartwright said. He tossed a blue shirt to Felix. "Put this on so we'll know you're a Knickerbocker."

Felix worked himself into the oversized shirt and grabbed hold of the wagon.

"All together now, lads," Cartwright called. "And, *push!*"

The cobblestones made the going rough at first, but as Felix and the others built up speed he felt the wagon bounce along without too much trouble. Turning was difficult, though, and as they ran the men debated the straightest path through the city.

"Fourth Avenue to Union, then Broadway south!"

"No, Broadway will be jammed! The Bowery."

Felix pushed with all his strength, but the cart had to stop as often as it started. Everywhere men and ladies poured into the street to see the smoke, making the already clogged avenue even worse. Cartwright rang the bell on the wagon and they nudged on, sending curious gawkers scurrying for the sidewalk.

And then they hit Union Square. The traffic was at a dead standstill.

"Make way! Make way! Emergency!" one of the firemen called.

But no one could move. The streets were so hopelessly packed it was almost impossible to cross the square on foot. Horses reared in the close quarters. Carriages scraped the sides of cabs and omnibuses. Men yelled obscenities at each other. Across the square a fistfight broke out. Cartwright

16

gave the bell an angry clang and slapped his hat on the tank. Through the tree-lined hills of Union Square, Felix could see their destination—the open expanse of Fourth Avenue south of the Bowery.

"Mr. Cartwright," Felix called. "The park!"

At first Cartwright didn't understand, but then he nodded and smiled at Felix and went to work again on his bell.

"Let us through! Make way! Push on to the park, lads!"

It took them a full quarter of an hour to ford the frozen river of carriages the short distance to the corner of Union Square Park, upsetting an apple cart and managing to turn another carriage completely around on the way. Felix wondered if they'd just made things worse, but it was the fire, not the traffic, that mattered now. The closer they got, the more Felix worried the fire was in Kleindeutschland. The entire skyline to the south was grayish black.

At last the Knickerbockers pushed their engine up the curb into the wooded expanse of the park. One or two of the stranded drivers close by cursed them, but Felix thought they were probably just sore at not having thought of it first. With a heave, the volunteer firefighters started their shortcut across the square. A couple of the men near Felix gave him smiles and patted him on the back.

The smiles soon turned to scowls, however, as none of them had ever reckoned how difficult it was to run up a park hill with a cast-iron tank. Felix dug in with his good shoes and gave it all he was worth, and with great effort the brigade slogged its way up and down the rolling hills of the park. An explosion to the south—a gas line, one of the men guessed—brought screams from the ladies caught in the throng of carriages around the square. Felix redoubled his efforts. There was another sea of vehicles to cross when they reached the other side of the square, but like a needle through leather they eventually found their way through, and the angry glares from the volunteers became smiles and weary pats on the back again.

South of Union Square Felix and the Knickerbockers were back at a trot, the streets clear of everyone now but rescue workers. Everyone else had fled farther north.

"The size of that smoke cloud, three or four buildings must be on fire," one of the company guessed. "Perhaps a whole city block."

The sky was black as coal as they drew near, and to Felix's relief it wasn't Kleindeutschland that was on fire. It wasn't three or four buildings that were burning, though. It wasn't even three or four blocks. *All of lower Manhattan* was on fire. Local fire brigades were already on the scene, and more poured in from all over the city: First two, then five, then nine, then fourteen, and more, but Felix began to despair that there would never be enough. Buildings burned down Water Street as far as Felix could see.

The heat from the flames was blistering as the Knickerbockers searched for an unoccupied cistern to drop their hose in. The air itself wobbled, as though the fire was melting it. Against the overpowering heat was the strange sensation that it was snowing, and Felix watched as burned-out cinders the size of quarters fell on everything, turning the Knickerbockers' bright blue uniforms to the color of thick gray ash. He could taste it too; it was like he had licked a stovepipe. The heat and the ash made Felix's eyes water, but his tears evaporated almost as quickly as they came.

The Knickerbockers pulled to a stop as the blaze rose from the roof of a five-story building beside them. The wind off the East River carried the fire like swirling leaves across the street, where it set the canvas awnings of another building ablaze. Suddenly the fire brigade was not on the edge of the inferno, but inside it.

Felix spun. Fire was everywhere around him and he panicked. His family seemed very far away from him now, more than a passenger ticket away, more than an ocean away. He felt sealed off from his family back in Bremen by a wall of flame, and for the first time in his life he thought he might die before seeing his mother and father again.

A hand on his shoulder stopped his spinning.

"Keep your head," Cartwright told him. "I never meant you to come this far, lad, but I'll see you safely home."

The Knickerbockers pushed on to William Street to escape the blaze, but the air there was too thick to breathe. One of the men collapsed, choking and gasping, and Felix helped haul him up onto the cart before they retreated to Hanover Street, where one of the company knew a cistern

19

could be found. No brigade had yet laid claim to it, and the Knickerbockers pried off the lid to the underground reservoir and snaked down their hose. Two of the brawniest members of the brigade took to the hand pump, and soon water was gushing through the network of hoses Felix helped put together. Water splashed from the nozzle into the broken windows of a clerical office, but after half an hour it was obvious to Felix that they weren't doing any good. If anything, the fire was getting worse.

From the look on Cartwright's face, he thought the same thing.

"The fire's too strong," he yelled over the clang of the bells, the rush of the water, and the roar of the flames.

"What can we do?" Felix asked. His skin was coated with a thick film of sweat, and his tongue tasted like burned matches.

"Maybe farther back—Wall Street, or Pine—"

Glass shattered and rained down on the sidewalk as the fire ate its way down through the floors of the warehouse behind them.

"The dry goods!" Cartwright yelled. "Salvage what you can before the buildings collapse!"

Men traded out places at the hand pumps to keep the water coming while the rest of the brigade smashed their way into warehouses with axes and hooks. Felix stood back, waiting until the doors were knocked down and the entrances sprayed with water to rush inside with the others. The first storehouse

Felix entered was filled with bolts of cloth—suit material like the kind he ran back and forth to Lord & Taylor. He and Cartwright began heaping the stuff in the middle of the street. Rolls of cottons, woolens, and silks joined bags of coffee beans, mounds of lace, stacks of paper records, bottles of liquor—anything and everything that could be saved.

Conditions grew worse and worse. One team barely escaped a vicious backdraft. Another became trapped when a second story fell in, and the men had to be rescued with axes.

"That's it, young squire," Cartwright told Felix. "You're confined to the wagon."

A man in a fire chief's hat rode up on a horse before Felix could argue.

"The fire's out of control, Mr. Anderson," Cartwright said. "We're doing all we can to save the goods in these warehouses, but—"

Felix saw the fiery piece of debris fluttering down toward the pile of stores in the street before anyone else, but there was nothing he could do—nothing any of them could have done. The moment it touched down the lace caught fire, then the cotton, and almost at once the mountain of dry goods was a blazing bonfire that drove them off the street.

"Fall back!" the fire chief called. "Retreat!"

The fire truck was trapped on the other side of the pyre, but the pumpers ran it through, singeing themselves and the cart in the process. Cartwright and the others turned what was left in the tank on the boys who'd come through the flames to make sure they were extinguished, and then everyone fell back to Wall Street.

"The glow and the smoke are so strong that crews from Philadelphia and New Haven turned out in their own suburbs, thinking the blaze was in their own cities," the fire chief said, his horse dancing backward, the only one among them with the sense to run. "The Pennsylvania and Connecticut crews telegraphed to say they're on the way, but they'll not be here in time to prevent the conflagration from jumping Wall Street."

Felix knew what that meant. Lower Manhattan was all businesses and warehouses, but beyond the road where a real wall had once stood were residences. Apartments. People. The thirty thousand souls who called the island their home. If the fire blew north, it could overtake City Hall and the Five Points slums. If it blew to the northeast, it might spread as far as the crowded tenements of Kleindeutschland—Felix's home.

"Powder then?" Cartwright asked.

The fire chief nodded. "Some of the boys are already rowing across to the Navy Yard in Brooklyn, but they may not be in time."

"We'll round up what we can from the groceries," said Cartwright.

"Godspeed," Mr. Anderson told them, and he rode off to find the next brigade.

"We need powder, and lots of it, lads!" Cart
announced to the Knickerbockers. "Take it from wl
you can, and meet back here!"

Felix ran with Cartwright, ignoring the command to stay
with the wagon.

"Powder, sir?"

"Gunpowder. We'll blow up the buildings that have not
yet caught fire and deprive the inferno of its fuel."

The idea sounded crazy to Felix. Fight fire with gunpowder?

They found a grocery on Pine Street and another on Nas-
sau where they collected small amounts of gunpowder. What
he knew to be only a few minutes' run felt like a lifetime to
Felix, the heat and howl of the fire at their heels like some
kind of wild animal. Soon though they rejoined the other
Knickerbockers, and the buildings up and down the block
were divided up by team. Cartwright took their small barrel
of gunpowder and Felix followed close behind.

"We'll want to place it near a supporting column," he told
Felix. "We need to bring the whole building down before the
fire reaches it."

Felix held the cask while Cartwright broke down the door
with an axe. Inside it was dark and cluttered, with crates and
boxes stacked on the floor and behind counters.

"Can we at least empty the stores first?" Felix asked.

"No time," Cartwright said. "If any of these buildings
catches fire before they all go up, none of this will do any

good. There—there's a post near the back. We'll put the gunpowder against that and—"

And Cartwright was gone, dropping from Felix's sight with a cry and a cracking thud. Felix felt a foot step off into nothing, then caught his balance and stumbled back before he fell. As his eyes adjusted, he saw the large black hole in the floor.

"Mr. Cartwright!" he called. "Mr. Cartwright, are you all right?"

There was a soft moan from below, then a match struck, illuminating Cartwright's pained face.

"Basement storage," he grunted. With the light, Felix could see ropes dangling on pulleys. The hole was built to haul crates up from the hold below.

"Do you—do you need me to pull you up?" he asked.

Cartwright shook his head, wincing. "There's a staircase. Near the back. But I think I've broken my ankle."

Felix worked his way to the rear of the building, sliding one foot in front of him the whole way to avoid any more pitfalls. He set the cask of gunpowder by the support beam and found the stairs, taking them two at a time. Cartwright waited for him at the bottom. Felix helped him to his feet and supported him as they climbed back upstairs.

"We'll have to send someone else in to light the charge," Cartwright told him. "I'll never be fast enough like this."

Explosions thundered nearby as Felix helped Cartwright hobble outside. Clouds of wood and dust blasted from the

24

collapsing structures, shattering the windows and shredding the awnings of the buildings on the other side of the street. One by one the warehouses came toppling down into heaps, the fire behind them flinching back from the detonations.

Felix dragged Cartwright into the lee of an alleyway across the street, and together they watched as bright sparks landed on the roof of the building they'd just escaped.

"Hurry—tell the men—"

Felix plucked the box of matches from Cartwright's vest pocket. "No time!" he called, already running back toward the building. Cartwright yelled for him to stop, but Felix knew that by the time they could find someone else to run inside and light the charge it would be too late. The line had to be drawn here, now, and like Cartwright said, if one building survived, the fire would push through.

Felix dashed inside, slowing around the hole in the floor and then running to where the small powder keg sat on the floor. It wasn't enough to let the fire outside reach the explosive and blow it up—by then the flames would have spread from rooftop to rooftop and crossed Wall Street to the businesses and homes on the other side. It had to be done now, and it had to be done quickly.

Felix eyed the long fuse on the keg, then bent it double so it would ignite twice as fast when he lit it.

"I am the fastest boy in Manhattan," Felix whispered. "I am the fastest boy in all of New York." He struck a match and readied himself like he was a runner on first base. "I am the fastest boy in America."

Felix lit the fuse and ran. He ran harder and faster than he had ever run in his life. The fuse hissed furiously behind him. Felix made the turn around the hole in the floor like he was rounding third base and he sprinted for the dim light of the front door like it was home. He was almost there, almost there, almost—

The blast lifted Felix off his feet and threw him into a headfirst slide over the sidewalk. *Ace!* Felix thought, and then he hit the ground and his world went black.

3

Felix awoke in a strange room and a strange bed. A dim light came in through the lone window in the wall and Felix blinked, trying to focus his eyes. The first thing he saw was Uncle Albert's face.

"Worthless boy," Uncle Albert said. He smiled softly.

"Worthless? This boy? He very likely saved the city." Felix turned. Alexander Cartwright sat on the other side of his bed, holding a cane.

"Do not overstate the matter," Uncle Albert said.

"Where—?" Felix tried.

"The Brooklyn City Hospital," Cartwright said. "Or what will be."

Felix saw now that there were three other beds in the small room, all with patients in them. He tried to sit up, but pain in his stomach and legs pushed him down again.

"Don't stir," Uncle Albert said. "You're still unwell."

"The explosion caught you as you ran through the door. It threw you all the way across the street. Do you remember?"

Felix closed his eyes. He remembered flying through the air—scoring an ace.

"The building?" Felix asked.

"It came down in time," Cartwright said. "The fire was contained, but it's been burning for days."

"Days?"

"You've been unconscious for some time," Uncle Albert said. "Your aunt Jenell has been very worried about you."

"Though she hasn't been the one at your side day and night," Cartwright said. Uncle Albert blushed, something Felix had never seen before, and he stood with his hat in his hand.

"My legs feel strange," Felix said. "Cold."

Uncle Albert put a blanket on Felix's legs. "I—I must go and tell Jenell," he said. "She will want to know you are awake." Uncle Albert put a hand to Felix's shoulder, then left quickly. Cartwright stood with the help of his cane and went over to the window.

"It's still smoldering, you know. They say the smoke plume can be seen two hundred miles away. It's all gone now. The last of what was New Amsterdam lays in ruins."

"New Amsterdam?"

"What they once called New York, when it was a Dutch settlement. Didn't you know? That's where we got our name—the Knickerbockers. That's the word people use for the Dutch settlers and their descendants. It's from that Irving novel, I think."

Felix had no idea what novel Cartwright was talking about, but it didn't matter.

"I wonder how many Knickerbockers there really are left in New York," Cartwright said. "Everything's changing so fast. I imagine everything that burned down will be replaced within a year. Newer, bigger, better."

"Your leg, sir," Felix said. "Is it greatly injured?"

"What, this?" Cartwright said. "A sprain. I'll be running the bases again in no time." Cartwright caught himself, as though he had said something he hadn't meant to, and turned again to the window.

"Your uncle tells me you stowed away to come here, young squire. That you ran away from home. I wonder, were you running *to* America, or away from something there?"

"Both, I suppose," Felix said. "Things were so bad in Bremen. No work, no food. And everyone said there was both in America, that a man could make his fortune here, no matter where he came from or what he started with. My father had no money to come, so I ran away and hid on a ship. I came here to work and make money and earn enough to bring my family over so we could be happy again."

"Do you regret it, coming here?"

"Oh no! I miss my family, but I've almost saved enough to bring them to America, and then I can show them Broadway and the fine ladies in their dresses and the pigs and the five-story department stores—and baseball!"

Cartwright laughed. "I think maybe baseball *is* America.

29

The spirit of it, at least. Something we brought with us from the Old World and made our own, the way we made this country." He turned from the window. "I'm getting ready to run away myself, I think. West, to California. They say the hills are full of gold."

Uncle Albert came back in then, bringing Aunt Jenell with him. She smothered Felix in her embrace.

"I think I'll turn you over to your aunt and uncle," Cartwright said, but Uncle Albert and Aunt Jenell wouldn't let him leave without pumping his hand and thanking him again and again. Aunt Jenell even surprised Cartwright with a hug.

"Good-bye, young squire," Cartwright said. He shook Felix's hand. "I hope this doesn't slow down your dreams."

"What does he mean, this slowing down my dreams?" Felix asked when Cartwright was gone.

"Mr. Cartwright was so kind," Aunt Jenell said. "He paid for all your hospital care. We couldn't have afforded it otherwise."

"But Felix, my boy," Uncle Albert said, "we've had to spend the money you saved to bring your family to America. I'm sorry. The fire, it has put so many people out of work, including me. When the warehouses burned, there was less cloth to be cut, and with less cloth to be cut, they do not need so many cutters. I've been let go."

"All the money I've saved? But—" Felix didn't understand, wanted to demand how they could just use up the money he'd put aside, but the way his aunt and uncle stared at the floor in shame told him they must have had no choice. "But . . . there will be work again, won't there?" Felix asked. "Cartwright said everything will be rebuilt."

"But not soon enough for us," Uncle Albert said. "We had very little savings. You know that. We—we've had to move from our apartment in Kleindeutschland."

"Albert has found us work here in Brooklyn. Sewing suits."

No, Felix thought—not that. Not living in the darkness, working his fingers to the bone for pennies like the Neumans.

"But my job as a runner—I can still do that. If there are pieces to be sewn, there must be someone running them to the department stores!"

Albert and Jenell shared a sad look, and his aunt put a hand on Felix's leg.

"Felix, your legs—they were injured in the explosion."

What? No—it couldn't be. But the strange cold sensation he had . . . Felix ripped the sheets and blankets off. Underneath, his legs were blackened and scarred.

"They've given you a drug, to combat the pain," Uncle Albert told him. "They say the pain will get better, but that it will never go away."

Felix didn't want to cry, but the tears came whether he wanted them or not. He was the fastest boy in New York. The fastest boy in *America*. His legs had taken him across

Germany and across an ocean to a new world. It was on his legs that he had planned to carry his mother and father and baby sister away from the blight and the famine and the poverty of Bremen. It was on his legs that his family's future depended, and now here they lay, ashen and crippled like Lower Manhattan itself.

Aunt Jenell wrapped him in another hug and let him cry.

Uncle Albert carried Felix home from the hospital the next day, even though Felix could walk passably well. What he couldn't do was run, and Felix wondered what the point of having feet at all was if he couldn't do that. His shoes too, the beautiful shoes his father had made for him, his only connection to the family he'd left behind, had been so mangled and burned in the explosion that they were unusable now. Felix didn't want to see them, had told his uncle to throw them away, but Uncle Albert had insisted on keeping them. The leather, he said, could be used for something else.

On the way to their new flat Felix saw a group of boys playing three-out, all-out in a pig field. They were in between innings, chasing each other around with the ball to see who would bat next, ignoring the pigs the way the uptown ladies and gentlemen did on Broadway.

Felix turned his head away so he couldn't see, and told his uncle to keep walking.

Their new apartment was much like the Neumans', only

they shared it not with more Schneiders but with another family, the Smiths. They had been Schmidts, but changed their name to something more American in the hopes of landing better work. Uncle Albert was considering doing the same.

There were two bedrooms in the Schneider/Smith home—one for each of the families—and a small kitchen where they all shared meals and sewing work. Felix's new job was stitching the broad, flat pieces of suit jackets together while Aunt Jenell pieced the sleeves. Uncle Albert, a master tailor, did the more complicated parts. Like the Neumans, they had no windows in their flat, and in the summer the heat was stifling. By midday Felix was so sweaty the needle would slip right out of his hand.

When the runner came to pick up their work, Felix would disappear into one of the bedrooms.

Life went on this way for more weeks and months than Felix could count. Uncle Albert didn't change their last name, but he did join a Christian church, which gave them Sundays off. Sometimes Felix would take his free day and wander down to the docks at the end of Flatbush Avenue and watch the city across the East River recover in stages. First one warehouse, then another, then a tall office building, a bank, a dry-goods store. Like Cartwright said, always newer, bigger, better.

Felix saw too the huge masted steamers with flywheels amidships, like the one he had stolen away on to cross the

Atlantic, unloading thousands of new immigrants upon the docks at the Battery as they had once delivered him. Felix remembered his first steps into this crowded new world of hope and promise, and he longed to be one of them again, a greenhorn fresh off the boat, ready to make his fortune and bring his family to the New World. There on the Brooklyn pier, Felix resolved to start again.

That night while everyone else slept, Felix found a wine cork in the kitchen and wrapped yards of twine and thread around it. When that was done he pulled out the pair of shoes his father had made for him, and with Uncle Albert's shears he cut away the charred leather and trimmed what was left into wide strips. Then, using a thick needle and the laces from his useless shoes, he began to sew the leather strips around the outside of his twine ball. When he was finished, Felix scratched a small *S* on his new baseball, an *S* for Schneider.

Cartwright had said that baseball *was* America, and somehow, some way, Felix would find a way to get back in the game. Even if it took him a lifetime to do it. Even if it took him *nine* lifetimes to do it. Felix would play ball again.

Second Inning: The Red-Legged Devil

Northern Virginia, 1864

1

"I reckon that's the best baseball in Spotsylvania, Virginia," Stuart said.

"I reckon this is the *only* baseball in Spotsylvania, Virginia," Louis Schneider said. He flipped his father's baseball high in the air and dashed forward to catch it.

"Louis! Will you stop!? We could be set upon by Rebs any second!"

Stuart's skittishness was understandable, if a little tiresome. Louis had been there for Stuart's rookie engagement in the Civil War—what the career men called "Seeing the Elephant"—and had seen Stuart come away the worse for it. After their first battle, most men went one way or the other: They either got crazy, or they got scared. Stuart got scared. He'd been a jumble of nerves ever since, and the whole time they'd been on patrol today he'd jumped and twitched at every little sound.

Louis sighed and stowed the baseball away in his

haversack, extracting a copy of *Beadle's Dime Baseball Player* to look at as the two walked their patrol.

"Where on Earth'd you find that?"

"My pa sent it to me. He's a top rail player, only he could never go pro because of his legs. Got messed up in an explosion."

"In—in the war?" Stuart asked.

"No, fighting a fire when he was a kid. That's why I joined the Army—because he couldn't."

Stuart peered at Louis. "Just how old *are* you, anyway?"

"Sixteen," Louis lied. "Say, it says here the National Association voted the fly rule in. No more catching a ball on the bounce."

"Uh-huh."

"What? I'm serious," Louis said, but he knew Stuart was still on about his age.

Stuart stopped and tensed, gripping his rifle in both hands. Louis looked ahead and saw a little general store at a crossroads. A thin trail of smoke rose from the chimney pipe.

"Say, you don't suppose it's *open,* do you?" Louis asked.

"You're not thinking of going in there! Louis, we're deep into Virginia. What if the owner is a Confederate?"

Louis grinned. "I'm counting on it. Follow my lead."

Louis bounded up the steps into the store but froze inside the door. To his amazement, it was stocked like a Brooklyn Heights grocers. There were barrels of fresh apples, carrots, and pecans, hunks of salt pork, sacks of flour and cornmeal and potatoes, shelves of fresh bread, rows of eggs. For a moment, he and Stuart stood in the doorway drooling. It was all Louis could do to keep from lunging for the first scrumptious morsel in sight and not cease eating until he was arrested or shot, whichever came first.

The shopkeeper came out from a small pantry in the back and stopped short when he saw them. Louis and Stuart weren't wearing Union blues, but they weren't wearing Confederate grays either. The shopkeeper's hand disappeared beneath the counter and came back with a pistol, which he laid down beside the register.

"I'll have no trouble now, you hear?" he told the boys.

Louis stepped forward with his hands in the air. "And we don't aim to cause any."

The shopkeeper nodded at them. "What kind of costume is that, anyway? French? Hessian?"

"We're the Brooklyn Fourteenth," Louis told him. "We're with the Army of the Potomac."

Beside him, Louis could hear Stuart hiss. The grocer picked up his gun again.

"This ain't a commissary, neither Union nor otherwise. You either got money or you don't—and I charge double for Yankees."

That told Louis all he needed to know. Heedless of the shopkeeper's gun, he strolled through the aisles, surveying the goods like he was shopping.

"Louis, let's get out of here," Stuart whispered for all to hear.

Louis ignored him and spoke to the grocer. "Oh, I've got a bit of money," he said. "But I'm afraid it's just this worthless Confederate stuff." He pulled a few small bills out of his pocket and set them on the counter. "I understand it's not good for much of anything. Like everything else down here."

The shopkeeper raised himself up, insulted.

"So long as the Confederacy still stands, boy, those notes will be good in my store."

"Is that so?" Louis asked. He took off his haversack and withdrew two handfuls of bills—almost five hundred dollars in Confederate money—and put them on the counter.

"In that case," Louis told him, "we'll take everything you've got."

✥ ✥ ✥

They didn't really buy everything, of course—just as much as they could carry. But that was plenty enough for a first-rate feast, and when they returned, Louis and Stuart were hailed by their fellow soldiers as heroes to the nation.

"It was all Louis," Stuart told them, regaling the rest of the Brooklyn Fourteenth with the story as he lazed by the fire, licking the chicken grease off his fingers.

"Lucky Louis!" one of the boys said with a laugh.

"Lucky nothing—where'd you come by so many Confederate bills?" asked Corporal Bruner.

"Well, I'll tell you," Louis said. "Every night after a fight,

I wait 'til late and sneak back onto the field of battle and go through the Rebs' coats."

"You can't be serious!"

"Why not? They do it to themselves so's there's hardly a thing left anyway—except all that no-account cash. I was just collecting it to take home as souvenirs. I never figured on buying anything with it. Never thought I'd have the chance."

"Lucky Louis," somebody said again.

Not lucky enough to earn a promotion, thought Louis, although he'd certainly put in his time. He'd lied about his age three years ago so he could march to Washington in '61 with the Fourteenth and beg to go to war. They let him march, but perhaps suspecting he was underage they only made him a drummer. Louis had taken over as standard bearer when Johnson took a bullet to the head at Antietam, and then had a rifle thrust in his hands at Fredericksburg. He'd battled the graybacks at Chancellorsville, spent three days dodging bullets at Gettysburg, fought in the Battle of the Wilderness, and been in half again as many skirmishes in between. Maybe he was lucky after all. Of the eleven hundred boys and men who'd left Brooklyn to the cheers of their city, only one hundred and forty-three remained. The rest, like Stuart, were fresh fish from home.

Louis took out the baseball again and flipped it between his hands. He wasn't lucky, he thought. It was the ball. His father had given it to him the day he left for the war, telling

41

him to bring it back in one piece. Louis figured his father wouldn't have let that ball go without knowing he'd get it back, which meant as long as he had it, he couldn't help but come home safe and sound. He ran a thumb over the *S* scratched in the leather, the *S* for Schneider.

A sergeant who'd been with them from the first clapped a hand on Louis's shoulder.

"Have a game with that ball of yours?" he asked.

"Could do," Louis told him. "If I can ever get up off this spot again."

The sergeant laughed. "Let us know. There's a lad from the Tenth Massachusetts who's challenged us to a match."

"I'm happy to beat the bean eaters any old time they wish," Louis told him. "But only if they'll play by New York rules. I'd rather the game not last three days."

Soldiers suddenly began scrambling for their caps and coats. Stuart leaped to his feet and knocked over the kettle before falling to the ground himself.

"What is it?" he asked. "Are we under attack?"

Louis stood. "General coming!" a sergeant yelled, running through the camp. "Make ready to present! General coming!"

Louis buttoned up his uniform and helped Stuart to his feet. They scurried to attention under the watchful eye of Lieutenant Tinker as a horse's hoofbeats drew closer.

"Atten-*tion!*" Tinker cried, and the Fourteenth stood straight.

The man who rode up was known to Louis and the others

who had been with the regiment the longest: He was General Abner Doubleday, the man who had commanded the Brooklyn Fourteenth at Antietam and again at Gettysburg. He was a stout man, as most generals were, with a hulking brown mustache, long tall nose, and receding line of dark curly hair. Louis counted him brave if not brilliant for his actions on the battlefield, though none of the boys thought the worse of him.

Doubleday pulled his mount to a stop before them and surveyed their lines.

"The Brooklyn Fourteenth," he said. "The Red-Legged Devils."

They had gotten the nickname after Bull Run, where it was said they had fought with hell's fury. General McDowell even let them keep their red breeches and hats as badges of honor when the rest of the army was issued standard blues. The Fourteenth's uniforms, like their boys, were supplied by the City of Brooklyn herself.

Doubleday rode up and down the lines inspecting them, then stopped to speak.

"On many a weary march, and many a hard fought field, I have personally seen your courage and devotion. Your name is a household word in the army. You are the elite of our division."

Louis stood a little straighter.

"You original members who mustered in during the formation of your regiment—you who have survived Bull

Run, South Mountain, Falmouth, Antietam, Fredericksburg, Rappahanock Station, Chancellorsville, Sulphur Springs, Gettysburg, Groveton, The Wilderness, Gainesville, and Spotsylvania Court House—*twice*—you brave few who remain have earned your nation's respect and gratitude. You have also earned your release from the Army of the Potomac."

Lucky again! Louis looked at those in Company K who had been around from the beginning. One or two of them were crying, but whether they were tears of joy or sorrow Louis didn't know. For his part, it was as though a great weight had lifted off his shoulders. His father's baseball had seen him through.

"Tomorrow morning you will take a train to Baltimore, and thence to Jersey City and home to Brooklyn, where your city fathers are even now, I am told, making ready a celebration of some consequence." The general sniffed the air and moved his horse closer to one of the campfires. "Although I gather you've already had something of a celebration here today."

A ripple of laughter rode through the company.

"I do swear, I have never known a regiment so full of shrewd devices to avoid unnecessary hardships as the Brooklyn Fourteenth. Where in tarnation did you—no, I had better not know."

"If you'd care to have a game with us," called Corporal Rugge, "we plan to play baseball next!"

The general laughed. "I have no talent or interest for base-ball," said Doubleday. "But I would very much like to sample whatever is brewing in that pot over yonder."

"Company *dis*-missed!" cried Lieutenant Tinker. The soldiers relaxed and fell out of ranks, and the general worked his way back to the homemade still, congratulating those who would be sent home.

Stuart hugged his friend. "You've made it, Louis! Lucky Louis, you're headed home for Brooklyn!"

"Perhaps I'll be home in time to see the Atlantics play the Eckfords for the championship."

"If the Putnams don't win it!"

"Have you heard? They've put up a fence around the Union grounds and are charging ten cents admission to see their games!"

Stuart shook his head. "Paying admission will be the ruin of baseball. What's next, paying the players?"

Louis smiled. For once Stuart wasn't listening for the snap of twigs and the report of rifles.

"Come on," Louis told him. "Let's go have a game. And we won't charge the trees and rocks any admission to watch."

They had more than enough to play among their own company, and the officers set to choosing up sides. The Fourteenth had a serviceable piece of oak they used for a bat, and the bases were measured off according to the New York rules. The fly rule was agreed upon, as most players thought catching the ball on the fly was more manly anyway, but

45

"stealing" bases, a new practice introduced by Ned Cuthbert of the Philadelphia Keystones, was deemed unsportsmanlike and prohibited. General Doubleday was solicited to call balls and strikes, but he had other companies to see and so the teams made do with Lieutenant Tinker.

That day Louis heard it said that a more delightful afternoon of baseball was never had in Virginia nor, it was argued, at any time in Manhattan or Long Island. He had to agree. Corporal Bruner pitched as well as James Creighton of the Brooklyn Excelsiors, and Stuart drew applause for a fine diving catch made on a fly to the outfield.

On Louis's third time at bat there were Red-Legged Devils standing on first and second with the score tied at six aces apiece. Louis was eager to have another go at Bruner's dastardly "dew drops," the balls that seemed to float across the plate as leaves descend to the forest floor, and his mates cheered him on from the sidelines. Bruner lofted the ball and Louis waited, waited, waited—and then swung, striking the ball high in the air toward Stuart in center field. Louis watched him track back on it as he ran, then, surprisingly, Stuart broke off his pursuit of the ball and turned to stare at the edge of the woods.

"Wait, I think there's somebody—" he started to call out, but he never finished. The pop of a rifle and the telltale puff of blue-gray smoke came out of the woods, and Stuart's leg exploded. In a moment the air was full of bumblebees, whizzing lead balls that cracked into the trees and the dirt.

Louis's run toward third became a sprint for his life. The shots brought men in their long johns scurrying from the Union camp with rifles in hand, and while those playing the game looked for holes to crawl into, the rest of the Red-Legged Devils came charging into the clearing to meet the Confederates in the forest.

What started as a skirmish turned into a full-scale battle, giving Louis and the other ballplayers time enough to go back for their rifles and rejoin the fight. The Brooklyn Fourteenth drove the rebels into the forest again, and then the Confederates, receiving reinforcements, pushed the Union soldiers back to their camp. When dusk fell there was no clear winner, as was so often the case in engagements like this, and Lieutenant Tinker received orders to break camp and retreat.

Louis marched with his company two miles inland under cover of night, and they set up their tents by a small stream. The camp canard had the rest of the regiment moving on to North Anna, some two days away, while Louis and the rest who had received their release would be transported to the nearest railway station when it was safe and then ferried northward and homeward.

But Louis couldn't go back to Brooklyn. Not yet. He had, alas, lost two things on the field of battle he could not leave behind: his friend Palmer Stuart, and the best and only baseball in Spotsylvania, Virginia.

2

"You can't go back."

Louis took the powder and shot out of his haversack and weighed them, then handed them to Corporal Bruner.

"Without a rifle too? Are you crazy, Schneider?"

"Too heavy," whispered Louis. "Need to travel light."

The camp was sleeping but for the pickets who kept watch. Louis looked around, trying not to think of it as the last time he would see his friends. Those who were headed home tomorrow were probably dreaming of family and hot baths and tables full of food. He didn't have to guess what nightmares the others who were staying dreamed of.

"It's not worth it, Schneider. You go home tomorrow," Bruner told him.

"Stuart's still back there," Louis said. "He was my friend. I can't just—"

"Stuart's dead and you know it."

Louis considered that.

"He only took a ball to the leg. I saw it."

48

"I saw it too. He's dead."

The cool night air was sharp, and Louis could see his breath hanging in front of him like some still image caught on tintype. In it, he felt the truth of the situation laid bare.

"If he's dead, I'll find my ball and be back before light."

Louis could feel Bruner's eyes on him in the dark. "Is that what this is about? That baseball?"

"I can't go back without it," Louis told him. "It's my lucky baseball. Besides, my pa would kill me."

"You go back there and Johnny Reb'll do the killing for him. If you're lucky. Or be taken to some Confederate prison camp if you're not."

They'd all heard the tales of the Southern prison camps. Compared to that, death did seem the better alternative. Louis hefted his haversack to his shoulder just the same.

"Your family's gonna be right sore you went and got yourself killed the night before you was heading home. Especially over a baseball."

How could Louis make him understand? It was more than a baseball. Louis's pa had given it to him when he left, with the order to bring it back in one piece. But they both knew he hadn't been talking about the baseball. His pa couldn't allow that Louis might get blown to bits like Stuart, or Kurlanski, or Jones, or any of the hundreds of other boys Louis had seen get mustered out the hard way on the field of battle. In time Louis had begun to think of the ball as himself, or the ball as a part of him maybe—he hadn't really tried to make sense of it. All he knew was that one way or another, both of them would end up back in Brooklyn one day, having a game with the boys at Pigtown.

"I'll be back before light," Louis said again. He and Bruner shook hands, and Louis tromped off through the forest the way they had come earlier that day.

The picket post was more on guard tonight, but when they saw Louis they smiled.

"Ain't you got enough souvenirs already?" one of the boys on duty whispered. The regulars were used to Louis slipping away to collect money from the dead graybacks, and he usually jawed with them on the way out. Tonight Louis gave them a wave but passed by without a word.

The moon was a sliver in the dark sky, which was good and bad. Good that it would be hard for anyone to spot him; bad that it was hard for Louis to see anything himself. He found the road to Spotsylvania Court House and worked his way alongside it through the woods. Occasionally he'd come to a cleared field and have to crouch along the roadside, trying to stay low and unseen. He reached instinctively to touch the baseball in his haversack, then remembered it wasn't there. Louis got scared on the battlefield—no man he knew could say he didn't—but now he began to feel as Stuart must have, that there was always someone lurking around the next corner, behind the nearest bush, the closest tree, someone waiting to send a lead ball buzzing his way

50

with his name on it. Poor Stuart had been right once, and once was all it took.

A dark figure appeared in the road ahead, and Louis flattened himself in a ditch, feeling the cold wet grass against his face. He wished for all his life he had his father's baseball back. Or his rifle. He cursed himself for leaving it behind.

The shape grew closer, and with his ears attuned to every little sound, Louis heard a man's boots scraping along the hard dirt path. *Thunk,* scrape. *Thunk,* scrape. Something was off about the way he was walking, and Louis dared to raise his head to take a look.

The scraping stopped.

"Who's there?" came a voice.

Louis buried his head again in the ditch and cursed silently.

"Be you grayback or bush hog, show yourself, varmint!"

Louis slowly lifted himself and stood. Better to die on his feet than facedown in a ditch—and in the dark, there was always a chance he might be able to run.

Louis squinted and tried to see the other man in the dark. He was only a shadow, but from his silhouette Louis could see he was leaning on a pole or a stick. Or a rifle.

"Friend or foe?" the man asked.

"That depends on what color uniform you're wearing," Louis said.

"Union blue," the man told him. "Army of the Potomac, First New Jersey Brigade."

"I hail from just across the river, friend. Brooklyn Four-teenth."

Louis stepped close enough so they could see each other in the dim light.

"Private First Class Louis Schneider," he said, shaking the man's hand.

"Corporal Giuseppe Silvestri."

"You coming from Spotsylvania?" Louis asked.

He nodded. "You coming from the camp? Am I close?"

"About another mile," Louis told him. He saw now the man had a leg wound, and he grimaced. It wasn't as bad as Stuart's, but the shirt he'd tied around it was already soaked with blood.

"You taking French leave, son?" He meant was Louis running away.

"No, I'm headed back to Spotsylvania to check on a friend I left behind. Is it much farther?"

"'Bout another hour or so, best I can reckon. Not much to go back for that didn't hobble away or get carried away though."

"You run into any Rebs from here to there?" Louis asked.

"No. You're the first ghost I've seen."

"Same here," Louis said. "Just keep down this road, then take the right junction at the forge. You'll come along the advance pickets, and they can get you into camp."

"Much obliged, Private."

Louis gave the man a quick salute, and they parted ways.

He stayed on guard the rest of his walk, but if the corporal hadn't seen any Confederates, ambling along at his cripple's pace, Louis figured he wasn't likely to meet the Army of Northern Virginia on the way.

In an hour or so the terrain began to look familiar and Louis picked his way off the main road into the woods where he thought they had been encamped. He caught a whiff of gun smoke on the air and he knew he was close. Soon he was upon the smoldering campfires of the day before, the roasted chicken and the baseball game distant memories now. It was late at night—or early the next day—and Louis shook his head and blinked his eyes to keep himself alert.

He started stepping over bodies before he ever reached the field. The soldiers, both Union and Confederate, lay faceup, which meant the surgeons had been here. After a battle the surgeons would roll in with their ambulances and stretchers and take some of the injured, but not all. Those that were only slightly wounded, like the corporal Louis had met on the road, were left to make their own way back to camp or to a field hospital; those with mortal wounds were left to die. In Louis's late-night skulks back to battlefields he had always made a point of waiting until well after the surgeons had finished their business.

It was brighter out in the open of the field, though still dark, and men laid out all over the field looked like they were sleeping. Louis knew better. He made his way quickly to where Stuart had been playing center field. He hoped not to find him, for that would mean the surgeons had gotten him and thought his wounds operable—but there he was, lying faceup and staring at the moon with dead eyes.

Louis closed Stuart's eyes and said a short prayer over him, then cast around for his baseball. He found it lying a few yards away in the tall grass and returned with it to Stuart's side.

"I'll find your folks," Louis whispered. "I'll tell them how brave you were." Louis looked at all the dark shapes around him. "Somebody'll come and bury you. Somebody'll come and bury you all."

"No, wait!" came a voice, making Louis jump. A hand clutched his ankle.

"Gah! What the devil!?"

At first he thought it was Stuart, come back from the dead to ask if Louis heard something rustling in the woods, but then Louis turned and saw another dark shape lying on the ground nearby, its dark arm snaking out to him, holding him so he couldn't get away.

"Don't bury me!" the thing squawked. "I ain't dead yet!"

Louis tried to pull away, but the thing held on like a viper.

"Get off! Get off!"

"Are you the Angel of Death?"

"What!? No, I'm—"

Louis's eyes adjusted and he could just make out the boy's gray uniform. He was a Confederate. He immediately thought of his gun, sitting against a tree miles away at the

Union camp. His eyes searched the darkness for a bayonet, a rifle, anything he could use to defend himself.

"Please," the Rebel said. "I don't know what's happened. Why is it so dark and quiet?"

"It's the middle of the night," Louis said. "That's what happens at night. It gets dark."

"Are you a medic? Can you take me back to my regiment?"

"What? Take you back to your regiment?" Couldn't the fool see Louis was a Yankee? "I'm not a—"

The Rebel's head turned this way and that, like he couldn't see a thing. It was dark, but not that dark. Louis bent low and waved a hand in front of the soldier's face. He was blind as a bat, his face and eyes charred like the inside of a furnace.

"You're not a what?" the Confederate asked. "Are you still there?"

"Of course I'm here," Louis told him. "You've got hold of my leg."

The Rebel let go and Louis stepped back out of his reach, trying to think what to do.

"Sorry. It's just—it's so dark. And my head hurts. Can you take me back to my regiment? Are they far gone?"

Louis studied the Rebel. He could see now he was around his own age, maybe even younger, and his gray Confederate uniform looked three sizes too big. His blind eyes searched the darkness eagerly, hoping for some shape or shadow that might give him his bearings.

Louis considered his options. He could leave the boy, which didn't seem right, or kill him, which might have been a mercy but was out of the question. During the heat of battle, killing another man was one thing. It was kill or be killed, and both sides accepted that. Killing this boy here and now would be akin to murder—even if he might have been the one to take Stuart down in cold blood.

An idea struck Louis. Why not take him back to the Union camp as a prisoner of war, maybe see if he could get a promotion out of it? Even on the eve of going home, a promotion would mean a better pension, which his family could sorely use. But without a weapon, how to convince the Reb to come with him?

"All right. On your feet," Louis said. "We're . . . we're going to find your regiment."

The boy was so profuse in his thanks Louis began to feel sorry for the lie, but there was no other choice.

"Try to find my pack," the boy said. "It's just inside the wood line. It's the one with the baseball bat in it."

Louis paused.

"The what?"

"The baseball bat. It's a white haversack with the handle sticking out. I left it near an oak tree."

Louis slipped away and found a white oak a few paces into the woods. Behind it was a haversack, just as the boy had said, a bat handle sticking up out of the top. Louis slid it out to have a look. It was the finest bat he had ever seen. Not a broom handle or a whittled-down tree limb, but a real, honest-to-God lathe-turned hickory bat, such as Louis had only seen in the hands of the finest players on the Excelsiors. The barrel was heavy and perfectly smooth, and the long handle had a knob at the end to keep it in the batter's hands as he swung. Louis took a practice swing with it right there in the forest, enjoying the *whhht* it made and the power it held.

He brought the bat and the sack back to the boy, who was sitting up now. He had his hands in front of his eyes, but turned at the sound of Louis's approach.

"I'm blind, ain't I?"

"I think so," Louis told him.

The boy sobbed once. "My rifle. It exploded. I remember now. I never even got a shot off. My rifle blew up in my face. The next thing I knew, I woke up here, in the dark, and I heard your voice. Are you—are you a surgeon?"

"No. They've come and gone. I just came back to find a friend of mine."

Louis's hand found the ball in his pocket.

"Where'd you get this bat?" he asked.

The boy was crying now. Not hard tears. Soft ones, like he'd just lost a friend. "My pa. He's—he's a carpenter. He makes them for some of the boys who play."

"I've never seen its equal," Louis told him. He sat down on the grass next to the Reb.

"I was going to be mustered out tomorrow," the boy said through his tears. "Go back to Louisville."

"Me too!" Louis said. "Mustered out, I mean."

"Where are you from?"

"Um—farther north," said Louis.

"What, like . . . Nashville?"

Louis didn't have the faintest idea where Nashville was. "Close to," he said.

The boy dried his eyes and Louis clapped him on the shoulder.

"All right then. On your feet. We've got a train to catch."

3

The boy's name was Jeremiah Walker, and he played second base.

"I swear, I've seen him do it!" Louis told him.

"Look, I may be blind," Jeremiah said, "but you can't tell me nobody ever made a baseball curve."

"I'm telling you—his name is Candy Cummings. He's one of the boys comes round to play ball with us. Lives out near Red Hook. He got to throwing clam shells on a curve one day and reckoned he could do the same thing with a ball."

They passed the spot on the road where Louis had met the corporal, and he knew they had a mile yet to go. He was enjoying the baseball talk so much he almost hated to get there.

"Clam shells?" Jeremiah said.

"I swear. I saw him skunk some of the best hitters in . . . my hometown." Louis had come dangerously close to saying Brooklyn, and he worried now that Jeremiah might have heard of Red Hook. He'd have to be more careful.

"You only count catches on the fly, right?" he asked.

"'Course. Though there's some that still play off the bounce. They ain't finding too many takers, though."

"Back home," Louis said, careful not to give anything away, "there were only three clubs that played that way when I left. I expect they've given it up by now."

"How many unhittable balls do you allow before you grant the batter first base?"

"Three," Louis told him.

"Your umpires count every pitch?"

"No. Just when things start to get out of hand one way or the other."

"What about bunting?" Jeremiah asked. "Do your teams look upon it favorably, or—"

Louis put out a hand to stop the Confederate.

"What? What is it?" Jeremiah said.

Louis hadn't heard anything and he hadn't seen anything. Instead he was beginning to wonder if there wasn't something else he should do with Jeremiah. He couldn't believe he was even considering it, but he knew in his heart he could not take the second baseman in as a prisoner of war. Not even for a promotion.

"I think we need to turn here," he said. He led Jeremiah off into the woods and circled around.

"Isn't this—isn't this the direction we just came from?" Jeremiah asked.

"Hey, who's the one with the eyes here? Trust me."

Jeremiah got quiet, but soon they were talking baseball again as Louis guided them through the woods. He eventually found a wide, dark field with trampled grass, which meant either the Army of Northern Virginia or a herd of elephants had come this way. Though he knew it was crazy, Louis followed the trail.

The two walked for hours, never running out of baseball talk. They had just begun discussing the merits of stealing bases when a voice in the darkness interrupted them.

"Who comes there?"

Neither of them spoke, and Jeremiah nudged Louis.

"Uh, friend!" Louis said.

The sentry waited. Louis heard a rustling. "And the countersign, friend?"

Jeremiah turned his blind eyes toward Louis like he was waiting for him to answer.

"Jeremiah," Louis whispered. "I can't—I don't know—"

A confused look passed over his friend's face, then Jeremiah turned toward the voice in the darkness and said, "Blueberry pie, friend."

There was a pause, and Louis waited for the lead to start flying if Jeremiah's memory had gotten knocked to Tuesday when his rifle exploded.

"Advance friend, blueberry pie," came the response. There was more rustling, which Louis took to mean they were no longer in the sentry's sights. "Need a hand there?"

"No!" Louis and Jeremiah said together, and too quickly.

"No," Jeremiah said. "Thank you kindly. We're not bad off, just got a little . . . turned around on the way home."

"Godspeed," the sentry told them. "And be a little quicker with the countersign next time, boys. There's Yankees on sacred soil."

"We will, sir. Thank you," Jeremiah said. He nudged Louis and they were off, giving the picket a wide berth.

When they were a little ways into the woods, Louis spoke.

"I uh, I don't know what I was thinking. I must have forgotten the password."

"I think I can forgive my guardian angel that one transgression," Jeremiah said.

Louis stopped him. The time for lies was at an end. "Jeremiah, I'm not an angel. I'm a devil. A Red-Legged Devil. I'm not a Reb, Jeremiah—I'm a Yankee."

Jeremiah didn't look as shocked as Louis thought he would be.

"I know," he said.

"You know? What, because I didn't know the countersign?"

Jeremiah pulled away from Louis and reached out until he found a tree to anchor himself.

"I don't figure it's something you'll ever need to know," he said, "but Nashville is *south* of Louisville. By a far piece. Any Southern boy'd know that. Heck, an Ohioan would know that."

"Right," Louis said, disappointed he hadn't known.

"And you ain't gonna find too many clam shells anywhere but the ocean, and you didn't say you was from Charleston or some such."

"I could have been from Norfolk! That's on the ocean, isn't it?"

"And I don't know what city you're from where 'only' three teams still count fly outs on the bounce. There ain't but four teams in Louisville, perhaps ten in all of Kentucky."

"Okay, okay. I get it. As a spy I'm not worth a plugged nickel."

"Not only that," Jeremiah said, "you talk like a Yankee."

"Oh yeah? Well, you talk like a cotton-picking Rebel!"

Louis and Jeremiah laughed, then grew quiet.

"What I can't figure," Jeremiah said, "is what we're doing at the edge of the Confederate army camp. When I had you pegged for a Yank, I thought for sure we were off to your side, not mine."

"Why come along then?" Louis asked.

Jeremiah shrugged. "I can't see. What was I going to do? Clonk you on the head and set out on my own? I figured a Union prison camp was better than running into trees until a bear ate me."

"That was the plan. A prison camp, I mean. Then I changed my mind."

"Why?"

"I don't know. You were going home tomorrow and so was

I, and . . . well, I guess I figured anybody that liked baseball that much couldn't be too bad a person, Reb or not."

Jeremiah fumbled with his sack and withdrew his baseball bat.

"If you've a mind to clonk me now," Louis told him, "I think it only fair to remind you that I *can* see you coming."

Jeremiah smiled. "Here," he said, holding the bat out to Louis. He meant for him to have it.

"No. I couldn't," Louis told him. "Your pa made that."

"And just what am I going to do with it?" he asked. "Go on, take it. This whole thing—this whole thing was a mistake to begin with. We weren't supposed to fire, you know. We were just watching the game on a lark. Then Samuels got twitchy and went and shot that boy, the center fielder. It wasn't right, but we had to take it up then, or else have you boys on our heels."

"Look, maybe it's just a flash burn," Louis said. "You might get your sight back after a time. Then you'll need that bat again."

"If that happens, my pa can make me another. Here. Take this back to—what, New York?"

"No! *Pfft.* Not New York. *Brooklyn.*"

"Is that close to Nashville?" Jeremiah asked.

"Very nearly," Louis said, smiling.

"Here." Jeremiah stepped forward until Louis had to take the bat or be struck by it.

"Wait, I'll trade you," Louis told him. He hesitated a

moment, then pulled his father's baseball from his pocket and put it in Jeremiah's hand. The Rebel turned it over, feeling the surface of it.

"This is a fine baseball."

"The finest," Louis said. "My pa made that when he was a boy."

"Sounds like you don't want to part with it."

"It's my good luck charm," Louis told him. "But I think you need it more than me."

"You sure about that? Looked around at where you're at lately?"

Louis smiled. "I'll be all right. I'm going home tomorrow, and I'm not going to let anybody stop me."

Jeremiah held out a hand and they shook as friends.

"Too bad we couldn't have settled this whole thing over a game of baseball," Louis told him, "trading fly balls instead of lead ones."

"Better for your side we didn't," Jeremiah said. "You'd have lost for sure."

"Oho!"

"You'd best be heading on," Jeremiah told him. "I can make it from here."

Louis looked about at the forest. It had started to glow with the first hint of morning.

"I think you'll be bouncing off the trees from here to Richmond," Louis told him. "Better let me take you a little farther in."

This time Louis kept his eye out for sentries and spotted a campfire through the bracken before the picket spotted them. The boys shook hands once more and took their leave, Louis with a new hickory bat, Jeremiah with a new baseball. Louis hoped his father would understand, and he suspected he would.

Over his shoulder he heard Jeremiah Walker call to the sentries for help, and Louis took off for Brooklyn as fast as his red devil legs could carry him.

Third Inning: A Ballad of the Republic

Brooklyn, New York, 1894

1

"I'm Cap Anson!" one boy called.

"I'm Oyster Burns!" said another.

The boys had rechristened Pigtown the Polo Grounds, and now they were giving themselves upgrades by pretending to be their favorite players.

"I'm Fred Pfeffer!" Tommy Collum said.

"Fred Pfeffer, Fred Pfeffer," sang Joseph, the biggest of the boys. "With him it's always Fred Pfeffer. He's like an el conductor. 'Tickets please. Tickets. Where's your tickets? Tickets.' Same thing over and over."

They all had a laugh. On the edge of the group Arnold Schneider laughed with them.

"I'll be King Kelly," he said.

"King Kelly!?" Joseph said. "Does he even *play* anymore?"

"He played for the New York Giants last year!" Arnold said. "He turned a triple play against Brooklyn."

"Yeah, so did my gran," Joseph said. The boys all had another laugh. "All right, me and George choose up sides."

69

One by one all the boys were chosen by the captains. All the boys but Arnold. He was the smallest and worst player there, and he knew it, but he still watched the captains, hoping one of them would take him today.

"You bring that good bat, Arnie?" Joseph asked.

"No. That bat's my dad's. He got it—"

"In the war. Yeah, yeah, we know. You want to play, you bring that bat next time."

"But with me the teams are even," Arnold said.

"He's right," said George. Arnold's heart leaped.

"Here, catch," George said. He threw the ball to Arnold, but it was too far over his head. Another boy caught it and threw it back.

"Here you go, Arnie."

The ball sailed over his head again. And again. Arnold knew this game. They were playing keep-away. He stopped trying to catch the ball and glared at them, his hands clenched and his fists shaking.

"Boat-lickers," he said.

"Oooooh," Joseph laughed. "I'm soooo scared."

Arnold wanted to cry, but he would never do that again. Not in front of the boys. Instead he walked away as fast as he could.

"Good-bye, King Kelly!" Joseph taunted, and Arnold broke into a run.

When Arnold finally slowed down to wipe the tears off his face he realized he had run halfway up Bedford Avenue.

He was in the Eastern District with the vaudeville theaters. He passed Hyde & Behman's and the Empire Theater, stopping to read the placards outside announcing the nightly acts. Above him, the Broadway–Brooklyn line rattled by on its elevated platform, and he watched as ladies and gentlemen in their fine clothes went scurrying for shop awnings to escape the soot and smoke that drifted down from the train.

Electric lights hummed at the entrance of the Gayety Theater, and a name on the board outside caught Arnold's eye as he passed. He rushed back to read the sign:

"Appearing all this week: O'Dowd's Neighbors! Featuring Weber and Field, Dutch Knockabouts; Haines and Vidocq, back talkers; the Braatz Brothers, acrobats; John LeClair, balancer and juggler; Drummond and Tahley, musicians; Alice Raymond, cornet player; Mike 'King' Kelly, famed baseballer; William Wheatman, maker of faces . . ."

Mike "King" Kelly, famed baseballer! Arnold couldn't believe it. King Kelly? Here, in Brooklyn? On the vaudeville stage? He rushed to the door to look inside, but he only saw the lobby. The doorman eyed him and he rushed back to the sign. "Mike 'King' Kelly, famed baseballer." Why had they buried him so far down the list of performers? Wouldn't he be the star attraction?

Admission was fifty cents, and Arnold didn't have to pat his pockets to know he didn't have enough coins. There was no chance his parents would give him money for a vaudeville show either. They wouldn't even like that he'd been in the theater district.

Music and laughter trickled out of the Gayety Theater. The show had already started. Arnold *had* to see King Kelly.

There was only one thing for it. He'd have to sneak in.

A group of young men and their ladies came strutting down the lane and stopped to consider the playbill. They would be perfect. Arnold tried to watch them without being obvious about it, silently willing them to decide to take in the show. A well-timed outburst of laughter sold them on the matter, and they moved as one toward the doorway where the men made a great show of paying their ladies' way in. Being on the short end of ten, Arnold slipped around them out of sight of the ticket seller and ducked inside.

The theater was little more than half full, and Arnold slunk down a side aisle and slid into a seat. He waited for someone to point a finger, to grab him by the shoulder, but no one seemed to have noticed he'd snuck in, and he relaxed. King Kelly wasn't on the stage now anyway—it was an acrobat routine with trained tumblers. After that came a man and a woman who played violins, then a face contortionist who made Arnold laugh, and a comedian who did not. He began to fear he had missed King Kelly entirely, when the master of ceremonies stepped onto the stage to announce the next act.

"Ladies and gentlemen," the emcee said, "the Gayety Theater is now proud to present that legendary Rascal of Round Ball, that Scoundrel of Swat, the Dandy of the Diamond— Mr. Mike 'King' Kelly in, 'He Would Be an Actor, or, The Ballplayer's Revenge'!"

King Kelly pranced out onto the stage with a glass of beer in one hand and a baseball bat in the other. It was him, sure enough. He wore the blue and white uniform of the Boston Beaneaters and a bright red scarf tied under his collar. His dark black hair was smoothed back under his white cap, and his big bushy mustache had just a hint of curl at the ends.

Kelly drew a polite smattering of applause and Arnold leaned forward in his seat.

"Ah, it's great to be back here in Brooklyn," Kelly said, his Irish accent rolling off his tongue. "Why, it was here, against your very own Brooklyn Bridegrooms, that I robbed Monte Ward of a home run. I remember that day very clearly," he said, settling in to a story he'd clearly told many times. "'Twas getting on toward dusk when Monte stepped to the plate, and we all knew the umpire would soon call the game on account of darkness. But the score was tied two apiece, you see, and the Grooms had something cooking with two outs in the ninth. Pinckney and O'Brien stood on second and third, and a hit of any kind would send us packing back to Beantown."

Kelly took a long draw off his beer, but not so long as to lose the audience.

"Now, it's gotten so dark I can hardly see Clarkson on the

mound, let alone the batter. But I hear the crack of the bat and see the infielders turn, and I know a scorching sphere is headed my way. I go back, back, back into the big vast swirling darkness of Eastern Park—you lot have been there, so you know what I mean—and I reach out as high as I can and I *jump* as high as I can," Kelly said, pantomiming the catch as best he could with his beer in lieu of a glove, "and I come down with me hand raised high in the twilight, dashing the hopes of the Brooklyn faithful!"

The hometown crowd gave him a good-natured boo, and he smiled.

"'Out number three!' yells the ump. 'Game called on account of darkness!' So I run back to the dugout with me glove closed tight, and our manager, old Frank Selee, comes forward with the rest of the boys to congratulate me. 'Kel,' says he, 'that was the finest catch I've ever yet seen.'

"'And you still haven't,' says I, and I opened my glove. There wasn't a thing in it. The ball went a mile over me head!"

What a marvelous trick! Arnold clapped himself silly, and the audience roared with laughter. Kelly saluted them all with his beer.

"Tell us about the ten-thousand-dollar transfer!" someone yelled.

"What'd you do with all that money?" called another.

"I ate strawberries and ice cream every day," Kelly said with a grin.

"Yeah, and the bartenders got the rest!" someone heckled.

Kelly told a few more stories from his playing days, then recited "Casey at the Bat," changing out mighty Casey's name for his own. When he was finished, he left the stage to the sound of the house band playing "Slide, Kelly, Slide" and great applause.

Not even the promise of the Salambos, fire-handlers from Brazil, could keep Arnold in his seat. He dashed down the aisle and out of the theater, turning down the side alley where he hoped King Kelly would emerge. He guessed the wrong alley, though, and by the time he had run around to the other side King Kelly and another man were already halfway to the street.

"Mr. Kelly!" Arnold called. "King! King! How about an autograph!"

Kelly stopped and turned, smiling magnificently.

"One of me fans, Hiroshi!" he said to the other man. Arnold slid to a stop in front of them, and he could see now Kelly was accompanied by an Oriental—a Chinaman or some such—dressed in brightly colored silks and sporting a braided ponytail like a girl might wear. There was something crawling on the man's right shoulder, and Arnold jumped in fright as a black monkey leaped from the Oriental onto Kelly's back.

"Me gentleman's gentleman," Kelly said. "Me valet Hiroshi. Now laddie, what's your name?"

"A—Arnold," he said. "Arnold Schneider."

"Right. Now, let's see here." He searched the pockets of

his coat. "Aha. Here's me fountain pen then. What have you got for me to sign, Arthur?"

Arnold's heart sank. Here was King Kelly before him, ready to sign his famous autograph, and Arnold had nothing in his pocket but three pennies and a bit of fluff. Now the boys at Pigtown would never believe him.

"It's—it's Arnold, sir. And I'm sorry, but I don't—"

Arnold stopped. Kelly suddenly had the most peculiar look on his face, like he had fallen asleep with his eyes open. The ballplayer's face lost all expression and his body began to sway.

"Mr. Kelly, are you all right?"

Hiroshi tried to catch Kelly before he fell, but he was too late. The monkey jumped from the sinking ship and King Kelly dove headlong into the gutter, splashing face-first into the muck.

Arnold rushed to Kelly's side and tried to turn him over.

"What's happened!? What should I do? Should I go for a doctor?" Arnold asked. He looked up at Hiroshi's blank face and realized he probably didn't understand a word Arnold was saying. "I—I'm sorry," Arnold said loudly. *No speak Chinaman.*

Hiroshi sighed. "I'm Japanese," he said with a distinct New England accent. "And no, he doesn't need a doctor. He needs a paddy wagon. King Kelly is drunk."

2

Arnold and Hiroshi carried the unconscious Kelly back to his boardinghouse, though to call his temporary place of residence a "boardinghouse" was generous. It was unclean and overcrowded, what Arnold's father would probably call a "flophouse." A man behind a counter shielded by chicken wire watched the three of them suspiciously as they crossed the lobby, and Arnold kept his head down as they dragged Kelly toward the stairs.

"Does King Kelly really stay here?" Arnold asked Hiroshi.

The valet grunted. "If they haven't thrown his bags into the alley yet."

"No pets!" the man behind the chicken wire yelled. Hiroshi stopped and clicked some command to the monkey, and it leaped down and scurried out the front door and into the night.

"Wait, where will it—" Arnold started to ask, but Hiroshi was already moving again.

The stairs were just as full of people as the lobby, and

Arnold wondered if these were people who couldn't afford a proper room. Some slept; others stared into the dim haze of the place, not registering Arnold and the others as they passed.

At the second-floor landing, Kelly roused for a moment and seemed almost lucid.

"What's all this then?" he asked. He straightened, and Arnold and Hiroshi backed away, watching to see if he could stand. He noticed neither of them, instead focusing on a homeless man huddled in the stairwell corner.

"You look a mite cold, friend," Kelly said. He struggled with his long coat, the removal of his arms giving him particular problems in his inebriated state. Arnold noticed that Hiroshi made no move to help him. At length Kelly escaped his coat and ceremoniously draped it over the man in the corner.

Kelly turned to his valet and smiled.

"Very noble, sir," Hiroshi told him, though his tone said he thought otherwise.

"And what's your name, laddie?" Kelly asked.

"Arnold—" he began to tell him again, but Kelly's eyes lost their focus again and he fell forward. Arnold was relieved when Hiroshi put a hand to Kelly's chest and stopped his fall, but was equally horrified when the manservant pushed him hard the other way, sending Kelly crashing to the stairs.

Arnold stared at Hiroshi in disbelief, but the manservant said nothing, simply taking one of Kelly's hands and dragging him up the stairs. Arnold rushed to help, doing his best to keep King Kelly's head from *thunk-thunk-thunking* on the stair treads.

King Kelly's room was tiny, even smaller than the one Arnold had all to himself at home. There was little more than a bed in one corner and a chair in another, the washroom shared by all somewhere else down the hall. Broken plaster hung from the ceiling, and the room smelled of sweat, liquor, and vomit.

Hiroshi went to the window, wrenched it open, and whistled. Arnold thought this very odd, until the little black monkey leaped in, having somehow scaled the outside of the building. The valet gave the creature a bit of treat from his pocket, then settled into the chair.

Arnold looked around the room and shook his head. "I thought he lived on strawberries and ice cream."

The manservant laughed. "Maybe once. He talks like he still does, just like he keeps me around, to make people think he's still rich. But he squandered all his money, and now he keeps himself in booze and pays my meager salary with these vaudeville shows. That coat he so generously gave away just now was the only one of its kind he owned. Now the poor mick'll freeze to death before he drinks himself to death."

"Begging your pardon, sir," Arnold said, "but you don't sound much like a Japanner."

The valet rubbed his face in his hands. "I lived in Boston

for twenty-five years before this sot hired me to carry his bags for him."

"Shouldn't we get him up off the floor?" Arnold asked.

Hiroshi afforded his employer a disdainful look and went back to feeding the monkey. "Have at it," he said.

Kelly was slight for a man, but Arnold still had trouble hefting him up off the floor. He started with his head and arms, then tried lifting him from the waist, turning his body sideways to roll it onto the mattress. Hiroshi did nothing to help. Just when Arnold though he had Kelly's lower half securely on the bed his top half slid off and *thunked* to the floor.

Kelly woke with a start.

"That is a smashing hat," he said.

Arnold blinked, then put a hand to his head. He was just wearing an ordinary boy's cap.

"Smashing hat," Kelly said. He started to giggle. He righted himself and plucked Arnold's hat from his head, then stood and smashed the cap beneath his heel. "*Smashing . . . hat!*" He laughed, then spied his own top hat, which had fallen to the floor.

"*Smashing hat!*" he cried, putting his foot through the top of his own hat. As strange as it all was, Arnold couldn't help but laugh with him.

Kelly's eyes fixed on the bowler his manservant wore.

"No," the valet warned.

"Smashing hat, Hiroshi!" said Kelly, and he chased the

Japanese man around the room. The monkey flew screeching from Hiroshi's shoulders and perched on the bed, and the neighbors pounded on the wall for them all to be quiet. Kelly made a swipe for Hiroshi's hat, but the manservant was too quick for him. To save his hat, Hiroshi took it off and tossed it through the open window.

"There. No smashing my hat," he said.

Kelly went to the window and leaned out.

"You've lost your hat, my good man. Just let me fetch it for you—"

King Kelly had a leg out the window before Arnold and Hiroshi grabbed him and pulled him back inside. Kelly fought them the whole time, as though he had no idea what peril it would be to fall three stories to the street.

When they'd pulled him a sufficient distance away from the window, Hiroshi reared back and slapped Kelly hard across the face. Kelly had certainly been silly, but Arnold couldn't believe how cruel his manservant was. Neither could King Kelly.

"What on Earth—what did you strike me for?"

"You just tried to jump out the window."

That thought, more than the slap, seemed to sober Kelly up. The red color drained out of his face and he slumped on the bed, looking around as though seeing the room for the first time.

"Who are you, laddie?" he asked Arnold. "What's your name?"

Arnold told him again.

"I'll get you some coffee," Hiroshi said.

"No, no," Kelly said. "I feel fine. Fit as a fiddle." He stood. "Why, I haven't felt this good since I won the batting title with Chicago. What year was that, Hiroshi?"

The valet was at the window, trying to see where his hat had fallen. "You know darn well what year it was."

"1886," said Arnold. "You hit .388. You also led the league in runs for the third straight year."

"Say, I like this lad!" Kelly said. "Aye, 1886 it was. The season old Cap Anson had those Pinkerton boys follow me about. I grew so tired of private eyes watching me every move that I decked one at the train station before I alighted. It wasn't 'til we were back in Chicago I found the poor lad wasn't really a detective. That was my last season with the White Stockings to be sure!"

"They sold you to Boston for ten thousand dollars," Arnold said.

"Aye, made A. G. Spalding a great deal of money, I did."

"You made a fair bit yourself," Hiroshi said from his chair in the corner. "And just where is that two-thousand-dollar salary now? The three-thousand-dollar 'bonus' for the use of your likeness? The endorsement fees for the King Kelly bats, the 'Slide, Kelly, Slide' sled, the shoe polish with your name on the can?"

"You know," Kelly told Arnold, ignoring his manservant, "I was once given a silver bat by the *Cincinnati Enquirer* when I played in the Queen City, in honor of hitting the first home run at the Avenue Grounds. That very bat is still on display in a store window in me hometown of Paterson, New Jersey."

Hiroshi gave a short, harsh laugh. Arnold didn't understand what was so funny about that, but Kelly didn't seem to mind. He wobbled back and forth, then caught himself like he was trying to stay awake.

"Have ye—have ye ever heard the story of how I substituted meself for Dimples Tate while he was trying to catch a foul ball?"

"Why don't you tell him the story of how you hit .189 your final season with Boston?" his valet asked. "Or how you made ten errors in just eighteen games last year with the Giants?"

But everything Hiroshi said was lost on Kelly. He was fast asleep again, sprawled out on his bed. The Japanese manservant buried his head in his hands.

"If you hate him so much, why are you still here?" Arnold asked.

"That's a very good question."

Hiroshi got up from his chair and called the monkey to him with a whistle. He pulled a suitcase out from under the bed, opened it to check the contents, then stood.

"You're—you're *leaving?*" Arnold asked.

"Might as well. Kelly can't pay his rent, let alone me. I'm going back to Boston."

"But what about next season?"

"There isn't going to *be* a next season, kid. Not for King Kelly, not on the baseball diamond. He hasn't told anyone, but the Giants cut him. Not even his old friend Monte Ward will have him. He's finished."

"But the stage, the vaudeville halls. People will still pay to hear his stories."

"Anson, hat. Fetch my hat," Hiroshi said, and the little monkey leaped to the open window and was gone.

"Kelly barely makes enough on the stage to keep him in beer and cigarettes," the valet told Arnold. "He drinks more than he earns every night. He's not the ten-thousand-dollar beauty anymore, but he still lives like it."

Hiroshi was clearly done with Kelly, but all Arnold could think about were the records the old ballplayer had broken, the songs that were sung about him, the picture of King Kelly sliding into second that had replaced the pictures of Custer's Last Stand in every public house in Brooklyn.

Anson the monkey climbed back into the room with Hiroshi's hat. The valet took it from him and dusted it off.

"That silver bat he won," Arnold said, still staring at Kelly. "You laughed. Did he really not win it?"

"Oh, he won it all right, and it's right there in a shop window in Paterson for all the world to see, just like he said. Only the shop is R. J. Robinson's Pawnbroker and Loan. He sold it to pay his bar tab." Hiroshi put his hat on his head and opened the door to leave. "*Sayonara,* kid. The job's yours now. And tell Kelly he can keep the monkey."

✜ ✜ ✜

Water sloshed onto King Kelly's face and he sat up like a man stuck with a pin.

"Whaaaa—! Who? What?" he sputtered.

Arnold felt a little bad for dumping a bucket of cold water on him, but didn't figure he had much other choice. He flipped the bucket over and sat down on it next to Kelly.

"I'm dreadful sorry to have to wake you like that," Arnold said.

"W—what day is it?" Kelly asked.

"Saturday." The monkey jumped on Kelly's back and perched there.

"And where am I?"

"A boardinghouse."

"I meant what city, laddie."

"Oh. Brooklyn."

Kelly put a hand to his head, as though it pained him to think.

"Ah. Yes. Brooklyn. And you are—?"

"Arnold, sir. Arnold Schneider."

Arnold waited for some sort of recognition to dawn on Kelly's face, but it didn't.

"I met you last night," Arnold told him. "I asked you for your autograph."

"Well, I certainly hope ye haven't been waiting all this time to get it."

"No. I came back to help you out." Arnold stood. "I'm your new valet."

"Are you now? And just what's happened to Hiroshi then?"

"He went back to Boston."

Kelly nodded. "So. You're me new valet, eh? And just how old *are* you?"

"Ten," Arnold told him.

"Aha. And what is our first order of business today, laddie?"

"To get you cleaned up."

❖ ❖ ❖

Arnold waited outside the Turkish bath in Brooklyn Heights with Anson the monkey for what seemed like hours. Kelly's treatment had cost Arnold a fair bit of what little money he'd saved for himself, but it was necessary. While Kelly'd been inside, Arnold had run the ballplayer's shirt, pants, and collar down the street to have them cleaned with kerosene at the dry cleaner too.

After a time Kelly strolled out of the bathhouse looking positively regal. His face was flush, his hair was slicked back, and his mustache stood at attention.

Anson jumped from Arnold's shoulder to his master's.

"I don't believe I have ever sweat so much in me entire life," Kelly said. "All right, valet. You've got the whisky wrung out of me, and me clothes have never looked finer." He straightened the red handkerchief tied around his newly pressed collar. "Where to next? Have I an audition at Prospect Hall?"

"No," Arnold told him. "You're playing Pigtown."

3

Arnold Schneider was a hero.

Just about every boy in Brooklyn heard that King Kelly was at the Pigtown field, and they rushed down to crowd him and pepper the baseball star with a thousand questions. Kelly answered them all with a wide smile, though just slightly smaller than the smile Arnold was wearing.

"What was it like winning the pennant?"

"Which time?" Kelly asked.

"The first time."

"With Boston!"

"Tell us about being sold for ten thousand dollars!"

"What'd you do with the money, Kel?"

"What's your monkey's name?"

"Anson," he managed.

"You mean like Cap Anson? What was it like to play with him?"

"Oh, he's a tough player, all right, but an even tougher manager. The first day of practice he ordered me to lose twenty pounds and put me through the mill with special meals and supervised dog trots. 'Course I have a new boss now," King Kelly said. He smashed Arnold's hat farther down on his head and rubbed it around. "This one's got me cleaned up and living straight again."

For the first time in his life, everybody wanted to stand near Arnold, to talk with him, to be his best friend. He was giddy with the rush of it all.

"Tell us about Corcoran," one of the boys begged Kelly.

"And George Gore!"

"What about Fred Pfeffer?" Tommy Collum said.

"Fred Pfeffer, Fred Pfeffer!" Arnold taunted, and everyone laughed. They laughed!

"Ah, now Freddy was a great friend of mine," Kelly told them. "A great friend indeed. He and I used to go out drinking, ah . . . *lemonade."* Kelly smiled. "Freddy was a proponent of 'inside baseball.' Do ye know what that is? So-called 'scientific baseball.' He even wrote a book on it."

The boys begged Kelly to show them how it was done, and he asked for a bat and ball. Arnold handed him his own bat, the one his father had brought home from the Civil War.

"Now this here is a fine bat, a fine bat indeed," Kelly said, weighing it in his hands. He stood back from the boys and gave it a swing. "Trade you me glove for it, Arnold."

The boys gasped as Kelly gave Arnold his baseball mitt.

It was thick and padded like a pillow, the kind that was in fashion among the catchers in the National League. Arnold marveled at it. None of the boys could afford a proper glove like this. It was heavy, like a great mitten with a leather-clad lump of stuffing forming a U along the base of the palm. Where the broad thumb met the rest of the mitt there were two small strings of leather to hold them together. The other boys watched on quietly as Arnold put his hand inside the massive thing. He was just able to bend it along its middle, and for a moment he imagined himself clamping down tight on an Amos Rusie fastball.

"Marvelous piece o' cowhide, ain't it?" Kelly said. "A trade then?"

"I—I can't," Arnold said, and he told Kelly the story of how his father had traded for the bat during the war. He sighed and handed the glove back. "I wish I could," he said.

"Ah well, you can have me glove anyway, laddie. No trade."

Arnold felt the wave of envy from the boys around him, and he knew he would never be picked last again. Ever.

Kelly put Arnold behind the plate and arranged the rest of the boys all around the infield.

"Scientific baseball is about playing the percentages, see?" Kelly said. "If you know Oyster Burns always pulls to the left side, why, you tell your fielders to shift that direction. If

Big Dan Brouthers likes to give the ball a Baltimore chop, you play your boys in, see? That's scientific."

Kelly showed the boys how to drill themselves on the basics of inside baseball, then taught them a few tricks they wouldn't find in any book: how to fool base runners into thinking you'd overthrown their bag when there was really an outfielder standing behind them to catch it, how to keep an extra ball in your pocket in case you lost one over your head, and how to skip bases when the umpires weren't looking. After that they played a few innings until Anson the monkey snatched up the ball and led the boys on a wild chase for it all over Pigtown.

"I've had a fine time, laddie," Kelly told Arnold, "but I'd best be getting back. I've a show to do tonight, and I find me act goes better when I've had a little something to drink first. And I don't mean lemonade. I'll tell you, lad, I'd rather face ten thousand angry baseball enthusiasts on the diamond field than go before a friendly audience in a theater."

"Kel, is it true what your valet said? That you won't play again next season?"

"Not won't, laddie. Can't. I'd play if I could, but no one will have me."

"But you're not old. Cap Anson's older than you are and he's still playing first base for the White Stockings."

Kelly sighed as the boys laughed and scrambled across the field after the monkey.

"I don't know how he does it, laddie. Cap Anson. Truly I don't. They keep moving the mound around for starters, and the pitchers don't throw underhanded anymore. Nowadays it comes in hard and fast, kicking and screaming into the catcher's mitt. Amos Rusie, Cy Young, Kid Nichols—pitchers are bigger and stronger and wickeder than ever before. And they hurt like hell to catch, by the way, even with all o' that padding. And now I hear they're actually thinking of counting foul balls as strikes. Mark my words: There won't be a batting average over .250 in all the league." He shook his head. "Baseball tain't like it were in the olden days, laddie. Me days of playing in the big leagues are through. It's the stage for me now, even though I'm not on Broadway. Heck, I'm in Brooklyn and I'm not even playing Prospect Hall."

King Kelly whistled and Anson broke off his game of keep-away and came scurrying back with the boys behind him.

"Time for me to be off, lads," Kelly told them. There was a general moan, but it turned into well-wishes and good-byes soon enough, and then calls for a new game when Kelly had gone.

"Me and Arnold are captains!" Joseph called.

Arnold knew he should have felt triumphant. He was a legend. He had brought King Kelly, the Ten-Thousand-Dollar Beauty, to Pigtown. But how long would it last? How long before he was little "Arnie" again, picked last every game and only allowed to play because of his bat—and now his glove. When the excitement of King Kelly went away, what would be left?

There was only one thing for it, he decided. King Kelly would have to stay.

The sun was just setting over the towers of the Brooklyn Bridge as Arnold made his way north toward Bushwick. He couldn't wait to tell Kelly his news.

"And now the pitcher holds the ball," he said, repeating lines from "Casey at the Bat." "And now he lets it go."

He stopped mid-run and took a swing with his father's bat. "And now the air is shattered by the force of Kelly's blow!"

He cheered for the hit—Kelly had gotten a double, not struck out like Casey had—then broke into a jog the rest of the way to the Gayety Theater, where King Kelly was appearing again that night. Three ladies with big poofy dresses were making their way inside when he arrived, and he slid in behind them. He had just stepped into the lobby when a hand grabbed him and yanked him back. The hand was attached to an ugly brute with a scraggy beard and a wandering eye.

"Awright. Let's have your ticket then, boy."

No! Arnold had to get inside to see King Kelly tonight. It couldn't wait. "I, uh—" he stammered, "I'm here to . . ." He looked down at the bat in his hands. "I'm here to bring King Kelly his bat!"

The ticket taker gave him a piercing look with his one good eye, then let him go.

"Shoulda used the stage door then," he said. "Kelly's back-stage."

Arnold tipped his cap and ran to the front corner of the theater. Up on the stage he could feel the hot gas lights that burned along the edge, and he felt the eyes of the audience on him as though he might be some part of the act. He quickly ducked behind the heavy red curtain.

One of the Dutch Knockabouts pointed Arnold toward a room at the back of the theater where many of the acts were preparing to go onstage. Arnold cast about and finally found King Kelly in the corner, already dressed in his light blue Boston uniform and cap. As he approached, Arnold couldn't help imagining him in a different color uniform.

Kelly squinted as Arnold approached.

"Well, if it tain't me shadow!" He turned. "How the devil did you get down here, lad?"

"I told them I was here to bring you your bat for tonight's show," Arnold said. He handed him his father's bat, which Kelly again weighed appreciatively.

"Well, it's a fair sight better than the one they run me out there with." He nodded to a bat in the corner. "Give her a try."

Arnold picked up the bat. It was light as a feather.

"Stage prop," Kelly said. He took a drink from a glass sitting next to him, then refilled it from what looked like a whisky bottle. "Just a little something to fortify me for when I go out in front of the cranks," he explained. "I've always found that—"

"I've got you a tryout!" Arnold interrupted. He could contain himself no longer. "A tryout with the Brooklyn Bridegrooms!"

Kelly sat speechless for a moment.

"You, er, what?" he asked finally.

"I skipped out on the game at Pigtown after you left and I went to Eastern Park and talked to the Bridegrooms' manager, Foutz, while he was shagging fly balls in the outfield. He said for you to come by the field tomorrow before the game, and he'll see."

"He'll see . . . what?"

"You. In action. The way you played today at Pigtown, you're a far sight better than either of Brooklyn's catchers."

"That was against a bunch o' guttersnipes, laddie! Good as you lot are, you're hardly National League caliber."

"Game time is one o'clock," Arnold went on. "Foutz said to be there an hour before the game. You can even use my bat!"

Kelly stared at the bat in his hands. "Maybe . . . maybe I *could* still play. I did tell Monte I still had a few good seasons left in me, and I meant it."

"You'll be great, Kel. It'll be just like it was before. And you can come play ball with us at Pigtown some mornings. Not every morning, I know, because you'll have practice, but it'll be a kind of a practice, see?"

Kelly gave Arnold his big famous stage smile. "Sure, laddie. Absolutely. Just like it was before. You're a good kid, Arthur."

"Arnold."

Kelly picked up his glass and drank it in a single gulp.

"Arnold then," Kelly said. "You're a good lad, Arnold. But tell me. Promise me one thing, lad."

"Anything, Kel."

The ballplayer refilled his glass.

"I want you to promise me you'll never take a drink."

"Sure, Kel. Of course."

Kelly ignored his own advice and finished off another glass. His face twisted into a grimace, and Arnold watched him shiver as the drink went down.

"Better skedaddle, laddie. It's just about time for King Kelly's big act."

❖ ❖ ❖

Sunday morning Arnold ran all the way up Kings Highway and out to Eastern Park on the far side of town.

"I'm here with King Kelly!" he told the man at the ticket window, dashing inside before he could argue. Arnold had remembered to bring Kelly his father's bat the night before, but not Kelly's glove, and he'd need that for the tryout.

96

The Grooms were already taking batting practice, and Arnold searched for King Kelly and Dave "Scissors" Foutz, Brooklyn's left fielder and manager. He didn't see Kelly, but Foutz stood near the dugout making out a lineup card.

"Mr. Foutz! Mr. Foutz!" Arnold cried. The manager took a moment to recognize him from the day before and made his way over to the stands.

"Brought me Mike Kelly, have you?" Foutz said, his voice heavy with doubt.

"You mean he isn't here?" Arnold asked. It had to be past noon already. "He said he would be here. And he knows the way to the park. He's played here before."

"Look kid, I don't know if you're pulling my leg or if someone's pulling yours, but take my advice. Leave it alone. Even if Kelly could play, that man's got a monkey on his back."

"I know all about his monkey!" Arnold said. "The monkey's name is Cap Anson."

Dave Foutz had a good hard laugh at that, although Arnold didn't see what was so funny.

"That's good, kid. Maybe you do know him after all. But believe me: Kelly's through."

"No! He must have overslept is all," Arnold said, running up the aisle. "I'll have him here before game time!"

"Kid, wait!" Foutz yelled, but Arnold was already gone. Outside the park he hopped one of the trolleys heading west, paying a nickel for the privilege but saving much time. He hopped off near the Eastern District and dashed the rest of the way to Kelly's boardinghouse, ignoring the look of the man behind the chicken wire as he ran through the lobby and up the steps.

"Kel! Kel!" Arnold said, bursting into King Kelly's room. Only it wasn't King Kelly's room. A stranger rolled over in the bed, cursing at Arnold and throwing a shoe at him as he pulled the door closed. Did he have the wrong floor? The wrong room? He retraced his steps. No, this was the room Kelly had been staying in.

Back in the lobby Arnold went up to the man behind the screen.

"Do you know if King Kelly has changed rooms?"

The man put down his newspaper and frowned.

"You know Mike Kelly?"

"He's my friend," said Arnold.

"You know where he is?"

"No. I was hoping you could tell me."

The man harrumphed. "Well, your friend bailed owing me twelve dollars. Don't know how he got his things out with him, but he did. Must have climbed out the window. You gonna pay me the twelve dollars?"

"I—I don't have twelve dollars."

"Yeah. Right." The man flicked his newspaper back open. "You tell that bum he owes me twelve dollars."

Arnold ran to the theater. The story was the same there.

"The louse slipped out after his last act owing more'n his pay in whisky," the stage manager told him. "If you're looking for him, I'd try any saloon in walking distance. Oh," he said before closing the door, "and tell him he won't be playing *any* stage in Brooklyn until he pays off what he owes."

There were a dozen or more bars in the Eastern District, and Arnold tried them all. In those that weren't empty or locked up tight he found some owner or barmaid who had heard of Kelly and seen him in the past week, but he had paid a call to none of their establishments last night. And every one of them was looking to settle up with him. One of them even handed Arnold Kelly's bar bill. It came to fifteen dollars and seventy-five cents.

Arnold walked back toward Kelly's boardinghouse in the vain hope that he might see Kelly, or one of the other performers, or find some clue as to where he'd gone. He had just resolved to return to the ballpark, thinking perhaps Kelly had only been late and they had missed each other, when an item in a shop window caught his eye.

It was his father's baseball bat. His father's baseball bat was in the window of a Fulton Street pawnbroker's shop.

Arnold burst into the store, almost tearing the bell on the door from its hinges. A stout man wearing a pin-striped vest and a large, thick mustache looked up from tinkering with a pocket watch.

"Looking for something in particular?" he asked.

"That bat in the window," Arnold said. "It's mine!"

The man smiled. "It's yours if you have fifty dollars."

"Fifty dollars!?"

"That bat is a collector's item," the man told him. "It's signed by King Kelly himself. Ever heard of him? He's a bit before your time, but he was one of the greats."

"No," Arnold said, though not in answer to the man's question.

"Had that bat made especial for him by a man in Kentucky. A Falls City original that is. What they call a Louisville Slugger."

"No. I mean, yes, that bat was made by a man in Louisville, but it was given to my pa during the war. It wasn't made for King Kelly."

The man shrugged his shoulders. "It was King Kelly's bat. I can authenticate it as such. He came into this shop himself right before closing last night and sold it to me."

Arnold felt like his heart had been ripped out of his chest.

"You looking to sell that glove?" the man asked. "Might be able to give you a dollar or two for it."

Arnold looked down at the glove in his hand. He had almost forgotten he carried it. The glove he had traded for his father's bat, without meaning to. The glove his hero King Kelly had given him. Arnold went to the front window to look again at the bat on display. He could reach out and touch it, but it wasn't his father's bat anymore. Arnold had lost it. He'd given it away and King Kelly had sold it.

"Said he needed train fare out of town," the man behind the counter said, as if he could read Arnold's thoughts. He went back to tinkering with the watch. "Some opportunity in Boston. You suppose that means he'll be back with the Beaneaters next season?"

"No," Arnold said, pushing his way outside. "Mike Kelly is all washed up."

Fourth Inning: The Way Things Are Now

Coney Island, New York, 1908

1

Walter wandered the grand boardwalk along the yard out-side the Brighton Beach Hotel while his parents checked in. It was early spring, just before the start of the baseball sea-son, and the salty air from the roaring surf was still cool and crisp, like a last gasp before the long hot summer to come. A few brave souls were even wading in the ocean, their navy blue two-piece suits dark against the bright white of the sandy beach.

Walter heard a familiar *crack* and a cheer. Farther down the boardwalk, part of the yard that separated the hotel from the ocean was parceled off into a baseball field, and he rushed to watch. As the batboy for the Superbas, Walter saw more baseball games than probably any other boy in Brooklyn, but the sound of a bat hitting a ball still excited him.

There was a small but enthusiastic crowd of hotel guests watching the game—gentlemen dressed in suits and hats, and ladies wearing extravagant summer dresses, all loung-ing on reclining beach chairs under umbrellas while colored waiters served them drinks and treats. This was where New York's well-to-do vacationed, and the baseball game was being played for them, and them only.

And it was being played by Negroes.

The runner on second base danced back and forth trying to rattle the pitcher, waving his arms and making silly sounds that made the hotel guests titter with laughter. The pitcher wheeled and pretended to throw the ball to the second baseman, who made believe he'd caught it. The runner played along, getting into a rundown between second and third as the fielders tossed a phantom ball back and forth between them, trying to tag him out. The ladies and gentlemen roared with laughter.

This isn't baseball, thought Walter. *It's a minstrel show.*

The runner slid safely into third base and the invisible ball was thrown back to the big pitcher, who focused again on the batter. The pickoff and rundown might have been fake, but there was nothing phantom about his next pitch, except that the batter had no way of hitting it. It was a blur of motion, a momentary vision that made you think a baseball had been thrown, but you weren't quite sure. Until the umpire called it a strike. The ball was tossed back to the pitcher—there it was, made of real laces and leather, proving that something had actually been thrown—and then he did it again, and again, the batter taking a pathetic, halting swing at the last one before being rung up on strikes.

The players changed sides.

"Who are they?" Walter asked.

"Waiters," said a gentleman lounging next to him. "Some of the hotel staff."

"Cubans," his lady friend said. "Up here for the season. They only play for fun."

The last three pitches didn't look like somebody playing for fun, Walter thought, but he kept it to himself.

"Hey, nice hat," said a boy behind him. Walter turned. Three boys around his age had come up to him. The oldest one might have been thirteen.

Walter touched the Brooklyn Superbas hat he wore. "Thanks. I'm the batboy for the Superbas."

"No," said the big kid. "I mean, 'Nice hat, sheeny. I think I'll take it.'"

Walter clenched his fists. "What did you just call me?"

"You heard me, kike," the kid said.

"I'm not a Jew!" said Walter. It wasn't the first time he'd been called a Jew, and not the first time he'd gotten into a fight over it.

"Sure you're not, Bergstein. With that nose you've got, your mom must have doinked a rabbi."

Walter launched himself at the big one, fists flailing. It was a fair fight for about two seconds. He got in one good blow before the kid and his two friends ganged up on him and beat the stuffing out of him. It would have been smarter to try to break away and run, or even curl up on the ground

107

in a little ball, but Walter clawed and fought, getting himself bloodier in the process.

"Cheese it. Pinkertons!" one of the boys said, and suddenly they were gone. And so was Walter's Superbas hat, the official hat he'd been given with his batboy uniform. He tried to sink to his knees, but a hotel security man pulled him up roughly by the arm.

"All right, we don't stand for any roughhousing here at the Brighton," the man said, his accent thick with Irish.

"I didn't start nothing," Walter said.

The Pinkerton man eyed him. "I'll bet. I know your kind."

"Walter!" his father called. His parents rushed up to him. "Walter, we've been looking everywhere for you."

"Walter, what happened to your face?" his mother asked. "And your clothes!"

"Been fighting," the Pinkerton man said. He gave the same appraising eye to Walter's parents as he had to the boy. "You guests?"

"Er, no," said Walter's father. "They're out of rooms."

"The concierge was kind enough to recommend the West Brighton Hotel," Walter's mother said. She licked a handkerchief and wiped at his face with it. Walter squirmed.

"We won't be troubling you anymore," his father said.

The Pinkerton released his prisoner and nodded. "West Brighton's the place for you," he said. "Now move along."

Walter's father dragged him away, sparing him at least the ministrations of his mother.

"What were you thinking, getting into a scrap at the Brighton? Not a week goes by I don't get called into school for your fighting, but on vacation?"

"They jumped me!" Walter protested. "They called me a sheeny!"

"That's enough of that talk," his mother scolded. Walter saw his mother and father exchange a look.

"Why aren't we staying at the Brighton this year?" he asked. "We stayed here last year."

"I told you, they're out of rooms."

"They have a *thousand* rooms," Walter said. "How can they be sold out? It's not even summer. I thought we had a reservation."

"The West Brighton is just as nice," his mother said, and her tone put an end to the conversation. Walter sighed.

✤ ✤ ✤

The West Brighton *was* just as nice, only it was twenty times smaller. Even so, they had plenty of rooms open.

"The name is Snider," Walter's father told the clerk. Walter thought he'd misheard his father. Their name was Schneider, not Snider. But then his father spelled it for the clerk—S-N-I-D-E-R—and that was how they were entered into the hotel register. Walter started to open his mouth, but a nervous shake of the head from his mother cut him off.

A colored porter carried their bags to their hotel room. Along the way, Walter saw something else different about the West Brighton Hotel. There were Jews here. Lots of them. Russian Orthodox Jews with full beards and long curls who'd been flooding into New York the past few years. The Schneiders—now suddenly the Sniders—were silent until the porter deposited them in their room and closed the door behind him.

Walter could barely contain himself. "Why did you tell that man our name is Snider?"

His father sat on the bed and put his head in his hands. "Please, Walter, not now."

"But our name is Schneider, not—"

"Don't you think I know what our name is?" his father erupted.

Walter's mother avoided the argument by unpacking their bags into the bureaus in the room.

"It's those Russian Jews that have been coming over," said Walter's father. "Why can't they be . . . more *American?* If they would just blend in more, not cling to the old ways so much. Didn't President Roosevelt say there should be no more hyphenated Americans?"

Walter began to put it all together.

"You mean they kicked us out because they think we're Jews!?"

"They didn't kick us out," his father told him. "There were no rooms left."

"But we're not even Jewish!" Walter cried.

"I told you—"

"Did you tell them we're not Jews? What made them think that?"

"Walter—"

"You didn't even tell them? You just let them send us away?"

"I'm sure the hotel manager is a good man," his father said. "Put yourself in his shoes. If the other guests don't want us there, he loses business. It makes no sense for him to hurt himself."

"So we get hurt instead?"

"No one's been hurt."

"The West Brighton is just as nice," Walter's mother finally said. "I like it smaller anyway."

Walter shook with anger. "But we're not Jews! Schneider isn't even a Jewish-sounding name!"

"But Felix Schneider was a Jew, and there's no reason to remind anyone. From today our name is Snider. Not Schneider. Understand?"

"What am I supposed to do, go back to school and say 'My name's not Schneider anymore, it's Snider'?"

"There are plenty of people who change their names to fit in," his mother said.

"Sure. When they step off the boat as greenies at Ellis Island! Not a hundred years after they got here!"

"Don't yell at your mother!" his father told him.

"But I don't understand! We stayed there *last* year and nobody said anything!"

"It's just the way things are now," his father said.

"So," his mother said, "what shall we do before lunch? It says here there's croquet and horseshoes on the front lawn."

Walter got up and left the room. He slammed the door behind him, then sprinted the length of the hall and down the stairs before his father could come after him and punish him for it. He didn't want to play horseshoes or croquet or do anything at the West Brighton. He wanted to be back at the real Brighton hotel.

And he wanted his hat back.

2

Walter felt a thousand eyes on him as he walked among the guests at the Brighton Beach Hotel. He was sure every single one of them was staring at him and thinking *Jew*. That he *wasn't* Jewish made it all the more infuriating. He and his family weren't *anything*. They didn't go to temple and they didn't go to church. They weren't Jewish-American, or German-American, or any kind of -American. They were just *American*.

What was it then that made all these people see him as a Jew? It couldn't be his last name, no matter what his father said. Schneider just sounded German, and there were plenty of Christian Germans. He put a hand to his face. Was it his nose? His curly hair? His complexion? Did he have "Jew" written somewhere on him he couldn't see, in some language he couldn't read?

Walter saw a Pinkerton security man strolling down the Brighton Beach boardwalk and scurried off into the long, crowded field at the foot of the hotel. As big as the place was

113

it would be quite a coincidence to run into the same Pinkerton twice, but it didn't hurt to be careful. For all he knew they'd put a sign up in the Pinkerton break room: "Warning: Be on lookout for fighting Jew."

The colored waiters were still at their game, and Walter found a discreet place to sit and watch. There were more antics—coaches goading players into stealing bases, players speaking what sounded like Spanish, trick throws, hidden balls, primitive acrobatics. But mixed in with all the silliness there was some real baseball being played. After two seasons as the batboy for a National League team—even if it was one of the worst National League teams—Walter knew good baseball when he saw it.

The big Cuban pitcher he had seen earlier was the best of the lot. When he and his team weren't clowning around, he would rear back and fire the baseball at his catcher with all the force of a cannon. Walter half expected to hear an explosion and see smoke as the pitcher released the ball, but instead the only sound and sight were the ball smacking the catcher's mitt, and the dust and dirt that *poofed* out of the leather. In all the time he watched, Walter never saw one batter even make contact with a pitch.

What an addition this pitcher would make to the Brooklyn Superbas! Despite their superlative name the team was truly mediocre, finishing fifth in the National League the last two seasons. A pitcher like this could make them instant contenders!

Walter thought about approaching the pitcher after the game, but in the middle of the eighth inning he spied one of the boys who had beaten him up. He didn't have Walter's hat on, but he wasn't with his friends either. Walter stood and rounded the field, careful to keep an eye out for the other boys or the Pinkertons. The boy he stalked was the smallest of the three, probably nine like Walter. Maybe ten. It didn't matter to Walter how old he was—he was about to get the thrashing of his life.

The boy wandered away from the baseball field and Walter followed him down to the beach, where row after row of dressing tents stood unused. When no one else was around, Walter sprinted up behind the boy and shoved him into one of the empty changing rooms.

"Hey, what gives?" the boy cried.

Walter popped him one in the nose before the boy got his bearings, and then the fight was on. The little guy wasn't a good brawler but he was scrappy. It was a nasty bout, with biting and clawing and hair-pulling. Once or twice Walter thought they might go tearing through the canvas of the tiny tent, but he eventually got his knee in the boy's back and the kid's face down in the sand where he could rain down on him with his fists. The boy coughed and sputtered and begged for mercy, but Walter wasn't in a merciful mood.

"Did you just fall off the tater wagon? Huh? Did you? *I'm—not—a—Jew*," he said, punctuating each of the last words with a blow.

When he'd beaten the fight out of the boy he got up. The boy was breathing hard, but he didn't make a move.

"Tell your pals I'm gunning for them," Walter said. He kicked sand on the boy and ran far away from the Brighton Beach Hotel, in case the boy or his parents set the hotel security after him.

Farther down the boardwalk the blaring carousel tunes and piped music from Coney Island's amusement parks called to him. Screams and laughter came from Steeplechase Park, where people rode mechanical horses around a great railed track, *pings* and *dings* rose from the arcade games, and everywhere barkers called out, trying to get people to drop a dime on their show, their ride, their attraction.

Competing with the barkers were the soul savers, railing against the sins and depravation across the street. The Salvation Army, the American Temperance Society, the Women's Christian Temperance Union, the Templars of Honor and Temperance, the Anti-Saloon League. They camped out on the boardwalk in their sandwich boards and uniforms and hurled warnings and damnation at all who passed.

"Each of these bottles represents crime and corruption!" one of them cried, tossing full bottles of whisky out into the sea. "Alcohol is an abomination, a plague on our cities and our communities and our families!"

Walter bought a hot dog at Feltman's, ate it in four

116

bites, then headed for Luna Park. For as long as he and his family had been coming to Coney Island, Luna Park had been his favorite amusement park. It was huge, and always packed full of people—at least in the vacation months, which is when Walter always came. He knew the place like the back of his catcher's mitt. All he had to do was look up and find the giant Electric Tower in the middle and he instantly knew where he was in the park. The tower was covered with electric light bulbs and glowed like the sun night and day.

By nightfall Walter had ridden the Virginia Reel, the Helter Skelter, the Whirl of the Whirl, and Shoot the Chutes—Luna Park's feature attraction—twice. For Shoot the Chutes you rode a cable car to the top of a five-story incline, and then boarded what looked like a long metal cigar to slide down into the lagoon below. Walter thought the ride had to go a hundred miles an hour. After his second trip, when his money was running low, he went to one of the theaters to see what the barker advertised as a "baseball movie."

He was disappointed to find that it wasn't a real moving picture show, just one of those gimmicks where they set slides in front of a projection bulb and show them on a big screen. Still, the photographs were funny, and the guy singing at the piano got laughs with a song about a girl named Katie O'Casey, who was mad for baseball. Walter especially liked the chorus:

"Take me out to the ball game,
Take me out with the crowd.
Buy me some peanuts and Cracker Jack,
I don't care if I never get back.
Let me root, root, root for the home team,
If they don't win it's a shame.
For it's one, two, three strikes, you're out
At the old ball game."

From the pictures Walter wondered if the person who took them had ever really *been* out to the old ball game himself, but he liked the song well enough. From the sound of the applause, the rest of the audience liked it too.

Getting up after the show, Walter spied the pitcher from the baseball game at the Brighton Beach Hotel. He and some of his Cuban friends were just leaving from the back of the theater.

"Hey! Hey you—pitcher!" Walter cried, realizing he didn't know the man's name. "Wait!"

The pitcher didn't hear him, or didn't know he was the one being yelled at. Walter worked his way across the theater, but the Cuban and his friends were already gone by the time he got there.

He couldn't find them outside right away either. Walter slipped in and out of the crowd, hopping up and down to see, and finally spotted them going into the men's bathroom.

The *colored* men's bathrooms.

Walter frowned. The men had dark skin, but Cubans weren't "colored." He waited outside, thinking maybe the men didn't know any better. They were, after all, from another country.

A white couple gave Walter a strange look for standing in front of the colored bathrooms and he moved to a nearby bench, his ears burning red. When the Cuban and his friends finally emerged, Walter had to hustle to catch up.

"Hey, uh, Cubans! Wait up!" Walter called.

The men didn't hear him or didn't care. They didn't stop. Walter ran around in front of them.

"Cubans, wait! Stop," Walter said. The men stopped. *Wait, how am I going to talk with these guys?* Walter thought suddenly. *I don't speak Spanish.*

"Wait-o. Me-o Walter-o," he said slow and loud.

The men stared at him openmouthed.

"Me see you play-o base-o ball-o today-o."

One of the men blinked. "I think this boy's brains are scrambled."

"Wait, you speak English?"

"Uh, what language did you think we'd speak?" the pitcher asked. He had a long drawl like Nap Rucker, the Superba pitcher from Georgia.

"Spanish. Aren't you all Cubans?"

The men looked at one another sheepishly. One of them laughed.

"Oh. Right," the pitcher said. "Well, we, uh, we been off the island a long time."

One of the men snorted and turned around so his face was hidden from Walter.

"Great! Even better," Walter told him. "I saw you pitch today. You were amazing!"

The big pitcher smiled. "Hey thanks, kid."

"I mean it. You were better than half the pitchers in the National League."

"More than half," one of the other men said. The others nodded and chimed in their agreement.

"Listen, I'm the batboy for the Brooklyn Superbas. Why don't you come try out? The team gets back tomorrow from playing exhibition games down South. I'm sure I can get Coach Donovan to give you a look, and I can already tell you you're better than anything the Superbas have got. They're the turds of misery."

"Ain't that the truth," one of the Cubans said.

The big pitcher gave Walter a sad smile. "Aw, look kid. That's awful nice of you, but I can't."

"But why not?"

The pitcher looked around at his chums, who were trying not to laugh.

"Look son, I'm sorry to fool you, but that Cuban thing's all an act."

"What?"

"We're Negroes, son. We're colored, see? I'm even part

Comanche, but my black daddy means there ain't no way they gonna let me play ball for no National League team, no matter how good I am."

"But—at the hotel. They said you were Cuban—"

"Nobody really believes that, kid," one of the others said. "All them white folks, they know we're colored. But if the hotel tells them we're Cuban they can *pretend* we're Cuban so they don't have to fess up to watching Negros play ball, see? That way they can all sit there and drink their mint juleps and enjoy a nice afternoon of baseball without having to get all riled up about it."

"That's the stupidest thing I've ever heard!" Walter said.

The Negroes agreed with him.

"Weren't always like that. Time was, right after the war, when a black man and a white man played ball right along-side each other."

"Who was it made the old American Association? Moses Walker?" one of them asked.

"First and last," the pitcher said. "But that was twenty years ago."

"The good old days," said another.

"Why can't it be like that now?" Walter asked.

The big pitcher shrugged. "That's just the way things are now."

Walter was getting tired of people telling him that.

"It's a nice dream, kid, but it's only a dream," the pitcher said. He and his friends moved away.

"Wait, I don't even know your name," Walter called.

"Joe Williams," the pitcher called back. "But you can call me Cyclone."

Walter left Luna Park that night mad at the world. Which was bad news for the second of the three boys who had beat him up that morning. Walter caught him coming out of Steeplechase Park alone and he beat the tar out of him right there on the boardwalk.

3

It felt like the Pinkertons were out in full force the next day at the Brighton Beach Hotel. Walter wondered if the special attention was for him, but even as he thought it he knew he was just being silly. Still, there *had* been a rash of hotel guests getting beat up. He smiled at the thought and ducked behind a trash can to avoid passing a security guard.

Walter had hoped there would be a baseball game on the lawn this morning, but there was a band playing John Philip Sousa music there instead. That meant he was going to have to sneak into the hotel. But he and his family had stayed there last season, back when it was all right to look like a Jew, and he had a good idea of where the dining hall was. There were fewer places to hide in the halls—and fewer avenues of escape—but he had to find Cyclone Joe.

The dining hall was an enormous room with hundreds of long tables and huge chandeliers that sparkled in the late-morning sunlight. Thousands of guests ate brunch, the noise from their chattering like the hubbub at a ballpark.

In between the tables, dozens of colored waiters moved in a complicated dance, delivering silver platters with the grace of a shortstop catching a ball, sideswiping second, and throwing on to first.

Walter realized someone had come up alongside him and he jumped, worried he'd been copped by a Pinkerton. Instead it was just a colored waiter in a white service jacket.

"Can I help you find your party, young sir?"

"Oh, I'm—I'm not with anyone here. I was actually looking for one of the waiters. Joe Williams. Cyclone."

The colored man blinked in surprise. He looked like he might ask why, but swallowed his question and bid Walter follow him. They went through a set of double doors that led to a long hallway. Farther along, waiters came with empty platters and emerged with full ones.

"You wait right here, young sir, and I'll see if Cyclone is about."

Walter waited for what felt like a long time, and when Cyclone Joe didn't appear he snuck down the hall and peeked in through the round windows on the swinging doors. It was a vast kitchen, hazy with the smoke and steam of food being cooked for five thousand people. Walter pushed his way inside.

One or two of the colored cooks near the door gave him a second glance, but they were too busy to do anything about him being there. The stream of waiters coming in with new food orders was never-ending, and Walter found a place in the corner out of the way of the constant traffic.

Until he saw Cyclone Joe Williams come through the door. Walter jumped out at the big pitcher, who was so startled he juggled his tray. Luckily it was empty.

"Dang, you liked to scare the bejeezus out of me, son! What are you doing here?"

"I got you a tryout, Cyclone! I wired the manager of the Superbas on my parents' hotel account and got you a tryout with the team when they get back to Brooklyn this afternoon!"

It seemed like the entire kitchen got quiet all at once. Cooks and waiters all down the line stopped what they were doing and listened in on the conversation. Cyclone swallowed hard, and Walter could feel everyone's eyes on them.

"I told you, kid. They ain't gonna let a Negro pitch the National League."

"They might if they don't know you're colored."

Cyclone shook his head. "Son, they ain't never gonna believe I'm no Cuban."

"Not Cuban," Walter told him. "Indian. You said yourself you're half Comanche, right?"

Cyclone glanced up at the kitchen staff. They were all still watching them.

"There's plenty of Indians that play in the National League," Walter told him. "Bill Phyle, Chief Bender, Zack

Wheat. All we have to do is tell them you're Comanche and you can play!"

Cyclone didn't look sold on it. "I don't know, kid."

"You're light skinned enough," one of the kitchen boys told him. "You might could pull it off."

"Can't hurt to try," said another. "Not like they's gonna lynch you right there in Washington Park."

"Says you," said someone else.

"They can't say no," Walter told him. "The Superbas need you."

"The Brooklyn Cyclone," one of the other kitchen boys said appreciatively.

"All right," Cyclone said. "What time?"

✤ ✤ ✤

Walter left the kitchen on top of the world. That afternoon he would deliver Cyclone Joe Williams to the Brooklyn Superbas—not as Cyclone Joe Williams, of course, but as Joseph Deerskin, Comanche Indian—and be a hero to an entire borough. With Cyclone Joe Williams as the team's ace pitcher, they might even challenge the Chicago Cubs for the National League pennant.

Outside on the lawn a blue baseball cap with a large letter B caught Walter's eye. It was his Brooklyn Superbas hat, and it was being worn by the boy who had taken it from him— the big ring leader who had called him a kike. Walter's fists clenched.

The lawn was too open, too visible, and worse, the boy was walking with what looked like his parents. But the weekend was almost over. When would Walter have another chance to get his hat back? And how could he show up at Washington Park today without it?

Walter arranged himself on the path to meet the bully and his family face-to-face. The kid saw him coming a few yards away and grinned like Teddy Roosevelt. He thought he was safe next to his parents—not that Walter thought he could take him in a straight fight anyway.

The family walked up to Walter, who blocked their way.

"Oh, hello," the mother said. "Are you a friend of Henry's?"

Henry snorted.

"No," Walter said. "But he's been borrowing my hat."

"This ain't his hat," Henry started to tell his parents. That's when Walter popped him in the nose, while he wasn't looking. Henry's mother let out a tiny scream as blood spurted from the boy's busted nose. Henry clutched at his face, wailing, and Walter snatched the hat off his head before the boy's father could stir himself into action.

"Help! Someone help! That boy just attacked my son!" Walter heard the man cry. He was already off to the races though, and the ladies and gentlemen out for their Sunday walks parted for him rather than try to stop him. At the last moment a Pinkerton man appeared out of the crowd, but Walter slid around him like a runner avoiding a catcher's tag, tumbled another yard or so, and then picked himself back up to run before the detective could lay a hand on him. Laughing, he ran for the train station that would take him north to Park Slope and glory.

✧ ✧ ✧

The reaction to Joseph Deerskin was not what Walter had anticipated. The Brooklyn players made no move to welcome him to the clubhouse, standing stiff and staring at him like he was something poisonous. Old Patsy Donovan, the Superba's Irish manager and sometime right fielder, chomped on his cigar.

"'Joseph Deerskin,' eh?" he said.

"Just wait 'til you see his tommyhawk pitch," Walter said.

Cyclone glanced at him, but Walter focused on the manager. He knew he was the one he had to convince.

"Where'd ye play last season, Deerskin?" Donovan asked.

"The San Antonio Black—" Cyclone said, catching himself. "The San Antonio Broncos, sir."

"San Antonio, eh? Down to Texas? You're a long way from home, laddie."

One of the players gave a short, hard laugh. Donovan looked up at the team as if gauging them.

"I'm sorry. We've no openings at pitcher this season," he said.

"But we need a pitcher," Walter argued. "Last season you brought in *three* new pitchers. How can there not be any room?"

"Look here, lad, I took you on as batboy because you came in here talking about King Kelly—hell, because you even knew who King Kelly *was*. That means a lot to an old Irishman like me, but this . . ."

"Don't worry yourself, Walter," Cyclone said. He nodded to Donovan. "Thank you for your time, sir."

"No, wait! You've got to see him pitch, Mr. Donovan. He'd be the best pitcher in the National League."

Behind him, one of the Superba players coughed.

"We just don't have the money, Walter," Donovan told him. "I'm sorry."

"No, let's see him pitch," one of the players said. Walter turned. It was one of the boys from Georgia. "I want to see this 'tommyhawk.'"

Walter beamed. "You won't be disappointed. I guarantee it."

The team took the field at Washington Park for practice, splitting up to play an intra-squad game. It was a warm spring afternoon, the clouds high in the bright blue sky over the long low grandstand behind home plate.

Cyclone hung back before taking the field.

"They know, Walter. We ain't fooling anybody. I should just go."

"No! They're going to give you a tryout. When they see how good you are they'll have to take you on the team. And you *are* Indian. That's not a lie."

"It ain't the whole truth neither."

"Are we going to see some pitching today, or are you just

gonna stand around jawing with the batboy?" one of the players called from the field.

Walter stepped back from the field and Cyclone took the mound. The broad-shouldered giant worked the ball in his hands, then slipped on his glove and went into his windup.

Fap! The ball smacked into the catcher's mitt as the first batter took a swing and a miss. Walter jumped and clapped, glancing around to see the team's reaction. Their faces were as stony as they were in the clubhouse, and he stopped cheering.

Fap! Another fastball the batter couldn't catch up to. Walter had to keep himself from cheering.

Cyclone kicked his leg for a third pitch and fired, but this time the batter turned his bat down and bunted the fastball into the ground in front of the plate. The catcher sprang from his crouch and pounced on the ball, then threw down to first—and well over the first baseman, who didn't even jump to try and catch it. The ball went into right field, and the runner was on second before the ball made it back in to the pitcher.

"That's a two-base bunt," one of the players said.

Walter didn't understand. That was no hit, it was an error, clear and simple.

Cyclone took a deep breath on the mound and worked the ball over in his hands before pitching again. This time the batter got a piece of it, knocking an easy ground ball down to the shortstop . . . who let it go right between his legs. Walter was furious. It was a play any kid on any street in

Brooklyn could have made with his eyes closed. The runner scored and the hitter was safe at first.

Cyclone struck out the next batter—despite his attempt to bunt—and struck out the next one looking. The following batter popped up into foul territory near Walter. He backed off as the first baseman came over to catch it, then stared openmouthed as the usually sure-handed Superba let it drop. The first baseman stared back like Walter's father when Walter got in trouble at school for fighting. Like he was disappointed.

Suddenly Walter understood what was happening. The Superbas weren't rusty. They were deliberately misplaying the ball behind Cyclone. This was their way of saying they would never play with a colored man on the field.

The Superbas booted, overthrew, and dropped ball after ball, and Cyclone endured seven unearned runs in the two innings he pitched.

"I think we've seen enough," Donovan said, and Cyclone made no complaint. He tipped his hat to the manager and said nothing to Walter as he left the field. There was nothing to say.

Donovan came over to where Walter stood and they watched as the Superbas went on practicing with a new pitcher. Walter couldn't help but notice they didn't make an error.

"I'm sorry, lad," Donovan said. "It never would have worked. Even if the boys took to him, the other teams would just walk off the field."

"He would have been the best pitcher on the whole team, and you know it," Walter said.

Patsy Donovan didn't say anything to that. He didn't have to.

Walter stared out the window of the train back to Coney Island without really seeing anything. It felt like there was a cloud in his brain, fogging everything up. At Coney Island he didn't head for the West Brighton Hotel or the Brighton Beach Hotel, but instead walked along the boardwalk with his head down and his hands buried in his pockets. Coney Island flashed and danced, but he wasn't watching. Bands played and preachers scolded, but he wasn't listening. Walter didn't even feel the wind off the water or the wood beneath his feet.

At the end of the pier Walter stood and stared out at the dark ocean, wondering what was at the bottom. When he was little, he had thought there was treasure there, Spanish gold or pirate plunder. Now he thought that maybe there wasn't *anything* down there, that it was a great empty pit of nothingness.

Walter pulled off his beloved Brooklyn Superbas hat and flung the thing as far out into the water as he could. He watched it splash down, then bob, and then sink, settling in with the rest of the trash at the bottom of the great black sea.

Fifth Inning: The Numbers Game

Brooklyn, New York, 1926

1

"Mrs. Radowski! Mrs. Radowski, it's Frankie!"

Frankie knocked again more loudly so Mrs. Radowski could hear her. The old lady's hearing wasn't so good anymore. Mrs. Radowski's place was right next to Frankie's house, so close that on summer nights Frankie could reach out her window and almost touch it. Most nights, summer or not, Frankie could hear Mrs. Radowski singing some low, sad song in Russian—but at least that was better than what came from the Polish house on the other side.

Mrs. Radowski opened the door all the way when she saw who it was.

"Hello, Frances! You would like to come in for a biscuit, yes?"

"Not this afternoon, Mrs. Radowski. I'm working. Do you want any numbers today?"

"Oh! Yes, please."

Mrs. Radowski found her change purse and handed Frankie a quarter.

"Twenty-five cents today?" Mrs. Radowski usually only bet a penny.

"Yes. Today is good. I win today. I feel it. What is winning on twenty-five cents?"

"One hundred and fifty dollars," Frankie told her.

The old lady patted Frankie's baseball cap. "So clever, young Frances. You should go to university."

"You sound like my pop. Same numbers, Mrs. Radowski? Four-zero-six?"

Mrs. Radowski nodded. It was always the same with her—four-zero-six. Her dead husband's birthday. Frankie waved good-bye and knocked at Mr. Nolan's three doors down. Mr. Nolan spent all Saturday in his undershirt and underwear, no matter the temperature. He took a nickel bet on eight-three-five. He was one of Frankie's few regulars who liked to mix things up. The Steins across the street bought five-five-five for a penny, the same amount the McAllisters on the corner spent on three-five-seven. Three-five-seven was one of the popular ones, even though in the two years Frankie'd been running numbers it had never hit.

Frankie finished her street and worked her way up and down the next couple of blocks. When she'd collected all the numbers for her territory she ran up Flatbush Avenue past the big ticker-tape board at Prospect Park Plaza that showed the sports scores, and then over to the blind pig on Sterling where they ran the policy bank. The front entrance was a dry cleaner's, but the service door led to the saloon in the basement.

Frankie rapped three times, waited, then rapped again. The peephole slid open.

Frankie waved. "Heya Amos!"

The door *plinked* and *clanked* as it was unlocked, and Frankie slipped inside.

"Heya Frankie," Amos said, his deep voice booming. Amos was huge—the biggest man Frankie had ever seen, colored or not, but he was a real softy at heart. Amos smiled. "No notes again today?"

Frankie tapped her noggin through her cap. "Got it all right here, Amos."

He shook his head as he bolted the door. "I don't know how you do it, Frankie. Me, I got trouble remembering my telephone exchange."

"Greenwood 3-6420," Frankie told him.

"That's right! But how did you—"

"I heard the barkeep ask for it one day when you were late and they called around looking for you."

Amos shook his head again. "Too smart for your own good, girl. Best get on in to Mr. Jerome. He'll be waiting for you."

The only two customers in the place sat at the bar hunched over their drinks as Frankie passed through the blind pig. She only ever came on afternoons, when the crowds were light. Her pop told her blind pigs were just places to go and have a drink anyway, joints that would have been dive bars before the Anti-Saloon League types had pushed Prohibition through. It was the speakeasies that were supposed to have singing and dancing too. Frankie would love to see that, but she supposed her father would tan her hide for it.

Billy Sparks was running through his numbers with Mr. Jerome when Frankie got to the counting room. She stood in the corner and figured up the combined earned run averages of the Brooklyn Robins pitchers while she waited. Billy always took a while. He had to write everything down, and it took him and Mr. Jerome the better part of half an hour to decipher his pigeon scratch.

When Frankie's turn came she gave Mr. Jerome the numbers and the bets as fast as he could record them. Mr. Jerome never said anything, but Frankie could tell he liked having someone who could give it to him straight, the way the men at the bank liked it when she worked everything out on her father's deposit slips before he got up to the counter.

Frankie was halfway through the numbers when the door opened and Mickey Fist stepped inside. Mickey Fist owned the blind pig and ran the local numbers game. He had a flat nose and a square head, and he looked like a gorilla stuffed into his big monkey suit. Mickey Fist was about the same size as Frankie's father, but all his weight was in his thick shoulders and arms. Frankie heard he got his name by putting his fist through a door and knocking a guy out cold on the other side, and she believed it.

"This the kid?" Mickey Fist asked.

Mr. Jerome nodded. "Keep going, Frankie."

Frankie didn't know if she was in some kind of trouble or not, but she gave the rest of her take to Mr. Jerome as usual while Mickey Fist listened in. When she was finished she handed over the pocketful of money she'd collected and waited while Mr. Jerome did the count. When he was finished he nodded at his boss.

"She ever get one wrong?" Mickey asked.

"Never."

"What's eight times eighteen?" Mickey asked her.

"One forty-four."

"A hundred and fifty-six times seven?"

"One thousand ninety-two."

"Divided by twelve?"

"Ninety-one."

Mickey Fist looked to Mr. Jerome, who was scribbling with his pencil. He looked up and nodded.

The boss looked Frankie up and down.

"How old are you, kid?"

"Eleven."

"You play it straight, a coupla years we could find a place for you in the organization. You like that?"

"Yessir," Frankie said.

Mickey Fist nodded and left. Frankie let out her breath, and Mr. Jerome did the same. He straightened his glasses.

"You did good, Frankie. Real good."

Mr. Jerome paid Frankie her cut and she went back out into the blind pig. Mickey Fist was talking to another man at the bar.

"I'm telling you, I was there," the other man said. He slapped a newspaper down on the counter and pointed to it. "The numbers in the *Times* and the numbers at the park don't match up. I bet the numbers that came up at Belmont. That means I oughta get paid."

Frankie knew immediately what was going on. The numbers game worked like this: The players bet money on three numbers between zero and nine. The numbers used to be pulled out of a hat, but that was too easy to fix and people wouldn't play. Then somebody got the bright idea to use the daily numbers the newspapers published from the local race tracks. Mickey Fist used Belmont Park. The *New York Times* printed the total take from the Win, Place, and Show bets from the Belmont, and Mickey used the last dollar digit in each one to come up with the daily winning number. If the *Times* said the Belmont took $2,597 for Win, $703 for Place, and $49 for Show, the daily numbers were 7-3-9. It was a good system. The players could check their own numbers in the paper, and since there was no way to fix the numbers everybody knew the game was legit.

Except the *New York Times* didn't always list the numbers right. Like today.

"Sorry pal," Mickey was saying. "You know the rules. We use the numbers printed in the *Times*."

"But they're not *right*, I tell you."

"I get what you're saying, friend," Mickey said. He squared his body toward the other man, making it plain just how much bigger he was. "But we only use the numbers in the *Times*." Mickey made a show of straightening the other man's tie. The guy didn't flinch, but he didn't bat Mickey Fist away either. "And what is it they say? 'If it's in the *Times*, it must be true.'"

Mickey nodded to Amos, who escorted the man out. Conversation over.

A clock on the lamppost outside told Frankie she still had an hour before game time, so she wandered through Flatbush looking for her father. She found him on Carroll Street, whistling and twirling his baton, and ran up from behind him and jumped on his back.

"A robber!" he joked. "Help! I'm being mugged!" He swung her around and she tickled him until he deposited her on the steps of a brownstone.

"How do you always know it's me?" she asked.

Her father reset his policeman's cap and tugged at his shirt to make himself look smart again. "Sweetheart, a real bandit'd lay me out cold on the sidewalk, not ride me around like some steeplechase pony." He took a break from his patrol and sat down on the step next to Frankie. "You run your numbers?"

Frankie showed him her haul. Fifty-five cents. Numbers rackets were illegal—just like blind pigs and speakeasies—

but Pop and most of the other cops looked the other way. Frankie knew most of them went to those places to have a drink when they got off duty anyway, her pop included.

Her father reached into his pocket and pulled out another dime.

"Here. So you can have something to eat at the park."

Frankie kissed her father on the cheek. "Thanks, Pop."

"Who they playing today?"

"The Giants."

"Easy win for the Giants then," he said.

"Brooklyn might win!"

"Those bums? They couldn't hit water if they fell out of a boat."

Frankie's father had been a batboy for Brooklyn a long time ago, but he hated them now, and would never tell Frankie why. He had to be the only Giants fan in all of Brooklyn—or at least the only one who was tough enough to admit it.

"You wait and see. The Robins'll win the pennant this year."

"If you like Brooklyn so much, why do you wear that old Giants hat of mine?" he asked, rubbing the cap on her head. She batted him away and fixed her hair under her hat.

"It's mine now. I like it," she said. She stood to go. "Mickey Fist talked to me today. Said I had a future in the organization."

"Your future is in college, not a numbers racket. I'll see to that if I have to work two jobs for the rest of my days. Three jobs."

"No girls go to college, Pop. That's just the way it is."

Her father frowned. "It doesn't have to be."

"I'll see you later, Pop. All right?" Frankie said, heading off.

"Be home by dinner," her father called. "I'm making meat loaf!"

"Okay, Pop!" Frankie yelled back. She was already turning the corner, on her way to Ebbets Field.

2

There were twelve ticket windows at Ebbets Field, twelve turnstiles, and twelve baseball bats and baseball-shaped lights in the chandelier that hung in the rotunda—Frankie counted them. The grandstand stretched all the way down the right field line and most of the way down the left field line, with a view of a few scattered buildings over the center field wall where Montgomery Street and Bedford Avenue came together. The left field wall was 383 feet from home plate, but right field was just 301 feet away, making it perfect for lefty pull hitters like Babe Herman.

The stands were already beginning to fill, even though the Robins weren't playing all that well again this season. It didn't matter to Frankie, and it didn't matter to anybody else either. Brooklyn loved the Robins. They might have been bums, but they were Brooklyn's bums.

The game was about to start, and Frankie didn't bother finding the left field bleacher seat listed on her ticket. Instead she climbed to the upper deck and looked for a good spot.

She liked to see the action from above. The players might be tiny, but at least she could see the game straight on, not from one side or the other.

There was a whole row of seats close to the front that was almost empty, and Frankie slid across and sat down like she belonged there. A man two seats away from her wrote in a notebook resting on his knee. He had big ears and he held his chin out like he was sucking on a cough drop. He looked up at Frankie, then went back to his writing. Frankie started filling out the lineups in her scorebook.

"What paper are you with?" the man asked her.

"What?"

"Are you with the *World Telegraph and Sun*? The *Daily News*?"

Frankie looked at the guy like he was screwy.

"Sorry. You're sitting on Press Row, so I assumed you were with one of New York's esteemed periodicals."

"Oh cripes," said Frankie. "Does that mean I have to move?"

The man smiled. "No. Stay. Please. It'll be nice to have the company for once. My name's John Kieran. I write for the *New York Times*."

"Frankie Snider," she told him. "I write for P.S. 375, but only when they make me."

Kieran laughed. He nodded at Frankie's hat. "I see you're a Giants fan."

"Can't stand 'em."

"But . . . you're wearing a Giants cap."

"Doesn't mean I have to like 'em."

"A girl named Frankie who sits on Press Row but only writes for school, and who wears a Giants cap but is . . . a Brooklyn fan, I take it?"

"Of course."

"Of course," Kieran repeated. "Do I contradict myself?" he said like it meant something. "Very well then, I contradict myself. I am large. I contain multitudes."

"You don't look so big to me," Frankie told him.

"Indeed."

"Who's playing center?" Frankie asked.

"Gus Felix." Kieran turned toward her. "So, if you sneaked up here, did you sneak into the stadium too?"

"Of course not! I do honest work. I get paid."

"Do you now? We've already established that you're not a member of the fourth estate."

"Are you smart or something?" Frankie asked.

Kieran smiled. "Something." The game started on the field below them, but he seemed more interested in talking to Frankie. "Come now. Information, please. What is it you do for a living? Besides go to school, I mean."

"I run numbers."

"Ah. Yes. Very honest work indeed. And do you wager some of your honest pay on those numbers once in a while?"

"*Chuh.* No. The numbers game is a sucker's bet."

"Curiouser and curiouser. How so?"

Frankie sighed. It was getting difficult to keep score and talk at the same time. "Look, do the math. Mickey Fist's numbers game pays six hundred to one. You bet a penny and win, you make six bucks. You bet a dollar, you win six hundred. Sounds good, right? Only nobody hardly ever wins. You gotta pick the right digits, in the right order. That's a one in a thousand chance, see? It's a sucker's bet. And the marks who play, they think they're not suckers because they only bet a penny or a nickel or a dime. But you bet a penny every day for a year, you spend $3.65. You win once every thousand times, that's like once every two and a half years. Two and a half times 3.65 is nine dollars and thirteen cents. You just spent nine dollars to make six."

"It does seem rather ridiculous when you put it like that."

"Yeah, and Mickey Fist is the one laughing his way to the bank. Say a thousand people bet a penny every day. That's three thousand six hundred and fifty dollars a year, which ain't bad. Now let's say he's got one winner every week—which he don't, but let's just say he does. Six dollars a week times fifty-two weeks is three hundred and twelve dollars. Subtract that from his yearly take, and he's made $3,338, free and clear."

The Robins got the third out, and Frankie flipped her scorebook over for the bottom half of the inning.

"Worst thing is," she told Kieran, "the folks who can't afford it are the ones who play all the time. They see that six hundred to one and their eyes light up. And yeah, they win once in a while, but they'd be better off spending that money when they had it the first time. Mrs. Whitt had her electricity turned off last week. The Orvilles have four boys and haven't eaten meat in a month. This old lady that lives next door to us, Mrs. Radowski, her husband is dead and her only boy died in the war in Europe. Pop says she's broke, but she still finds a coin to play the numbers almost every day."

They watched as the Robins got something going with a double and then a single.

"So tell me something," Kieran said. "Why do you run numbers on your street if you know your neighbors can't afford it?"

Frankie shrugged. "It's just a job I'm good at is all. Besides, it's their money, right? I can't tell them what to do with it."

Kieran went back to scribbling in his notebook, then snapped it shut.

"Finished," he said.

"With what?"

"My story about today's game."

Frankie looked down at the field. It was still the first inning, and the Robins had two men on base with only one out.

"But it's only just started."

Kieran crossed his legs, leaned back, and tilted his hat forward on his head.

"They're all pretty much the same," he said. "I go in right

before the paper goes to press and change the one or two things I got wrong."

"You mean, like who won?"

"Well, yes, occasionally there are some inconvenient facts that have to be worked in. Although with the Brooklyn Robins I can say they lost, and I'm not often wrong. 'Hope is the thing with feathers,' Emily Dickinson once wrote, yet Brooklyn's poor Robins proved featherless yet again today at Ebbets Field.' Something like that. You see how easy it is?"

"Yeah, well, you better start rewriting, mister. The Robins have the bases loaded with only one out, and Babe Herman's up to bat."

Kieran leaned forward to watch. "Ah yes, not the best hitter in New York named Babe, but perhaps a close second."

Herman smacked a double to right, and Frankie stood and cheered. Hank DeBerry scored from third, but then things got crazy. Chick Fewster, who was on first when Babe got his hit, rounded second and slid into third. Dazzy Vance, who had been on second, got caught in a run-down trying to score. Meanwhile, Babe Herman, who'd kept his head down the whole time and run as hard as he could, tried to stretch his double into a triple.

And somehow three Brooklyn Robins ended up standing on third base at the same time.

The Giants catcher tagged them all and let the umpires sort it out. Five minutes later, Herman and Fewster were called out. Babe Herman had doubled into a double play.

Frankie looked across at John Kieran, who leaned out over the rail with a huge grin on his face. He caught her looking and laughed.

"Oh, now I'm going to *have* to add that!"

❖ ❖ ❖

None of Frankie's neighbors won the numbers game that day, but that didn't stop them from betting again. Frankie made enough to go back to the ballpark on Sunday, and she kept score from Press Row until John Kieran showed up late in the third.

"You're just in time," Frankie told him. "The Robins have three men on base."

"Oh?" Kieran asked. "Which base?"

"Ha-ha."

Kieran sat down a seat away from Frankie and opened up his notebook.

"Want to know what's happened?" she asked.

He held up a hand. "No need."

"Why do you come if you're not even going to watch?"

"Oh, I watch the games, Frankie. I watch and enjoy. Particularly the Brooklyn Robins. Who wouldn't like a team with names like Chick Fewster, Trolley Line Butler, Rabbit Maranville, Snooks Dowd, Buzz McWeeny. *Buzz McWeeny,* for heaven's sake! And did you know that this ballpark sits in the exact same spot where a pigsty once stood? They called it Pigtown. Priceless."

"Maybe you'd prefer Yankee Stadium then," Frankie told him.

"Oh, it's very fancy. And Lou Gehrig, Tony Lazzeri, Babe Ruth—they hit a great many home runs and win a great many ball games, if you like that sort of thing. But a foolish consistency is the hobgoblin of little minds. I much prefer the capricious Brooklyn Robins. You never know what's going to happen next."

"Then why don't you write about what really happens?"

Kieran searched the high blue sky for an explanation. "It's like—it's like reading a book to review it. Somehow having to break a book down into its parts to critique it sucks all the joy out for me. I greatly prefer to write my story in advance, and then sit back and enjoy the sum total of the afternoon. Besides, the truth is subjective."

Frankie didn't know what that meant. "I like baseball because it's mathematical," she said. "You know, geometry and algebra and stuff."

"I'm vaguely acquainted with the concepts, yes," Kieran said. He wrote another few lines in his notebook.

"A guy gets a hit, it changes his batting average," Frankie said. "He scores a run, it changes the pitcher's ERA. He makes an error? Count it on the board. There's numbers everywhere. Even the positions are numbered."

"You're quite fond of numbers, I take it."

Frankie recorded the last out of the inning in her scorebook. "Numbers are the one true thing in the world."

"That's a rather bold statement," Kieran said. "And I dare say there are a few poets out there who would disagree with you. You don't think numbers can be made to lie? Here. Take today's pitcher, Burleigh Grimes. Besides his wonderfully Dickensian name, Burleigh Grimes sports a 3.71 earned run average."

"Nothing wrong with that."

"Indeed. It's very good. But consider this: He allows roughly the same number of base runners per inning as fellow Robin Jesse Barnes. Yet Master Barnes possesses an ERA of 5.24."

Frankie frowned. "Well, not every guy that gets on base scores."

"My point exactly. So might we consider Burleigh Grimes 'luckier' than Jesse Barnes? If they are, in fact, comparable pitchers in terms of base runners allowed, how else can we reconcile the differences in their earned run averages? To wit, does Burleigh Grimes' far better ERA mean he is a far better pitcher, or just far more lucky?"

"Okay, so ERA is a measure of luck," Frankie told him. "It's still mathematical."

"Sticking to your guns, eh? All right. How about two players with an equal number of home runs—only one of them hit half of his with men on base, and the other hit none with men on base? The numbers say they are equally dangerous, but is that true?"

"That could just be the fault of the guys batting in front

of him. Maybe he'd hit more with men on if his teammates hit better."

Kieran shook his head, but he was smiling. "I see this is going to be a difficult argument to win."

Below them, Brooklyn slugger Babe Herman came to the plate.

"All right, let's take a different tack," Kieran said. "How many home runs has Babe Herman hit this season?"

"Nine."

"And have you seen him hit all nine?"

"Well, no. So what?"

"So what if he really *hasn't* hit nine. How do you know?"

Frankie frowned. "Because other people saw them. Because the papers said so."

"Ah. And 'if it's in the *Times,* it must be true,' correct? Or have you never seen the paper make a mistake?"

"Well, sure. They make mistakes all the time. Just the other day the Belmont take was wrong. That's what Mickey Fist uses for the numbers game, the last three digits of the Win, Place, and Show takes. But there were other people there who saw it, who know what the numbers really were."

"So those numbers—the right ones—those were the ones used for the payout?"

"No. It was the numbers in the papers. Those are the official ones for the game."

"Aha." Kieran nodded and thought for a moment. "So the numbers lied. They cheated someone out of his winnings."

153

"Nobody cheated, it was just a mistake."

"But someone *could* cheat, couldn't they?" Kieran said, keeping his eyes on the game. "They could, say, change the last three digits to the numbers one, two, and three, in place of whatever they really were."

"I guess, but it's almost impossible," said Frankie. "They'd have to change the numbers on the machines before the papers got printed."

"Of course. And who in the world could do that?" Kieran asked. He snapped his notebook closed. "Well, it's been fascinating talking with you, Frankie, but I think I'll visit the Brooklyn Museum this afternoon. The Robins don't seem to have that certain je ne sais quoi today."

"They're winning," Frankie pointed out.

"Yes. Perhaps that's what's wrong. Well, my story's written regardless." He stood and arranged his hat on his head. "Besides," he said, "I can always go in tonight and change it at the last minute if I need to."

Down on the field, Babe Herman hit his tenth home run of the year.

At least, Frankie *thought* it was his tenth home run of the year. Now she wasn't so sure anymore.

✦ ✦ ✦

The next morning, Frankie read John Kieran's story about yesterday's Brooklyn game. It left out a few things, but everything in it was right. She didn't know if he'd just made a lucky guess or if he had gone in late, like he said, and changed something. After digesting all the box scores on the page, Frankie flipped to the Belmont take to see if any of her players had hit the numbers.

"Jeepers!" she cried.

Her father jumped, dropping the knife full of jam he was about to put on his toast. "What is it? What's wrong?"

Frankie couldn't believe what she was reading.

The last three digits on the Belmont takes were one, two, and three. In that order.

3

Frankie dashed to the newsstand on the corner of Rogers and Fenimore, grabbed a *Daily News,* and flipped to the sports pages at the back.

"Hey, no reading," said the guy behind the counter.

Frankie read anyway, skimming until she got to the Belmont numbers. The last three were not one, two, and three. She slapped the *Daily News* back on the stack and pulled out a *Telegraph.*

"Hey, this ain't no library, kid."

Frankie found the Belmont numbers just as the newsstand keeper rounded on her. Seven, seven, two—just like in the *Daily News.* Just like everywhere, she expected, everywhere except the *New York Times.*

Frankie shoved the newspaper at the stall keeper and took off, hearing him curse at her all the way down the block. She didn't care. She suddenly understood what Kieran was trying to tell her yesterday. He was trying to tell her he could fix the numbers game.

Frankie ran up the steps to Mrs. Radowski's front door and knocked.

"Mrs. Radowski! Mrs. Radowski, it's Frankie!"

The locks and chains clicked and clinked, and the door opened up to the nice old lady who lived next door.

"Hello, Frances. You would like to come in for a biscuit, yes?"

"Um, sure, Mrs. Radowski."

The inside of the old lady's place was dusty and smelled like mothballs. There were little white doilies all over everything too—the tables, the chairs, even the mantel. Frankie looked at the pictures there while Mrs. Radowski went into the kitchen. There was a picture of her husband, mugging for the camera in a picture booth at Coney Island. Next to that there was a picture of her son, in his army uniform. Frankie barely remembered him.

Mrs. Radowski set a tray of cookies on a table by the fireplace. For some reason she called cookies biscuits, but they were real cookies, and good too. She asked if Frankie wanted some milk with them, and Frankie nodded.

"You're here for my numbers, I suppose," she said, and she started to look for her change purse.

Frankie stopped her. "Mrs. Radowski . . . why do you play the numbers? I know you don't have much money."

"Oh, well, I play because I have so little, you know?" She toyed with her necklace. "I think if I win big, maybe I never have to worry about money again, yes?"

157

"But the odds are terrible," Frankie told her. "How many times have you won in the last year?"

"Well, none," she conceded. "But you have only to win once, yes?"

Frankie thought about laying it all out for her, the way she had for Kieran, but she didn't think Mrs. Radowski would understand. Or care. She was already opening her coin purse.

"Mrs. Radowski, if you won once, would you stop playing?"

"Well, I don't know—"

"If you won big, I mean."

She fiddled with her necklace again.

"Well, if I win, why should I not keep playing?"

Frankie sighed. It was going to be like this no matter who she asked, she was sure.

"Same numbers, then?" she asked. "Four-zero-six?"

Mrs. Radowski nodded and pulled out a penny. Frankie waved it off.

"Let's make it a quarter," she told her. "It's a good day today. I feel it."

Frankie made her rounds, having similar discussions with a few of her favorites on the block, then checked the clock on the jewelry store at Bedford and Linden. They would expect her numbers at the blind pig within the hour, but she had one more person to talk to first.

Frankie found her father walking his beat near the hospital, but she was so tired from running she didn't even try to jump on his back.

"Whoa there, Frankie, what's the matter? Take a deep breath."

Frankie clutched her knees and waited until she stopped panting.

"Is something wrong, Frankie?" her father asked. He lifted her chin so he could see her face.

"No, Pop. I just wanted—I just wanted to see—if you wanted to play the numbers game today."

Her father frowned. "You know I never play the game, Frankie. It's a sucker's bet. You told me so yourself." He leaned down to look her in the eyes. "You're not playing the numbers, are you?"

"No, Pop. Of course not. It's just that today, well . . ." She couldn't decide how to tell him. "Today . . . today would just be a really good day to place a bet."

Her father narrowed his eyes. "Frankie, what have you gotten yourself mixed up in?"

"Nothing I can't handle, Pop."

Her father crossed his arms, looking bigger and tougher than ever, but he didn't say a word. In her head, it was like Frankie could hear the minutes ticking away.

"I'm due at the blind pig any time now," she told him. "I just thought you might want to bet a little something is all."

Her father gave her the eye, then pulled his change purse and counted out two dollars in coins.

"And don't tell 'em it's from your old man."

"I'll break it up three ways. Bet it for Mr. Wesker, Miss

159

Richmond, and the Coopers down the street. They'll never know they won for us. They never play."

"And I don't suppose I need to pick a number then, do I?" her father asked.

Frankie smiled, which only made her father's frown deepen.

"I hope you know what you're doing, Frankie. Mickey Fist is no man to cross."

In the back room of the blind pig, Frankie gave Mr. Jerome her bets. He wondered why seven of her players had chosen the same number, but she told him it was the anniversary of the day Mrs. Radowski's husband died and everybody on the street was doing it in his honor.

Mr. Jerome shrugged. "Don't matter to me what excuse they use to give us their money."

Game time was early that afternoon, and Frankie lost no time getting to the ballpark and taking her seat on Press Row. Kieran sometimes didn't arrive until the first or second inning was under way, but she was too nervous to wait, and ran back down to the main concourse. He was nowhere in sight. Frankie ran up and down both sides of the concession area, then stood under the baseball chandelier to watch the crowds pour in. In a few minutes she got anxious and went searching again. What if Kieran had decided to spend the day at the Brooklyn Botanical Gardens and just make up something about the game later?

Frankie was cursing Kieran's name when she caught a glimpse of his long prim face and white fedora hat. He was down on the field by the dugout talking to big Babe Herman, the Robins' notorious slugger.

"Mr. Kieran!" she called. "Mr. Kieran!"

Kieran said his good-byes to Herman and climbed into the stands.

"Believe it or not, Frankie, I was actually *interviewing* someone for once. You know that double Herman hit that turned into a double play? The big lunk actually blames his *bat*. Says it's defective. You'll never guess what he said he's going to do with it—"

"Mr. Kieran, I need to *tell you something.*"

Kieran crossed his arms. "All right. What's so important it couldn't wait for the third inning?"

Frankie looked around at all the people who were listening to their conversation.

"I want you to . . . come buy me a hot dog," she told him.

"I think you have an elevated idea of what writing twenty column inches a day actually pays," Kieran told her, but Frankie grabbed his jacket and pulled him up to a more private spot on the concourse.

"All right, now what is this all about?" he asked.

"I just wanted to tell you," Frankie said. "I sure hope four-zero-six comes up in tomorrow's numbers game. A lot of my players bet on it."

"Oh. Oh yes. I see," Kieran said. "Four-zero-six, you said?" He jotted the number down in his notebook.

"I hope not *too* many of your neighbors chose that number," he said.

"Only the ones who really need it," Frankie said.

Kieran put his notebook away. "Well, I certainly hope the numbers fall their way. Now, you'd better hurry to your seat if you want to see the first pitch."

"You're not coming? What about the game?"

He patted the notebook in his pocket. "Why watch it when I've already written the article? Besides, I have one or two short errands to run." He tipped his hat and winked. "Until tomorrow, Frankie."

✣ ✣ ✣

Frankie was quiet all through dinner. Her father kept looking at her like he wanted to ask her something, but he didn't. Frankie knew one thing for sure—she couldn't keep working for Mickey Fist, not after this. If it worked, if Kieran did his part, then Mickey Fist and Mr. Jerome had to pay out. They had to pay out, or word would get around that they were welchers and no one would play their game anymore. Even so, they'd still see it for a fix, and they were bound to be unhappy about it.

Tomorrow couldn't come soon enough, and by morning Frankie was tired from a fitful night's sleep. She dragged herself out of bed and splashed water on her face before daring

162

to check the paper. Her father wasn't there that morning—he must have had to check in at the precinct early—but he had left the *New York Times* folded to the Belmont numbers under a bowl of grapefruit.

The last three digits were four-zero-six.

Frankie ran her numbers route that morning just in case the whole thing went over without anybody noticing, but she still waited as late as she could to go in. Amos met her at the door, but he wasn't his usual talkative self and he wouldn't meet her eyes when she said hello. Frankie got a tight feeling in the pit of her stomach, but she went on inside anyway. There were one or two men at the bar again today, but Mickey Fist and Mr. Jerome were waiting for her when she got to the counting room.

"Here she is," Mickey Fist said. "Our little girl who's so good with numbers." He leaned against the wall behind the accounting table, his thick arms folded across his chest. Mr. Jerome shot Frankie a look of warning.

"I've got my daily numbers," she said. Her voice came out like a squeak, and Mickey Fist smiled.

"If they're anything like yesterday's numbers, I ain't sure I want them." Mickey pushed himself off the wall and came around behind her.

"I—I don't know what you mean."

"Sure you don't. Seven people on *your* route bet four-zero-six, and that number just happens to be printed in today's *Times*."

"They just got lucky is all—" Frankie started to say.

Mickey Fist leaned in close to her ear. *"Too* lucky, little girl."

"It was the—it was an anniversary," she stammered. "They were just—"

"Save it." Mickey Fist picked up a *Times,* folded almost exactly like her father had folded his, and jabbed at it with a meaty finger. "The numbers ain't even right. I don't know how they did it, but somebody messed with the Belmont take. We ain't paying."

Frankie didn't understand. How could they not pay? What were they going to tell all their customers? She knew she should have said something, but she was too scared of Mickey Fist to argue.

"That just leaves what we're going to do with you," he said. His breath on her neck was warm and smelled like bacon. "I think we'll start with who put you up to it."

There was a knock at the door and Frankie's father burst through wearing his street clothes. She recognized him now—he had been one of the men she saw hunched over the bar on her way in! She almost ran to him, but his eyes told her to stay where she was.

"What is this?" demanded Mickey Fist.

Amos followed in her father's wake. "Sorry, boss. This fella started raising a stink, then he come busting through the door—"

"Leave it," Mickey said. He stood face-to-face with

Frankie's pop. Frankie was right—they were almost the same size, but where her father was all chest, Fist was all arms.

"I've come for the winnings," her father said.

Mickey Fist laughed. "And who are you?"

"Sergeant Walt Snider, NYPD," her father said, flashing his badge. "We've had complaints."

Mickey Fist blew up. "What is this, a shakedown!? I pay good money to keep my operation in the clear. I ain't paying a red cent!"

"You pay to run an honest game, Mickey. You don't pay up, people talk and we get calls. How long do you think we can turn a blind eye to you cheating folks out of their money?"

"Me? Cheat? That little girl there, *she's* the one running a fix."

"This little girl?" Frankie's father said. "You expect me to believe that?"

"She's smart, this one. But somebody else had to help her out. Somebody at the paper—"

Frankie's father got up in Mickey Fist's face. "You gonna let it get around that you run a dishonest game, *and* that an eleven-year-old girl took you to the cleaners?"

Mickey Fist clenched his fists.

"Go ahead, Mickey. Hit me. See how long that police protection lasts when you nail a cop."

Mickey grinned. "So you're in on this too, huh?" He gave them all a few minutes to sweat, then cracked his neck and took a step back.

"Jerome, how much do we owe?"

"Two thousand, nine hundred and ten dollars," he croaked.

Mickey Fist gave Frankie's father one last glare, then marched around and opened a cabinet at the back of the room. It was stacked with bills and bags of coins.

"Give 'em their cut, Jerome, and tell 'em I don't expect to see either of them ever again."

Mickey Fist brushed Frankie's father on the way out, but her pop didn't rise to the bait. Mr. Jerome counted out the cash with shaking hands, even though Frankie could see it hardly made a dent in the stash in the cabinet.

"You could have really made something in the organization," Mr. Jerome told Frankie as he handed over the money.

"She did," her pop said. He collected the money for her and stuffed it in his pockets. "And now she's through."

Frankie's father steered her out the door past Amos, who gave them the slightest of nods before letting them by.

"All under control, huh?" her father asked when they got to the street. Frankie said nothing. After a few blocks Frankie couldn't hold it in any longer and burst into tears. Her father sat on the steps of a brownstone and pulled her into his arms.

"I'm so sorry, Pop," Frankie whispered.

He held her away so she could see the authority in his eyes. "Don't you *ever* do something stupid like that again, you hear me?"

Frankie nodded, and her father wrapped her in his arms again and let her cry it out.

"That money is for you to go to college, and you're going to make it, do you understand me? You're smarter than me, maybe the smartest Snider there ever was, and I'm going to see you do something with it, you understand?"

"Yes, Pop," Frankie said, and she buried her tears in his big broad chest.

After the winnings had been handed out to Mrs. Radowski and the others, Frankie's father put his uniform back on and went to work. Frankie went to the ballpark, where she found John Kieran lounging in the front row of the upper deck with his white hat pulled down over his face.

"You know, I think I can see my house from here," Frankie said.

Kieran tipped his hat up. "You missed the start of the game. Brooklyn's got two men on."

"Oh yeah? Which base?"

Kieran smiled. "I was starting to worry about you."

"Me? I got everything covered. Thanks to my pop. Lost my job, though."

"Ah, more's the pity," he said. Then he snapped his fingers. "Wait a moment. Now that I think of it, I *did* just hear a young person is needed to operate the ticker tape sports board at Times Square. She would have to be good with numbers, though. Are you good with numbers?"

Frankie jumped up and hugged Kieran, then sat down

beside him. They enjoyed their afternoon quietly for a few outs.

"So, did you already write your story?" Frankie asked. "Who's going to win?"

"Brooklyn. Four to two," he said. "Give or take a few runs."

Kieran ordered two hot dogs with everything from a vendor, and Frankie watched him pull out a wad of bills to pay for it.

She whistled. "Look who's Mr. Rockefeller now."

"Well Frankie, it just so happens I got very lucky in today's numbers game . . ."

Sixth Inning: Notes of a Star to Be

Fort Wayne, Indiana, 1945

1

The reaction to Kat when she walked into the visitors' locker room was not exactly what she had hoped for. She had come right from the Fort Wayne train station and she was still wearing the clothes she'd left Brooklyn in: her best dress and a pair of her mother's real spiked heels. The only thing she carried was her mother's tattered old scorebook, which she clutched with both hands like a life preserver. Everything else was in her suitcase, including her glove.

The other girls stopped changing into their uniforms and stared. Kat gave a little wave and heard someone snort.

Ms. Hunter, the team chaperone, cleared her throat. "Everyone, meet the newest Grand Rapids Chick: Katherine Flint from Brooklyn, New York."

"Kat," she corrected. "Everybody calls me Kat."

A couple of the girls laughed, and someone made a little "meow" sound.

An older man in a baseball uniform walked in and the girls suddenly looked busy. Kat figured he must be the manager.

171

"This the new girl?" he asked.

Kat held out her hand. "Kat. Katherine. Flint," she said, nervous. The manager didn't shake her hand.

"You play infield or outfield?"

"Well, either one, I guess, but—"

"Ziggy's leg is twisted, so you'll play second today. Get suited up," he said, then disappeared into his office again.

Kat ran her hands down the side of her dress, looking for pockets that weren't there. Why had she packed the last of her gum in her suitcase?

A lanky blond girl lacing up her spikes eyeballed Kat and shook her head. "We're gonna lose twenty to nothing."

Kat had tried out for the All-American Girls Professional Ball League last year when she was fourteen, but they told her she was too young. This year they had told her the same thing, but then just after the start of the season she got the call—there were already so many injuries the league was giving her a chance. Could she meet the team in Fort Wayne, Indiana, by the end of the week?

Darn tootin' she could.

Ms. Hunter brought Kat a uniform like the rest of the girls wore, a belted dress with a tunic that buttoned up the side. In the middle of the tunic was the round logo of the Grand Rapids Chicks. Kat looked at herself in the mirror. The skirt had no pleat to it, and Kat felt like she was wearing a parachute. Worse, the hemline came down to her knees. She felt a little corny putting on a skirt to play baseball or softball or whatever it was they were calling the game the girls played. Ever since the war had started, girls everywhere had been wearing pants and dungarees. But Kat wasn't getting paid to design uniforms, she reminded herself, she was getting paid to play baseball. She would have worn a sack cloth if they'd asked her to.

"You'll do great, Katherine," Ms. Hunter told her. "And I've found a glove for you to use in the game."

"I don't suppose there's anyplace I could get a stick of Orbit, is there?" Kat asked. Orbit was her favorite kind of gum.

"Marilyn," Ms. Hunter called. A girl almost the same age as Kat came running over. "Marilyn, can you run to the concession stand and bring back a pack of Orbit gum for Kat?"

Ms. Hunter gave her a nickel and the girl hurried off.

"Thanks," Kat said. She ran her hands down her sides and caught herself again. If she didn't get control she'd be touching wood again soon—and in a dugout with all those bats, that could be a problem.

Kat saw one of the players nudge another and nod at her. "Straight off the train and already she's making demands."

Not a good start, Kat thought.

Before the team took the field, the manager came back to give them a pep talk, such as it was.

"All right girls, listen up. We're awful. The papers say the Chicks can't buy a win, but I'm gonna prove them wrong. You beat the Fort Wayne Daisies today and I'll give each of you a five-dollar bill. Including Ms. Hunter."

That was the sum total of his speech.

Kat marched up the staircase with the other girls into the bright sunshine of an Indiana afternoon. She was blinded at first, but when she finally was able to look around she saw . . . people. Hundreds, maybe *thousands* of people! As many as might be at a Brooklyn Dodgers game. The stands all up and down the first and third base lines were packed and the fans cheered as the team stepped onto the field.

Kat spun where she stood and laughed. For a moment her laughing was the only sound she could hear, the crowd and the band and the loudspeakers fading into the background like someone had turned down the volume on the wireless of her life. She couldn't remember the last time she'd felt the sun so warm on her skin, or laughed so hard, or felt so alive. She was a million miles away from her father's war letters, her mother's ten-hour-a-day job, Hattie's victory garden. For the first time in years she wasn't worried about blackouts or scrap drives or food rations. Kat was a Grand Rapids Chick—a professional baseball player!—and she wanted this feeling to last forever.

When Kat came back to her senses she was the only one left on the field. The Chicks were already in their dugout, and they stared at her like she was a void coupon. Kat quickly dipped down under the awning and started touching the ends of baseball bats sticking out of a box.

"Looks like they're recruiting from the nuthouse now," the tall blond girl said. Embarrassed as she was, Kat couldn't stop—until Marilyn the bat girl came running up with a pack of Orbit. Kat almost kissed her.

"Thank you thank you thank you," she said, ripping the pack open and popping a stick in her mouth. She immediately felt better, and the urge to touch the bats was gone.

Every last one of the girls in the dugout stared at her like she was crazy.

"*V* for victory time, girls!" Ms. Hunter called. "*V* for victory."

Kat was confused, but she followed the other girls out onto the field where they formed a V shape with the girl at the point standing on home plate. A *V* for victory in the war against Germany and Japan, Kat guessed. She ran to the last place on the end of one of the letter's arms just as the band began to warble "The Star-Spangled Banner."

When the anthem was over Kat ran to second base by way of first. Touching the bag was one of her rituals, and to break it would mean she'd lay an egg for sure. That didn't make the look from the girl at first base any easier to swallow, though.

No, Kat thought, definitely *not a good start.*

Kat held her own at second, handling three chances in the first two innings just fine. In the meantime, she liked watching the pitcher, the tall blond girl who'd said the Chicks were going to lose with Kat in the lineup. She had a big windmill windup, and she'd swing her long arm in a circle a few times before slinging the ball at the plate. *Pow!* The ball would pop in with such force that Kat didn't know how anybody could hit it.

Luckily she didn't have to, and the Daisies pitcher wasn't nearly so crafty. When Kat came up to bat in the third the pitcher laid a fat one right across the plate that Kat laced to right for a hit. She got another single in the fifth and a double in the seventh and scored both times. But neither time was she met at the plate by her teammates, and they gave her the silent treatment in the dugout like they didn't want her there. Kat took a seat at the far end of the bench, away from all the players, and touched the end of every bat in the box.

Thanks to Kat the Chicks won the game—their first in six tries, she found out later—and the manager made good on his promise of five bucks each to the girls. Even so, none of the girls would speak to her, and on the bus ride back to their hotel she was the only girl to sit by herself. As she peered out the window at the passing streetlights, Kat wondered if coming here had been a terrible mistake. The team didn't want her, and if they didn't want her, well, she could just go home to Brooklyn . . . But the thought of going back to that life, that world, almost brought her to tears.

Just when she thought things couldn't get any worse, Ms. Hunter told her she'd be rooming with Connie Wisniewski, the tall blond pitcher who'd made fun of her in the dugout. Kat waited for the rest of the girls to pull their luggage out of the bottom of the bus and hauled her own bag into the hotel by herself. She eyed a couch in the lobby and wondered if she'd be sleeping there tonight.

Kat found her room and put the key in the lock, half expecting the bolt to be latched. It was unlocked, but that was just the first of the surprises. The entire team was crammed into her room, and they cheered for her as Connie Wisniewski swept her up in a hug.

"What? But, I don't—" Kat tried to say.

"I'm so sorry for being snippy," Connie said. "You just looked so small and dolled up when Ms. Hunter brought you from the station, and we haven't won in so long."

Girls clapped Kat on the back and introduced themselves, laughing about how hard it was to keep giving her the cold shoulder while she single-handedly won the game for them.

"It was all my idea, I'm afraid," Connie told her. "Consider this your initiation."

Ms. Hunter came by and shooed the other girls off to their own rooms.

Kat gasped. "My mother's scorebook! I gave it to Ms. Hunter before the game!"

Connie caught her at the door. "Calm down, calm down." Connie pulled the scorebook from her satchel and handed it to Kat. "I wondered when you'd notice."

Kat wiped tears from her eyes. "If I had lost this—it's got every game me and my mother have ever seen in it, all the old Brooklyn Robins games she went to as a kid."

"Yeah, well, there was one missing, so I added it at the end."

Kat flipped through to the last used page. It was today's game—the Grand Rapids Chicks versus the Fort Wayne Daisies. Kat hugged Connie.

"The first of many, kid. You're gonna be here a long time, Kat. I know it."

Connie peeked out the door down the hall, then flipped open her suitcase and pulled out a pair of pants.

"Come on. Get dressed."

"Get dressed? For what? It's after curfew."

Connie went to the window and slid it open. "We're sneaking out to a party."

"What, are we going to climb out the window like monkeys?" Kat asked.

Connie looked back, one leg already over the sill.

"Of course not. How many monkeys do you think have ever climbed down a hotel fire escape?"

✤ ✤ ✤

The party was in a cemetery. The Fort Wayne catcher lived in her own place beside a graveyard, and that was where she threw shindigs when visiting players came to town.

Kat touched trees as they made their way deeper among the tombstones.

"Don't get spooked," Connie told her. "We haven't once been loud enough to raise the dead."

Not that they weren't trying, Kat thought. Someone had brought a portable phonograph player, and Frank Sinatra was crooning "Saturday Night (Is the Loneliest Night of the Week)" with a backup chorus of Daisies bobbysoxers. The rest of the girls sat on gravestones sipping beers and smoking cigarettes.

"Hi-de-ho!" a woman called, and she hopped down to give Connie a hug. Connie introduced her as Pepper Paire, the star catcher for the Fort Wayne Daisies.

Kat ogled the cemetery and the broad, bright sky full of stars. "I can't believe I'm here," she said.

"In a cemetery?" Pepper asked.

"In a cemetery, in Fort Wayne, in Indiana, in the league."

"First day," Connie explained.

"Ah," said Pepper. She smiled. "Yeah. You know, back home during the Depression, I used to play on this little softball team sponsored by the local grocery. If we won, we each got to go back to the store and fill up a bag with as much stuff as we could cram into it. Now I get paid a hundred dollars a week."

"More'n my pa ever earned in a week, that's for sure," Connie said.

Pepper raised her bottle. "Pennies from heaven," she said.

"Where are you from?" Kat asked Pepper.

"Los Angeles."

Kat moved closer to her, making sure not to step on any graves. "What's it like? California, I mean. I've only heard stories."

179

"It's always sunny in Los Angeles," Pepper said. "Sunny and warm. Not like here. And there's movie stars all over. You see 'em in the drugstores, in diners, walking along on the streets. There's professional softball leagues for girls too. They pay you if you're good enough. Not like this, but enough to make a living."

"I always wanted to play ball for a living," Kat said.

Pepper smiled. "Who doesn't, kid? Who doesn't?"

There was an argument over what would be played next on the phonograph. Eventually the Bing Crosby fans won out and the graveyard was serenaded by "Swinging on a Star." Kat stared up at the constellations. She'd never seen so many stars in the sky, not from New York, where lights burned night and day.

"I don't think she heard you," Connie said.

Kat blinked. "What?" Had someone asked her a question?

"She looks like she has a lot on her mind," Pepper said. "She needs to talk to Mrs. Murphy."

Pepper beckoned for Kat to follow her, and they walked alone to a quiet part of the cemetery. The catcher stopped in front of a small, simple gravestone that said only: "Hope Murphy."

"Kat, meet Mrs. Murphy," said Pepper. She brushed the top of the stone like she was cleaning it. "How you been, Mrs. Murphy? I've been on a road trip, so I haven't had a chance to drop by and say hello."

Kat looked around, wondering if this was another initiation.

"I come out here sometimes and talk to Mrs. Murphy," Pepper said. "I tell her all my deepest, darkest secrets."

"Who is she? I mean, did you know her?"

Pepper shook her head. "Just another gal like us. All she ever did and was, all that's left is her name." Pepper put a hand on Kat's shoulder. "You tell Mrs. Murphy whatever it is you've got on your mind. She'll listen. She's good at that."

Pepper left Kat alone at the grave. Kat looked around, sure a gang of players was waiting to jump out and laugh at her the minute she started talking to the stone.

"Um, hi," Kat said. "I um, I don't . . ." She looked around again. There wasn't anywhere Pepper or the other girls could be hiding, and the party carried on behind her. "I guess I do have something to say. Something I've never told anybody. I don't—I don't want the war to end. I want my dad back safe of course, but I wouldn't be here, now, without the war. There wouldn't even *be* a girls' league. And my mom, she's so smart, so good with numbers, but she only got a job as an engineer because all the men are off fighting. And Hattie, she's smart too, and she could go to school, get a good job if she wanted. The whole world's different now because of the war, and I know that there's less food and things to go around, and everybody's working so hard, and people are dying, but—"

Kat closed her eyes, ashamed of what she was saying.

"I wish it could be like this forever."

Kat backed away from Mrs. Murphy and tripped on another stone. She hadn't realized she was standing on someone else's grave.

2

Coach Meyer moved Kat up a couple of places in the lineup at home against the Rockford Peaches. She came to bat in the second with two girls on and no outs, and took time to do her pre-hitting ritual: Touch both ends of the bat, touch both toes, and draw an *H* in the sand, for "hit."

"You gonna hit sometime before the war ends, rookie?" the catcher asked.

Kat nodded to the umpire that she was ready and the pitcher went into her windup. The first pitch was a hanging curveball, and Kat sent it high and deep to right, where it banged off the wall of a lock factory for a home run. The crowd went dizzy. Connie, who was coaching first base that day, cheered Kat as she ran the bases, and the Chicks poured out of the dugout to celebrate with her when she reached home plate.

"You put one in orbit!"

"Like her gum!"

"You're the cat's meow, Kat!"

"She's a killer!"

"Killer Kat!"

Kat tried to get back to the dugout, but Alma Ziegler wouldn't let her.

"You gotta run the gauntlet," she told Kat. Was this some new initiation? A girl pointed Kat toward the first base line, where Kat saw Grand Rapids fans beckoning to her. Still not sure what she was in for, she ran over and found that every one of them wanted to shake her hand or clap her on the back.

The Chicks won their second game in a row, and the girls took Kat out on the town for dinner and then loaded up on the bus again for the next day's game in Kenosha against the Comets. Kat stuck with Connie, and together they sat mesmerized for a moment by the passing streetlights outside their window.

"Round and round the lake we go, where we stop, nobody knows," Connie whispered. "I probably been around Lake Michigan more times than Chief Pontiac."

"Have you been in the league a long time?" Kat asked.

"Just since last season. I came in with the Chicks when they were in Milwaukee. We won the whole thing, but nobody came out to see us. Same thing happened to the Millerettes in Minneapolis. But Grand Rapids has been great, same as Kenosha, Racine, Rockford, and the rest. Good crowds, good people."

"One of the fans today," Kat said, "when I went over to 'run the gauntlet'? One of them slipped me a dollar bill!"

Connie laughed. "I know! They do that sometimes. Teeny Petras made fifty dollars that way last season! Sent every bit of it back to her mother in Jersey."

"I also—I also got this." She handed Connie a slip of paper with a man's name and telephone exchange written on it.

"Ohhhh, no." Connie wadded the paper up and tossed it back over her head. "You're too young for that sort of thing. Looks like I'm gonna have to stick to you like glue, kid. Keep you away from Grand Rapids' more *sinister* element."

Kat smiled. She knew Connie was only kidding about the sinister element, but she was glad to have a friend. She was glad for so many things right now, and immediately felt guilty for it. She took a paper gum wrapper out of her pocket to fold it into little squares.

"So what's with you and the gum and the bats?" Connie asked.

"The bats?"

"Touching all the bats in the dugout."

Kat blushed. "I—I sometimes get nervous and have to touch all the wood I can see." She reached over and touched the wood frame of the bus window.

"You loony or something?"

"It wasn't always this bad, but once my dad got drafted—"

"Europe or the Pacific?"

"Europe. He's fighting in France." Kat unfolded the little wrapper and took a cigar box with a bear on the cover from her bag. The box had been her father's once. Inside, there were two cigars and a framed photo of him in his army uniform. Underneath that there was a stack of Orbit wrappers, all folded and unfolded again, one for each day he'd been gone. Kat added the new wrapper to the stack and touched all four corners of the wooden frame.

"I've never missed a night," Kat said of her little ritual. "It's stupid, but I like to think it keeps him safe."

"I'm sure it does, Kat."

Kat took a deep breath and stared out the window. The city streets of Grand Rapids had turned into the rolling farmlands of Michigan. She wanted her father to come home safe, wanted the Allies to beat Hitler, wanted her family to stop scrimping and saving and eating nothing but potatoes and carrots from their victory garden. But out here, in the vast flatlands of the Midwest, she was already starting to forget about all that.

And the forgetting felt good.

A murmur of laughter came from the poker game at the back of the bus, and Kat turned in her seat. It was late and she knew she should be sleeping, but she didn't want to miss a thing. It had been like this last night, and the night before, and Kat wondered if she would ever want to go to sleep again.

A broad, dark shape made its way down the aisle and stopped beside them.

"Katherine, are you awake?" It was Ms. Hunter, the chaperone.

"Yes, ma'am. I'm sorry."

"No need to be sorry, dear." Kat could practically hear the chaperone smiling in the dark. "I'm sure you're excited. Things have been such a whirlwind that I didn't have time to give you your beauty kit."

Connie snorted. Ms. Hunter put a booklet in Kat's lap, and in the occasional glow from the passing streetlights she could read the cover: "A Guide for All-American Girls: How to Look Better, Feel Better, Be More Popular, by Mme. Rubenstein."

"It's hard to walk in high heels when you've got a charley horse," Connie told Kat.

"You don't have to read it now," Ms. Hunter said, "but the league wants you to read it soon, and to always be as attractive and healthy and charming as possible."

"And play to win," Connie added.

"Of course," said Ms. Hunter. "And play to win."

Kat flipped through the packet, dismayed that she had homework to do.

"There are really only a few important things to remember," Ms. Hunter said, like she could read Kat's mind. "Always wear a skirt and look your best. Don't get your hair cut short, and never wear Oxfords or masculine-looking shoes. And the biggie: No fraternizing with opposing players."

"No what?"

"You're not supposed to be chummy with the girls on the other teams," Connie translated. "They don't want the league to look like a sorority."

"That's it," Ms. Hunter said.

"But last night we—"

Connie elbowed Kat, who quickly shut up.

"I'm sure Connie or one of the other girls can steer you clear until you get into the swing of things, but if you have any questions, do come to me, all right, dear?"

"All right, Ms. Hunter."

Kat flipped through her beauty manual again and saw that the last page was blank but for a headline: "Notes of a Star to Be." She liked that. "A Star to Be." It reminded her of Hollywood and all of Pepper Paire's stories of California. Kat looked out the window, trying to see the stars, but she couldn't see past her own reflection.

"So where'd you learn to hit like that?" Connie asked.

"Hmm? Oh, back in Brooklyn. I practically grew up at Ebbets Field, and there was always a stickball game going on around the neighborhood. I just played with the boys, learned to hit whatever they could throw. My whole family's mad for baseball. No time for that now, though. Dad's off in France, mom's an engineer building battleships, and Hattie, that's my sister, she runs the house."

And I ran away to play games.

Connie caught Kat thinking. "You miss them? Your family?"

Kat looked at her face in the window.

"No. Is that bad?"

Connie shrugged. "Some go one way, some go the other."

A car beside the bus started honking and flashing its lights. The girls craned forward to see what was going on as the bus slowed down and pulled over. There was some discussion between the bus driver and whoever it was who had flagged them down, and soon he came back with an armful of soda crates.

"Local Coca-Cola fella says he wants to donate a few cases to the team!" the driver announced. The girls hooted and hollered, and some of them leaned out the window to thank their benefactor and blow him kisses as he unloaded more from his trunk. Each girl took a bottle as they got passed back, and more cases were stacked into the front seat of the bus before it pulled back out onto the road.

"I tell you, this is the life!" Connie said.

Kat couldn't agree more. She tapped the top of her bottle three times before popping it, and Connie looked at her suspiciously.

"Keeps the fizz down?" Kat tried.

"Uh-huh." Connie clicked bottles with her and they drank.

The pit stop for Cokes had riled the girls up again, and Alma Ziegler—the girl Kat had been playing for while she was hurt—crab-walked her way forward from seat to seat. At the front of the bus Alma turned her jacket inside out and put her cap on backward to the calls and whistles of the team.

"My fellow All-Americans, let us pray," she said.

The girls were still buzzing, and half of them were laughing uncontrollably.

"I said let us pray, you creeps! Now shut it!"

There were stifled snorts throughout the bus, but everyone got quiet.

"My friends, many games hath we strayed from the winning path."

"Amen, sister!" Connie cried out. There were more laughs.

"And long have we toiled under Meyer, who God knows ain't no Moses."

"Aw, shut it and let me get some sleep," the manager called from the front of the bus. He was met with raspberries.

"And lo, Saint Feller and Saint DiMaggio and Saint Williams and the rest have left and gone to war."

Connie and the other girls put their caps over their hearts, and Kat hurried to do the same.

"In short, dear sisters, it is high time for a Sermon on the Mound."

The girls pelted Ziegler with their caps, and she very unpreacherly shot one of them back at a girl. In a moment she had her eyes closed and her hands raised in mock prayer again.

"Is there a rookie in this house of worship tonight?" she asked.

There was more whooping from the back of the bus, and Kat felt her ears begin to redden.

"I said, is there a rookie among us tonight!? Come forth, rookie, and be saved!"

"I thought I already had my initiation," Kat whispered.

"You did," said Connie. "This is different. This is a baptism."

Connie nudged Kat into the aisle and the team cheered. Not knowing what to do, Kat staggered down the aisle of the still-moving bus and stood before Ziegler. The veteran put her hand on Kat's cap and then pushed her to her knees.

"What is thy name, rookie?"

"Kat. Katherine Flint."

"Kat Katherine," Zeigler said, getting laughs, "you come today to the church of women's baseball from Hoboken, New Jersey."

"No, Brooklyn, New Y—"

"Don't interrupt me, sister. You come to us from Hoboken—or wherever—and offer yourself to this most holy of games. Do you give of yourself freely and clearly to baseball?"

"I do."

"Do you accept the central tenets of our faith—the run, the hit, and the error?" she said, then quieter, "But not so much the error."

"I do."

"Are you in body, mind, and spirit—particularly body— truly *in the game?*"

"I am!"

"And when my leg gets better, are you going to play some other position so I can have my old job back?"

Kat laughed. "Yes!"

"Good. Now that that's out of the way—are you going to get a hit tomorrow, sister?"

"Yes!"

"Are you gonna play your little rookie heart out tomorrow, sister?"

"Yes!"

"Let me hear it!"

"Yes, sister!"

"Then let it be known to all here who bear witness, that from this day forth you shall be known as 'Killer Kat' from Brooklyn—not Hoboken—and that you are, fully and truly, a Grand Rapids Chick. I now baptize you in the name of Tinker, and of Evers, and of the holy Chance."

Ziegler lifted Kat's cap, and she felt something rain down on her head. Too late she realized it was a bottle of Coca-Cola. Kat jumped up, sputtering.

Alma Ziegler laughed. "Say hallelujah, sisters!"

The bus rang out with hallelujahs. Kat pushed the sticky wet hair out of her face and smiled.

"Hallelujah," she whispered.

3

"We ain't got forever, you know," the catcher told Kat as she went through her hitting routine again.

Kat grinned at her as she stepped into the batter's box. "Hallelujah, sister," she said, getting a strange look from the catcher. It didn't matter. Nothing anybody else thought or did mattered. Kat was a Grand Rapids Chick, and nobody could take that away from her. She pounded the fourth pitch she saw into right center, and Connie, coaching first base again, windmilled her toward second. Without looking Kat knew the throw was coming in, that the play would be close, and she slid feet first into the bag.

"Safe!" cried the umpire.

Kat popped up. "Hallelujah!" she told the umpire, almost laughing.

"Hallelujah!" Connie echoed at first, hopping up and down. The Chicks had won five straight games, and Kat had climbed higher and higher in the lineup.

Kat was so happy she almost didn't feel the sting, but

then it came on like an electric burner heating up. Her exposed leg beneath her skirt was all scraped up from her slide, like she'd slid on concrete. It hurt like all get out, but Kat fought back the tears. It didn't matter. Nothing else mattered. She was a Grand Rapids Chick.

And the town of Grand Rapids loved Kat almost as much as she loved it. Cars honked and people waved as the girls made their way down the street. Restaurant managers gave them the best seats in the house. Strangers sent them drinks. Little girls asked for autographs. Kat couldn't imagine a better life, and the page in her guidebook, "Notes of a Star to Be," quickly filled with her memories and her hopes and her dreams.

But there was one dream Kat had she did not want, a dream that came to her again and again, night after night, a dream that would not stop until she tore herself from sleep, panting and sweating. In Kat's dream, she was tapping on the ends of bats. She knew it was a dream, because there were hundreds of thousands of bats, more than she could ever count, but she could never rest until she had touched them all.

But tonight as Kat touched the bats her tapping grew louder and louder, until it was a knocking, a pounding . . .

Kat woke with a start to someone knocking on the door of the hotel room she shared with Connie.

"Wake up, girls!" Ms. Hunter called through the door. "Wake up!"

Kat's vision was fuzzy, but she could see she still wore the clothes she had worn out last night when Connie had taken her to meet some friends on the Racine Belles. She pulled the covers up to her chin, afraid Ms. Hunter might come inside. The knocking was more insistent, and Connie worked her pillow over her head.

"Go away," she moaned. "It can't be afternoon. We just went to sleep."

"It's victory in Europe!" Ms. Hunter called through the door. "It's over! The war in Europe is over!"

Kat shot straight up in bed. Connie did the same. The knocking stopped and they heard Ms. Hunter banging on the next door down the hall.

"What did she say?"

"She said the war in Europe is over," Kat said, still dazed.

Kat heard clapping and cheering out on the street, and Connie rushed to the window.

"Jeepers, look at 'em!" Connie marveled.

The street was alive with people. It was like the indoors was too small to hold their happiness, like they had to get outside before their joy blew out all the doors and windows. People were crying and singing and dancing and hugging. Down the hall, some of the other girls were tearing up toilet paper and shoving it out the window like confetti. Church bells rang across the city, and car horns joined in the hullabaloo.

"Let's go down!" Connie said. She grabbed Kat's hand and pulled her out the door but stopped when she could feel Kat holding back and turned to see her tears.

"Kat, what is it?"

"I'm happy. I am," Kat blubbered. Her tears spilled out like boiling water. "It's just, I just got here and all and—"

"Oh, Kat," Connie said. "Are you worried about the league?" Connie pulled Kat into a hug. "You batty kid! This isn't the end—it's just the beginning!" Connie held her out at arm's length. "The league is stronger than ever! We're not going away just because Hitler's been squashed. Why, someday your own daughter will be playing for the Chicks. I guarantee it. And think of your pop! He's safe now. You won't have to be collecting those gum wrappers and tapping on wood anymore."

Kat gasped. "My Orbit wrapper!" She pulled an empty wrapper out of her pocket. "I forgot to put it in with the others when we got home last night!"

"But see? It doesn't matter!" Connie told her. "It's victory in Europe!" Connie whooped and dragged Kat with her down the steps. On the sidewalk, a man Kat had never met before picked her up and kissed her. The lady behind him gave Kat a bear hug, and little children ran among the revelers waving American flags and flying little toy airplanes. Kat looked around for Connie, but she had already disappeared into the crowd.

Maybe Kat was wrong. Maybe the league would go on. Maybe this life would go on, long after the war was over. Maybe forever. Maybe people had seen the way things could be and would never go back. She wiped her eyes again, and suddenly thought what a disappointment Mme. Rubenstein would find her right now—just out of bed, clothes rumpled, hair a mess, eyes red and puffy from crying. Kat started to laugh, and soon she couldn't stop. It hurt to laugh, but it was a good kind of hurt, like pulling a splinter.

Farther down the street there was a fountain, and anybody who wouldn't jump in was being thrown in. Connie was dancing on the edge, and Kat jumped up and took her in with her, crashing into the cold pool, cackling all the way.

Their game that night was canceled. Everything was canceled, and for one glorious night, all of America took the break it *hadn't* taken ever since the attack on Pearl Harbor more than three years ago. But in the morning it was back to business as usual. There was still victory in the Pacific to work for, and it wasn't going to be won playing in fountains and dancing in the street. Still, everywhere Kat went that day there was a smile on people's faces, and when she got to the ballpark she learned it had been sold out for hours.

Kat gave Marilyn a nickel for a pack of Orbit and the bat girl dashed off as the players began to get changed. Meyer posted the lineups, and Kat, Grand Rapids' newest star, was batting third. Connie gave Kat a punch in the arm to congratulate her as Marilyn ran up to them.

"That's fast," Kat said. "Back already? Somebody get this girl a contract!"

But Marilyn wasn't back with Kat's gum. She was back

with a Western Union telegram. It was from Kat's sister, Hattie, back in Brooklyn.

"It's probably to tell me we won," Kat said. "Like I wouldn't hear."

Connie frowned and sat on the bench beside Kat to read over her shoulder. Kat tore into the envelope and read the thing through.

"Oh my God, Kat—"

Kat read it through again.

And again.

It was a short message. All it said was:

"Father killed in action May 8. Body buried in France. Mom says stay and play."

Connie hugged her. "Oh, Kat. I'm so sorry."

"It's not true," Kat said. "May eighth. That's V-E Day. That's the day the war ended. How could he die on May eighth? This isn't right." Tears fell even as she said it. She knew it was right, knew her sister would never have played such a terrible joke, never written unless she was absolutely sure. She knew it was true because she had not put the gum wrapper in the cigar box that night. She hadn't touched her father's picture frame to keep him safe. She knew it was her fault her father was dead.

"My fault," she sobbed.

"No, Kat. No," Connie said, rocking her.

Kat found her glove through her tears and stood to join the other girls on the field. Connie caught her hand.

"Let me tell Ms. Hunter and Meyer," Connie said. "They'll understand you can't play today."

"No. Please. I have to play today. I have to play today, because tomorrow I have to go home."

"What? No. Why? What good would that do?"

"I have to be there for my mother. Help Hattie—"

"If your mother is designing battleships, I don't think she needs much help. And besides, look, she even told you to stay."

Kat sobbed. She hadn't missed her family before, but now she did. Now she wanted to bury herself in her mother's arms and cry like a baby.

"There's a time and a place for everything, Kat, and this is your time. Your place. You're a star."

"*V* for victory, girls!" Ms. Hunter called. "Come on. Let's go."

Kat wiped her face with her glove, and Connie let her go. Kat walked up the steps and out onto the field to take her place in the V. She knew the sun was shining and the flags were waving and the crowd was cheering, but to her the world was a different place. To her it was still and quiet, and *she* was the only one moving, her weeping the only noise.

The national anthem played, and Kat cried. She cried for her father, she cried for her mother, she cried for Hattie. But most of all she cried for herself, because she knew Connie was right. She knew she was going to stay.

Seventh Inning: Duck and Cover

Brooklyn, New York, 1957

1

There was a trick to flipping baseball cards. Just the right flick of the wrist, just the right release, just the right spin so that it fluttered and floated to the ground and landed heads-up on the picture side or tails-up on the stats side. There was a knack to it, an art, and Jimmy Flint was the undisputed card-flipping king of PS 161.

"You gonna flip sometime this century, Clyde?" Eric said.

Eric Kirkpatrick was the biggest, ugliest kid in the fifth grade. Legend had it he'd been held back not once, but twice. He was also just about the only Yankees fan in the whole neighborhood, probably just because everybody else was a Dodgers fan. But Jimmy didn't care about any of that right now. Jimmy had taken three straight cards from him, and now Eric's beloved Yogi Berra card was facedown on the playground cement. All Jimmy had to do was land his next card faceup beside it and both cards would both be his.

"Stay back! Give him room!" Jimmy's friend Ralph said,

203

pushing away the small circle of watchers their game had attracted.

Jimmy drew the next card from his stack—Jim Gilliam, second baseman for the Dodgers. Jim Gilliam was just about his favorite baseball player of all time, the Brooklyn Dodger who'd taken over at second base for Jackie Robinson when Jackie moved to the outfield. Jimmy had a special fondness for second base; his mother had played second for the Grand Rapids Chicks back when there was a women's league, and Jimmy himself had spent the last three months of one of those seasons at second base, growing inside her. He figured if ever there was a born second baseman, he was it.

"Come on, already! Recess is about to end!"

Jimmy kissed his card, took a moment to get the angle just right, and flicked it. Time slowed as it fluttered end over end, then settled to the ground. It was faceup. He'd won!

The boys around them erupted, cheering and clapping him on the back. Jimmy added both the cards to his stack and his friend Ralph raised Jimmy's hand like he was a winning prizefighter.

"Ladies and gentlemen—the undisputed winner and champ*een*, Jimmy Flint!"

"Gimme that back," Eric said.

"What?"

"Gimme that card back. You cheated."

"Cheated how?" Ralph demanded. "He won fair and square!"

"Back off, monkey boy," Eric said.

Jimmy's black friend took a step back with the rest of the crowd, and Jimmy couldn't blame them. He was right in Eric's sights, though, and there was nowhere for him to run.

"Bet you come from a long line of cheaters, don't you, Skinflint? Bet your dad was a cheater. But—oh, that's right, you don't know who your dad is, do you?"

Jimmy clenched his fists, but he knew he would never take a swing. Eric would wipe the pavement with him. The circle of boys hid them too well for him to call for help too; Jimmy couldn't see Mrs. Holloway at all.

Eric stepped closer. "Come to think of it, I haven't seen your mom around the neighborhood in a while either. She off looking for your dad?"

Eric's friends snickered.

"My mom's in California. She's a scout for the Dodgers!"

"You sure about that, Skinflint?" Eric flicked a finger at the Keep the Dodgers pin on Jimmy's jacket. "Or did she finally skip town for good like your stupid ball team?"

"Get bent!" Jimmy said, then immediately wished he hadn't.

"What's that?" Eric said. "Did I just hear you tell me to get bent?"

The class bell rang, and Mrs. Holloway called for everyone to come inside. Eric Kirkpatrick shoved Jimmy and he fell, losing his stack of cards and scraping his hands on the cement. Eric kicked the loose cards around with his sneaker and took back all of the ones he'd lost, including the Yogi Berra card.

"You're the one who's going to get bent, Skinflint," Eric said. "After school."

"Skinflint's going to get bent!" one of Eric's goons repeated as they walked away.

✤ ✤ ✤

Back in the classroom Jimmy sulked at his desk. The rest of the class was buzzing because Mrs. Holloway had turned on the radio. The only other time Jimmy could remember listening to the radio in class was two years ago, when Johnny Podres had twirled a shutout to beat the Yankees in game seven of the 1955 World Series. It was the only World Series the Dodgers had ever won—and the way things were going, the only World Series they would *ever* win. At least for Brooklyn.

But this time their teacher tuned in to hear a very different enemy, one far scarier to Jimmy than the dreaded Yankees:

Sputnik. The first man-made spacecraft, built and launched by the Russians.

It was everywhere on the radio, on every station. The Russians had beaten the Americans into space.

"It's a satellite," Mrs. Holloway explained. She drew a crude picture of the Earth on the blackboard, then drew a circle around it, punctuated by a small white dot. "It circles the Earth like our moon does, only much faster and much closer."

"It looks like a baseball Duke Snider hit into orbit," Ralph said. That got some laughs, but Jimmy wasn't in the mood.

"Wait—" the NBC announcer said. "Our observers tell us Sputnik is just now passing over the Eastern Seaboard!"

Half of Jimmy's class left their desks and rushed to the windows to look for it, but Mrs. Holloway waved the students back to their seats. "Sit down. Sit down. You won't be able to see it right now. You'll have to wait until sundown, and you'll probably need binoculars or a telescope."

They might not be able to see it, but they could hear it. The radio played the signal live as it passed overhead, a speck in the sky.

Beep, beep, beep, beep, beep, beep, beeeeeeep, beep, beep, beep—

It was monotonous. Endless. Inhuman. Jimmy got goose bumps.

Ralph leaned forward to whisper in Jimmy's ear. "Man, that's creepy."

"What—what does it mean?" Betsy Walker asked.

"It means the Commies can drop atomic bombs on us from space!" Eric said from across the room. Mrs. Holloway's fifth-grade room exploded into chatter and she tried to calm them down again.

"Children, children! Please, calm down." Mrs. Holloway shot Eric an exasperated look. "The Russians are not going to drop atomic bombs on us from space, or anywhere else.

Because they know if they do, we'll drop atomic bombs right back on them."

"But then we'll *all* be dead!" Betsy Walker wailed.

"Yes, and no one wants that, now, do they?" Mrs. Holloway said.

The radio announcer signaled that the station was going to a commercial, with more Sputnik news to come. "And later, of course, more of our ongoing coverage of the crisis in Little Rock, Arkansas, where federal troops—"

Mrs. Holloway switched off the radio. "Enough of that. You'll have nightmares enough as it is. Please open your arithmetic books." The students moaned, but did as they were told.

Jimmy still heard the *beep, beep, beeeeeeep* of Sputnik in his head, but if he couldn't figure some way to sneak out after school the Russians didn't matter: Eric Kirkpatrick was going to kill him first. While he was supposed to be working on long division Jimmy calculated the many ways Eric could devise to bring him down. When he was supposed to be learning about adjectives in English class, Jimmy outlined how Eric could modify his face. In music he noted that Eric could beat him like a wood block; in science he experimented with the hypothesis that Eric would dissect him. By the time social studies came around at the end of the school day, Jimmy was convinced he would end up stuffed in a locker like a mummy in a sarcophagus.

Which gave him an idea.

✤ ✤ ✤

That afternoon Jimmy stood in darkness, straining to hear the slightest sound in the hallway. School had been out for almost an hour, and in the silence all he could hear was the echo of Sputnik's robotic laugh in his head: *beep, beep, beep, beeeeeeep—beep, beep, beep, beeeeeeep—*

A door handle *ka-chunked* somewhere down the hall, and Jimmy held his breath. Eric couldn't have hung around this long looking for him, could he? Jimmy closed his eyes and said a silent prayer as a pair of sneakers squeaked down the hall, closer and closer and closer, until they stopped just outside his locker.

"Psst. Hey, Jimmy. You still in there, man? The coast is clear."

"You sure?" Jimmy whispered.

"I followed them all the way to the soda shop. They're gone, man."

Jimmy torqued his shoulder around to reach the latch and opened his locker.

Ralph shook his head at him. "Man, I can't believe you stuffed yourself in your own locker."

"Better than getting pounded by Eric Kirkpatrick," Jimmy said when he had worked his way out. "Now I just sneak down the back stairs and—"

The doors down the hallway *ka-chunked*, and Jimmy froze.

"You sure they didn't follow you back?" Jimmy whispered.

"Yeah. Positive," Ralph said.

Multiple sneakers squeaked their way closer.

"Um, pretty sure?" Ralph amended.

"Run!" Jimmy said, and the moment they took off they heard the other sneakers pick up the pace. Jimmy and Ralph dashed out the back doors, leaped down the flight of stairs to the sidewalk, and flew down Crown Street. A quick glance back over his shoulder told Jimmy all he needed to know— Eric and his gang were after them.

"Split up!" he cried when they hit the corner of Nostrand Avenue. Ralph took a right and Jimmy took a left toward Montgomery and Ebbets Field. At Ludlam Place Jimmy ducked down the bottom steps of a brownstone and hid, knowing he couldn't outrun the gang forever. He did his best to fade into the stone wall of the stairwell as they ran past, and it seemed to work. He waited until they had turned the corner down the street just to be sure, then doubled back.

As he ran home, Jimmy kept one eye on the sidewalks and one eye on the skies. He couldn't decide which was worse: Eric Kirkpatrick or the Russians.

2

Jimmy got to school early the next morning, hoping to avoid meeting Eric and his friends. Between Sputnik and Eric Kirkpatrick, Jimmy hadn't even been able to sleep. Nobody was in the hallway, and the clock on the wall told him class wouldn't start for another hour, but it was worth the wait. He put his book bag in his locker and went inside Mrs. Holloway's room to practice his card flipping, secure in the thought that he had at least delayed his beating until the first recess of the day.

He was in his seat talking with Ralph about *The Adventures of Rin Tin Tin* on television when Eric Kirkpatrick came into class, right before the bell. Eric watched Jimmy the whole way to his seat, and Jimmy knew he'd only made things worse by playing keep-away. As bad as it sounded, maybe he should just have let Eric and his gang beat him up yesterday, or come to school on time and let them catch him in the hall. Then again, maybe if he stayed away from Eric long enough he'd just give up.

Across the room, Eric popped his knuckles and grinned at Jimmy.

Or maybe not.

The bell rang and Mrs. Holloway began setting up the film screen. Yesterday the radio, today the projector—it was shaping up to be an interesting week. Usually Jimmy was as excited as the other students in the class to have a film, not so much because they liked films, but because they could close their eyes and pretend to be watching while they napped. Today, though, Jimmy was too focused on self-preservation.

"Today's film is called *Duck and Cover,*" Mrs. Holloway said, "and what with all the talk about Sputnik and the Russians, the principal thought we should start showing it again. This film should answer a lot of the questions you had yesterday about an atomic attack. Alice, if you would please get the lights?"

The lights went off, and the classroom resounded with the fake farting noise their pants and skirts made when they all slouched down in their seats at the same time. A girl in the back corner giggled.

"Pay attention, please," Mrs. Holloway said.

The film began with a cartoon turtle in a helmet walking down a path, enjoying a nice spring day. His name was Bert the Turtle, a song told them. Behind Jimmy, Ralph snickered. If he hadn't been so wound up, Jimmy would have too. This was kids' stuff.

Suddenly a monkey dangling from a tree hung a fire-

212

cracker in the turtle's face. Bert ducked into his shell. The firecracker exploded.

"Bad monkey!" Ralph said, and the class laughed. Mrs. Holloway shushed them again.

When the smoke cleared, the tree and the monkey were gone. But Bert the Turtle, the narrator told them, was safe because he had ducked and covered.

The film then showed a classroom not unlike Jimmy's, where the teacher was showing them how to duck under their desks and cover their heads when an atomic bomb exploded.

"We all know the atomic bomb is very dangerous," the narrator told them. "Since it may be used against us, we must get ready for it, just as we are ready for many other dangers that are around us all the time."

"Yeah, like Eric Kirkpatrick," Ralph whispered.

Jimmy didn't know how Ralph could joke around right now. All he could think about as he watched was Sputnik circling overhead. *Beep, beep, beep, beep, beep—*

"You will know when it comes," the narrator said. "There is a bright flash, brighter than the sun, brighter than anything you've ever seen." The film went white, and then cartoon houses and trees were knocked down and thrown around. This was what Sputnik could do: Drop a bomb that would blow up his house, his block, his school, Ebbets Field—*everything*. Kill his mom, his grandmother, his great-grandfather. Him.

There were two kinds of attacks, they were told—with warning and *without* warning. When there was a warning, they would hear air raid sirens, and must get to shelters as quickly as possible. "But sometimes the bomb might explode without any warning!" the narrator said. When they saw a flash, they were supposed to duck and cover, no matter where they were. The film showed pictures of students in the cafeteria, boys riding bikes, children playing on playgrounds. They showed families having picnics, people sitting in buses, men driving tractors. Each time the flash came and the people ducked and covered. But if an atomic bomb could knock down buildings and destroy his neighborhood, Jimmy wondered, what would it do to people?

Bert the Turtle came back at the end. "Remember what to do, friends. Now tell me right out loud—what are you supposed to do when you see the flash?"

Some kids in the film answered back, "Duck and cover!" but none of Jimmy's classmates said a word. The movie ended, and the loose end of the film *slap-slap-slapped* against the empty reel. Mrs. Holloway switched off the film projector and turned on the lights.

"What are you supposed to do?" Mrs. Holloway asked. "Let's hear it."

"Duck and cover," Jimmy answered with the class.

"Right. Let's practice. Ready? Just like in the film. There's a *flash!* Quickly, down under your desks."

Jimmy and his classmates slid out of their seats and crawled under their desks. Most of them, at least.

"Eric, get down under your desk," Mrs. Holloway said.

"I ain't afraid of no atomic bomb. This is sissy stuff."

"Don't be silly. Now duck and cover."

Jimmy watched as Eric slid out of his desk and crouched, not really ducking or covering. For his part, Jimmy wasn't going to play around. He pulled himself as tightly into a ball as he could and shielded his neck and head with his hands.

"Good, Jimmy. Good, Ralph. Cover your neck better, Betsy," Mrs. Holloway said, going up and down the rows.

"Man, this is what you ought to do when Eric Kirkpatrick comes after you," Ralph whispered. "Duck and cover."

Jimmy knew his friend was kidding, but right now he wasn't as worried about Eric as he was about the atomic bomb. All he could hear in his head was Sputnik flying overhead.

Beep, beep, beep, beep, beep, beep, beeeeeeep—

✣ ✣ ✣

Just because he was afraid of the atomic bomb didn't mean Jimmy was eager to get beat up. At the first recess of the day he avoided Eric by telling Mrs. Holloway he wasn't feeling well and asking to stay inside. He *wasn't* feeling well, not after the film, but it was really just a ploy to buy himself a little more time. Like the Russians, Eric Kirkpatrick could attack at any time, and if Jimmy couldn't really duck and cover to avoid him, at least he could hide out in his turtle shell a little while longer. He skipped the other two recesses of the day the same way, which amused Eric and his friends to no end.

"What's the matter, Skinflint? You scared of something?" Eric asked on the way outside. Jimmy just kept his head down, silently plotting a way to escape that afternoon without being caught.

Ralph stayed with Jimmy after school while he did everything he could think of to delay leaving the classroom. He volunteered to beat the erasers, wash the blackboard, even sweep up.

"Man, what you gonna do now?" Ralph asked him when he was finished.

"I don't know. Do you think they'd let me spend the night?" he joked.

"You want me to go check out in the hall, see if they're there?"

Jimmy checked the clock. "No. There's a Keep the Dodgers rally at Ebbets Field I wanted to go to anyway. Maybe if I can slip past them I can lose them again on the way."

"Man, you are one brave dude," Ralph told him.

Jimmy stepped into the hall, expecting to see Eric and his friends right away—but they weren't there. He glanced up and down the hallway. They had to be lying in wait for him somewhere.

"Where are they?" Ralph asked.

Jimmy went to his locker, half afraid Eric was hiding inside, waiting for him. He wasn't, of course, but that just meant he was waiting to jump him somewhere else. Jimmy collected his books and headed for the front stairs. Eric and his friends weren't in the stairwell, but when he reached the bottom step Jimmy froze. Through the bank of doors that led outside to the front steps of the school, he could see Eric Kirkpatrick waiting for him. Suddenly his bravado ran out.

"I—I'm gonna go out the back way."

"Yeah. Sounds like a good idea to me," Ralph said. Together they jogged up the stairs and down the hall to the back stairs. Jimmy was just about to push his way outside and make for home when he saw two of Eric's gang hanging out on the back steps. He ducked back inside.

"They covered both the exits!" Ralph whispered. "Man, they must really want to get you bad. What are you gonna do now?"

Jimmy retreated into the stairwell—and noticed for the first time that the stairs kept going down beyond the ground floor.

"Hey, where do these stairs go?"

Ralph shrugged. "Basement, I guess."

Jimmy jogged down the first flight of stairs to the turn.

"Can you see me from up there?"

"No."

"All right," Jimmy said, coming back up. "I've got an idea."

Ralph burst through the back doors and almost made it past Eric's buddies before they grabbed him.

"Whoa there, monkey boy. Where you going in such a hurry?"

"Yeah, and where's your little friend?"

"Eric got him. Coming out the front door."

"Swell," one of the boys said.

"Please, no—leave him alone."

"Heh. Some hero you are," the other boy said. He shoved Ralph against the wall and headed for the door. "Come on," he told his friend. "I don't want to miss the fun."

Ralph gave Eric's friends time to go inside and climb the stairs, then pulled the door open and whistled softly. Jimmy came running up the stairs from the darkness below and slipped outside. Together the two friends ran as far as Nostrand Avenue before they stopped to say their good-byes.

"I owe you one," Jimmy said.

"Great. How about you give me your Jim Gilliam card, then?"

"What!? No way!"

"Gil Hodges, then."

"Deal." They shook on it, and Ralph took off for their street while Jimmy headed for Ebbets Field.

There was a small group of people assembled at the corner

of Sullivan and McKeever when Jimmy got there. Some of them wore sandwich boards with slogans on them and sang songs trying to convince the Dodgers to stay in Brooklyn. A woman wearing a "Keep the Dodgers" pin and a Brooklyn cap sat behind a little table nearby, and Jimmy gave her the pages of signatures he'd collected for the petition to get the Dodgers to stay. The woman added them to an impressive-looking stack on a clipboard and offered Jimmy a pin, but he told her he already had one.

A man with a bullhorn led the crowd in a Dodger fight song, and Jimmy sang along as loud as he could. But even as he sang, Jimmy couldn't help but wonder who heard them, or who was actually going to read the petition. The season was over. The Milwaukee Braves were playing the New York Yankees for the World Series, and his mother and the rest of the Dodgers' front office were already in California getting ready for next season. It suddenly felt silly to work so hard to keep the Dodgers in Brooklyn when they clearly didn't want to stay, and Jimmy slipped away before the song was even finished.

Jimmy shuffled up the steps to his great-grandfather's house and went inside. Great-Grandpa Snider was watching television, and Jimmy plopped down beside him. They watched in silence until Jimmy's grandmother appeared in the doorway to the kitchen.

"I thought I heard someone come in. Did you have a good day at school, Jimmy?"

"Yes ma'am."

Grandma Frankie waited like there was something more.

"Your teacher called. Mrs. Holloway. She said you didn't go out for recess at all today. Said you seemed all mopey."

Jimmy stared at the ground.

"You're not getting sick, are you?"

"No ma'am."

"So what about it, then? Why won't you go out to play?"

"I just—I just needed some time to work on my Keep the Dodgers petition," Jimmy lied.

"Oh, Jimmy. You know that man never meant to keep the Dodgers here. He was just looking for a reason to leave."

"I know."

"Dinner'll be ready in a half an hour," she told them, disappearing into the kitchen.

Jimmy couldn't bring himself to get up, so he sat and watched *What's My Secret?* with his great-grandfather. They put the new contestant's secret up on the screen so the viewers at home would know what the panel was supposed to guess. It said: "Every time Sputnik goes over my house my garage door opens."

"What's his name?" Great-Grandpa Snider said out of nowhere.

"Whose name?"

"The boy who's giving you trouble on the playground."

Jimmy flushed and clammed up. His great-grandfather looked away from the TV at him.

"I don't know any red-blooded American boy who doesn't want to go outside for recess. You're not a Commie, are you?"

Jimmy laughed and Great-Grandpa Snider smiled.

"No, sir. And his name is Eric Kirkpatrick."

"Bigger'n you? Ugly cuss?"

"You know him?"

Great-Grandpa Snider laughed. "I've known a lot of him over the years. So what are you going to do about it?"

"Duck and cover," Jimmy said.

His great-grandfather harrumphed. "So that's the plan? You're gonna run away all your life?"

Jimmy shrugged. "At least until junior high."

"I tell you," Great-Grandpa Snider said, "you better do something about it now, or you're going to be ducking and covering your whole life. That's what my pa did, and it wore him down."

"But what can I do?"

"Fight back. If he's bigger'n you, step on his toes. Then, when he's hopping around cussing, pop him one in the nose."

Jimmy didn't know what to say. He'd never heard his great-grandfather talk like this.

"Better yet, shoot him a knee to the groin. Don't matter how big a man is, that'll take him down every time. No matter what you do, you find a way to fight back, or you'll be a victim all your life."

"Y—yessir," Jimmy said, sliding off the couch. "Thanks."

Jimmy went out back into their small yard. It was almost twilight, and he lay down on his back to see if he could spot Sputnik flying overhead. Next door, the Ramirezes' radio was tuned in to the news, where the broadcaster was talking about "Mutually Assured Destruction." Then they replayed that *sound*, the sound of Sputnik drawing a bead on them from orbit: *Beep, beep, beep, beep, beep, beep, beeeeeeep, beep, beep, beep*—

The Russians were in space, the Dodgers were going to California, and Eric Kirkpatrick was going to pound him to a pulp.

Other than that, his life was perfect.

3

Jimmy watched the second hand ticking away on the clock above the chalkboard in Mrs. Holloway's classroom. *Tick, tick, tick*—it beat with the haunting regularity of Sputnik. But Sputnik was death that could come without warning, and Jimmy's more immediate concern was the death that was coming *with* warning: Eric Kirkpatrick, who had come over to Jimmy's desk that morning to tell him in no uncertain terms that there would be no escape this afternoon.

Tick, tick, tick—skipping recesses and lunch, Jimmy had five hours and twenty-three minutes left until the end of the day, and maybe the end of his life.

When it was time for math Jimmy and the rest of the students pulled out their arithmetic books, but the teacher told them they wouldn't be using those books anymore. They had ordered new math textbooks, books about geometry and algebra, and the students would begin using them within the week. They would be getting new science textbooks too.

"This is math you would be learning later, in junior high,

223

but the school board has decided to step things up a bit. I'm sure you'll all do fine," Mrs. Holloway said. She gave them all an encouraging smile. "Instead of your usual math work today, we're going to watch a film to help prepare you for what's to come. Can someone fetch the film projector for me? Jimmy?"

Jimmy jumped. He'd been staring at the clock and not really paying attention.

"And who will go with him?" Mrs. Holloway asked.

"Ooh! Ooh! Me!" Eric Kirkpatrick said, waving his hand frantically in the air.

"Why, Eric. I've never known you to be so . . . enthusiastic about helping," Mrs. Holloway said. "You and Jimmy then. Off you go."

Jimmy couldn't move. He knew exactly why Eric had volunteered to go with him to get the projector. This time he was going to get Jimmy before he had another chance to slip away.

"Remember—duck and cover!" Ralph whispered from behind him.

Jimmy rose like a condemned man and met Eric at the door. Eric beamed at him.

"Back in a flash," Eric told Mrs. Holloway, and he opened the door for Jimmy with mock politeness.

Jimmy walked alongside Eric down the hallway, wondering when the attack would come. Not here, he realized, not around the other classrooms. Eric would wait until they were alone together in the A/V room.

He could just run away, but to where? If he ran back to class he'd be a laughingstock. If he ran home his grandma would just send him right back. He could run off to the movie theater, spend the day there in the dark, and then head home after school was over, but then what about tomorrow? And the day after that? And the day after that? No, Great-Grandpa Snider was right: To run now would mean he'd be running away all his life. He'd have to *move* to get away from Eric Kirkpatrick, and that wasn't going to happen.

But fighting him wasn't going to happen either. Great-Grandpa Snider might have been able to stand up to bullies, but Jimmy couldn't. He'd never been in a real fight in his entire life, and he was sure if he started this one—or even fought back—it would only make things worse on him.

Jimmy was beginning to think that maybe duck and cover was the best option after all.

Eric pushed him inside the A/V room and closed the door behind them. The place was filled with film projectors on carts and reel-to-reel tape machines, and had the metal/plastic smell of the future. Oddly, Jimmy wondered if this is what Sputnik smelled like.

"No running away this time, Skinflint."

Eric knocked him backward into a cart, and while Jimmy was trying to keep himself from falling Eric punched him in the stomach. It was like running into his bike handlebar times a thousand, and Jimmy fell to his knees, groaning.

"You think you're pretty smart, don't you, Skinflint?"

225

Jimmy kept his eyes on the floor.

"You got nothing wise to say this time? That's what I thought. All right, Clyde. This is how it's gonna go. I'm gonna pound you, but if you say anything about what happened and get me in trouble, we'll just do this again, see? Mrs. Holloway asks, and you tell her you—"

Eric was interrupted by something howling outside—a siren. They both froze.

"What gives?" Eric asked.

Jimmy knew that sound. They'd just heard it the day before in class.

"It's a civil defense siren!"

Eric ran to the window. "I—I see it! I see a bomb!"

"Duck and cover!"

Jimmy and Eric dove underneath a strong-looking wooden table, and Jimmy covered his head and neck with his arms.

"You think it's the Russians?"

"Of course it's the Russians, Skinflint! Who else would it be? But did you see a flash? I didn't see a flash. They said there would be a flash!"

Jimmy didn't see anything. He had his eyes shut so tight they made faint radiating patterns against the back of his eyelids. Over the wail of the siren, Jimmy kept hearing the drone of Sputnik. *Beep, beep, beep, beep, beep, beep, beeeeeeep*—

This was it. He would never see his mother again, never see Grandma Frankie or Great-Grandpa Snider again. His house, his school, Ebbets Field—his entire world would be gone.

And then the siren stopped. In the sudden silence, Jimmy could hear their breaths against the cold tile floor.

"You think it's over?" Jimmy asked. "I didn't hear any explosions."

"I don't know—but I ain't getting up until somebody tells me to get up."

The two boys waited under the table, hands over their heads, for what seemed like ages—but Jimmy wasn't going to get up until Eric did. Just when his legs were starting to cramp up, Jimmy heard the door to the A/V room open.

"Oh, boys! I'm so sorry." It was Mrs. Holloway. Jimmy and Eric raised their heads. "The drill is over now. You can come out."

"Drill?" Eric asked.

"We didn't know when it would come, but we announced it to the class when the sirens went off."

"But Eric saw a bomb. He said so."

"Saw a bomb?" Mrs. Holloway said. "I'm not sure you would actually see one falling. Exploding, yes, but not falling."

Eric ran to the window. "No, I was sure I saw it. Look— there it is!"

Jimmy and Mrs. Holloway went to the window with him. There, in the distant sky, was a small oval object with tail fins.

"That's a blimp!" Jimmy said.

"An easy mistake," Mrs. Holloway said. "You two did very well in the duck and cover drill. Very well indeed. Now let's get that projector and get back to class."

His classmates were jabbering away when Jimmy got back to class, and Mrs. Holloway let them talk while she set up the film.

Ralph leaned forward. "Hey, you're not dead!"

"No, and neither is anybody else."

"What are you talking about?"

"We didn't know it was a drill! We were still ducking and covering when Mrs. Holloway came and got us!"

Ralph had himself a good laugh over that, and Jimmy punched him in the arm.

"It's not funny!"

"Hey, okay, okay. So does that mean Eric is still after you?"

Jimmy looked across the room to where Eric was laughing with his friends, probably telling them all about how he beat up little Jimmy Flint. Somehow he doubted he was telling them how the two of them ducked and covered the rest of the time, thinking it was the end of everything.

"No," Jimmy said. "I think it's over."

✤ ✤ ✤

But it wasn't. On the way home from school that afternoon Eric and his buddies caught Jimmy and Ralph on the cement playground and surrounded them.

"Heya, Skinflint," Eric said. "It's time to finish what we started."

Jimmy couldn't believe it. Not after what they'd been

through, not after what they thought had happened. It's not like he and Eric had become buddies hiding under the table, but Jimmy figured it had shown both of them there were bigger things to worry about than who beat who at card flipping.

Eric cracked his knuckles. "Now, where were we?"

Jimmy backed up, but one of Eric's buddies shoved him forward. If Jimmy didn't think of something fast, he was going to get it. He looked around frantically for a teacher, a parent, but there was nobody around. There *was* something in the sky, though—

"Look! Up in the sky! It's a bomb!"

"What? Huh? Where?" Eric's gang said, and everyone looked where Jimmy was pointing.

"That's not a bomb, you moron!" one of Eric's buddies said. "That's a blimp!"

"The spaz don't even know the difference between a blimp and a bomb!"

Eric's gang broke up in fits of laughter, but Jimmy saw right away that Eric wasn't laughing. He was glaring at Jimmy, warning him silently with his eyes not to say anything more.

"Did you see a flash? They said there'd be a flash. Are you sure you didn't see it?" he said, overplaying it so he was sure Eric got the message. From the scowl on Eric's face, Jimmy knew he understood. If Eric beat him up, Jimmy would tell everybody how he'd ducked and covered, and mistaken a blimp for a bomb. He might still put Jimmy in a body cast, but Eric's reputation as a tough guy would be ruined forever. It felt wrong to make fun of Eric for being scared. Jimmy had been just as frightened, maybe even more so. But Jimmy wasn't the one picking the fight.

"Come on, Eric, pound him!" one of the boys said.

Eric sneered at Jimmy, then gave in. "Not today."

Eric's buddies couldn't believe it.

"Not today, Skinflint," Eric said, pointing a finger at his nose. "But one day, when you least expect it—" He smacked a fist into his open hand. *"Boom."*

He was just making a show of being tough for his gang, and Jimmy didn't say anything more. He didn't have to. He and Eric both knew what would happen if he made good on his threat. And it wasn't just his word against Eric's—Mrs. Holloway knew all about him ducking and covering from a blimp too.

Eric turned and walked away, and his confused friends followed him.

Jimmy let out a breath he didn't realize he'd been holding.

"What—what just happened!?" Ralph asked. "He was gonna pummel you!"

"He was, but it's over. For real, this time."

"What do you mean it's over? He just said one day when you least expect it, boom!"

"He won't do it," Jimmy said. "Not now and not ever."

He looked up into the sky, trying to see Sputnik. "And I don't think the Russians will either." He was beginning to understand now, and it felt like a great weight was lifting off his shoulders.

"What are you talking about?"

Jimmy smiled and told Ralph all about Mutually Assured Destruction as they looked for a place to flip cards.

Eighth Inning: The Perfectionist

Brooklyn, New York, 1981

1

It was shaping up to be a perfect summer day, but Michael Flint didn't notice it. Not right away, at least. He was too focused on perfecting his curveball to notice anything else. His grandma Kat had taught him how to throw one, but he still hadn't mastered it. He was doing everything he was supposed to: He held the ball deep in his palm, he nestled his first two fingers along one of the seams, he rolled his hand to give the ball downspin. But the ball either ended up breaking far too early and bouncing home, or it flattened out and didn't break at all—the dreaded "hanging curveball" that was so easy to hit. Every now and then he got one just right and it dropped into the catcher's mitt like a Tom Seaver curveball, but he couldn't do it perfectly every time and so he *never* did it. At least not in a game.

The rest of the team began to arrive for their morning game at the Prospect Park baseball fields, and Michael and his catcher Carlos Reyes finished up their workout to join them.

"You've just about got that curveball down," Carlos told him.

"Yeah. But not quite."

"When the baseball strike ends, you should watch Fernando Valenzuela throw. He has the best curveball in the majors."

"Fernando has the best *screwball* in the majors."

Carlos grinned. "Yes, but his curveball is the best too."

In the dugout Michael found his closest friend on the team, Adam Rosenfeld, and tossed his glove on the bench beside him. Adam was a curly-headed eleven-year-old from Richmond, Virginia, who could never sit still. He played just about every position on the team, was a star football player, and could beat Michael handily at any video game.

"Me and Raul saw *Raiders of the Lost Ark* last night," he said.

"Again? How many times is that?"

"Seven. How many times you seen *Empire?*"

Michael shrugged. "Ten or twelve."

Coach Clemmons clapped his hands as he came into the wire-fence dugout. "All right, troops, big game today. Big game."

Michael and Adam rolled their eyes at each other. Every game was a "big game" for Coach Clemmons, even though it was the middle of the season.

"Who's ready to get off the schnide? Hmm?" He clapped again. "I want to see some focus out there today, all right, boys?" He made his way down the bench. "Let's take good swings today, all right? Keep your eye on the ball. We're going up against their best pitcher." Coach Clemmons got to Michael. "But they're going up against *our* best pitcher, right, Michael?"

Michael shrugged, even though he knew it was true. They all knew it was true. If the coach could run him out to pitch every game he would, but the league rules wouldn't allow it.

"We've lost three straight," Coach Clemmons told Michael. "I'm counting on you to be our stopper now, all right? And just remember, not every pitch has to be perfect, Mikey. Most batters will get themselves out, and the guys behind you can do the rest, all right? We may not be able to hit a lick, but we can field like nobody's business. All right?"

Michael nodded and Coach Clemmons went back down to the front of the dugout, clapping to rally his team.

"All right, you're our best pitcher now, all right?" Adam said, riffing on Coach Clemmons. "You don't have to be perfect, all right? Just all right. All right?"

Michael held up his hands and laughed. "All right! All right!"

"All right," Adam said.

The Bob Smith Ford team took the field first, and Michael and Adam chatted while their Fulton Street Pawn and Loan teammates took their swings.

"So you've seen *Empire* all those times," Adam said as they watched George Robinson ground out to short. "Who do you think Yoda meant when he said, 'There is another.' You know, when he was talking about other Jedis besides Luke."

"Han Solo. Has to be."

"No way," Carlos said. "He says he doesn't believe in all that stuff."

"So what? He doesn't have to believe in it. The Force is what it is."

"I think it's Lando," Adam said.

"What? No."

"Well who then?"

"I think it's R2-D2," Carlos said.

Michael and Adam busted out laughing.

"You guys settle down back there and focus, all right?" Coach Clemmons called. "Now come on. Let's hear a little baseball chatter, all right?"

Michael wiped tears from his eyes. "Come on batter. Get a hit," he called, trying not to laugh.

"*Um* batter, *um* batter," Adam said, but he was overcome by another laughing fit and had to stop.

"What? Who says R2-D2 can't have the Force?" Carlos said.

"Dude. He's a *robot*. Robots can't have the Force. Only living things."

"Says who?"

The last batter struck out swinging and the bench shuffled to its feet to take the field. Michael shook his head, still laughing, as he climbed up on the mound. He threw a few warm-up tosses and then the first Bob Smith Ford batter stepped up to the plate.

"Easy out, now, easy out," Adam called from first base.

Michael set up his off-speed pitches with his fastball, fast, slow, fast again, and got the lead-off batter to pop out. The second batter saw a steady diet of fastballs, this time in and out, out and in. He struck out swinging on four pitches. The third batter was Bob Smith Ford's best; he'd hit two doubles off Michael last time they'd played, and Michael didn't want to let him do that again. He worked him inside, inside, inside, not letting him get those big long arms around on anything. He got a piece of one that shot a mile in the air and came down in fair territory around third base, where Ramon hauled it in for the last out of the inning.

Back in the dugout Michael started kidding Carlos about C-3PO maybe having the Force. Adam nodded at something behind him.

"Little brother alert," Adam said.

Michael's little brother, David, stood on the other side of the chain-link fence, a messy ice cream cone in his hand and the other half on his face.

Michael sighed. "What?"

"You want to play Atari later?"

"I'm kind of doing something right now, David. I'll worry about that later, all right? Sheesh. Now get out of here."

David stayed where he was and scarfed his ice cream cone.

"Go on, beat it!" Michael said. David turned to go back to the stands. "Wait, wait," Michael said. "Tell Grandma Kat I'm opening up too much on my follow-through and ask her what I should do."

David took another bite of his ice cream cone.

"So go *on,* you little Ugnaught."

David left again.

"What a dork."

"So, you think you'll play Atari later?" Adam asked.

"Yeah. Probably."

Coach Clemmons called Michael out on deck, and he went to the plate to bat when Ramon grounded out. Michael's helmet was a little too big and his bat was a little too small, but he wasn't a very good hitter anyway. Good enough to bat seventh, but that was only because Tim and Alberto were a lot worse.

Michael managed to work a two and two count and got his aluminum bat on the next pitch, but all he did was float a weak liner to second base for the third out. He tossed his bat and helmet back in the dugout and Adam brought his glove out for him as the teams changed sides. The next half inning he made quick work of the Bob Smith Ford batters, notching two strikeouts and a fly ball to right. He still wasn't locating his pitches where he wanted them, though, and David wasn't back when he came off the field. He tried to find his family in the bleachers, but he couldn't see them.

"Useless," Michael said.

The next half inning he went back to the mound to face the bottom three hitters in the Bob Smith Ford lineup. He got a strikeout, a ground out, and then the ninth batter, probably the lamest on the team, made Ramon have to dive to save a sure double down the line. But Ramon was so good and the runner was so slow he still threw him out at first.

Michael threw his glove against the chain-link fence and kicked the dirt floor when he got back to the bench.

"It doesn't have to be perfect," Coach Clemmons called. "Let's show a little respect for the game down there, all right?"

Michael caught sight of his brother on the path behind the dugout and called him over.

"David! David, what did Grandma Kat say?"

David had a little red and white bag of popcorn, and he stuffed a handful in his mouth.

"Abow wha?"

"About me opening up too soon! Not locating my pitches."

"She seb if yow're piding pewfec yow're nob dobing anbyfing wong."

"In *English*, please?"

David swallowed. "She said if you're pitching perfect you're not doing anything wrong."

"But I'm *not* pitching perfect."

"Yes you are," Adam said. "Nobody's reached first base in three innings. That's perfect." Adam laughed. "Hey, just six more innings and you've got a perfect game!"

"Right," Michael said. Like he could *ever* be perfect.

241

2

Fulton Street Pawn and Loan didn't score in their bottom half of the inning, even though they did muster two hits. In the bottom of the fourth Michael faced the other team's top three hitters again, registering a strikeout and a ground out to Adam for the first two outs of the inning. Then the big doubles hitter came to the plate, and Michael knew he wouldn't fall for a barrage of inside pitches again. He looked in to see what Carlos was thinking.

Carlos put down the sign for an inside fastball.

Michael sighed. With just a fastball and a changeup, his off-speed pitch, he didn't have many options. He nodded to Carlos. Even if they didn't go there the entire at bat, he could throw an inside fastball that at least set the batter up, make him think that's what they were going to do again this time.

But Michael didn't want to "waste" a pitch—to throw one that did nothing but delay confrontation. Instead he aimed for the edge of the plate, looking maybe to get a called strike if the umpire was in a generous mood and the big hitter was expecting junk.

The hitter took the pitch. "Strike one!" the umpire cried. The big guy slumped his shoulders and looked back at the umpire, questioning the call without saying a word. His coach said something about it, though, giving the umpire an earful from the dugout.

Carlos threw the ball back to Michael and he looked in again. Fastball inside. Michael shook his head. Carlos wanted a repeat of the first at bat, but Michael knew this guy wouldn't let another close strike go by without doing something with it, and he wasn't going to swing at something too far in. Behind the plate, Carlos shrugged, as if to say, "Okay, what then?"

Carlos put down the sign for a fastball away. Michael nodded. It was worth a shot, and the hitter might be expecting more inside stuff. But Michael would really have to waste one now. If he put it anywhere near the plate the hitter would tattoo it to right field.

Michael took a deep breath, aimed, and let his fastball fly. The hitter was ready for it, eager for anything he could reach out for, and he lunged after the fastball like a golfer.

"Strike two!" the umpire called. Michael snapped the ball back in his glove and nodded to Carlos. They had the guy on the ropes. He peered in for the sign.

Carlos dropped two fingers.

The curveball? Was Carlos crazy? A third of the time it

243

bounced to the plate, and a third of the time it floated in like the fattest, most hittable pitch the batter had ever seen. Sure, there was that other third of the time when it broke just right, when it came in looking like a fastball and then dove away at the last second, leaving batters flailing, but there was no way he could take the chance. He shook Carlos off.

Carlos's catcher's mask tilted sideways, and Michael knew he was wondering: "If not now, when?"

Michael sighed again. Carlos was right, and he knew it. The pitch wouldn't *get* to be perfect if he didn't use it, and a two-strike count was the time to try it. He motioned for Carlos to cycle through the pitches one more time and nodded at the sign for curveball.

"Drop in there," Michael whispered as he went into his windup. "Drop in there drop in there drop in there."

He released, staring the ball down as it flew closer, closer, closer—

—but didn't drop. It hung like a fat breaking ball, and the big Bob Smith Ford hitter took a late, greedy hack at it. The ball pinged off his bat and flew straight back into the chain-link fence backstop behind the plate—*thwack!*—rattling the No Pepper sign.

The big hitter glanced back at Michael like he couldn't believe the gift he'd just been given, and he kicked at the dirt for not blasting the ball for a home run.

"All right, enough of that, then," Michael said. He got a new ball from Carlos and they went back to square one.

244

Another fastball away? No. Another fastball inside? No. An off-speed pitch *way* outside? *No.* Everybody always wanted to waste pitches when they had a two-strike count, like they had three balls they could throw anywhere. What was the point of wasting a good count just to run it back to three balls and two strikes?

Carlos called time-out and jogged to the mound.

"You gotta call something, amigo. I say try the curveball again."

"No," Michael said. He grasped for something, anything he could use to get him out. "Changeup low. Bottom of the strike zone."

"Why not waste a couple first? Get him guessing."

Michael shook his head. "He's too smart for that. Let's go with the low changeup."

Carlos shrugged and jogged back to the plate, and Michael kneaded the ball in his hands. When his catcher was set he went into his windup, then slowed his delivery down, aiming for the bottom of the strike zone. The ball took an eternity to get there, and he watched as he followed through. The hitter waited, waited, waited, hitched his shoulder, then swung—

The bat met the ball with the resounding *ping* of aluminum, but he drove the ball down, into the ground. It tore a divot in the earth four feet in front of home and bounced to short, where George made quick work of it and threw the batter out at first. Michael pumped his fist and slapped Carlos on the back as they ran back in the dugout, four innings in the books.

Four perfect innings.

Michael was up first for Fulton Street Pawn and Loan, and he grabbed his helmet and bat and walked out to the plate while the other pitcher took a few warm-up tosses. Perfect through four innings. That was something, but a lot of pitchers had been perfect for four innings. Perfect for nine innings was a different thing altogether. There had only been ten perfect games in the history of Major League Baseball. Grandma Kat loved to tell the story of being there for Sandy Koufax's perfect game in 1965, but good as he was, Sandy Koufax had never thrown another. Tom Seaver and a host of others hadn't thrown *any*.

A perfect game was practically impossible, wasn't it? Especially for Michael. He'd walk someone, or there would be a bloop hit, or one of his teammates would throw one three feet over Adam's head at first for an error. Besides, none of that was going to matter if they didn't get some runs. The score was still 0–0.

Michael did his best at the plate, but the pitcher was too good for him. Even when he could guess what was coming he still couldn't do much with it, grounding back out to the mound and getting tossed out easily at first.

Coach Clemmons clapped as he ran back into the dugout—Coach Clemmons clapped for everything, from a home run to a strikeout—but nobody said anything to Michael as he made his way down to the end of the bench. He sat next to Adam and Carlos, but neither of them said anything either.

"So I've got another idea," Michael said. "About who the other Jedi is." He paused, trying to build suspense for his punchline. "It's Chewbacca!"

Michael grinned, expecting Adam to laugh and Carlos to get upset that they were still making fun of him, but Adam just looked at his feet and Carlos worked at cleaning the dirt from his cleats.

"It could be Chewbacca," Adam said.

Michael looked around at his friends. What was wrong with them? Had he done something to make them mad?

Before he could ask, the last batter of the inning struck out and Coach Clemmons was rallying everyone back out onto the field. Michael walked up on the mound, still wondering what he'd said to make his friends upset. But if something was wrong Carlos didn't show it behind the plate. He was all business as the bottom half of the inning got going, and they made quick work of the next three batters in the lineup, setting them down one-two-three.

Coach Clemmons clapped as Michael ran past him into the dugout, but he didn't say anything. The whole bench was quiet, and Adam and Carlos sat near Michael but wouldn't even look at him. Michael's little brother, David, standing right beyond the chain-link fence and eating a Moon Pie, was the only one who even acknowledged his presence.

"Everybody's talking about you," David said.

"What?"

"In the stands. Everybody is talking about your perfect game."

Adam and Carlos glared at David, but said nothing. So *that's* what this was about. His teammates all knew he had a perfect game through five innings, and nobody wanted to say or do anything to jinx it.

"Mr. Robinson says it's impossible."

"Shut up," Michael said.

"Dad thinks you can do it, though."

"Shut up," he said, Adam and Carlos joining him this time. His friends frowned at Michael as if to say, "Don't jinx it!"

Coach Clemmons called Carlos's name, and he got up to go hit.

"I'm telling Mom you told me to shut up."

"So go tell her and leave me alone!"

David turned to go.

"Wait!"

Michael ignored the glare from Adam and went to the back corner of the dugout to whisper through the fence with David. "What does Grandma Kat say?"

David shrugged.

"Ask her what she thinks I should do about that big guy, their number three hitter. I have to get him out one more time. Ask her what I should do."

David took another bite of his Moon Pie.

"So go already!"

David wandered off, and Michael watched as Carlos hit into a double play. Four pitches later Ramon was down on strikes and the half inning was over. It was time for Michael to face the bottom of the sixth.

He walked out to his position more slowly this time, try-ing to calm down and think about how he was going to get the next three batters out. It was the bottom three hitters again, but Michael didn't want to fall asleep and let one of them sneak something by like the ninth batter almost had last time. Michael climbed the mound and took off his hat to wipe the sweat away. It was mid-morning now, and the summer sun was shining right down on him. He looked around at the bleachers to find his family and realized for the first time that the crowd was larger than it had been before. The stands were full, and there were people scattered up and down the foul lines.

And they were all looking for perfection.

Michael pulled his cap back down tight and looked in at Carlos. The first batter they worked up and in, up and in, and then down and away. Strikeout. The next batter swung at the first pitch and drove it to right. The crowd gasped and Michael's heart skipped a beat, but then he saw it was routine and watched as Raul put it away. After his near heart attack, Michael vowed to put the last batter away without letting him make contact, and he struck him out on five pitches.

The crowd burst into applause at the strikeout, surprising Michael and his teammates. There were even more people watching now, people who must have come from one of the other six Prospect Park fields where games were being played. Michael and his teammates stood at their positions for a few seconds, unsure of how to handle their newfound attention, then came to their senses and ran off the field.

Michael now had no company at the end of the bench, silent or otherwise. Adam and Carlos found excuses to be at the far end of the dugout, and Michael sat all alone. It wouldn't have mattered anyway. The dugout was as quiet as a classroom during a test.

"All right, boys," Coach Clemmons said, breaking the strange silence. "Top of the seventh. I don't think I need to tell anyone how much we need a run right now, do I?"

Nobody answered.

"All right then. Let's do it. And come on, I want to hear a little chatter in here. I want everybody to loosen up, all right? Who's seen that new *Clash of the Titans* movie, huh?"

Michael had seen it, but he didn't want to talk about it. Neither did anybody else on the team, it seemed. All he could think about was the perfect game. Where was David? Had he gone to talk to Grandma Kat, or was he off at the concession stand again? Michael took off his hat and rubbed at his temples. He wanted this, wanted perfection more than anything. A perfect game, and he was three innings away. But how would he get through that lineup one more time?

The Fulton Street Pawn and Loan lead-off hitter drew a walk, then stole second. It was the first runner they'd had in scoring position all game, but Michael was only half paying attention. In his mind, he was going over every pitch he had thrown that game to every batter. How had he gotten the number two batter out in the fourth? What had the number six hitter done with the off-speed pitch he'd thrown him in the second? Michael closed his eyes and tried to think. *Think.* What could he do to keep things perfect? He did *not* want to screw this up.

A bunt got the runner to third as Michael hurried down the bench to Tim's little brother, Chris, who kept score for the team.

"I need to see the scorebook," Michael told him.

Chris was a few years younger than Michael, maybe nine like David, and he was usually quiet around the older kids on the team. Now a thirteen-year-old was talking to him, and Michael wasn't just any thirteen-year-old: He was the one pitching a perfect game, the one nobody wanted to talk to.

Chris looked to the other boys for help, but nobody would look at him.

"I—I—" he started, then just handed Michael the book, despite the fact that he should be recording the run Fulton Street Pawn and Loan was scoring right then off a sacrifice fly.

The crowd cheered the run but Michael ignored them, poring over the ledger for the other team. Strikeout, ground-out, pop foul, strikeout—the scorebook wouldn't tell him the pitches he'd thrown, just the outcomes, but he could reconstruct the rest himself. As he stared at the boxes on the page, the impossibility of it all stood out even more. Out, out, out, out . . . eighteen boxes, eighteen hitters, eighteen outs. Not one person had reached first base. No hits, no errors, no walks. No hitter had even gotten to a full count. The enormity of it, the craziness of it, was almost overwhelming.

The half inning ended without another run scoring, but Fulton Street Pawn and Loan now led one to nothing. Coach Clemmons came back into the dugout clapping.

"All right," he told his team. "All right!" He looked at Michael. *"All right."*

Any other day the boys would have been laughing, but not today. Michael understood what his coach meant. The team had gotten Michael his one run, the one run he needed to win, and that was all he was going to get.

Now it was up to him to go out and be perfect.

3

Carlos put down two fingers, asking for the curveball. Michael wanted to call time-out and kill him.

Instead he shook him off—vigorously this time, hoping he got the point. Carlos slouched again and went through the other signals, trying to find something they could both agree on. Michael already had two outs in the seventh inning. The last batter he had to retire was the big number three hitter, and they were running out of things to throw him. Michael took a deep breath, wishing he'd heard back from Grandma Kat before the start of the half inning.

Carlos put down a single finger—a fastball—but didn't indicate left or right. A fastball, right down the middle, to Bob Smith Ford's best hitter. Well, it was something he certainly wouldn't expect, but he was too good a hitter not to do something with it, even if he didn't see it coming. No, Michael would nibble at the corners of the strike zone before he gave him a fat fastball to hit.

He took a sign he liked from Carlos and pitched. He

meant it to be low and inside, but it wasn't perfect. The ball came back toward the plate more than he meant it to, and he watched in horror as the big hitter attacked it, driving the ball deep to right center. Raul broke right and Tim Clemmons in center broke left, and the big crowd sitting in the bleachers rose to their feet. All Michael could do was watch as the ball sailed farther and farther and Raul and Tim drew closer and closer—then Raul was sliding out of the way so he wouldn't hit Tim, and Tim was reaching as high and far as he could, and both players went tumbling as the ball disappeared between them.

And then Tim Clemmons popped up triumphantly with the ball clutched in his glove. The umpire, who'd run all the way out past second base to watch, signaled "out" with his fist. The audience cheered, and Michael waited on the infield to rub Tim's hat around on his head in thanks.

Twenty-one outs. Six more to go.

Michael went to his solitary place at the end of the bench and the wall of silence descended again between him and his teammates. They sat so far away now Michael felt like he had some disease no one else wanted to get. No one but David, who stood behind him eating a snow cone.

"There's a reporter here," David said. "From the *Canarsie Courier*. Somebody called him."

"David, what did Grandma Kat say? You talked to her, right?"

254

David shrugged. "She said you had to just keep doing whatever it was you were doing."

Michael grabbed the chain-link fence in his fingers and rattled it. "That's not good enough!" he said, drawing stares from a couple of his teammates, who just as quickly looked away. Michael lowered his voice. "David, I can't just keep doing what I've been doing. They've seen it all before, and my arm is getting tired. What am I supposed to do?"

"I dunno," David said. He shrugged again and took a bite of his snow cone.

If the chain-link fence hadn't been there Michael would *so* have killed his brother. Instead he tried to calm himself down. He could kill David *after* the game.

"Just . . . Look, tell her to come down here, all right? Tell her I need to talk to her."

David took another bite of his snow cone and walked away.

"Adopted. He has to be adopted," Michael muttered.

His turn to bat came up again that inning, but this time he didn't care. He took his bat and his helmet and stood in the batter's box, but he was hardly aware of the pitches coming his way. Instead he was looking at the players in the field he knew he had to face again. The third baseman, the shortstop, the pitcher, the left fielder, the right fielder, the second baseman. What did he know about each of them that he could use to get them out? And were they looking at him right now, trying to figure out how they were going to get a hit?

The umpire called strike three and Michael walked back to the dugout, where Coach Clemmons was clapping and exhorting the next batter to get a hit, ignoring Michael completely. He didn't care. He didn't want to talk to anybody anyway.

One out later Michael was back on the mound. Foul territory was now full of people, the crowd so large there was an audible murmur from them. The opposing coach clapped and urged his players to get a hit. Michael's own teammates stood silently behind him, waiting for whatever would come.

Michael squeezed the ball in his hand so tightly it hurt. He worried that he didn't have enough gas left, that he didn't have any more tricks up his sleeve, that he'd make a mistake or somebody would get lucky. That he would be a failure in the eyes of however many hundreds of people were watching. He called time-out and walked around the mound once more, but Carlos didn't run out to meet with him and none of the infielders came in to talk to him. He was in this alone.

The ump gave him a moment, then Michael stepped back up and went at it. He got a fly ball to second from the first batter, a strikeout of the second, and a ground ball to third for the last hitter, and suddenly the inning was over, as easy as any he'd ever pitched.

And he was three outs from perfection.

The crowd cheered as he walked off the field, but he could

sense the expectation in their voices. He went back and sat by himself at the end of the bench, wondering again if he had what it took to be perfect.

David appeared again, eating a hot dog.

"David! Where's Grandma Kat?"

"She won't come."

"What!?"

"She says you're not supposed to talk to somebody with a perfect game. She won't even say 'perfect game.' She just keeps working her way up and down the bleachers, touching all the wood."

Michael leaned close to the fence to whisper to his brother. "I'm running out of ideas here, David. I don't know how I'm going to get the next three batters out. I don't even know how I got the *last* three batters out. She didn't say *anything?*"

David took a bite of his hot dog and chewed on it, and Michael wished he could choke people with the Force like Darth Vader.

David finally swallowed. "She said there's a time and place for everything."

"That's it? 'There's a time and place for everything'? What's that supposed to mean?"

David shrugged. "So you think you'll play Atari later?"

Michael didn't even bother to answer. On the field behind him, Adam grounded into the last out of the inning, and it was time for Michael to take the mound one last time. He looked around at the empty bench. The team had already left without him, none of them wanting to be the one to jinx it by jostling him or talking to him. Coach Clemmons opened his mouth to say something to him as he passed, but instead just nodded. Michael walked out to the mound.

The crowd burst into applause as he came out of the dugout, and he wondered if he was supposed to tip his cap. That didn't feel right, though, like he'd be thanking them for applause he hadn't earned yet. Instead he went to the mound and took a few light tosses with Carlos. The umpire seemed ready to give Michael as much time as he needed, but Michael just wanted to get it over with. He signaled the umpire he was ready, and the ump called, "Play ball!"

Michael Flint felt like the loneliest boy in all of Brooklyn. He scratched at the dirt of the mound with his cleat, raised his glove to just under his eyes, and stared in at his catcher's signal. He turned, stepped, and threw, threw as hard as he possibly could, and the ball flashed, a brilliant white thing in the midday sun, rocketing toward the catcher's mitt . . . and then over the catcher's mitt, and over the umpire, and into the backstop behind, where it *thwacked* into a pole.

The crowd murmured, and Michael could hear their words in his head. *He's cracking. He's lost it. He can't be perfect.*

Carlos threw him a new ball and Michael worked it over in his hands while trying to clear away the voices in his head. Those weren't the voices of the crowd. He couldn't really hear them. They were the voices inside him, telling him he couldn't do it. But why couldn't he? He didn't know what he was doing that was different from any other time he'd pitched, but even so the magic had been there all day long. Why did it have to stop? He stepped off the mound, taking the time the umpire had been willing to give him before, and readjusted his hat while he gathered his thoughts. Maybe today was one of those days where everything just clicked. Maybe it had nothing to do with him at all.

Maybe today was perfect.

Michael climbed back up on the mound and shook off Carlos's signals until he had the one he wanted. After the first blazing pitch into the backstop, the hitter was expecting more of the same, so Michael threw the next pitch as slow as he could, aiming it right for the middle of the plate. The batter whiffed on it early enough to swing twice if he wanted to, and the crowd *oohed*. One ball and one strike. Now that the batter was off balance, Michael gave him another changeup—strike two—and then the high heat to finish him off.

Two outs to go.

The next batter was a pinch hitter, somebody he hadn't seen before, but the kind of guy who's not a starter for a reason. He flailed at the first pitch, and Carlos wisely called for a pitch away and Michael got him fishing again for strike two. Ahead 0 and 2, Michael threw the kid an inside pitch that was impossible to hit but he swung at it anyway, strike three.

One out to go. One batter left.

Michael turned around on the mound, facing the outfield and his teammates. They watched him now, stared at him, and he could feel the eyes of everyone in Prospect Park. It was like they were holding their collective breath, waiting to see if perfection was possible. Michael couldn't decide if he wanted to know the answer or not, but he couldn't just walk away. He had to finish the game, one way or another. He turned and faced home plate and a new pinch hitter.

His first pitch was a fastball, and the batter took it for strike one. Michael felt a surge of optimism. Maybe it was possible. Maybe he could be perfect. He just needed to push it that last little bit.

He got the ball back and sent another fastball toward the plate, this one too high and too fast, so high and fast Carlos had to go up to get it. Michael lost his hat throwing it, and the batter didn't bite. Michael was pressing now and he knew it, grabbing at the magic rather than letting it work on its own, but he was desperate.

Michael got the ball back and picked up his hat, dusting it off. He pulled it back down over his mop of sweaty hair and took another deep breath, his grandmother's lone piece of advice coming back to him.

There's a time and place for everything.

Michael reached back, grabbed for some of that magic, but threw another fastball high. Ball two. He was going to be patient, this batter, make Michael work for it. The Bob Smith Ford coach had saved his best for last.

Michael could feel the sweat running down his back. He had put everything he had into those last two pitches, and he didn't have anything more. His fastballs were starting to feel like changeups, huge red and white targets that were as slow as Christmas coming. He couldn't speed it up, and he couldn't slow it down any further. This was it. This was all he had left.

Two balls and one strike. Michael couldn't afford another ball called here, so he took a little something off—though not so much as to make it a proper changeup—and aimed for the corner of the plate. A swing and a miss! He'd evened the count to two balls and two strikes.

If ever there was a time to waste a pitch, this was it, but Michael still refused. If he threw a wide pitch well outside the strike zone, there was little chance this hitter would chase it, and all that would do would force the issue next pitch on a full count, where the batter knew he couldn't make a mistake, wouldn't throw a ball. Michael waved off the waste-pitch signal Carlos gave him and nodded for the inside fastball. He'd try to hit the corner, catch him looking.

His arms like rubber, his legs like logs, Michael stepped into his windup and pitched it right where he wanted it, the magic back. The batter flinched but didn't swing. The ball popped into Carlos's mitt. Michael felt relief beyond relief, could see now what kind of day it was, a *perfect* day, and started to jump for joy—

And the umpire called the pitch a ball.

The crowd booed and hissed, but Michael knew it had been a close one. He'd put it out on the edge hoping for a strike, the kind of pitch that had to be perfect.

But he wasn't perfect. He was never going to *be* perfect. He had twenty-six outs, three balls, and two strikes, and he was as close to perfection—and imperfection—as he was ever going to get. If he could freeze that moment, preserve it, he could forever be one strike away from glory, the applause for what he was *doing* never-ending, the disappointment for what he had *not* done never felt.

And that was when Michael Flint noticed what kind of day it was.

He had glimpsed it a few seconds before when he'd thought the game was over, when he'd truly relaxed for the first time all day. He looked for it again now and there it was, all around him. The kind of day where a little dirt on his hands felt good, where the high blue sky was just right for catching fly balls, where grounders always bounced into his outstretched glove. It had been that way all along, but it hadn't belonged to him or to anybody else. It was *baseball's* day, a day when the Earth said, "Here's the best I've got," and baseball said, *"That's pretty good, Earth, but I'll show you perfect."*

It was a day like Michael had never known and knew he would never see again. Like Sandy Koufax and his perfect game, it was a special gift in a special time and a special place, one that he shouldn't examine too closely, one he could never duplicate. No matter how much he worked, no matter hard he tried, it was the kind of perfect day that would come only when *it* wanted to, when the sun smiled and the grass laughed and wind sang *hm-batter-hm-batter-hm-batter-swing*.

It wasn't up to Michael anymore. He saw that now. He stepped back up on the mound, worked his fingers into the right grip, shook Carlos off until he dropped two fingers for a curve, and let the ball fly.

Ninth Inning: Provenance

Brooklyn, New York, 2002

1

The room was on fire.

That's the way it looked through Snider Flint's blurry eyes. He woke in a sweat to a piercing alarm, louder and harsher than his bedside alarm clock. *The smoke detector.* He snapped awake, feeling the full blast of heat on his face, seeing the orange flames licking up under his bedroom door, through his walls. *Through his walls?* Was that even possible?

He scrambled back on his bed, away from his door. Smoke collected on the ceiling in great billowing clouds, as though it were some kind of monster, alive. Snider coughed and slid off the end of his bed to get away from the black air.

"Mom?" he called, choking. "Dad!?"

The window *thump-thump-thumped* behind him and he jumped.

"Snider! Snider, wake up!" It was his father, standing on the porch roof just beneath Snider's second-story window. He had his hand to the glass, trying to see in. "Snider, the house is on fire! You've got to crawl out the window!"

Snider stood where his father could see him, covering his mouth and nose with the sleeve of his T-shirt while he wrangled the difficult latch on the top of his casement window. It finally gave, and he hefted the heavy old window up enough to crawl through. In the distance, Snider could hear the siren of a fire engine and realized it was coming for *his* house.

"What happened?" Snider asked as his father helped him onto the roof. "Where's Mom?"

"She's already out. The Hendersons are helping her get down. Are you all right?"

Snider coughed again and nodded. Heat radiated from the house behind them, making his eyes burn. Glass tinkled and shattered.

"Come on, let's get out of here," his father said. Snider held his father's hand as they inched their way barefoot down the rough shingles, the fire hissing and roaring behind them.

Snider's dad slipped. He hit the roof with a *thump,* letting go of Snider to throw his arms out and catch himself. Snider tried to grab him and lost his footing too. His father flattened himself out on the roof and slid to a stop, but Snider skidded on past, out of reach. He rolled over on his stomach and clawed, kicked, dragged, but he kept sliding sickeningly down, down, down.

There were screams below—his mother, the neighbors— but they were as helpless as Snider as his feet caught on the gutter and then hammered past, his weight and speed too much for it to stop him. Half off the roof, half on, Snider grabbed for the gutter, but the flimsy metal thing ripped away from the wall and Snider went spinning, falling, into darkness.

Snider cried out and woke in a sweat to the memory of falling and fire. He shot straight up, his sheets already a tangled mess at his feet, casting around in the dark to figure out where he was.

"Snider. Snider, it's all right. You're all right," a voice said. It was Snider's uncle Dave, and Snider immediately remembered where he was. This was Dave's little apartment above his antiques store. An electrical fire in the old wiring in Snider's house had burned it to the ground, and Uncle Dave was sharing his place with Snider and his parents while they continued the impossible search for an affordable apartment to rent while their new house was being built. Snider was on the living room couch and Dave was beside him on the floor on an air mattress. Snider's parents slept in Dave's bedroom.

"Do you need anything?" Uncle Dave asked. "A glass of water?"

"No," Snider said. He turned over and buried his face in the back of the couch, ashamed that his uncle had heard him screaming again. He hated that he didn't have a room of his own anymore, that everything he owned was stuffed into a duffel bag at the end of the couch, that it was impossible to

269

be alone. It wasn't his uncle's fault, but he still wished he was anywhere else but here.

Snider pulled the blanket back up over the cast on his broken leg and tried to sleep, praying he didn't dream of fire again.

✤ ✤ ✤

Dave's two-room apartment was never smaller than when he and Snider's parents were all getting ready to leave for work in the morning. Snider kept his blanket pulled up over his head as they came in and out of the bathroom, bustled about the kitchen, and watched the morning news where he pretended to sleep.

"Snider," his mother said, "I want you to be ready to go to Paramus this afternoon."

"I don't want to go to New Jersey," he mumbled.

"You need a whole new set of clothes."

"Where am I going to put them? On top of the TV? Under the couch?"

"We're all having to make sacrifices, Snider. Your uncle David most of all. You're just going to have to get used to not living on your own terms, at least for another year."

Snider sat up. "Another year? But the insurance people said they could have a new place built in six months."

"That's if we want one of those contemporary in-fill monstrosities. We're having them rebuild the old house instead."

"Rebuild the old house? You've got to be crazy!" Snider

maneuvered his broken leg on the couch while his mother went around the room assembling the things she needed to take to work. "It was too small. And too old. It's like we were living in an ancient ruin. I just thought we couldn't afford to move."

"Your uncle David and I grew up in that house, Snider. It meant a lot to me," his dad said.

Dave stood in the kitchen and sipped from a mug of coffee, listening to the argument.

"So wait," Snider said. "People are paying all kinds of money to tear down old houses like ours and build *new* ones, and you're going to have them build the same old house when you could have something bigger and modern for *free?*"

"In-fill housing ruins neighborhoods, Snider. And besides, it's ugly."

"This is so lame! And you don't care that this is going to take an entire year? I'll have to start high school somewhere else. I'll miss my freshman year with my friends!"

His mother sighed. "We're in *Fort Greene,* Snider, not Hoboken. You'll see your friends plenty. And we're *trying* to find a place to rent in Flatbush. Now will you please be ready to go to Paramus this afternoon?"

"I'm getting all Mets jerseys."

"You're getting *no* Mets jerseys," his mother said.

"Three Mets jerseys."

"One Mets jersey."

"Two Mets jerseys."

"Two Mets jerseys, and not a single complaint when we try on dress clothes."

"Whatever," Snider said.

His parents left for work, and Snider hopped over to Dave's computer to check on his fantasy baseball team and to see if any of his friends were awake and online. Nobody was up, of course. Why would they be? It was summer, and none of them had to sleep in the same room where their parents made toast. Most of them wouldn't be online later either. They'd be out at the pool or at the ball field or the park. Snider *thunked* his way back over to the couch and started flipping through the cable channels, ready for another exciting day of watching ESPN News for Mets highlights.

Uncle Dave finished cleaning up from breakfast and came into the living room, where he picked up the TV remote and turned it off.

"Hey, what gives?"

"Come down and see me in the shop when you're showered and dressed," Dave said, leaving before Snider could argue.

❖ ❖ ❖

Snider *ka-thunked* his way down the narrow back staircase to Dave's shop. The small storage area at the bottom was a cluttered mess, like a single attic with the junk of an entire neighborhood piled up to the ceiling. Among the stacks Snider saw an old bugle, a Japanese sword on a stand, and an ancient-looking game console with dials instead of joysticks, but rather than stop and look he turned sideways and crab-walked himself on his crutches through the piles of collectibles into the front of the shop, where his uncle Dave sat at a computer entering items for sale into an online auction site. Snider flopped on a stool behind the counter and waited.

Uncle Dave spared him a glance over his shoulder, then kept working.

"Pretty rough on your parents back there, weren't you?"

Snider huffed. "Is that what this is? The part where you tell me how much my parents love me and how tough this is for them too?"

Dave swiveled in his chair. "No. This is the part where I tell you to get over it."

"What?"

"It's time for you to get over the fire, to get over your broken leg and your lost summer, and start pulling your weight around here."

Snider burned with shame and anger that his uncle would bring up the fire.

"Look—"

"No, *you* look. Your parents are both working full-time jobs while they haggle with insurance agents, comb Flatbush for an apartment big enough to live in and cheap enough to actually pay for, meet with architects and builders, and reconstruct your lives. What have you been doing?"

"I'm fourteen. What *can* I do?"

"What are you good at?"

"Baseball."

"Too bad. Your leg's broken. What else?"

Snider shifted uncomfortably. "Video games," he said, just to be perverse.

"Great. Maybe we can put you to work crafting shirts in an online game and sell the gold you make to other players."

"Ha-ha."

"Or wait," Dave said. "I've got a better idea." He stood and handed Snider a broom. "Clean out the back room."

"Hello? Broken leg, remember?" he said, rattling his crutches.

"All right. Fine. Here," Dave said, plunking a cardboard box in front of Snider. "You like working on the computer so much, use it to find out how much this stuff is worth."

"Whatever," Snider said.

Uncle Dave gave his seat at the computer to Snider and went to work in the back room. Snider rolled his eyes at the box and opened it. It was a lot of baseball junk at least, but most of it wasn't anything to get excited about: a moldy old catcher's mitt, a used scorebook, a silly-looking beauty guide for an all-girls baseball league.

There was also an old wooden bat, and a baseball that should have been thrown in the trash a long time ago. The baseball was made of dark brown leather, almost black, with white stitches instead of red. The seams didn't go in a wavy pattern either, they were sewn in an X shape. The stitches were all torn up, though, and two of the leather flaps were so loose Snider could see the wound string inside the ball. One of the flaps had a little letter *S* scratched into it too.

Snider surfed the Net for a half an hour, found some comparable junk, typed up prices for the stuff in the box, and printed it out.

"Here," he said. He handed the sheet to his uncle and went back upstairs to see if the afternoon Mets game was on yet.

2

The next morning Snider settled onto the stool behind the counter of Fulton Street Antiques and Collectibles wearing his new Mike Piazza Mets jersey. Uncle Dave was talking to an actual customer—something even more rare than the baseball cards in his display case—about an old lunch box.

"A Jetsons lunch box," the customer said. "What a fabulous piece!"

"It's a 1963 original," Dave told him. "Hardly any scratches on it. Just a little normal wear around the edges. The sticker is the original Aladdin sticker. No rust on the thermos inside, cup and stopper in pristine condition."

The customer turned the lunch box over in his hands. "What are you asking?"

"Eight hundred."

Snider nearly fell off his stool, but the customer nodded like that was about what he expected. He handed the lunch box back to Uncle Dave.

"It's great stuff," the man said. "I don't suppose you have a Star Trek lunch box, do you? One of the 1968 ones, with the *Enterprise* on one side and the picture of Kirk and Spock beaming out on the side?"

"No, I'm sorry."

The customer smiled. "I had one of those when I was in fourth grade. I loved that thing. I remember, Friday nights I was allowed to stay up late and watch TV. I'd watch *The Wild, Wild West,* then flip the station to *Star Trek.*"

"Good stuff," Dave said.

"I have no idea what happened to that lunch box. I'm sure my mom just threw it out. Anyway, thanks a lot."

"You bet," Uncle Dave said. He put the Jetsons lunchbox back on a shelf as the customer left.

"Not the right price?" Snider asked.

"Not the right lunch box," Dave said. "Most collectors, they collect things because they have a sentimental value to them. The comic book collector whose parents never let him read comics when he was a kid, that guy who remembers watching *Star Trek.*" Dave smiled. "The antiques store owner who never got over selling all his Star Wars toys at a garage sale when he was fourteen. Didn't you lose anything in the fire you can't replace?"

"No."

"I see. So, to what do I owe the pleasure of your visit this morning?" Dave asked.

"The TV remote has mysteriously disappeared."

"Why not just get up and change the channel whenever you want? Oh—right. Your broken leg. Bummer. Well, since you're here—"

Dave slapped the price sheet Snider had typed up onto the counter in front of him.

"What? You said look up what the stuff was worth, so I did."

"Come on—this is price guide stuff. A third grader could have done this. Here, look at this baseball," he said, pulling it out of the box. "I don't just want to know how old this is. Who used it? How was it made? Who owned it before us, and before that, and before that? Or this bat. Whose was it? Was it used in a game? What's this on the handle—postage stamps? Why are there postage stamps on a bat handle? Where's your natural curiosity?"

"Well, I *am* curious about what happened to the TV remote."

Uncle Dave ignored that. "Who wore this cap? Did the Knickerbockers use this ball?"

"The who?"

"The first modern baseball team." Uncle Dave pulled each piece out of the box and laid them on the counter. "You find the provenance of something, its origin, you start to find its story. You find its story, you find its *real* value. Here." Uncle Dave took a pair of cleats off a hook on the wall. "Just a crusty old pair of cleats, right? If these had belonged to your dad when he was a kid, they would have been thrown out a long time ago and they'd be rotting in some landfill. Who wants to own Michael Flint's old shoes, right?"

Snider shrugged.

"Okay, so ordinarily, these shoes are worthless. But what if I told you they were worn by Pelé in his very last professional game with the New York Cosmos?"

"Who?"

"Pelé? The greatest soccer star in history?"

Snider shrugged. Uncle Dave sighed and slid the paper over to Snider. "Okay. How about this: You find the *real* value of anything in that box and I'll give you a ten percent commission on the sale."

Snider perked up. Ten percent of an eight-hundred-dollar lunch box was eighty bucks.

"Twenty percent," he countered.

"Fifteen."

"Done," Snider said.

Uncle Dave shook his head like the thrill of the hunt should have been enough to tempt Snider, but Snider didn't care. Fifteen percent of eight hundred dollars was . . . well, he didn't have a calculator handy, but it was more than eighty bucks.

Snider started with the ball that Uncle Dave had been so crazy about, searching the Internet for any references to old X-seam balls marked with an *S*—or *any* kind of ball marked with an *S*. Nothing. The ball was a dead end, so Snider turned his attention to the bat.

It looked similar to a modern bat, but the handle had a smoother rise to the nub and the barrel had a smaller, fatter sweet spot. The wood was dark brown but faded in spots, and the handle had stains on it like pine tar or something. The bat maker's logo was branded into it just below the sweet spot, the name BABE HERMAN was burned into the barrel, and the crown of the bat looked like it had been chewed on by one of the goats at the Prospect Park Zoo. But the strangest thing about the bat was the remnants of postage stamps Uncle Dave had pointed out. They were glued right to the handle, and there was a faint, illegible address printed off to the side, right on the wood of the bat, as though somebody had just dropped it into a mailbox to send it somewhere.

"Babe Herman." Was that Babe Ruth? Snider thought he remembered "Herman" being part of Babe Ruth's real name, but he didn't want to ask Uncle Dave. A Babe Ruth bat could be worth a fortune! He Googled the name, and was disappointed to see it wasn't Babe Ruth. That was George Herman "Babe" Ruth—that's where he'd heard Herman. This was another guy named Babe Herman who played around the same time for the Brooklyn Dodgers, only for some reason they were called the Brooklyn Robins then. Best he could tell from a fan site dedicated to the Robins, Babe Herman had been a heck of a hitter but a terrible base runner and fielder, so bad he sometimes got hit on the head trying to catch fly balls in the outfield. So much for the bat being worth a fortune.

There was more on the site, but Uncle Dave came back in eating a cup of yogurt. Snider closed the browser so Dave wouldn't see him getting too into it.

"So, um, I think this bat might have belonged to Babe Herman, this guy who played for Brooklyn a long time ago."

Dave filed some paperwork in a wooden file cabinet. "How do you figure that?" he asked.

"Well, it's got his name stamped on it."

Dave nodded but didn't look up. "Could be a factory bat. One of those models they sell at the store so you can own the same bat as your favorite major leaguer. Nobody's going to pay more than what you put on that sheet. Dig deeper."

"*Dig deeper,*" Snider muttered under his breath. "Dig you a *grave.*"

"What's that?" Dave asked from across the room.

"I'm digging away," Snider covered. He turned back to the computer. There were lots of hits for baseball almanac sites and statistical pages, and a few mentions of Babe Herman on websites built by middle-aged dudes who got all teary-eyed about the good old days of baseball at Ebbets Field. More than once he read about Herman doubling into a double play, when he and two other Robins ended up all standing on third base at the same time. The guy sounded like an idiot, but these website guys loved him. Maybe the bat could be worth something to one of these jokers after all.

The best stuff about Herman and the Robins was written

by a guy named John Kieran in the *New York Times*. From the looks of it he wrote about all kinds of New York sports from back in the day, but he seemed to really enjoy laying into the Robins. His stuff was hysterical: He'd start off with poetic stuff, then find some way to slam the team before the end of the first paragraph. The trouble was, that's all Snider could read for free. The rest of the articles cost money to read, and there was no way he was doing that.

Besides, how would any of it prove Babe Herman had actually used this bat? He was about to give up when he read the first paragraph of a Kieran story that started off with a description of Babe Herman stepping up to the plate, talking about how he spit a huge glop of tobacco juice on his hands and rubbed it all over the bat's handle. The brown stains! Snider sniffed the bat. Was that a faint tobacco smell? Maybe that stuff wasn't pine tar, maybe it was tobacco—which was actually pretty gross. The question was, were they Babe Herman's tobacco stains?

The article also said Herman knocked the dirt off his cleats with the bat, and Snider knew exactly what Kieran was talking about. He'd done that to his own cleats a thousand times playing on the Prospect Park fields, only his bat was graphite and indestructible. Well, except that it had melted with everything else in the fire. But smacking his shoes with it had never done any damage to it, not like it would have done to a wooden bat, and Herman would have had metal cleats that really chewed it up.

Snider stood and hopped until he was balanced on his one good leg, then took the wooden bat in hand and pretended to knock dirt off the bottom of his cast. The chewed-up part was perfectly placed.

Snider lost his balance and the bat slipped. It *thwacked* his cast and he yowled.

"Everything okay in there?" Uncle Dave asked. Snider noticed he didn't exactly come running.

"Yeah, great," Snider said. He winced and sat back down, leaning the bat against the counter.

The stamps on the handle were the next thing Snider had to figure out. Who would put postage stamps on a bat and drop it in a mailbox, and why? He did a couple of searches with Babe Herman and stamps, then just with stamps and bats, but got nothing useful either way—just more stuff about Babe Ruth and stamp collecting. But a stamp collector might be able to tell him something about the pieces on the bat, right? They put new stamps out every year. Maybe some stamp nut could tell him at least what year the bat was mailed.

Snider tried his uncle first, figuring he might know something since he owned an antiques store, but Dave shook his head.

"Not my thing," he said through a mouthful of granola bar. "You need a philatelist."

"A whatsit?"

"Stamp collector."

No duh, Snider thought. Dave went to an old paper Rolodex file and pulled out a card. "Here's the guy I send people to when they come in with stamps. He's here in Brooklyn."

Snider snagged a packing tube to carry the bat in and told Dave he was going out, checking the time on his phone to make sure he would get back in time to watch the Mets game that evening. A short subway ride later Snider was *thunking* his way down a sidewalk in Williamsburg, looking for the address of "Philo's Philately." He shuddered to think what his friends would say if they heard about *this.*

The stamp shop was on the top floor of a two-story walk-up that put his iffy crutch skills to the test, and Snider wondered, not for the first time that day, if any of this was even worth it. At the top of the stairs he paused to catch his breath, then rang the bell.

Philo—if that was really the dude's name—was a small, wiry man with thick glasses, a tall, thin neck, and a balding head. Everything about him was brown too—he had brown eyes, brown hair, brown corduroy pants, a brown collared shirt, and a brown sweater. He raised a suspicious eyebrow at Snider, the same kind of look Snider had seen on the faces of countless adults who wondered what kind of trouble a fourteen-year-old boy was about to bring them. Snider was tempted to just turn around and forget about it, but he'd already come all this way.

"Yes?"

"My name is Snider Flint. I'm David Flint's nephew. He sent me with a question about philly—philata—with a question about some stamps."

Uncle Dave's name worked like a magical key, and the brown man opened the door wide for Snider. "Ah. Mr. Flint has sent a great deal of business my way. Philo Cohen," he said by way of introduction. "How can I be of assistance?"

The inside of Philo's Philately was as brown as its owner, filled with dark wood chairs and tables and stained brown bookcases filled with brown-covered books. There was nothing brown about the insides of the display cases throughout the room, though. They were filled with every color of the rainbow, all in tiny inch-tall works of art.

"Sorry," Snider said when he realized he hadn't answered Philo's question.

"Not at all. Postage stamps are my passion, and too often I forget how *dazzling* they can be when one is not surrounded by them all the time."

"Ah, yeah. Right."

"Now, how may I help, Master Flint?"

Snider put the packing tube on a table and withdrew the baseball bat. Philo arched an eyebrow, but understood when Snider turned the handle to reveal the postage stamp fragments.

"Intriguing," said Philo. He beckoned Snider to bring the bat over to another table with a lamp and a magnifying glass on swinging arms.

"Why on earth would someone put postage stamps on a baseball bat?"

"No idea," Snider said. "And I know they're kind of torn up, but I was hoping you could at least tell me what year they came out."

Philo studied the bat handle under a powerful magnifying glass.

"Snider is an interesting name," Philo said.

"What?"

"Your first name. Is it a family name?"

"Yeah. It's like the last name of a whole other side of my family."

"Aha!"

"Aha?"

Philo pointed to one of the stamps under the glass with a pair of tweezers. "This one will be the thirteen-cent Harrison." He chuckled. "A makeup stamp. Postmaster New was a Benjamin Harrison man. Resented Woodrow Wilson getting a seventeen-cent stamp the year before."

"Yeah, I can see how he would hate that," Snider said, not really having any idea what the guy was talking about.

"And here, this one . . . torn, but obviously a two-cent Sesquicentennial Exposition stamp. You can even see the gum breakers here on the back where it's peeled up a bit—"

"That's great," Snider said. "But can you tell me what year the stamps came out?"

Philo Cohen stood. "Well, a sesquicentennial is one hundred and fifty years. That means this stamp was printed for the one hundred and fiftieth anniversary of the United States."

Snider glanced around for a calculator.

"1926," Philo said.

"1926? You're sure?"

Philo selected a brown volume off the shelf, flipped through a few pages, and turned it so Snider could see it. There, under the exciting heading "Postage Stamps of the United States First Issued in 1926" were full-color pictures that matched the torn pieces of the two stamps still clinging to the bat.

"Hey, that's great!" Snider said. "Can I get a copy of that page?"

Philo bowed slightly. "I'm happy to oblige. If you'll wait just a moment."

While the philatelist went to a photocopier in his office, Snider peered through the magnifying glass at the stamps. He turned the bat to see the stamp fragments better and saw again the illegible handwritten address. Under a bright light and a magnifying glass it wasn't so illegible.

"Spalding, Chicago, Illinois?"

Philo returned from his office. "What's that?"

"The address. It just says, 'Spalding, Chicago, Illinois.'"

"You'd be surprised at how diligent the U.S. Postal Service is about delivering to even the vaguest of addresses," Philo told him, "and people were far less careful about those things in the past, from what I've seen on vintage envelopes."

"But who is Spalding? I know I've seen that name just recently."

"If I may?" Philo said, turning the bat slightly. There, clear as day under the magnifying glass, was written in the bat's baseball diamond logo: "Trade Mark Spalding No. 200, Oil Temp. Made in U.S.A."

So the bat had been mailed back to its maker in 1926, and Snider was pretty sure Babe Herman had used the bat himself. So why had he sent it back to the bat company? And how could Snider prove it was Herman who sent it?

Snider thanked Philo and escaped before the philatelist could tell him the story of every single postage stamp on the premises. But instead of heading back to Fulton Street Antiques and Collectibles, Snider took the subway to Grand Army Plaza to hit the Brooklyn Public Library. John Kieran had steered him right the first time, and he wanted to go back and see what else the writer could tell him. With a year now—1926, Babe Herman's rookie year—a librarian was able to help Snider find everything John Kieran had written about the Brooklyn Nine for the entire year. Then he had to sit at a huge microfiche machine and scroll through every *New York Times* for that year until he got to the articles he wanted—but at least it was free. Still, it would have driven him nuts if Kieran wasn't as funny as the guys on ESPN.

Snider read for almost an hour until he found it, the

last piece of the puzzle about Babe Herman's bat. It was so perfect he almost shouted out loud. In an interview with John Kieran just a few days after the infamous double/double play, Babe Herman told the reporter with a completely straight face that he didn't blame himself, or his teammates, or even the umpires. He blamed his bat. It had to be flawed—that was the only answer to his recent struggles. The bat was defective, he figured, and that very day he had marched down to the post office and mailed the cursed thing back to the fellows who'd made it.

3

Uncle Dave munched on a carrot while he read through the photocopied pages Snider had laid out.

"Is it good enough?"

"You mean, does it prove this was really Babe Herman's bat? Yeah, I'd say so."

Snider nodded with what he hoped wasn't too much enthusiasm.

Uncle Dave examined the bat. "Better than that, you've proven this bat was used on a particular day, in a particular game. A *famous* game, no less. A provenance like this without an eyewitness is practically impossible. This is really impressive, Snider."

"What do you think it's worth?"

Uncle Dave took a bite out of his carrot.

"I don't know. Say . . . twelve hundred dollars?"

"Twelve. Hundred. Dollars!?"

"Just an educated guess, really. Collectible value is all about what the market will bear."

Snider pulled a calculator over and did the math. His commission on $1,200 would be $180. That was six tickets in the upper deck box seats at Shea Stadium. He rubbed his hands together.

"Okay, so now what?"

"Now we wait and see if someone's looking for a Babe Herman bat. We'll put it on display here in the shop and we'll list it online."

Snider's heart sank as he looked around the cluttered shop. Most of this stuff had been here as long as he could remember.

"So what am I supposed to do in the meantime?"

"Go back to the box. See what you can do with everything else. That baseball has to have a story."

Uncle Dave went to the computer to list the bat and Snider slumped on his stool. There had to be some way of finding a buyer quicker than just putting the thing up in the front window or waiting for someone to type "Babe Herman bat" into a search engine. He tossed up the ratty old ball from the box and caught it. He didn't know the ball's story, but the bat had a story. The trick was just figuring out who cared enough about that story to buy it.

Those fan sites. That's who cared enough to buy it—whoever took the time to post those websites Snider had found when he first searched online for info about Babe Herman and the Brooklyn Robins. When Dave was finished at the computer Snider hopped over and found the sites again. A couple of them hadn't been updated in a while, but one had a photo gallery with new pics added in the last six months, and it even had a forum where people could discuss their memories. There were very few posts—most of them by the host. That was the guy Snider wanted.

Snider wrote an e-mail introducing himself and giving a little background on the bat. He didn't want to go too overboard, though, in case the guy wasn't interested, and he didn't want it to sound like spam either. He read over the e-mail one more time, then hit SEND and went back to the box of baseball memorabilia. All morning long he tried every angle he could think of to find out more about the hat, the photo, the beauty guide, and particularly the baseball. Nothing. He even got the phone number of the Atlanta auction company Uncle Dave had bought the lot from and called to see if they could put him in touch with the original owner. They couldn't. The box had been part of an estate sale: Some man named Walker who had no close relations for Snider to call.

It was crazy to think the guy who ran the Brooklyn Robins site would e-mail him back that day—or ever—but Snider kept checking. Why not? He didn't have anything better to do. But it was more than that now. He'd come all this way and he wanted to see it out, to finish it.

And a hundred eighty bucks wouldn't be too bad either.

Snider was reading about how early baseballs were made when the e-mail alert chimed and he clicked over to find a response from the man with the Robins site. He was interested! He wanted to see the bat! His name was Brian McNamara, he was a teacher in New Jersey, and he wanted to come to Brooklyn later tonight—but it would be after the store was already closed. Snider called Uncle Dave in and showed him the e-mail.

"Tell him I'll keep the store open, and you'll be here to talk to him."

"Me?"

"Sure. It's your commission, right? This is your deal. That means you make the sale."

"What do I do? What do I say?"

"Tell him everything you told me. Show him all the research you collected on the bat. If he's interested, negotiate a price. Start at one thousand five hundred dollars, though. He'll want to haggle. And I know you know how to haggle."

Uncle Dave went back to work and Snider hit REPLY, but his hands hovered over the keyboard. He suddenly wasn't so sure he wanted to sell the thing, which was stupid. It was just a dumb old bat, right?

✢ ✢ ✢

Mr. McNamara was a white-haired man, older than Uncle Dave but not grandfatherly, with a neatly trimmed white beard and an easygoing smile. True to his word, Uncle Dave sat back and watched while Snider laid out his research for

293

the man. At first Snider was nervous and stumbled over the points he had spent all afternoon preparing, but McNamara listened patiently.

"May I hold it?" he asked when Snider was finished.

Snider looked to his uncle to see if it was all right, but all Dave did was smile.

"Sure, I guess," Snider said.

McNamara took the bat in his hands as though he were weighing it. He ran his hands down the length of it, pausing to feel the indentions where the Spalding logo had been burned on. He felt the chewed-up end, examined the torn postage stamps, smelled the handle, and Snider felt another pang at maybe parting with it.

"Can you imagine?" he said. "The very same bat Babe Herman used to hit that double off the wall in right center. They say he was such an incredible hitter that they had to put a fence on top of the right field wall at Ebbets to keep him from putting out the windows of the building across the street. I don't remember the fence, but then I didn't get to see many games at Ebbets before the Dodgers left town. My father took me to the very last game they ever played there in 1957. I was very young, but I can still remember the grown men and women weeping around me at the end."

Snider had a hard time picturing a stadium full of adults crying about a baseball team leaving town, but he didn't say anything.

"The provenance was your work, I take it?" the man asked Snider.

"Yes sir."

"It's a fabulous piece of detective work. How much are you asking?"

"One—one thousand five hundred dollars," Snider said, his voice cracking. He'd meant to be so much firmer about that, but the weird feeling he had about not wanting to sell it made him stumble.

The older man set the bat back on the counter and stared at it. Snider could tell he wanted it. But did he want it more than Snider did? How much would this guy pay for a piece of history, a mere piece of wood that had value far beyond the material used to make it?

"I'll give you one thousand dollars," the man said.

One thousand dollars! It wasn't what they had wanted to get, but a thousand dollars was a lot of money. Snider looked back at his uncle, but Dave just shrugged at him, as if to say: "It's your deal."

Snider cleared his throat. "Fourteen hundred."

"Eleven."

"Thirteen," Snider said, falling into the negotiation more easily now.

"Twelve hundred—and I'm afraid that's as high as I can go."

"Done," Snider said. *Twelve hundred dollars!* He'd sold the bat for twelve hundred dollars.

McNamara visibly relaxed, then smiled. "He's quite good at this, you know," he said to Uncle Dave, who had come over to handle the payment.

"His first find," Dave said. "He's a natural."

Snider stood with Mr. McNamara while Dave ran his credit card. It was gone. The bat he'd worked so hard to document, Babe Herman's bat, wasn't his anymore. The white-haired man put his hand on it again.

"Oh, this was an extravagance," he said, "but I had to buy it. For my father. He was there, you know. At the game where Herman ended up on third base with Fewster and Vance. He used to tell me stories about the Daffiness Boys when I was young."

"Are you going to give the bat to him, then?" Snider asked.

"Oh no. He's dead now. For the last few years he didn't even remember who I was, but he remembered the Dodgers, the Robins, all those games he went to as a boy. It was the only thing we could really talk about, the only connection we still had." He smiled sadly. "I suppose that's all we ever have in the end. Stories about the people who are gone and a few mementos to remind us they were here."

McNamara settled up and said his good-byes, and Uncle Dave locked the front door and turned off the lights.

"You did it," he said.

"Yeah."

Uncle Dave opened the cash register and counted out one hundred and eighty dollars. "Your commission," he said.

Snider fanned out the money, not so much to count it as to look at it.

"You wish you hadn't sold it?" his uncle asked.

"A little. Yeah."

"That happens. You became part of its story, if only for a few days. That's not easy to let go of. But you didn't have to sell it."

"I know," Snider said. He put the money in his pocket and worked himself up on to his crutches. "But that guy should have it. That bat was a bigger part of his life. It meant more to him than it did to me."

"You mean like your old house meant a lot more to me and your dad than it does to you?"

"Yeah, yeah, yeah. I get it. Beat me over the head with it, why don't you."

Uncle Dave raised his hands in surrender. "I'm just saying. All right. So, you think you can pull any more miracles out of that box?"

"Nah. I've been over this stuff a hundred times. There's a Sandy Koufax card worth maybe forty bucks, and this Jim Gilliam guy is worth like ten or fifteen, but there's no special story for either one of them. This Brooklyn cap is vintage—worth maybe a few hundred dollars—but I don't know who wore it or when. And I don't know who's going to want a photo of some Little League championship team from Long Island."

Uncle Dave pulled the tattered old brown baseball out of the box. "What about this?"

Snider took the ball from him. "Well, it's old. Like early eighteen hundreds old, based on the way it's stitched. It was handmade too—you can see the holes poked through are uneven, and the leather flaps aren't exactly the same size. And this piece—see underneath it?—there's some wear *inside* the ball, like this is leather from a shoe or something. Maybe the person who made it was a tailor or a shoemaker or something. I don't know. Only thing I know for sure is that somebody really loved this ball."

"What makes you say that?"

"Look at it. It got used so much it fell apart, and every time it fell apart somebody repaired it again, over and over. They even carved their initial into it too—*S.*"

Dave took the ball from Snider. "You couldn't figure out anything else about it?"

Snider shrugged. "I called the people who sold it. It was part of some guy's estate, but he's dead now, and there wasn't anyone left who was related to him. If he knew what its deal was, where it came from, it died with him. But it had to have some kind of story. Why else would anybody keep a junky old ball like this around?"

"Sentimental value," Dave said.

"Yeah. Which means it's worthless, I guess."

"Not to the person who kept it all those years," his uncle said. "And not to you. Here. You keep it. It's yours."

"But it's old. It has to be worth *something*."

"Okay. Give me ten bucks for it."

"Five," Snider said.

Uncle Dave laughed. "Deal. You drive a hard bargain, especially when you could have had it for free." He made change for Snider from the till. "There. Now it's official. You're part of its history. 'Purchased by Snider Flint in Brooklyn, New York, June 13, 2002.' There's just the small issue of a hundred-fifty-year gap in the provenance." He grinned. "But from now on, you'll know exactly what its story is, because you'll be living it."

Snider ran his fingers over the rough seams of the ball and brushed the carved letter *S* with his thumb—an *S* for Snider now.

"I wonder what happened to the guy who made this?"

Uncle Dave turned off the last of the lights. "There's no telling. Come on—there's a Mets game on TV, and I think I know where the remote is."

Author Notes

First Inning

Alexander Cartwright, considered by many today to be the father of modern baseball, was a bookseller and volunteer fireman, and his Knickerbocker Volunteer Fire Department gave its name to the baseball club Cartwright helped found. For their new sport, the Knickerbockers borrowed rules from older ball games like "town ball," "three-out, all-out," and "one old cat," and added some new rules of their own—like standard distances between the bases, foul territory, and, most importantly, no more throwing the ball at runners ("soaking" them) to get them out! In 1849 Cartwright left New York and, like so many other people, headed for California to try and get rich in the gold rush. He introduced the Knickerbocker baseball rules to towns and players all along the way, becoming a sort of Johnny Appleseed of America's game.

Second Inning

Contrary to popular belief, Abner Doubleday, who makes an appearance this inning as a real Union general, did not invent the game of baseball in a cow pasture in Cooperstown, New York. That myth was most likely started by sports-star-turned-sporting-goods-manufacturer Albert G. Spalding, who was desperate to convince the world that baseball was an American invention with no ties to older games or other countries. Despite zero evidence that Doubleday had ever even *seen* a baseball, much less invented the game, the idea was presented as fact, a Hall of Fame was built in Cooperstown, and the myth persists to this day.

Third Inning

As professional baseball became the national pastime, Mike "King" Kelly became one of its first great stars. A true showman, Kelly really did travel with a Japanese manservant and a pet monkey, and he is thought to be the first ballplayer to give autographs and the first to sell the rights to his name and image for product advertising. The song "Slide, Kelly, Slide" became a nationwide hit when it was released on a phonograph cylinder by Edison Studios, and after his playing career Kelly traded in on his fame to star on the vaudeville stage. In many ways, though, Kelly's story is as sad as that of the slugger in "Casey at the Bat." Heavy drinking cut short Kelly's playing career and his life. Already washed out of professional baseball, Kelly died when he was just thirty-six years old.

The title of this story comes from the subtitle of Ernest Thayer's "Casey at the Bat: A Ballad of the Republic," which was published in the *San Francisco Examiner* in 1888.

Fourth Inning

Hall of Famer Cyclone Joe Williams (later known as Smokey Joe Williams) was perhaps the greatest pitcher of his era, black or white, even though he never played a day in the majors. As far as I know, Cyclone Joe never tried to pass himself off as a Native American, but one black man during that time *did*. In 1901, Baltimore Orioles manager John McGraw tried to sign black second baseman Charlie Grant to a major league contract as an American Indian named Chief Tokohama. McGraw and Grant were busted before "Tokohama" could ever play a game, and baseball's color barrier remained unbroken for another forty-six years.

Fifth Inning

The 1920s were the heyday of wordy, "purple prose" sports writing, and John Kieran was one of its most famous figures. Kieran wrote for the *New York Times* sports section for almost thirty years, filling his sports columns with references to Latin, law, poetry, nature, and the works of William Shakespeare. In the hours before ball games, Kieran could be found visiting museums, zoos, parks, and libraries, and he had a habit of writing his articles in advance of the actual games. While I can't say that Kieran ever really conspired to fix a numbers game, he certainly seems like the kind of man who would have appreciated the effort.

One of Kieran's favorite subjects had to have been Babe Herman, who led the league in errors, put lit cigars in his pockets, twice stopped to watch long home runs while running the base paths only to be passed by the hitter and called out, and really did double into a double play. A teammate of Babe Herman said, "He wore a glove for one reason: Because it was a league custom." Years later during World War II when many of the younger players were called to military service, Herman was brought out of retirement to play for the Dodgers. He singled in his first at bat but tripped over first base and was almost thrown out. The Brooklyn fans gave him a standing ovation.

Sixth Inning

The All-American Girls Softball League was founded in 1943 by Chicago Cubs owner Phillip Wrigley, who wanted a women's league that would play in major league stadiums while the men's teams were on the road. The league played a cross between softball and baseball until the end of the 1945 season, when the name was changed to the All-American Girls Professional Baseball League, and overhand pitching and smaller ball sizes were adopted. Almost 200,000 fans turned out during the first season to watch the women play ball, and even though Wrigley's dream of women playing to packed major league stadiums never did happen, the league lived on in small Midwestern towns until 1954, when the AAGPBL played its last skirted season.

All the major characters in this story besides Kat—
from the players to the coach to the ball girl—were real
people.

Seventh Inning

Duck and Cover was an educational film shown to American
schoolkids, and, at least at the time I write this, can be seen
in its entirety on both Wikipedia and YouTube. Years later,
people argued that ducking and covering would provide little real help in the event of a nuclear attack, and that the film
did nothing but heighten kids' fears. That didn't stop the
film from being shown over and over again to students from
the late 1940s all the way, incredibly, to the 1980s.

Eighth Inning

As of the beginning of the 2008 season, there have been
only seventeen official perfect games in the history of Major
League Baseball. More people have orbited the moon than
thrown perfect games in the majors, and no pitcher has ever
thrown more than one. The ninth inning of Michael's perfect game in my story is loosely based on the ninth inning of
the perfect game thrown by Sandy Koufax of the Los Angeles Dodgers in 1965. I've tried to evoke the poetry of Dodgers radio announcer Vin Scully's call of that game in my
story, including a nod to my favorite line from his broadcast:
"I would think that the mound at Dodger Stadium right
now is the loneliest place in the world." The brief but thrill-

ing transcript of Scully's ninth-inning call of Sandy Koufax's perfect game can be found online.

Ninth Inning

In 2006, a Babe Herman Pro Model Signature Bat was sold to a collector at auction for $1,508. Tobacco stains and cleat marks proved it had been used in games, but there is no way to know if it was the same bat Herman used to hit into the famous double/double play. Oddly, the bat does bear the remnants of three postage stamps on the barrel, and faint, illegible writing that may be the address of Spalding, the bat's manufacturer. How or why the bat was mailed back to the factory no one knows.

Extra Innings

The story of the Gratzes is not nearly as exciting as the story of the Schneiders and Flints, but my own family history played a part for me in the writing of this novel.

Our family's American journey began in 1861, when nineteen-year-old Louis Alexander Gratz, a German Jew, landed in New York City with ten dollars in his pockets and no knowledge of English. A few months later he volunteered to fight in the Civil War, and less than a year after arriving in America, Louis Gratz was an officer in the Union Army. Louis, the main character in "The Red-Legged Devil" is named in his honor.

Though Louis Gratz never changed his last name, he did,

like some immigrant Jews, convert to Christianity to better fit in. Louis covered his tracks so well, in fact, that my family didn't even know we had Jewish ancestors until my grandfather began to research our family history more than a hundred years later!

To help research the Seventh Inning, I interviewed my father, who was a boy in 1957. He remembers duck and cover drills and collecting baseball cards when he was a kid. I was able to draw on my own childhood for the Eighth Inning, when I played youth baseball and worshipped movies like *Star Wars* and *Raiders of the Lost Ark*.

By 2002, I had grown up and moved away from home and had a family of my own, but still not a day goes by during baseball season that I don't talk to my father on the phone about some terrific hit, some great defensive play, or the sad state of the fantasy baseball team we share. Baseball, more than any other sport, has a magical way of connecting fathers and sons, mothers and daughters, grandparents and grandchildren, and ancestors back down the line. For that reason and many more, *The Brooklyn Nine* is, at long last, dedicated to my mom and dad.

Special Thanks

I owe a great debt of thanks for *The Brooklyn Nine* to editor extraordinaire Liz Waniewski—not to be confused with Grand Rapids Chicks pitcher Connie Wisniewski, although I more than once typed "Liz" instead of "Connie" in that inning. Editorial thanks are also due to Brad Anderson, who got his first big-league at bats against me, and Robyn Meshulam, who led the team in assists. And thanks as always to copy editor Regina Castillo, who of course bats cleanup.

In an age when information is a commodity, we're incredibly lucky to still have libraries where all that wonderful knowledge is free for the asking, and I am indebted to the libraries of Emory University, the University of Tennessee, Knoxville, and Appalachian State University for the bulk of the research I did on this book. I routinely cleared out their baseball and American history shelves for this project, and any mistakes that remain are my own.

And thanks of course to my wife, Wendi, and my daughter, Jo, who put up with my surly editing moods, my closed office door, and baseball on TV every night, and special thanks to all the Gratzes, past and present; I am just another chapter in your story.

CLIFF HANGER

CLIFF HANGER

A Martha's Vineyard Mystery

PHILIP R. CRAIG

CHARLES SCRIBNER'S SONS
New York

Maxwell Macmillan Canada
Toronto

Maxwell Macmillan International
New York   Oxford   Singapore   Sydney

Copyright © 1993 by Philip R. Craig

Charles Scribner's Sons
Macmillan Publishing Company
866 Third Avenue
New York, NY 10022

Maxwell Macmillan Canada, Inc.
200 Eglinton Avenue East
Suite 200
Don Mills, Ontario M3C 3N1

Macmillan Publishing Company is part of the Maxwell
Communication Group of Companies.

Library of Congress Cataloging-in-Publication Data
Craig, Philip R., 1933–
Cliff hanger: a Martha's Vineyard mystery/Philip R. Craig.
    p.   cm.
ISBN 0-684-19552-6
I. Title.
PS3553.R23C57   1993
813'.54—dc20   92–41167
CIP

Macmillan books are available at special discounts for bulk purchases for sales promotions, premiums, fund-raising, or educational use. For details, contact:

Special Sales Director
Macmillan Publishing Company
866 Third Avenue
New York, NY 10022

Map illustration by Aher/Donnell Studios

10 9 8 7 6 5 4 3 2 1

Printed in the United States of America

For my grandchildren, Jessica and Peter Harmon,
who live with their parents in the Colorado mountains
far, very far, from Martha's Vineyard
and the singing sea.

"There are always many more disordered
states than there are ordered ones."
—Stephen W. Hawking
A BRIEF HISTORY OF TIME

"Though lovers be lost love shall not;
And death shall have no dominion."
—Dylan Thomas
"And Death Shall Have No Dominion"

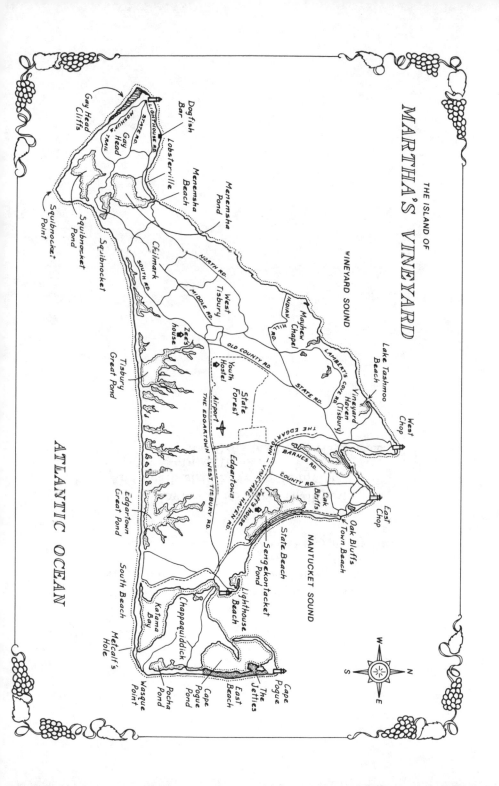

CLIFF HANGER

— 1 —

The first time, I thought that I'd just been involved in a near-miss accident. The second time, I thought I'd almost killed myself. The third time, I realized that someone wanted me dead. I couldn't imagine why. But then many a murder victim probably has a look of surprise on his face.

If the bluefish hadn't gone north early or if the bonito had arrived on time, maybe none of it would have happened to me, but late July found the waters around Martha's Vineyard so barren of fish that it seemed the usually fertile sea was dead, and I worked the beaches in vain. I didn't have any better luck fishing from the *Shirley J.*, either, partially because the midsummer winds were fluky and weak and an eighteen-foot catboat is none too swift in the best of conditions. Unlike the power boats, whose speed was not dependent upon the winds, the *Shirley J.* was slow to get out to the shoals and just as slow returning home, and I had little daylight fishing time between going and coming back. Not that it would have made much difference, since the shoals were almost as empty of fish as the shore and the guys in power boats weren't doing much better than I was in the *Shirley J.*

I was bored and eating the early summer's catch out of my freezer instead of fresh stuff out of the sea.

Of course I could have been eating shellfish. Martha's Vineyard, and Edgartown in particular, has some of the East Coast's finest shellfishing ponds, after all. I could have had clams, quahogs, mussels, or maybe even some oysters, in spite of the truism that you're really only supposed to eat oysters in months with an "r" in their names.

The "oysters are mushy and tasteless in warm months" theory is not necessarily gospel. I've eaten good Vineyard oysters in the middle of the summer.

But I didn't want any shellfish. Eating shellfish bored me.

Everything bored me. If I hadn't been bored, I never would have gone across Vineyard Sound to America, and if I hadn't done that, then . . .

The real problem was not the lack of fish. I had gone fishless before. The problem was that Zee had left the island for a month. I had learned about this plan for the first time in the spring, when we were down on Wasque Point on a very brisk May morning waiting for the bluefish to arrive.

Zee, wearing her waders, a sweater, a hooded sweatshirt, and her topsider jacket, did not look like her normal slender self. Her apparent bulk did not fool me, though, because I knew what she looked like in warm weather. She and I had been alternating between making casts out toward the light buoy to the south of the point (one way to determine which way "straight out" is, when it's too dark to see anything) and coming back to the truck for its meager warmth, and coffee from my large, stainless steel thermos jug.

I was as bundled up as she was, because it wasn't yet sunup and the southwest wind, blowing in from the sea, was cold. Moreover, the heater in my ancient, rusty Toyota Land Cruiser was none too good and you had to wear a lot of clothes to keep warm anytime the air was chill, even if you weren't going fishing.

When Zee came up to the truck, I would usually go down and make my casts, just so one of us would have a line in the water most of the time. Sometimes, though, we were both in the cab at the same time, drinking coffee and listening either to the C and W station from Rhode Island, which for some reason I can pick up well on Wasque, or to the classical station over in Chatham.

Gradually the sky lightened in the east, most brightly just to the left of where Nantucket lay right over the horizon, and then the sun inched into sight behind low clouds and climbed until it was a huge orange-red ball of fire coloring the sky and setting the ocean momentarily aflame. I put my rod in the spike on the front of the Land Cruiser, and dug out the slingshot I'd made from a piece of leather and two thongs. I picked up some choice pebbles from the edge of the surf. I smiled at Zee.

"Watch this."

I put a stone in the sling and whipped it down the beach.

"You see that? I hit that tree dead center."

I threw another stone. Zee got out of the truck.

"I used to do this when I was a kid," I said. "Yesterday I was reading Samuel again; you know, the part where David and Goliath are promising to feed each other's flesh to the birds of the air and the beasts of the field, just before David does Goliath in, and I remembered making these things, so I made this one. Nifty, isn't it? And I haven't lost the old skill either. It must be like riding a bicycle.'"

"There's no tree there," said Zee.

"Use your imagination," I said. "Watch this. There! I got it again. Great, eh?"

"You're a sick man, Jefferson."

"If you'll just call some fish in, I won't have to do this. Wow! Another hit! Ah, I have the golden touch! You want to try?"

"No. Put that away, and have some coffee."

"I used to make slingshots out of forked pieces of wood and strips of rubber from old inner tubes, too, and later I had a BB gun. Ah, this brings it all back." I grinned at her, put away the slingshot, snagged my coffee cup from the dashboard, and watched the birth of yet another day. There is no prettier place to see it happen. Zee leaned on the truck beside me.

"How did you manage to become such a saint, after such a violent childhood?" she asked.

"Moral vigor," I said. I waved at the ocean. "I have a hunch that just at the exact moment when I finish this coffee and walk down there and make my cast there'll be a fish out there waiting for the plug to hit the water."

"Sure," said Zee. "I think that's about the tenth time you've made that prediction this morning."

"I was just practicing before. This time I mean it."

"I'm going away for most of August," said Zee.

I drank my coffee.

"I'm going to a women's conference up in New Hampshire."

"You don't have to tell me where you're going."

"I thought you might want to know. It's a conference on 'Women in the Health Professions.' "

Zee was a nurse. "It's probably a good time to go," I said. "The fish will be going away and you'll get to miss the August People." Some of the island cops say the August People are more trouble than either the June People or the July People.

"I've been thinking about going to medical school," said Zee.

I hadn't heard that before. I finished the coffee and held the cup in my hand, looking at the rising sun. "You'd make a good doctor."

"I haven't decided yet. That's one reason I'm going to the conference."

I was still surprised about the medical school idea. "It must be some conference if it lasts a month."

"There are two conferences, actually. The medical one and then another one about women's lives. Some of the same people will be at both of them. Then I'm going to just take some time off and be by myself for a while. Maybe I'll even go see my folks."

"Sounds good," I said.

"I'm going to make a cast," said Zee. She took her nice

eleven-and-a-half-foot graphite rod out of its spike and walked down to the silvery-red water. The waves weren't too big, but the water was chilly if you let it splash up into the front of your waders. Zee walked the receding water down, made her long, straight cast, and stepped back before the next wave hit the beach. Out toward the whitecaps in the Wasque rip I saw her Roberts hit the water.

I looked to the west. A couple of trucks were coming along the beach. One of them looked like George Martin's Jeep and the other looked like Iowa's pickup. They were planning to hit the rip two hours before the turning of the west tide. Not a bad idea. Zee and I had arrived four hours before the turning and had nothing to show for it. So much for the Early Bird theory. As I looked west, I heard Zee yell and turned to watch a huge swirl surround her plug. A bluefish, sure as taxes!

"Get on there!" encouraged Zee, slowing her reel.

Another swirl, but no hit. Zee inched the plug in. A Roberts is about as good a surface plug as I know. It catches fish sometimes when nothing else seems to do. Zee flicked her rod tip and the Roberts jumped a bit at the end of her line. The bluefish took another whack at it and missed again.

"Come on!" said Zee, encouragingly. Another swirl. Her rod bent. "There!" She jerked up the rod tip to set the hook and the Roberts flew through the air. "Damn!"

I grabbed my rod and made my cast as I reached the surf. Zee's plug was back in the water and sure enough there was another swirl right on it.

"Look at that!" cried Zee. "There he is again! And again! He can't catch it, the rascal! Come on, fish, catch it!"

But the fish did not catch it. He swirled and flashed and hit it with his nose and chased it all the way into the surf, but he never got it.

Meanwhile, about two turns on the reel in from the end

of my cast, I was on. I felt the hit, set the hook, and heard the reel sing.

"Get him!" Zee grinned at me and made her second cast and a moment later we were both on, rods bent, lines cutting through the water.

They were fighters, and they walked us down the beach before we got them in. Nice ten-pounders, just up from the Carolinas. We were carrying them to the Land Cruiser when George and Iowa pulled up beside us and got out. There was a passenger in Iowa's pickup. A woman.

"Perfect timing," said George, taking his rod off his roof rack.

"What's that Madieras person doing here?" said Iowa. "Women belong in the kitchen, not out here catching us men's fish."

"I left a couple for you," said Zee, "but you won't catch them by standing around complaining."

"All right, all right," said Iowa, getting his rod and following George down to the surf. "Getting so a man's got no place to call his own. Damned women are every-where. I thought I told you not to bring her out here anymore, J.W."

"Just because your wife's too smart to hang around listening to you grouse all day doesn't mean I have to forsake the company of the fairer sex," I said.

"Nothing fair about Zee," said Iowa, making his cast. "She's caught a lot of fish that rightfully belonged to me. Whoops! On, by Gadfrey!"

And he was. And so was George. And moments later, so were Zee and I.

As I brought my fish in, I looked at the passenger sitting in Iowa's pickup. She was a youngish woman, one I'd not seen before. Several fish later, the young woman was out of the pickup, getting a closer look at the action on the beach.

"My niece," yelled Iowa over the sound of the surf. He

took a fish off his plug and gestured all around. "Gerry, these characters live off the fish they steal from me. That's George, that's J.W., that's Zee. She's the worst of the bunch. Everybody, this is my niece, Geraldine Miles. Visiting from Iowa City. Brought up all wrong. Doesn't know a damned thing about fishing. Trying to teach her how to live right!"

The woman smiled and Iowa was headed back to the surf.

"Gangbusters," said Zee an hour later.

The fish had gone, but we'd gotten our share and the five of us were standing by the trucks drinking George's coffee since Zee and I had almost finished our own before the fish had hit.

"Not bad, not bad," Iowa said. "Even a woman could catch 'em today."

Zee pretended to peek into his fishbox. "How many did you get onto the beach? One? Two? A bent rod doesn't mean a thing. They don't count until you land them, you know."

"You're hard," said Iowa. He had at least ten fish in his box and was feeling good.

Geraldine Miles drank coffee with us, smiled, and was quiet. She moved in an unnatural, awkward way, as though some of her bones hurt. She was a pretty woman about Zee's age, with brownish hair and a milky skin. At first I thought that she was shy. After a short time, though, I suddenly realized she was more troubled than shy. I studied her when she wasn't looking and decided that her smiles were more polite than real, that she was trying to be happy rather than actually being happy. The fact that she'd gotten up in the wee hours to come to Wasque with Iowa when she knew nothing at all about fishing suggested two things: that Iowa, who normally went fishing alone or with his dog or very occasionally with his wife, Jean, who did not share his fanatical love

of surf casting, was trying to get his niece occupied with things other than those troubling her, and that she was agreeable to such distractions.

Maybe she had come to the island to escape problems at home. I knew something about that, having come to live on the island for the same reasons several years before. Now I felt a sympathy for her, but had my own desire for distraction. Zee would be away for the last month of the summer, and I wasn't really up to thinking about that yet.

"I see you hauled the *Mattie* and put her back in again," said George. "Kind of early, isn't it? John Skye doesn't usually come down until the middle of June."

John Skye was a professor at Weststock College who hired me to keep an eye on his house and boat in the winter and to get both ready for his arrival for the summer. If you're going to live on Martha's Vineyard year-round, you take jobs like that. The *Mattie* was his big old wooden catboat. She floated at her stake in the harbor all winter and sometimes I had to chop ice away from her hull. In the spring I hauled her, painted her bottom and topsides, and dropped her back in. An old wooden boat will last forever if you keep her painted and in the water. Haul her out and put her in the barn, she'll dry up and fall apart.

I looked away from Geraldine Miles. "I got a call from John," I said. "Seems that he's making his house and boat available to a professor he works with. John does that sort of thing sometimes. If he's not here, he'll let other professorial types use his place. This guy and some students are coming down to the island to do a study of some sort. Everything's got to be ready and waiting for them."

"More for you to do now, but less to do later," nodded George.

"When are they coming?" asked Zee.

"Next week. They'll be here about ten days, I guess."

"And then John and Mattie and the girls will be here." Zee was fond of the Skyes.

"I don't think so. According to John, Mattie and the twins are going out to Colorado for the summer."

"There's no ocean in Colorado," said Iowa. "There's no bluefish. Why would anybody want to go there?"

"There's no ocean or bluefish in Des Moines, either," Zee reminded him.

Iowa was a retired high school superintendent. "Yeah," he said, "but I was smart enough to leave Iowa as soon as they'd let me go! Well, I suppose they can't fish for trout out there in the Rockies. That way the trip won't be a total waste of time."

"Not everybody likes to fish," said Zee.

Iowa's eyes widened. "Is that a fact? I never knew."

"John came from out there someplace," explained George. "Grew up on a cattle ranch before he came east. Mattie and the girls went out there to meet his mother after he and Mattie got married, and the three of them fell in love with the place."

"The twins are horse crazy," added Zee. "And they love the mountains."

"Well, the mountains are okay . . ." grumbled Iowa.

In the warming morning sunshine, Geraldine Miles pushed the sleeves of her sweatshirt up, then caught herself and pulled them down again, but not before I saw the bruises on her upper arms. Her eyes flicked around and met mine. She looked away.

"Not a bad choice of summer vacations." said George. "The mountains of Colorado or Martha's Vineyard. Too bad you can't be both places at once."

"Maybe they'll split the season," I said. "Half out there, half here."

"The perfect solution," said Zee. "I'd love to go to Colorado someday."

"The Vineyard will do for me," I said, wondering if that would still be true if Zee went off to medical school. How long did medical school take? Four years? And then there'd be a residency. How much longer would that be?

"Well, I'd like to go out there," said Zee.

"Good idea," said Iowa. "I'll be glad to help, if you'll just leave right now and stay away from my bluefish till the derby's over this fall. Now lemme see if I've got any money here . . ." He pretended to dig in his pocket.

Geraldine Miles smiled and the rest of us laughed. But I was wondering if Zee was developing a sugar foot. Was the wander-thirst on her? Was the island giving her cabin fever? First she was going to New Hampshire and now she'd like to go to Colorado.

As things turned out, I was the one who went to Colorado. I nearly died there, in fact.

— 2 —

Martha's Vineyard is verdant island surrounded by golden sand beaches. It lies about five miles south of Cape Cod and lives off its tourists. Ten thousand year-round islanders play host to a hundred thousand summer visitors who bring in the money which oils the island's gears. The year-rounders labor mightily in the summer, some working two or three jobs, some renting out their houses and summering illegally in tents or shacks; many then go on unemployment during the winter.

Island wages are low and everything else is expensive, but summer jobs are sucked up by college students who are looking for vacation jobs with access to sea, sun, surf, and sex, and who don't really care if they actually make any money before returning to school in the fall. More serious workers come from overseas, legally or illegally, and live wherever they can while working as hard as they can, since even low Vineyard wages are better than they can earn at home.

Day-trippers come across from Cape Cod, take tour bus

rides, buy knickknacks mostly made in Asia but sold with Vineyard logos in island souvenir shops, and go back to America having done the island in half a day. Other summer visitors come for their week or two of escape from the real world. The harbors are filled with yachts, and there are great summer houses owned by the people who come for the season.

John Skye was one of the house owners. He owned a part of what had once been a farm. The house had been built in the early 1800s, in the time before the island economy became dependent on tourism. In those days, islanders, like most coastal people, generally tried to make a living by combining farming and fishing, two of the toughest jobs imaginable. Tourism, by comparison, offered easy money, so when the island economy turned in that direction, farmers' sons and daughters left the farms for the towns and, years later, John had bought his house, outbuildings, and land pretty cheap.

Before I knew him, he and his first wife had come down every summer from Weststock, where he taught things medieval at the college. When she had died, too young, he had missed a season and gone instead back to southwest Colorado, where his people still lived. The next summer he was back on the island where, a year or so later, he and I had met on the beach and, in time, I became his caretaker, charged with closing his house in the fall, keeping an eye on it over the winter, opening it in the early summer, and caring for the *Mattie*.

The *Mattie* wasn't the *Mattie* when I went to work for John. She was the *Seawind*. She became the *Mattie* when John married Mattie, whose young husband had left her a widow with twin daughters when he drove his motorcycle into a tree at a high rate of speed.

And now Mattie and the girls had fallen in love with Colorado and John had a dilemma: where to spend the summer? Out by Durango, near the mountains they all loved, or on the island they all loved?

"If Colorado had an ocean, it would be no problem," John had said on the phone. "If they could just flood everything east of the divide, or maybe all of Texas, I could live out there for the rest of my life, but . . ."

"Everybody's got problems," I'd said.

"Except you. You've got it made, J.W."

"Who's this guy you're sending down, and when will he be here?"

"Jack Scarlotti. He'll be down May 25. He's our current hotshot junior faculty member. Sociology, Poli-Sci, or some combination of both, I think. Anyway, he's very dashing, very intense, very bright. The ladies all love him. Not a bad guy, actually. Teaches a grad seminar. Wants to take the whole class down to the island for a week so they can do field research among the locals, before the summer people really get there."

"The island as a laboratory. Natives living in isolation from the mainstream. That sort of thing?"

"I think that's it. Something like the deafness bit, maybe."

Presumably because of inbreeding, a lot of up-island people once suffered from a type of deafness. Some medical or academic type had studied the phenomenon and his conclusions had been written up and had attracted a good deal of comment.

"The politics of isolation," I said. "Professor Scarlotti's students do the legwork and write papers and he puts it all in a book with his name on it and uses it as a required text in all of his courses."

Skye laughed. "Spoken like a true scholastic, J.W. Where'd you learn about that trick?"

"From listening to you and your academic buddies at those cocktail parties you throw."

"I'll have to advise my colleagues to talk less about our trade. They'll give away all of our secrets. I'm going to have Jack come by your house for the keys. Then you can

take him over to the farm. Is that okay? I'll let you know
what boat they'll be coming on."

"Okay."

"I think you'll like him. He's a good guy even if he is
a whiz kid. I understand there'll be about ten grad students with him, both sexes. They should all fit in the
house if they don't mind sleeping double. I want nothing
to do with deciding who sleeps where, by the way."

"I'll make sure the place is clean, that there are sheets
and blankets and water and lights, and that the fridge has
bacon and eggs and bread waiting for them. I'll show him
where the A & P is, too. Can this guy sail?"

"He says he can. If he wants to go sailing, you can
show him the *Mattie* and where the dinghy is on Collins
Beach and where the oars and oarlocks are in the barn."

"No problem."

"I'll have him leave the keys with you when he leaves.
I'll be down in the middle of June."

"That'll give me time to clean the place up again. What
do you mean, you'll be down? What about Mattie and
the girls?"

That's when I learned that Mattie and the girls were
going to Colorado to stay at John's mother's ranch.

"So you'll be living the jolly bachelor life, eh?"

"That's an oxymoron. The bachelor life is not the life
for me. I have a theological crisis whenever Mattie has to
be away. Sleeping alone in a double bed is evidence that
there is no God."

"Why don't you just go out to Colorado with your wife
and avoid this existential predicament?"

"I thought you of all people would understand.
Bluefish, my boy! Clams! Quahogs! I haven't had a fresh
bluefish since last summer. I haven't had mussels. I
haven't had a clam boil. I haven't had one single littleneck
on the half shell. Life is not always easy, you know. We
have to face tough choices."

"Well, my favorite woman is right here, so I don't have to chose between her and fish."

"You're a lucky man."

A few days later, when Zee told me about her New Hampshire plans, I didn't feel so lucky, but at the time I could not but agree with John.

John's house was off the West Tisbury Road. In the wintertime, when the leaves were off the trees, you could catch a glimpse of the ocean from a couple of his upstairs windows. If some developer had gotten hold of it, he probably would have called it Ocean View Farm, or some such thing.

In preparation for the arrival of Dr. Jack Scarlotti and his band, I turned on the water and electricity, made sure there were no leaky pipes and that the toilets all flushed, and vacuumed and dusted the house, including the fine, big library where a few thousand of John's books tended to slow me down a lot as I examined titles and fingered through pages when I should have been working. I made sure there were blankets and sheets in the linen closets, opened screened windows so the place could air out, turned on the bottled gas for the stove, mowed the large lawn, and checked the barn and fences for needed repairs.

Behind the barn the grass was high in the field where the twins kept the horses that wintered at a farm up toward Chilmark. The horses would stay at that farm this summer, I reckoned, since Jen and Jill would be in Colorado with their mother instead of here. I liked the twins although I simply could not tell one from the other. I realized to my surprise that I would miss them. Was I becoming a sentimentalist?

I unlocked the tack room, where the twins kept their saddles and other riding gear and grooming supplies, enjoying, as always, the smell of leather and oils and the scent of horsehair and sweat that gets into tack, and the smell of hay and grain that is usually mixed in with it. Everything was fine, so I locked the door again and went

back to the house, closed the windows, locked up, and went home. As I drove I saw Geraldine Miles walking slowly toward me on the bike path that paralleled the road. The bike paths on the Vineyard are popular with walkers and joggers, and Geraldine was limping along with an intent look on her face. In the warm spring air, she wore long pants and a long-sleeved sweatshirt. I considered offering her a ride, but changed my mind. She was walking because she wanted to be walking. I drove past and she never glanced at me.

On May 24, I got another call from John Skye. Jack Scarlotti and company would be coming over the next day on the one-fifteen boat from Woods Hole.

I went to the A & P and bought juice, instant coffee, bread, oleo, bacon, and eggs. As is customary on Martha's Vineyard, I paid a lot more for the food than I would have on the mainland. Such is the price of island living. All businesses overcharge and claim that it's because of the cost of bringing in supplies on the ferries. The over-charges are, of course, much greater than the freight costs, but it is a convenient lie shared by the businesses, and islanders tolerate it because they must. Once the state sent down a Consumer Affairs official in response to complaints about unjustifiably high prices. The official agreed that island prices were outrageous and had little to do with freight costs, but could find no law against the practice of overcharging and went back across the sound to America, never to return. Some people were disappointed, but no one was surprised.

I put the food in John Skye's refrigerator and went fishing.

At home again, I filleted the fish on the metal-topped table behind the shed in back of my house and threw the carcasses into the trees. As long as the wind blew from the southwest, the scent of rotting fish would blow away from the house. Within three or four days, the bones would be stripped bare by insects and birds and

there would be no smell at all. Blues, like people, are biodegradable.

I set one fillet aside and put the rest in my freezer, then celebrated with a bottle of George Killian Red. George Killian Red is a product of the Coors brewery. Coors beer ("brewed with pure Rocky Mountain spring water") may be a bit overrated, but George Killian Red is a good beer that I enjoy.

My peas were ready, but there was also some asparagus coming up, so I picked that and managed to get it back to the house without eating it raw, proof that I have a will of iron. Asparagus out of the garden is so tender that it really doesn't have to be cooked at all, but on the other hand, a bit of butter doesn't hurt it. I put it in a pan with a little water and cooked it in the oven while I fried up the bluefish fillet, and made a sauce of horseradish, mustard, and mayo. In the fridge I had the last half of a loaf of bread I'd baked the day before (you always eat at least a half loaf of fresh bread as soon as it comes out of the oven), and in a bit sat down with another George Killian to a supper better than what anyone else I knew was eating. A Vineyard meal, the gift of the earth and sea. I wished that Zee was sharing it, but she was at the hospital on the four to midnight shift, alas. I managed to eat everything by myself.

The next afternoon at two-thirty I heard cars coming down my long, sandy driveway. Not too many cars come down my road, but these were right on time. The one-fifteen boat from Woods Hole gets into Vineyard Haven at two o'clock. It should take about a half hour to get your car off the ferry and down the road to my place. Dr. Jack Scarlotti could apparently read a map, because here he was with his students.

They were in two station wagons which stopped in the yard. I was pulling weeds in my garden and was glad for an excuse to stop. Weed pulling is not my favorite pastime. Car doors opened and people got out. Ten people

in their twenties. The eldest came toward me. He was one of those dark-haired, dark-eyed, tight-skinned people who almost glitter with intensity.

"Mr. Jackson?" He put out his hand. "Jack Scarlotti." His grip was quick and firm. He gestured at the people with him. "My students." A girl with glasses was hovering directly behind him. "My teaching assistant, Bernie Orwell."

Bernie Orwell thrust out a hand and we shook. Her palm was soft and a bit damp. "How do you do?" she asked.

I thought she looked tired. "I do reasonably well," I said.

Another young woman, slim and attractive, stood beside Scarlotti. He did not introduce her. I looked at him. "I'll get your keys for you. Then I'll take my car and let you follow me out to John's place. If one of your crowd wants to ride with me, I'll point out the post office and some other places you might want to know about."

"I'll do it," said Bernie Orwell. Although her voice was without expression, she was quick to serve, which was maybe one reason she was his teaching assistant instead of just another student.

"Good enough," said Scarlotti. "Interesting place you have here," he added, looking at my house with a studious eye.

"An old hunting camp. I put in heat, water, and electricity. Otherwise it's about the same as it was eighty years ago when it was built. You'll find John's house a good deal more civilized."

I got the keys and gave them to Scarlotti, then pointed Bernie Orwell to my rusty Land Cruiser. The other girl climbed into the front seat of the station wagon driven by Jack Scarlotti. The station wagons got themselves turned around and followed me out to the highway.

"A station wagon train," I said to Bernie Orwell. "Does that make me a station wagon master?"

"What? Oh. I get it." She smiled a distant metallic smile. She was older than most people wearing braces, but I guess it's never too late to straighten your teeth. Hers didn't look too bad. She glanced back at the following cars.

We drove into Edgartown and I pointed out the post office, the drugstore, the liquor stores, and, when we finally got past the normal traffic jam in front of the almost brand-new A & P, the hardware store down by the park.

"We call this Cannonball Park because of those stacks of cannonballs in it," I said. "It's got cannons, too, as you see, but they're the wrong size to shoot the cannonballs. Don't ask me why."

"Very well, I won't."

"That way's downtown," I said, pointing, "but we're going this way." I turned up the West Tisbury Road and drove until I got to John Skye's driveway. The station wagon train followed me down to the house.

"So this is his place," said Bernie Orwell in her dull voice. "He liked to talk about it."

Scarlotti and the students emptied out of their cars and looked appreciatively at John's farm. After seeing my place, they realized how well off they were here. Bernie Orwell went to Scarlotti's side.

"I know where all the stores are. We'll need to do some shopping. I'll make a list and get right back to town."

"Let's look at the house first, Bernie," said Scarlotti, smiling.

She shrugged, and flicked a glance at the other young woman. "Yes. Of course."

A tired dog, but one still willing to please.

I climbed back into the Land Cruiser. "You know where I live and my number's in the book. If you need me, let me know. I can fix most of the things that might break while you're here."

"Thanks."

"Do you know about John's boat?"

"I know it's moored in the Edgartown harbor some-where. He said we could use it."

"If you decide to go sailing, contact me and I'll show you the boat and John's dinghy."

"I doubt if we'll have time for sailing, but if we get our work done and the weather's good . . .'"

I drove away and didn't see any of them again until, two weeks later, the station wagons came down my drive-way and Jack Scarlotti handed me John's keys and drove off to catch the ferry back to America.

That afternoon I went up to John's house to clean up the mess. I found what I expected to find: overflowing trash barrels behind the house, breakfast dishes still in the dishwasher (which had been John's none-too-romantic-but-greatly-appreciated last year's birthday gift to Mat-tie), a lot of beer cans stacked on the back porch, and a very large pile of dirty linens which had been stripped from the beds. I also found three stray and unmatched socks and, behind the kitchen table, one earring. I opened windows to air out the house and spent the morning clean-ing up. I washed several loads of linens in the machine and hung them on the solar drying line, vacuumed the house, washed the dishes, and made a run to the dump (once a favorite shopping spot where fine and useful stuff could be found and taken home for further use, but now an efficient and expensive recycling facility where all lum-ber had to be cut into short lengths, glass and paper and plastics had to be separated into colors and grades, and it cost you money for every barrel of just-plain-rubbish you deposited).

When the linens were dry, I folded them and put them away in various closets, and decided that John's house was back in shape. I checked the barn and that, too, was fine.

I closed the windows and loaded the beer cans into the Land Cruiser so I could take them to a liquor store where

I could get a nickel apiece for them, thus adding a bit to the meager Jackson coffers and cleaning up the environment at the same time. Then I took a last turn around the house to see if I had missed something. I had.

Upside down in the flowers at the side of the front porch was a small green knapsack. It looked to me as if it might have been knocked off the porch when the gang was stacking stuff outside to be loaded into the cars. I got it and opened it up, looking for some ID. Inside were a variety of items: a zipped plastic bag containing lipstick, face powders, tiny bottles, and brushes; a Swiss army knife; pen, pencils, and notepaper; some Kleenex; cigarettes and matches; a plastic 35mm container with a bit of white powder in it and another film container with some pills; two books.

I wet a finger and tasted the white powder. Hmmmmm. I decided not to try one of the pills. I looked at the books. One was a book of social theory. Inside the cover was Bernadette Orwell's name. The other was a journal. I opened it up.

Its first entry was almost two years old and had to do with what Bernie Orwell had been doing that September day at Weststock when she began her senior year. She also wrote about how she felt, which was not great. I flipped pages shamelessly. A few entries later, Bernie was very happy with her courses and particularly happy because she was in a Medieval Literature class with Dr. John Skye, "a wonderful, wonderful person."

Lucky John. I wondered if he knew in what favor he had been held. I flipped ahead. If John hadn't known earlier, he surely knew later. Bernie wrote of lingering in his classroom, of seeing him in his office, of thinking of him at night. Bernie waxed up and down in her moods. No surprise, considering her film containers. Powder up, pills down was my guess. I found myself uncomfortable reading Bernie's secret words, but not so uncomfortable that I stopped reading. Instead, I flipped far ahead in her journal.

Last fall. Graduate school. Hot and heavy thoughts of Jonathan, who had not only become Jonathan instead of Dr. Skye or plain old John, but who, according to Bernie, was "so beautiful and brilliant" that she "trembled at the very thought of his touch." Good grief! So people really did write stuff like that. I wondered how anyone could think of John Skye as beautiful. Feeling suddenly like a voyeur, I closed the journal and returned everything to the backpack.

I went inside and phoned Weststock and asked for Bernie Orwell's address. They said they didn't give such information out. I got Jack Scarlotti's number and called that, but no one answered. I phoned John Skye. He obviously would know. But John said he'd get the address from the registrar and call me back. I found a beer in the fridge and drank it while I waited and wondered why John had told me he didn't have the address at hand. When John called back, he gave me an address in New Jersey, but said the registrar had been unclear about her Weststock address.

I scribbled a note to Bernadette Orwell and told her where I'd found her backpack and the earring in John's house, and that he'd given me her address. I put the note in the pack with the earring (which, after all, might actually have been hers and certainly was of no use to anyone else), and packaged everything up. I took the package to the post office on my way home, and sent it parcel post, thus robbing Uncle Sam of the first-class postage he would have required of me had I told him of the note inside. It's hard to hold your own against the government, but I try.

That evening as I was eating crackers and bluefish paté, the phone rang. It was Bernadette Orwell calling in a panic from Weststock.

"I'm terribly, terribly sorry to interrupt you, but . . ."

"Relax. I found your backpack."

"What? You did! Oh, thank you . . . !"

"It had fallen off the front porch. I got your address

from John Skye and sent everything to New Jersey. I didn't know your Weststock address."

"Oh! I just changed apartments . . . Well . . . Thank you! Thank you! My journal was inside . . . I've always kept a journal. Oh, I hope . . . You didn't . . . Oh, dear . . ."

"Don't worry," I said, "I don't read other people's journals. Only a real crumb would do a thing like that."

"Oh! Well, thank you again. You have no idea how worried I've been . . ."

"Think nothing of it," I said. Bernadette was in Weststock and her cocaine and pills would soon be in New Jersey. Everybody has problems. One of mine was being a real crumb sometimes.

— 3 —

I was wrapping smoked bluefish for my illegal markets when the phone rang. The Commonwealth of Massachusetts and the town of Edgartown insist that people who sell processed fish to restaurants and other purveyors of food should have very expensive and sanitary facilities to pre-pare that fish, but I prepare my smoked bluefish in my kitchen and smoke it in a smoker made out of an old refrigerator and electric stove parts salvaged from the dump long ago, before the environmentalists seized con-trol of the world. I maintain that if I've never poisoned myself or the guests at my table, my food won't poison anybody else either. Happily for me, some fine establish-ments on Martha's Vineyard agree with me and are glad to buy as much of my illegal smoked bluefish as they can get. Why not? It's the island's finest, after all.

It was mid-June and John Skye's voice was on the line.

"Just got down. Place looks fine. How are the fish running?"

"They've been up around Cape Pogue for the last couple of days. Not too big, but lots of them."

"The little ones are best. Have supper with me. I'll feed you my catch."

"Sure."

"Zee working nights? No? I'll give her a call. Maybe she can join us. All my own women are out west. Bachelorhood is no kind of life, my boy; you've got to have women around if you want to be happy. I'm going fishing. You want to come along?"

"Sorry. Delivery day."

"Ah. See you about six."

"Yes."

On the way to John's farm, I saw Geraldine Miles walking on the bike path. Her pace was longer and she was moving more easily than when last I'd seen her. She was young and her body was healing itself. Her face looked better, too. There was some color in it. I liked the way she looked.

At six, I parked my ancient, rusty Land Cruiser beside John's brand-new blue Jeep Wagoneer. John came out of the house, shook hands, and helped me take three cases of liquor from his Jeep and put them in the Land Cruiser. On Martha's Vineyard, booze, like all other commodities, is vastly overpriced, so when our friends come down from America they bring our orders for life's essentials with them. John handed me his receipt for the liquor and I paid him in cash. A deal. I found a bottle of Moselle in one of my boxes and followed John back into the kitchen, where I put the bottle in the freezer for a fast chill.

He took two glasses and a half gallon of Stoli from the same freezer, sloshed dry vermouth around in each glass and tossed it out, then filled the chilled glasses with icy vodka and dropped two olives in each glass. He handed one glass to me. The perfect martini.

"Cheers."

"Shalom."

The vodka was smooth and cold as a mortician.

"Damn fine."

"Sit."

We sat and looked at one another. I tried but failed to see him as beautiful. He was fiftyish, a bit over six feet tall and short on hair. He was developing a slight belly that embarrassed him not at all; he held that it was emergency rations in case of atomic attack. When not on the island, he lived in Weststock where he was a professor at the college, specializing in literature written in European languages not spoken for at least a thousand years. He had once told me that one of the things he liked about his work was that it was completely useless. Just the thing for a man as basically impractical as himself, he said. I found his claims of being incapable of handling practical matters to be greatly exaggerated since he seemed handy enough when he needed to be.

"You found the fish," I said.

"I did, indeed. I have a little fellow in the fridge who will feed the three of us nicely. Stuffed with my wife's prize stuffing recipe and ready to be popped into the oven. You will drool when you eat it, but the secret of the stuffing will not be revealed to you in spite of your pleas. Not even the beautiful Zeolinda Madieras, for all her manifest charms, will extract it from me."

"Is that the recipe I gave Mattie last year?"

"I was afraid you'd remember that. Oh, well. Yes it is, so you know what to expect. Julienned beets and carrots on the side and white rice."

"Is that my julienned beet and carrot recipe?"

"Now that you mention it. But I got the rice recipe off of the box."

"Sounds like an excellent meal."

"It will be. Well, here's to summer and the end of another academic year."

We sipped our icy martinis.

"I take it that Jack Scarlotti and his gang got back to Weststock in one piece," I said.

"Indeed. I got a bottle of very good Scotch as thanks. Young Dr. Scarlotti and his crew apparently did some good work while they were down here and Jack was settled down to devote his summer to organizing it and getting the results published. I am to get a copy of the book for my collection. I can probably get one for you too, if you want it."

"What were they doing?"

"I never asked, but I dare say it will be of great interest to some people."

"I doubt if I'm one of them, but if you get an extra copy of the book I'll take it."

"Smart thinking, J.W." John glanced out of a window. "I do believe that Zee has arrived."

She had, indeed, arrived, and naturally she looked terrific. As John waved her through the kitchen door, I met her with a chilled martini for which I got a nice-tasting kiss.

"I may have succeeded in training you, after all," she said.

"You mean the bit about the hardworking woman coming home and being met by a clean house, her man, and a martini?"

"That's it." She sat down and crossed lovely long legs. I ogled them shamelessly. She smiled and pulled her skirt up another inch. Then, surprising me, she allowed a little frown to ripple across her face and pushed the skirt down again.

What was that all about? And what was it that made a glimpse of forbidden flesh more exciting than a beach full of bikini-clad nymphets?

"Very nice, Zee," said John, "but I'll thank you to keep your clothes on. My wife is two thousand miles away, remember, and if you keep adjusting that skirt I might have a spasm."

"Don't listen to him," I said. "Adjust, adjust!"

"It's splendid to have this power," said Zee without expression in her voice. "No wonder women rule the world." Then she pushed away any frown that might have been on her face and lifted her glass. "Good to see you, John."

"And you."

"I saw that beautiful young professor and his doting students the other day. His students seemed to adore him."

"The good ones mostly do," said Skye. "He drives them hard, but they like it. The youngest associate professor at Weststock. Were he and his gang any kind of problem, J.W.?"

"I never saw them while they were here. The normal dirty linens, dishes, and rubbish were here when they left. I found an earring, three stray socks that I added to the rubbish, and that backpack I mailed to its owner. I'd call them a pretty good crew."

We ate in the kitchen.

"Say," said Zee, "this is good fish, John. I think I recognize the stuffing. Jefferson's recipe, isn't it? And these julienned beets and carrots!"

"Simple, but delicious," said John, modestly.

"Let me guess. Cook a pound and a half of carrots and a pound and a half of beets, then peel and julienne them and mix them up and heat the mixture through with some butter in a frying pan. Right?"

"Hmmmmph," grunted John.

"They look good and they taste great and they're easy to fix! Terrific for a bit of color on the table at Christmas or Thanksgiving. Jeff showed me how to make this dish. Where did you learn it, John?"

"Have some rice," said John. "You'll love it. J.W. showed me how to read the recipe on the box. And have some more wine. J.W. had me bring it over from the mainland."

"What's for dessert?" asked Zee, with a laugh.

"Cognac. My own, by God!"

Over cognac and coffee John learned of Zee's August plans. He looked at me. "Seems that you'll be the only one left on the island, J.W. I'm headed for Colorado in August."

"There are worse places than this to be abandoned by your friends," I said.

"How long since you've been off the island?"

I thought about that for a while.

"Last fall," said Zee. "We went to a Red Sox game at Fenway. Remember?"

"That was it." I get off once a year or so. It's usually enough.

"They even won," said Zee. "That was an unexpected bonus. We had a good time. Beer under the stands, popcorn and peanuts, all the stuff you're supposed to do. We even met an old cop buddy of Jeff's. He was there with his wife and kids."

"Brad Tracey."

"Nicknamed Dick, naturally. He and Jeff got to talk cop talk for a while. His wife was nice. Two nice kids, too." Zee's voice changed tone when she mentioned Brad's wife and children. Zee was getting close to thirty and I wondered if she was hearing the famous biological clock ticking inside her and if that might be one of the reasons she was going off to conferences in New Hampshire. It didn't seem the time to ask her.

"If you can hold the island down until September," said John, "I'll be back to do some fishing before the fall term starts. The girls will have to be home early in the month so they can start school, but I'll have a couple of loose days."

"I thought you scholarly types never really had a day off. I thought you were always thinking and thinking."

"Hey," said John, "I have to think all winter. When summer comes, give me a break."

After supper, we went for a walk in the evening light. There was a lane leading south from John's barn. It ran along between trees on one side and a meadow of high grass on the other. A hundred yards along, John snapped his fingers.

"Oops. Gotta go back. Got to call Mattie. Don't get lost."

We watched him move back toward the house.

"I don't think he really had to call Mattie," said Zee. "I think he got a look at your face and decided we should talk."

"Could be. Should we?"

"Half of me says yes, the other half says to hell with it."

I had to smile. "Me, too."

"Well?"

"Well. Well, well. Well, so far I've asked you to marry me several dozen times and you always say not yet. Now you're going away for a month to find out what you want to do with your life. If you decide to go to medical school, you'll be gone for years and I wouldn't be surprised if you didn't come back at all. If you decide not to go to medical school, you still might not come back. I want you to do what you want to do, but I don't like the idea of being out of your life. That's it, I think. I don't want to be out of your life, but I think that's the way you're leaning. But if this is what you want, then I think you should do it. Life is too short to spend doing things you don't want to do."

"You sound bitter."

"I'm not bitter. I don't like bitter people and I won't be one. But I'll miss you and I'm afraid you'll leave the island forever. That doesn't make me bitter, it makes me unhappy. But I've been unhappy before and gotten over it, so my unhappiness shouldn't concern you . . ."

We walked through the dimming light down the sandy

lane. "Look," she said. "I'm almost thirty years old. I'm not a kid. I want things I don't have. I want a normal family. I want a job that I can live with all my life. I love being a nurse, but why shouldn't I be a doctor? I love being with you, but I want children . . ."

"Marry me and you can have all the children you can handle. Or if you don't want the marriage, you can still have the children . . ."

She took my arm. "You don't even have a job, Jefferson."

"I have a lot of jobs. I fish, I look after some houses . . ."

"And you're the envy of every man who works nine to five, but . . ."

"But what? Are you telling me I should start chasing bucks? Why? I'm doing just fine. I've never missed a meal."

"But I'm not sure you're really husband material. A husband has responsibilities. A husband has to make sure his kids grow up right . . ."

"A role model?" I didn't want to be a role model. One of the reasons I'd come to the Vineyard and lived like I did was because I was tired of being responsible for other people.

"Look at you. You live in an old hunting camp on Martha's Vineyard, you go fishing and shellfishing whenever you want, you grow a garden, you cook like a dream . . ."

"I chase after you . . ."

She squeezed my arm. "And you catch me, too. Anyway, you live this wonderful life of yours and it's right for you. But I don't know if it's right for me or for a family . . ."

"You come by every now and then."

She didn't miss a step. "You're a terrific guy and a great lover and the best friend I have, but I'm not sure you'd be as good a husband and a father."

I tried to imagine being the father of her children. It

didn't seem to be a bad job. I wondered if I needed to change in order to be a father. I thought of my own father and wondered what he would think.

"And there's something else," said Zee. "It has nothing to do with you, but it's important. I'm tired of being somebody's somebody. I want to be myself. When I was little, I was my parents' daughter, then I was Paul's girl-friend, then Paul's fiancée, then Paul's wife, then Paul's ex-wife, then my Aunt Amelia's niece, and now I'm your girlfriend. It's not just that other people think of me as somebody's somebody, I even catch myself thinking of myself like that, and I don't like it. And here's something that maybe does have to do with you. I'm tired of defining myself in terms of my relationships with men. I think we women do that all the time and I don't think that you men do it at all, or at least not very much. Do you think of yourself as my boyfriend?"

"Sounds good to me."

"Do you?"

"No."

"You think of me as your girlfriend, don't you."

"When I'm feeling lucky."

"There. You see? I'm tired of that. I'm going away to think about that. All of those things. The one conference is about work and the other one is about everything else."

"I don't have any chain around your neck," I said. "I don't make you do anything you don't want to do . . ."

"You are bitter."

"I want you to be free," I said. "I want you to be free and to choose to come back so I can have you in my life. I want you to choose that out of all the other choices you may have. But I don't want you to come back and feel that you've missed your life and I don't want you to come back because you feel sorry for me. I don't like people who feel sorry for me or for themselves and if you ever start feeling that way, I probably won't hang around. If

you choose not to come back, I want you to make that choice with joy, because it's what you want."

We walked on. After a while I noticed that it was dark. "We'd better get back," I said.

We turned and walked back up the lane toward the lighted windows in John's house.

Outside of John's door, we paused. Zee looked up at me. "Do you love me?"

"Yes."

"Will you love me if I go away in August?"

"Yes."

"Because I am going to go."

"I know."

She put her head against my chest and I put my hand in her hair and pressed her against me. I could feel my heart beating.

After a while we went inside to escape the night. John looked at us thoughtfully.

Long afterward, I wondered if, far away, someone else had been looking out at the same darkness, his soul cold, his feelings twisted, forming the plan which would, in not too great a time, lead him to stalk me through that curious moral jungle where manhunters seek their prey.

— 4 —

Three days after John's supper, I got word about when they were going to open the Edgartown Great Pond. This annual exercise is to insure that salt water gets into the pond so the shellfish there won't die. The opening through South Beach is dug by heavy equipment and for a while the tides sweep in and out of the pond, allowing the fresh

water to escape and the ocean water to run in. After not very long, Nature closes up the opening again, but by that time the shellfish are in good shape for another year. Since I do my oystering in the Great Pond, I have a personal interest in those shellfish. Moreover, while the opening is open, it is a popular place for fishing, since both bass and bluefish are attracted by the bait that is carried by the tides in and out of the pond. For reasons which elude me, the exact time of the opening of the pond is not widely publicized, and fishermen play games trying to be among the earliest at the new opening. This year my hot tip turned out to be true, and I was there at dawn when the bass showed up.

I didn't normally fish for bass since I don't hunt for fish I can't keep, and the minimum keepable length for bass that year was 36 inches, which meant that most of the ones you'd catch you'd end up throwing back. The minimum length rule was in force because for years the bass population had been declining and efforts were being made to bring the fish back. I also didn't like to keep the bigger fish because they're mostly the females who lay the eggs.

But this year I did a bit of bass fishing, so I could tag them and let them go again. It was part of an effort to learn more about the migratory and other habits of the fish. The tagging was simple and, according to the island's resident marine biologist, painless to the fish: You ran a needle, threaded with a strip of plastic printed with the address of the Littoral Society in New Jersey, through the fish's flesh just behind the dorsal fin, knotted the plastic, and let the fish go. You recorded the size of the fish and the time and place of the tagging and sent that informa-tion to the New Jersey address. If the fish was ever caught again, the person catching it could send the plastic in along with information about the size of the fish and the time and location of the catch.

Lest I give the impression that I am a dedicated law

keeper and environmental moralist, I should confess that if I catch a bass when I feel like eating one I keep it no matter what size it is. Unless someone is looking, of course.

I had tagged five bass running about two feet and weighing six pounds or so and had just recaught a particularly dumb one I'd tagged not an hour before, when I saw a blue Jeep Wagoneer coming west from Katama. I had decided that if I was doomed to recatch fish that I didn't want in the first place I would quit fishing, so my rod was racked and I was having coffee when John Skye drove up with Iowa.

Iowa got out and looked around. He was disappointed.

"Where the hell's Zee?"

"Working."

"Damned shame. Any fish here?"

"Small bass."

"Get any?"

"No keepers. Tagged some."

"Good enough."

He got his rod from the roof of John's Jeep and stepped down to the surf. Iowa would fish in a bucket if that was the only water around.

"What's Iowa doing riding around with you?" I asked John.

"His pickup is in the shop. Tore up his muffler at the jetties. He'll have his own wheels again tomorrow."

"Didn't bring his niece with him this trip."

"She's home with Jean. Kid's had a tough time, I understand."

"Somebody roughed her up. Boyfriend, I'd guess."

"How'd you know that?"

I told him about the bruises. "I figure she's here to either get over the bastard or decide to go back to him. Women have a hard time leaving these guys, sometimes." It was a truth I could never really understand.

"You hit it on the head," said John. "Guy living with

her lost his job and started beating on her. She took it for a while, then got out. Came here. Iowa's a favorite uncle."

"I see her walking the bike paths. She's looking better. She going to stay?"

"I don't think she knows, yet."

"The guy know she's here?"

"I don't know."

When I was a cop in Boston, I learned a lot about women and the men who beat them up. I knew that men beat up women here on the island, too, but I wasn't a cop anymore, so I didn't have to deal with it. I had had enough of cop stuff.

"Maybe she'll be sensible enough to shake him."

"Sometimes the men come after the women who leave them."

True enough. About half the killings you read about in the Boston papers are the result of turf wars or drug wars. A lot of the others are men killing the wives and girlfriends who want to leave them or who have left them and been hunted down.

"Let's hope she's smart enough to shake him for good."

John nodded and looked for a new subject. "When I saw your truck, I thought Zee might be here. I didn't know she was working mornings."

"Maybe she isn't. I haven't seen too much of her lately."

"Oh." John dug around in his Jeep and came up with a thermos and a box of doughnuts. He pushed the open box at me. I found what looked like a blueberry-filled doughnut and took a bite. Skye squinted at me. We chewed doughnuts. He swallowed the last of his. "Maybe you should get off the island for a while. Why don't you come out to Colorado with me? Different country. Change might do you good."

"Maybe so." I remembered flying over the Rockies long ago on my way to Vietnam. The mountains had been covered with winter snow and had gleamed white in the sun.

"I'm going out there early in August," said John. "I'll be back in September. Zee'll be back by then, too." He raised an eyebrow.

"Um."

John drank coffee for a while. "Well, if you don't want to go that far, maybe you'll do me a favor and drive up to Weststock with me when I go, and then bring my Jeep back down here."

I looked at him.

"Get you off the island for a couple of days, at least," he said. "We can drive up together. I have to pick up some gear at home, then I'll fly west from Boston. I want the Jeep here when I get back so I can get a little fishing in before I go back to slaving over hot students. You can stay in the house up there in Weststock after I head to Durango, if you want. Go into Boston to see a show or two. Whatever."

Weststock was close to the New Hampshire border. Zee would be there somewhere. My ex-wife was not too far away either. She and her husband and their little kids lived north of Boston in a suburb where fewer bullets flew than had been the case in the city when I'd caught mine and she had decided that she didn't want to spend her life wondering if I was going to come home at all the next time. The two most important women in my life would both be within miles of Weststock, but neither one of them would want to see me.

Still, John's offer had appeal. I hadn't been to America for quite a while. Getting away felt like a good idea.

On the other hand, the fish still filled Vineyard's waters, my garden was flourishing, and in a few days the annual used-book fair in West Tisbury would allow me to turn in the books I'd finished reading during the past year and get another year's supply. Books, beer, fish, and fresh veggies on Martha's Vineyard made a winning combination, one which had made an islander (howbeit a transplanted one) out of me.

"I'll drive you up and bring the Jeep back," I said. "I don't know about staying over. There are still a lot of fish around . . ."

"Good. You'll be helping me out."

I left them there and drove home, where I yelled at a bunny who was looking thoughtfully through the chicken-wire fence that surrounded my garden, and went inside just as the telephone rang.

It was Manny Fonseca, the Portagee Pistoleer. Manny had for years taken great pleasure in insulting the Wampanoag Indians who inhabit Gay Head. Then, to his dismay and his wife's great amusement, he had discovered that he himself had enough Wampanoag blood in him to be an official Native American. After he had recovered from the shock, he gradually stopped telling his jokes about "professional Indians" and being "ready to pull yourself into a circle if you go to Gay Head," and "Fort Wampanoag," and in their stead began to develop some "white eye" wisecracks.

"Hail, Chief," I said. "What's going on in the pre-Columbian community?"

"Gottum new firestick," said Manny, whose idea of tribal languages was primarily acquired from the comic books all of us had read in our youth. "Got an electronic dot reticle scope, too," continued Manny. "Brand-new. I'm headed for the club to try it out. You want to come along?"

Manny's profession was as a finish woodworker, but his avocation was pistol shooting. He shot up his share of the family entertainment money at the Rod and Gun Club target range and was greatly involved in the buying and selling of guns and ammunition. If it was new and interesting and had to do with shooting, Manny bought it. He was, in fact, an excellent combat pistol shooter.

I was not into the sport. I had had a brief experience with real combat in a faraway land and had not found it

sporting at all. On the other hand, I didn't have anything else to do at the moment and needed some distraction. Among other things, I might find out what an electronic dot reticle scope might be.

"I'll see you there, Cochise."

I got my earplugs out of the gun cabinet where I kept the shotguns and rifle I'd inherited from my father and the police .38 I'd carried for the Boston PD. I was still into a bit of duck and goose shooting in the winter, but my gunning seemed to be slackening off more and more as time went by. If I hadn't enjoyed eating the birds so much, I'd have given it up completely. Still, the guns in their cabinet were so much a part of the house that I'd never considered getting rid of them.

The Rod and Gun Club was within sound of my house. I could hear the guns popping there while I sat in my yard or worked in my garden, and had grown so used to them that I often did not hear them at all. With the key that came with my R and G membership, I let myself in through the locked gate to the club and waited at the new target range until Manny showed up in his shiny Ford Bronco.

He was wearing his shooting gear: a black belt with a holster on the right side and extra clips and other gear attached elsewhere. He got out a satchel and walked down to the table at the twenty-five-yard marker.

"How?" I said, holding up a hand.

"You foreigners will regret making fun of us original Americans," said Manny. "If my ancestors had had hardware like this stuff I'm carrying, instead of clubs and stone axes, you never would have made a beachhead."

"You're not original Americans," I said. "You're a bunch of Asians who came across the land bridge up in Alaska. You probably ran somebody out who was here before you were."

"Nah. We've always been here. Probably we went

across the land bridge the other way and settled the whole damned world. You're probably one of my descendants. Look at this."

He opened the satchel and got out a long-barreled pistol mounted with a lumpy-looking sight that looked too big for the gun.

"Llama M-87 Competition Pistol," glowed Manny. "Got your built-in ported compensator, got your beveled rapid-load fourteen-round magazine with your rubberized base pad, got your oversized safety and your fixed barrel bushing."

"No kidding."

"Better yet, look at that scope. Thirty mm tube, coated optics, adjustable click-stop rheostat so you can adjust your red dot, lithium battery power pack, polarized filter, filter caps, glare shields, and a 3X booster. Nifty, eh?"

"The Pilgrims should be glad you guys didn't have that in 1620."

"Bet your ass. Let's put up some target and see what happens."

We walked down and hung three paper targets on the frames in front of the dirt backstop.

"What's the advantage of this fancy sight, Tonto?"

"Simple. You put the red dot on the target and that's exactly where your bullet is going to go. Especially good in dim light."

"There are those who say you shouldn't hunt in light that's so dim you can't really see."

"What do they know? Besides, now you can do it just fine. Got night sights, for that matter. See in the dark."

"Modern technology is awesome."

"I loaded both clips at home. Let's pop some caps." Manny put on his shooting glasses and stuck plugs in his ears. He slid a clip into the pistol and jacked a shell into the chamber. He locked his right arm, cupped his left hand below and around his right, and the gun boomed. I

looked at the targets. There seemed to be a hole near the bull's-eye of the center one. A tiny red dot danced near the bull's-eye, then steadied. The gun boomed again. Another tiny hole near the bull's-eye. Another boom. Another hole.

Manny made a small adjustment on the sight. "Shooting right," he said in that loud way people have of speaking when they have muffled their ears. He raised the weapon in one smooth motion. The red dot bounced on the target and then steadied. The gun jumped and boomed. "Better," said Manny. He emptied the clip carefully into the target, jacked out the clip, and slid in a second one. He put the gun on safety and laid it on the table and we walked up to the target. There were fourteen bullet holes near the center. We covered them with tape. It didn't take much.

"You try it," said Manny. "Just remember that the red dot tells you where your bullet is going to go. Don't yank the trigger, just squeeze it."

I plugged my ears, put on my shooting glasses, and took up the pistol. The red dot danced all over the target. I steadied my arm and the dancing slowed. When the dot touched the bull's-eye, I squeezed off the shot. A bullet hole appeared six inches to the left. Not good, Kemo Sabe. Again the red dot touched the bull's-eye and again I fired. High. I fired again. Closer, this time. Eleven more shots. One in the bull's-eye. It took fourteen pieces of tape to cover the holes.

"Well," said Manny, "if it'd been a man, you'd have hit him most of the time."

"If it'd been an elephant, I'd have hit him every time."

"We don't shoot many elephants on Martha's Vineyard," said Manny, reloading the clips.

"There used to be mastodons or woolly mammoths or some such creatures out west before you red-skinned savages killed them all," I said.

"I think those other guys did that," said Manny. "The ones you say we ran off when we came over the land bridge. Here, try again."

We shot his new pistol for a while and then shot another one, since Manny always shot more than one pistol when on the target range.

Two trucks pulled up beside my Land Cruiser and Manny's Bronco, and guys with guns and satchels got out.

"I guess we've used up our time," said Manny. He put his guns and gear away. I put my earplugs and glasses in my pocket and got our targets. "What do you think of the scope," asked Manny, as we walked.

"I think that Crazy Horse or Sitting Bull or whoever it was that did in Custer had a bunch of them at the Little Bighorn."

"Red dot, red power," grinned Manny, raising a clenched fist.

I gave him some money for my share of the ammunition we'd shot up and went home. After lunch I went to the Eel Pond and spent an hour and a half on my hands and knees digging soft-shelled clams. When I had my bucket full, I went home and put them in a bigger bucket full of salt water, so they could spit out the sand in their systems. Tomorrow I'd freeze them. You can steam frozen clams just like fresh ones and never know the difference, and I always liked to have a batch on hand in case an irresistible clam boil urge came over me unexpectedly.

Manny thought digging clams was a nonsensical way to spend time. I liked it. He liked to shoot guns at targets. Everyone to his own madness, I say. Almost everyone, that is. Some madness can be fatal.

5

It was mid-July and hot when I discovered I had to actually go downtown into Edgartown. This is a venture I undertake in the summer for only the most serious of motivations, since the lovely, narrow streets of Edgartown are filled with tourists and jammed with cars and there is never anywhere to park.

But I was out of books and the big book fair in West Tisbury was still days away, so I had to make a run to the library to keep myself going. Normally I have at least one book to read, since I keep one in each place I expect to be. I have a bedroom book that I only read before sleeping, a bathroom book that I only read while on the throne (poetry here, since it comes in appropriately short slices), a kitchen book, two living room books, and a car book for traffic jams. However, a cruel fate had touched my life: I had finished all of these books within days of each other and was suddenly bookless.

So downtown I went.

Edgartown is so quaint and lovely, so filled with flowers and greenery, so fairylandish and make-believe, that pedestrians think that cars are just part of the scenery and the middle of the street is as much for them as for automobiles. They are surprised and even resentful when they discover some car attempting to occupy the street they are walking in while ogling the sights, and only reluctantly move to the brick sidewalks as the car inches by. Edgartown summer cops do their best to keep both drivers and pedestrians moving, and actually do a pretty good job of it by late summer. In mid-July, they are still a bit green and have a hard time untangling traffic, and need wise advice from the chief.

I found him, walking down North Water Street, Edgartown's classiest street as well as the location of its excellent library. This surprise was almost as great as the one I had experienced only moments before when a car parked right in front of the library had pulled out just in time for me to pull in. Shocking.

"You look pale," said the chief, "and I don't blame you. An actual parking place."

"Perhaps you'll take my arm and lead me to a chair before I faint. What brings you up to this part of town? Don't tell me that the weed of crime is bearing bitter fruit on North Water Street."

"The weed of crime in this case was a lady in that big house there who phoned that somebody was trying to break through the back door. It turned out it was her cat that she'd forgotten she'd put out, trying to get back in out of the heat."

"Your story has done much to make me feel more secure on these mean streets. How's the summer going?"

He wiped his brow and replaced his hat. "Be glad you've turned in your badge. We have more jerks in jail than I can ever remember having before."

In every community the size of the island's winter population, there are about twenty people who cause ninety percent of all the problems. They are the vandals, the drunks, the druggies, the car racers, the thieves, the people who rob their parents, who beat up women and children, who trash houses, who hate cops, and who never seem to change.

"If you'll give me immunity and a whole lot of money, I think I know some guys who will shoot the guys who are giving you most of your trouble," I said.

"Hell," said the chief. "If you could just move a couple of families off of the island, I could retire. How's Zee?"

"Fine, I guess. I haven't seen her for a while."

He nodded and his eyes floated down toward the four corners, where Main met Water Street. Many cars were

not moving there. A summer cop in traffic trouble. The chief tugged on his hat brim and started on down the walk to do his duty.

"Protect and serve," I called after him and turned to see Geraldine Miles coming down the walk from the library.

She was wearing a wraparound skirt and short-sleeved shirt, and the bruises were no longer apparent on her arms. She was tanned and looked happy. There was a man with her, a tall, strong-looking guy about her age wearing new summer clothes: Vineyard Red shorts and a white shirt that said "Frankly scallop, I don't give a clam." He carried a canvas beach bag. His face and arms were tanned, but his legs were still white.

She looked at me, reached into her memory and came up with my name, and smiled.

"J.W. How are things on the beach?"

"You're looking well," I said.

"I am well. I'm very well. I'd like you to meet Lloyd Cramer. Lloyd, this is J.W. . . . I'm sorry, but I don't think I know your last name . . ."

"Jackson."

"J.W. is a friend of Uncle Dan."

Lloyd had a mouthful of good teeth and a strong grip. There was a tattoo of a skull on the arm attached to the hand that took mine. There was a tattoo of a knife with a wavy blade on the other arm.

"Any friend of Dan's is a friend of mine," said Lloyd in a hearty, Midwestern voice. "Pleased to meet you, sir."

Sir. I was only six or seven years older than he was.

"You're new in town," I said.

"I wrote to him and he came all the way from Iowa City just to visit me," said Geraldine in a happy voice. "Isn't that sweet?"

Lloyd shuffled his feet and put his arm around her shoulders. "After she left home to visit Dan and Jean, I realized how important she really is to me, so I just took

some time off and came right here to tell her that. We've got a lot of things to talk about and we're having fun doing it. Isn't that right, honey?"

"That's right," said Geraldine, taking his hand. "We're getting everything straightened out. Isn't this weather just wonderful?"

I thought that right now Geraldine would feel that a hurricane or a blizzard was wonderful weather.

"I'll let you get on with your talking," I said.

Lloyd put out his big hand again and I took it in my big hand.

"Nice to have met you, J.W.," he said as he gave me his friendly smile.

"How long are you going to be around?" I asked Geraldine.

She looked up at Lloyd and smiled. "Oh, not too much longer, I imagine. I think maybe I'll be headed back to Iowa City soon."

Lloyd beamed down at her. "Great to hear you say that, sugar. Hey, let's hit the beach. I gotta tan up these legs before I go back home." He looked at me. "You got a really beautiful island here, J.W."

He showed me his fine teeth and she waved and they walked up North Water Street, headed, I guessed, for Lighthouse Beach. They looked like a happy pair. I hoped that it would last, but I didn't share the belief of many women that their men would reform if given one last chance.

I thought, Good luck to you, Geraldine Miles, and went into the library.

Libraries are some of my favorite places. They're filled with books and information and give you the good feeling that no matter how much you've read there's an endless amount of reading material still ahead of you, so you never have to worry about running out. It's a nice certainty in an uncertain world. I calculated the time left before the West Tisbury book sale, and got myself three

books, including one about the popular inclination of con-
quering armies to burn books and destroy libraries.

The idea of destroying libraries was one that irked me,
and it occurred to me that maybe I took the book because
I was already irked that Geraldine Miles had gotten back
together with Lloyd and irked even more that I hadn't
gotten myself loose from my resentment that Zee was
going off to New Hampshire. Reading of the destruction
of the great libraries of Alexandria and Constantinople
was only one more irritant in my irritated life. I apparently wanted an excuse to be out of temper. I turned this
notion over in my mind and was not pleased with what
it told me of myself. I went home and called the hospital
and invited Zee to supper. She accepted.

She was still wearing her white uniform when she got
out of her little Jeep. She inhaled as she came into the
house.

"Ah, another delicious meal from the kitchen of J. W.
Jackson."

"Indeed. But first this." I gave her a perfect martini
and waved her back out the door. We went up onto the
balcony and I put a plate of smoked bluefish pâté, Brie,
and saltless crackers on the little table between our chairs.

We looked out over the garden and Sengekontacket
Pond to the sound where, in the haze of the summer afternoon, sailboats were leaning with the wind as they beat
for evening harbors. Along the road between the pond and
the sound the cars of the beach people were pulling out
and heading home.

"I was beginning to wonder whether I was ever going
to get another invitation to come here," said Zee.

"It's been a while," I agreed.

"In fact, we haven't seen each other very much since
May."

"True. My nose has been out of joint ever since you
told me you were going away next month. I've been
sulking."

"But you're over it now?"

"Over enough to want to see you a lot before you go off on your pilgrimage."

"Good. Me too. You're really over it?"

"I don't like sulkers, especially when one of them is me. I want to make up for the time I've lost. I know I'll miss you, but I'm not mad about it anymore."

"Good." She got up and came around and leaned over and kissed me. I kissed her back. She went back to her chair.

We sat and drank and ate and looked across at the boats and cars.

"I doubt if New Hampshire is as nice as this," said Zee.

"Well, you can always come home early."

"No, I'm going to do it all."

"A woman's got to do what a woman's got to do. A manly man like me understands that. It's a kind of code you have to obey."

"You're so sensitive I sometimes wonder how you survive. What's for supper?"

"A simple but elegant Scandinavian baked fish served with little boiled potatoes and fresh beans from my very own garden. Madame will find it quite satisfactory."

"Tell me more."

"Normally the chef never reveals his secrets, but I know I can trust you to be discreet. You cook a bunch of sliced onions in a skillet with butter until they're soft, then put them in a baking dish, put a pound or so of fish on top, add a couple of bouillon cubes and cover the whole thing with a couple of cups of roux. Easy and mega-delish. I like to use fish with white meat best, by the way. Today you're having cod caught up off Cedar Tree Neck. First, though, another drink."

I brought more martinis and we worked our way through the hors d'oeuvres. I felt happier than I had in a while. When the time was right, I went down and got

supper going. At seven, we ate, washing everything down with a nice Graves I'd been saving. Zee ate everything in front of her, leaned back, and patted her lips.

"Yum. You have not lost the touch, François."

"Note my modest smile. If you will place yourself on the porch, I will bring the coffee and cognac."

She did and I did and we watched the night darken around the house. She put her hand in mine.

"I've got to go home," she said.

"Sad words for one who has plied the maiden with his best booze and food."

"I have to go to work in the morning."

"You can go from here."

"I don't have a clean uniform here, J.W."

"Wear this one."

"This one needs to be washed. It has smudges from when I helped today's first moped accident up onto a table where we could patch him up. No, I've got to go."

"I want to see you a lot before you leave."

She put her arms around my neck. "Why don't you come to my place for supper tomorrow?"

"Can I bring a clean uniform with me?"

She laughed. "Yes."

The next day, early, I was on East Beach looking for bluefish that weren't there. Coming back to Wasque, I found Iowa with his head under the hood of his pickup. Two small bluefish lay at his feet.

"Glad to see you, J.W. By Gadfrey, will you look at this? Broken radiator hose! What next? First a muffler and now this. I have to get me a new truck. This one's beginning to fall to pieces. Your truck there is even older than this one. How in blazes do you keep it going?"

"Good Japanese engineering. You should stay away from American machines."

"By Gadfrey, maybe you're right."

"Actually I use the ride-it-a-day, work-on-it-a-day technique. I spend a good deal of time underneath this mon-

ster. I'll give you a ride into town then bring you back out. Toss your fish in my box."

"Damned glad you came along. Not another soul on the beach. Thought I was going to have to radio for help."

We drove through the dunes and then along the south side of Katama Pond until we got to the pavement.

Iowa looked at his watch. "Let's go to my place first, so I can put the fish in my big cooler. Have a cup of coffee. By that time the parts place will be open."

Iowa lived out near the big airport. In the early morning, there wasn't much traffic, so we were there in pretty quick time. As we pulled into his driveway, Iowa cursed and said, "What's that son of a bitch doing here?"

There was a car with Iowa license plates in front of the house. As we stopped behind the car, I could see the front door of the house hanging open. Suddenly Iowa's wife came running out. Iowa caught her in his arms.

"What's going on, Jean?"

Her voice was high. "He's in there, Dan! He broke in the door and came right in! He went into her room! I've called the police, but . . . He's in there with her now. I think he's going to kill her!"

I didn't have to be told who "he" was. I turned Jean to me. "Does he have a gun? A knife? Anything like that?"

"What . . . ? No! I don't know! I didn't see anything, J.W. . . . I tried to stop him . . ."

Jean was small and in her sixties. Far away, I could hear sirens. I put Jean back into Iowa's arms.

"Get out to the road and make sure the cops don't go to the wrong place by mistake. Go on!"

"My shotguns are upstairs in my closet," said Iowa. "He may have gotten to them . . ."

"No," said Jean. "He went right into Geraldine's room!"

"Get to the road," I said and turned and ran to the house. I slowed at the door, listened, and went in through the splintered frame.

The grunting of a man's voice and the moans of a woman came from a room down the hall from the living room. I went down the hall and into the room. Furniture was overturned and a throw rug was wadded in a corner. Geraldine Miles lay across the bed while Lloyd Cramer knelt over her, his left hand on her throat, his right rising and falling, striking with sodden thumps against the bloody thing that had been her face. I thought I saw a bit of bone through the blood. With every blow he grunted and between grunts he cursed her with vile and unimaginative names.

He heard me and turned as I came in. His face was glowing with a kind of happiness.

"I got the bitch," he said.

I took him by a shoulder and his belt and jerked him away from the bed. He hung on to Geraldine's throat and brought her with him. I let go of his belt and hit him as hard as I could under the ear. He let her go and staggered back against a wall. I went after him and his hands came up. He was possessed by the strength of a sort of madness. He got hold of my throat with his left and hit me with his right hand, a punishing blow which I partially blocked. He was a big man and in good shape, so I jerked away and kicked him in the knee. The sound of the knee-cap dislocating mixed with his cry as he felt the pain. As he reached for his knee and started his fall, I grabbed his hair with both hands, jerked his head forward and brought my knee up into his face. His nose disappeared in a spray of blood. I brought my knee up again. Then, hanging on to his hair, I drove his face into the floor. He lay there and didn't move.

Geraldine Miles lay on the floor. Her face was making little red bubbles. I put a finger on her pulse. It was faint, but still there. I heard the siren die in the yard. I turned and kicked Lloyd Cramer in the head. A moment later, the cops were in the room. There was an older cop and a young summer cop.

"You'll need a couple of ambulances," I said, and kicked Lloyd again.

"Hey!" said the summer cop. "Don't do that."

"Aw, just one more time," I said, and kicked Lloyd again. "This is the guy who did that to her," I said, pointing at Geraldine. "I'll wait for you outside."

"That'll be all right," said the older cop, looking at the figures on the floor. He looked at the summer cop, who was getting pale around the gills. "Joe, go out and put in a call for two ambulances and another car. Tell 'em it's a Domestic."

— 6 —

"They flew them both to Boston by helicopter," said Zee. "I was on duty when they brought them in. It was pretty bad. Her jaw and cheekbone were broken. She may have a fractured skull. I don't know whether they can save her eye. She had some broken ribs and a broken arm, and she was bleeding internally. He had a broken nose and a dislocated knee and head injuries of some kind. They both had blood coming out of their ears. I never like that."

We were having a drink at her house that evening. Normally Zee didn't talk much about her work. Like a lot of doctors and nurses, she had learned to put her work away when she went home. Unless they learn to do that, many people in the medical game would soon become dysfunctional. They are like cops in that respect. Of course, also like cops, some of them can't put aside the sights they see and the things their work obliges them to do, so you're never surprised to learn of doctors and nurses on the bottle or taking pills or other drugs. It's a professional hazard.

I had calmed down a lot since morning and no longer regretted that I'd been wearing only sandals when I'd kicked Lloyd Cramer. I had spent some time reminding myself that I had quit the Boston PD because I'd had enough of trying to save the world. But there was a perversion in me; I still doubted if I'd be sorry if I'd been wearing steel-toed boots.

"Is she going to be all right?" I asked.

"I don't know. I think he will be. As right as he ever was, anyway. Why do men do that to women?"

I thought it was for the same reason I might have beaten Lloyd Cramer to death if the cops hadn't walked in. "I think we hate the things we fear," I said. "I think we're afraid that those things will win out, that they'll ruin our worlds."

"How could she have frightened him? It doesn't make sense."

"Somebody said it's transference. We transfer our fear to someone we can hurt," I said. "Cramer's world is a bad one for him, so he beat up Geraldine because he couldn't beat up his real world, the one that scares him."

"That doesn't make any sense."

"We don't make sense when we take symbols so seriously that we'll kill for them. When we kill you because you're Catholic or because you're a different color, we're all crazy. I think we're the same way when we die for the Cause. The flag, our country, whatever. Fear makes us do it."

"It sounds to me like you're saying we're all like Cramer. I don't think I am, and I don't think you are, either."

"I think all of us have that little monster inside us. Most of us keep it caged up most of the time, but when we feel threatened, the cage door opens. I know that every time I've been angry, it's been because something frightened me. I don't get mad at things I don't see as dangerous."

"You're waxing philosophic this evening."

"I'm the guy who sent Lloyd Cramer up to you in pieces. I guess I'm just talking it out."

Zee looked at me in surprise. "You did that to him? I never heard your name mentioned."

"I got there just before the cops did. Afterward I talked to Iowa and Jean, and Jean said that Geraldine had come home and said she'd argued with Cramer and decided not to go back to Iowa with him. I think that after a while everything built up inside of him and he came after her. I stopped him, but I don't know if I was in time . . ."

She put her healer's hand on my knee. "Let's put the subject away. If I'd known you were involved, I wouldn't have brought it up. I'm sorry."

"Me, too." We sat for a while, then I said, "How are the Red Sox doing?"

"Now there's another sorry tale," said Zee. "Don't you have anything cheerful to talk about?"

I narrowed my eyes, wet my tongue, and licked my lips. "How about your primary and secondary erotic zones?"

She grinned and her hand patted my knee. "Now, now. You haven't had supper yet. I think you're probably too weak to even think about such things. I don't want you to hurt yourself. Get us more drinks while I start on the cooking and maybe we can talk about it later when you've got your strength up to a satisfactory level."

I got it up to a proper level later in the evening.

The next morning Zee went off to work and I hung around to wash up the breakfast dishes and make the bed before heading home. As I drove through West Tisbury I stopped at the general store and got a *Globe*. On the other side of the street was the field of dancing statues. I crossed and went walking among them, looking for a new one but finding the old ones quite adequate. As usual, they cheered me up. They told me not to take myself too seri-

ously, that life was comedy, that the universe was an ode to joy and whimsy in spite of death, in spite of pain, in spite of chaos. I heard the song of birds and saw them flashing through the trees. The wind stirred the grasses, and clouds floated across the blue sky. I willed Lloyd Cramer out of my life and felt better for it.

Too soon, as it turned out. At noon I heard the phone ringing as I was picking veggies (lettuce, radishes, a tomato, and a small zook) for a luncheon salad. It's always a toss-up whether I can get from my garden to the phone before it stops ringing. It rang again before I decided to try to get it. I put down my basket and galloped into the house. The chief was on the other end of the line.

"Just thought you'd like to know that Cramer signed himself out of the hospital this morning. He's gone and the last thing anybody heard him say was that he was going to get you and the bitch both. I've arranged for a guard to stay outside Geraldine Miles' hospital room. Do you want one too?"

"The guy's got a wrecked knee. How dangerous can he be? Besides, they're sure to pick him up before he can get here. Even Boston cops should be able to capture a man on crutches."

"Yeah, if they wanted him for anything. Right now, there are no charges against him. He could be anywhere by now."

"If he comes here, he'll have to come by plane or bus, and he'll be easy to spot and remember. Crutches and a face wrapped in bandages and all. His car's still down here, isn't it? And he can't drive it anyway, if his knee's no good. You going to call Dan and Jean Wiggins? Cramer might have a grudge against them, too."

"I did that already. They'll keep their eyes open and I'll have a car swing out that way every now and then."

"Well, you don't have to have a car swing out by my place. Thanks, anyway."

The chief rang off and I went out and got my veggies. I brought them in and washed them off and cut them up in a largish bowl. I added some salty olives and feta cheese I'd found at the A & P Deli, laced the works with some good olive oil and just a tad of vinegar, and *violà!*, an excellent Greek salad appeared. I ate it with home-made Italian bread and washed it down with a couple of bottles of Dos Equis, Mexico's best beer. International cuisine. Nothing like it.

That evening, I showered and got into my go-to-town clothes—a blue knit jersey with a little creature over the pocket and Vineyard Red shorts, both found almost new in the thrift shop, and boat shoes without socks. I know a guy at the yacht club who, on racing days, wears his captain's hat with scrambled eggs, his blue blazer and tie, his gray slacks and boat shoes, and a red sock on his left foot and a green one on his right, symbolizing port and starboard. I was not so formal because I was only going out to eat, not out to watch the races.

At seven, Zee's Jeep came down the long, sandy road to my house. She got out wearing a pale pink summer dress that perfectly set off her deep tan and long blue-black hair. She was dazzling.

"You're dazzling," I said.

"You look pretty Vineyardish yourself." Her teeth flashed between lips colored to match her dress. She came to me and put her face up and I kissed those lips, then licked my own as I looked down at her.

"We don't absolutely have to go out," I said.

"Yes, we do! I don't often get an offer to eat at the restaurant of my choice and you're not going to weasel out of taking me. So let's go to Edgartown. You can romance me later."

"Not a really bad idea. Food first and then lust. It worked like a charm last night."

"You have a long memory, Babar. It's one of the things I like about you."

We ate at the Shiretown, where I've never had a bad meal. Rack of lamb for me, salmon in a croissant-like crust for Zee, washed down with very satisfactory wine. Coffee, brandy, and a chocolate torte for desert. The bill came and I paid with cash. Zee stared, aghast.

"All that?"

" 'Farewell, paternal pension,' " I said. "But it was worth it." The J. W. Jackson criteria for judging restaurants are three: good food, reasonable price, and good service. If I get two out of three, I'm content. If I get three out of three, I'm in heaven. If I get one or less out of three, I figure I got ripped. That goes for every kind of place, from a hot dog stand to a four-star restaurant. I explained all this to Zee.

"Gee," she said, "what a sophisticated thinker you are. Tell me, have you ever actually been to a four-star restaurant?"

"I saw a picture of one once in the *Globe* food pages. Does that count?"

"Close enough for the likes of us," said Zee. "Let's go walk on the docks."

We did that, looking out at the lights of the anchored yachts and at the house lights on both sides of the harbor. Summer people were in the streets behind us, looking in shop windows and doing business at the ice cream stands and the clam shops. Zee's arm was in mine.

"It really is a beautiful place, isn't it?" said Zee.

"Yes."

"You can see why all these people come here."

"Yes."

"I'm going to miss all this."

"New Hampshire is beautiful, too."

"I know, but . . ."

"But it doesn't have an ocean? Yes it does. Down by Portsmouth."

"It doesn't have one where I'm going in the mountains."

"No, I guess not."

"I'm going to miss you, too."

"Good. The more, the better."

We walked up to North Water Street and then out to the Harborview Hotel, where we leaned on the railing beside the street and looked out toward the outer harbor. The Edgartown lighthouse flashed its endless message to the sea. There were lights on Chappaquiddick and stars and a sliver of moon in the sky. After a while, we walked back, got in the Land Cruiser, and drove to my house. The next morning Zee ran naked out to her Jeep and brought back a shiny clean white uniform.

"Smart," I said, reaching for her. "You nurses are smart."

She danced away. "Don't do that! This is my only clean uniform! Get away! I've got to go to work!" She ran around the room, snatching up pieces of her underwear. Then she stopped suddenly and put up her lips. I kissed them and slid my hands down her sleek brown body. "I really do have to go to work," she said a little breathlessly.

"I know." I held her a moment longer, then let her go and stepped away. She pushed a hand through her thick, tumbled hair, looked at me thoughtfully, sighed and smiled, and went into the bathroom to ready herself for the day.

I saw her almost every day for the rest of the month. We fished in vain from beach and boat. We fought the friendly crowds at the West Tisbury book fair and later those at the Chilmark library book sale. We brought home treasures from both. We went shellfishing and hit the Saturday morning yard sales. Then one morning she drove her little Jeep onto the early morning ferry to Woods Hole, and the world which had seemed such a good place was now, of a sudden, weary, stale, flat, and unprofitable.

For two days I fished in the fishless sea, made complex meals which were tasteless in my mouth, and tested previously untried beers which I found as flavorless as water.

On the second night after Zee left, the phone rang. It was John Skye.

"Well," he said, "my bags are packed and I'm ready to go. I've got a reservation for the seven o'clock boat tomorrow morning. You still want to come up to Weststock with me?"

"I'm ready to roll," I said.

— 7 —

It takes forty-five minutes for the ferry to cross the sound between the Vineyard and Woods Hole on the mainland. By eight o'clock the next morning we were in the line of traffic emptying from the boat and headed for Falmouth. From there we went north to the Bourne Bridge over the Cape Cod Canal and finally fetched 495 North and drove toward Weststock, which lies northwest of Boston and not too far south of the New Hampshire border.

It was a foggy, warm, damp day on the island and I was glad to be elsewhere. The ride in John's nice, new blue Wagoneer was smooth as a baby's behind and the countryside rolled past us like a motion picture image. It was quite unlike the rattle and bang of travel in my rusty Land Cruiser. "As we drove north, the fog and haze of the shoreline were left behind and we came out into bright sun. There was a lot of commuter traffic on the highway, but it moved along at its normal ten-miles-above-the-speed-limit pace and after a bit we were out of most of it. Green fields and trees flowed by us.

"I've got a luncheon meeting," said John. "At Weststock we like to clothe our business meetings with food whenever possible, since it seems to be true that food hath charms to soothe an academic breast, to soften deans, or

bend a knotted prof. Personally, I'd probably be more cooperative after a cocktail or two, but some of my colleagues get spiteful and too honest for their own goods when they tipple, so we eat instead of drink. Probably it's for the best. The drinkers can always meet later down at the Duke of Ellington, and usually do. Anyway, the meeting will probably last for a couple of hours, so I thought you could drop me off at the college and then go on up to the house and get yourself settled in."

"Sounds okay to me."

"Of course, if you'd rather come to the college, I'm willing to pass you off as a visiting scholar. You can walk the ivied yards and ogle the women like the rest of our younger colleagues."

"No thanks. I'll go to your place and then maybe take a stroll around town. It's been a while since I was up here."

"A wise decision. This evening, I'll take you to supper at the Duke and afterward we'll go upstairs to the Higher Realm and play some poker with the chaps."

"My poker-playing skills are pretty rusty."

"You'll be in good company. Most of the gang who play are good scholars but terrible poker players. They leave their brains in their briefcases and are easy picking for guys like Lute Martingale. You'll meet Lute tonight, if you decide to play. He's a sort of permanent part-time teacher and grad student here, but actually supports himself playing poker with rich undergraduate kids who've had a floating game on campus for as far back as I can remember. As long as you don't let Lute sucker you into a big pot, you'll be okay. The rest of us are suckers."

"Sure."

"You can trust me, I'm a professor!"

Two hours after leaving Woods Hole, we turned off 495 and drove north into Weststock, a lovely little village nestled near the large mill towns along the Merrimack River but untouched by the grime and smudge of those once

thriving industrial centers. Instead of great abandoned mills and rows of sagging tenement houses, Weststock's winding streets were lined with clean brick homes, white houses with flower gardens and green lawns, and small stores catering to the college community which dominated the town.

The college itself was a Georgian collection of brick and frame buildings built around yards and scattered with green playing fields. It had been established almost two hundred years before by enterprising New Englanders who thought they could produce a college at least as good as Harvard and Yale and who had been right. Weststock College was much smaller than either of its famous rivals, but bowed to neither in its claim to academic excellence, particularly in the liberal arts. It was, in fact, almost idiosyncratic in its insistence upon studies which, in John Skye's words, "taught its graduates nothing whatever which would help them earn money," but which nevertheless produced notable figures in the humanities and theoretical sciences.

It was not quite my kind of place, but it was ideal for John. I followed his directions to the college building of his choice and accepted the key to his house.

"I'll walk home after this is over," he said, getting out. "I'll see you there, probably about three or so. Stick the vodka in the freezer. Your room is the one in back, by the garage."

"Gotcha."

I drove across the campus, looking at the summer students in their shorts and sandals, books under their arms, small packs on their backs. Some walked the brick sidewalks, some sat on benches; others lay on the green lawns, books and satchels beside them. They talked, studied, lazed, and looked young and healthy. I tried to remember what it had been like to be that age.

One reason that it was hard for me was that when I *had* been that age, I'd been going to, living in, or being

shipped back from Vietnam. I'd come home after a very short tour with some metal in my legs, the gift of a Vietnamese artillery man or mortar man who had lobbed a shell right next to me while I was blundering around in the dark looking for his friends. Even now small pieces of the metal occasionally worked their way out of my skin. I hadn't gone to college until I was older, and when I had gone, it had not been to so pastoral a campus as this, but to Northeastern University in Boston, where you combine work and study as you go. My work had been as a Boston cop. It had all happened quite a while back, and none of it had happened in places as pretty as Weststock.

I turned up Main Street and drove up the hill past the town center, where youthful buyers were spending their parents' money in neat shops—clothing stores, bookstores, record stores, eating emporiums, furniture stores, and stores selling expensive objets d'art and decorations for the abode of the modern college student or academician. Weststock had long since bowed to economic reality and unabashedly directed its sales to the members of the college community.

Similarly, it had politically more or less given up the notion of town versus gown identities, although there were, of course, still a few hostile locals who felt oppressed by the college and whose youths occasionally engaged in fisticuffs with Weststock boys or, better yet, struck an even more wicked blow at Privilege by dating and mating with college girls. Lingering manifestations of this division were two bars which catered almost completely to clients in the particular camps. The Millstone was the bar of choice for townies, and the Duke of Ellington was the college pub. Some of the town's most famous fights had started when members of one group accidentally or purposefully entered the wrong bar. This had resulted in the hiring of large bouncers who now guarded the doors of the establishments.

John Skye, naturally enough, attended the Duke of

Ellington, whose owner, Morey Goldthorpe, was an ex-teacher of English literature. All descent English teachers, John had explained, secretly want to own a pub. Not just a bar, but a pub in the English tradition. And not just a pub in the English tradition, but a pub in the English tradition *as it ought to be,* not as most English pubs actually are. That is to say, it should have broad beams in the ceiling, should serve drawn beer, should have a dart board, chessboards, and dominoes, and should be a place where a man or woman could have a companionable pint without risking reputation, life, or limb. Morey Goldthorpe, unlike most other dreamers of pubbish dreams, had actually quit teaching and bought a bar which he had then transformed into the Duke.

Over the mirror behind the bar was a large sign announcing that drunks and loud arguments were not allowed, and that the management reserved the right to forbid service to anyone who disliked real ale. Instead of television, the Duke of Ellington, as its name and the namesake picture on its sign suggested, offered live jazz five nights a week. The Duke's clients were not obliged to listen to the music, but those who did not received silent frowns of protest from the regulars. If you liked jazz, you could come and listen even if you were a townie. Morey could not refuse service to a jazz fan.

Upstairs were the Goldthorpe quarters and two rooms known as the Higher Realm to which only members of the college faculty and their guests were allowed admittance. This undemocratic practice was Morey Goldthorpe's bow to his past profession and was strictly enforced. Weary professors could escape from their students and others by withdrawing upstairs to a private bar, a lounge, and several oak tables at least one of which served as the site of the faculty game, an illegal poker game such as the undergraduates' famous floating game, both of which the police overlooked because no one ever complained about them or admitted that they really existed.

I drove past the Duke and, two cross-streets later, turned left onto the avenue where John's large frame house sat back behind a large lawn and flower beds. I turned into the driveway, parked, and got out my bag. It was a clean, comfortable, tree-lined street of faculty homes. In the hot summer sun, the shade of the lofty trees was welcome.

I went inside and down a hall and found my room. The house was old-fashioned and had many fireplaces. There was one in my room with an ancient gas burner disguised as a log. The kind you lit with a match after opening a valve. I hadn't seen one of those in years and didn't even know they still had them. Only an antiquarian like John Skye would have such a thing in his house.

One thing I didn't need on an August day was a fire in the fireplace. I opened a window to air the room out and had just put the vodka in the freezer when the phone rang. It was John Skye.

"I was in Weststock but my brain must have been in Colorado," said John. "I left my briefcase in the Jeep. Can you run it down here for me? There's a secretary just inside that door I went in. She'll shuttle it on to me. Fifteen minutes?"

"Fifteen it is."

"You're a good man, Charlie Brown."

I locked the door and went out to the Jeep. It was a beautiful day, so I decided to walk to the campus. I got John's briefcase and stepped along. I wondered if a passing stranger would take me for a professor. Did professors wear pink button-down shirts found in the thrift shop? Did they wear chino shorts and Teva sandals without socks?

The test would be in the town center. When I got there, nobody paid any attention to me. Was this a good sign or a bad one? I wondered if I would appear more professorial if I grew a beard. What kind? A little pointy one or a big bristly one? Maybe just a moustache.

I walked through the town center and slanted across the road to enter the college campus. There was a nondescript blue car quite a way up the street, but I had plenty of time to cross before he got there. When I was about halfway across I heard the roar of an engine behind me and a simultaneous scream from a girl on the sidewalk I was approaching.

"Look out!" she screamed, and put her hands up to her face.

I turned, saw the grill of the car filling my vision, and dived for the gutter. Something touched my foot and tumbled me, and John's briefcase went flying. Then I was on the pavement, rolling, and looking at the rear of the car as it careened on its way. I caught a glimpse of a youthful face glance back at me. The face wore dark glasses and was topped by a mass of yellow hair. Then I was rolling some more and hitting the curb.

The girl who had screamed came across the street and other people, students all, I guessed, came running.

"Are you all right?"

"I think so."

"You're bleeding!"

True. Some skin was missing from my knees, calves, elbows, and hands. A shoulder hurt. I eased slowly up into a sitting position. I moved various parts of me. Everything functioned. "I'm okay," I said.

"You're bleeding!"

"I need a couple of Band-Aids."

"The infirmary is right over there," said a young man. "Should you try to walk?"

I got up. The young man and a young woman put their hands out as though to catch me should I fall. "I think I'm fine," I said. "Did that guy stop?"

There were confused replies.

"I thought it was a woman!"

"No, it was a guy with a weird wig. Or maybe hair down to here."

"I never saw his face, but the son of a bitch kept going! We should call the cops! What an asshole!"

"You'll get no argument from me," I said. "Would any of you recognize him if you saw him again?"

"I'd recognize that wig!"

"It wasn't a wig, it was a woman!"

"No, it wasn't!"

"How about the car?" I asked. "The license plate?"

There were shakings of heads and angry noises.

"Here, sir. I think this is yours." A boy handed me a Teva. The car had knocked it off my foot and he had found it down the street. I put it back on.

"Here. It didn't even open." The girl who had screamed handed me John Skye's briefcase. She looked pale.

"You saved my life," I said. "Thanks."

"Oh, I was so scared!"

"You should go to the infirmary, sir," said the young man who had pointed it out. "You should let them check you out and get some bandages on those abrasions. You're bleeding all over your clothes."

True on all counts. I looked at the girl who had screamed. "What's your name?"

"Amy Jax."

"You're a student here?"

"Yes."

"Amy, you've already saved my life, but I want you to do me another favor." I pointed to the building John Skye had entered. "I want you to take this briefcase through that door and give it to the secretary you'll find there. Tell her it's for Professor Skye." I gave her the briefcase. "One more thing," I said. "Lean forward."

She leaned and I kissed her forehead. "Thanks again, Amy Jax."

She actually blushed. Hands clapped approvingly around us. Amy went away with the briefcase and I allowed myself to be conducted to the infirmary by one of the young men who insisted on calling me "sir." Zee would have

said I looked like another moped accident and she would have been right.

After I was bandaged up, I did the right thing. I went to the police station and reported the incident. The guy behind the desk wrote everything down and said they'd certainly look into the matter. I suspected that he was a townie who probably wasn't too sorry that an obviously academic type like me had gotten bunged up a bit. On the other hand, maybe he was an old Weststock grad who probably wasn't too sorry that an obvious townie like me had gotten bunged up a bit. In either case, I was more work for a department that probably already had enough to keep it busy.

I smiled at him and limped out.

— 8 —

When I left the police station, I barely had time to get home and change my clothes before John was scheduled to some strolling in. I put on socks and slacks and a long-sleeved shirt to cover various bandages and got myself a drink, which I downed while walking around John's fine old house. I was getting a little stiff in the joints and hurting in small ways I hadn't noticed earlier. My hands were sore and I was also feeling a bit ethereal and shaken, the way you sometimes do after the danger is over. America was as risky a place as I remembered it being.

I got another drink and went into John's nice big library. Thousands of books, comfortable chairs with good reading lights, a worn oriental rug, a big, battered desk with a brand-new computer on it signifying that John was entering the twentieth century just as it was ending. I opened a book about Mencken and immediately read that

human existence is always irrational and often painful. Very Menckenish, but I didn't need to be told that because I'd just experienced the proof. I put the book back and tried a little John Gay. Gay, I learned, had written his own epitaph: "Life is a jest, and all things show it. I thought so once, and now I know it."

Cute. A footnote informed me that Gay's monument was in Westminster Abbey and that the *Dictionary of National Biography* considered the words on it flippant. Irreverent to the last, eh, John? I read some more.

A bit later, the phone rang. It was John Skye again.

"Hope you weren't wondering where I've been. Damned meeting went on for hours. Just as well, because if we'd cut it short, we'd all have had to continue it tomorrow. This way, we're done today! I don't think I'll bother to come home right now. I could use a drink. Why don't you meet me down at the Duke?"

"Why not? See you there."

I went out into the summer afternoon and walked downtown. The air seemed clean and good. I was very careful crossing streets. By the time I got to the Duke, I'd walked some of the stiffness out of my knees and hips. I knew that it would come back during the night, but I also knew that sooner or later it would go away for good.

It was about five o'clock. John was standing at the bar with a glass of dark beer in his hand. A tall, thin man was talking with him while nursing a glass of whiskey. He was one of those people who might be in his twenties or his forties. When I came up to them, the man looked at me with a gambler's deadpan eyes.

John smiled. "Lute, meet J. W. Jackson. J.W., meet Luther Martingale. Morey, a pint of bitter for Mr. Jackson!"

I shook Martingale's hand. It was smooth and strong. I wondered if he sanded his fingertips. Martingale placed a smile on his face. When he did, it made him look almost innocent.

"I've heard about you," I said. "I've been advised not to get in any big pots with you."

"My enemies are everywhere," said Martingale. "Don't listen to them."

"Part of that is true," said John. "He does have enemies everywhere. Mostly people who still think the poker money he won from them is rightfully theirs. Some folks just can't get it through their heads that once they toss their money into the pot, it's not theirs any longer."

"If it weren't for the lambs, the lions would starve," said Martingale.

My beer arrived. Martingale lifted his glass. I got a whiff of its contents. Scotch. "To the lambs," he said.

We drank.

People were beginning to fill the place.

"If we eat before the crowd gets here, we might even find a table," said John.

"Another round first," said Martingale. "On me."

"What the devil did you do to your hands?" asked John, noticing my missing skin for the first time.

"A funny thing happened to me on the way to your office," I said, and told them about my near miss on the street.

"Good God!" said John. "You really are all right?"

"Lost a little skin, is all."

He shook his head. "Mattie says that'll happen to me someday if I don't pay more attention to traffic when I walk to the office or back home. She claims that I am a classic absentminded professor and that someday after a truck runs over me, my last words will be 'Who was the Green Knight, really?' I think you deserve another drink, my boy. Morey! Another round!"

We drank to my survival. I was beginning to feel better. As the sign behind the bar said, Malt does more than Milton can, to justify God's ways to man.

Graduate students talking of things academic and otherwise continued to come into the bar. The noise level

gradually rose. John lifted a hand to someone across the room. I turned and saw Dr. Jack Scarlotti sitting at a table with the attractive young woman I'd seen with his group on Martha's Vineyard. Waitresses and waiters began to move among the tables. A second bartender appeared. We finished our round and found a table in a corner.

"Popular place," I said.

"It's the beer," said John. "Imported from Jolly Olde. Damned fine."

"Indeed."

"Good food, too. Pub fare. Simple but filling."

"And better than you get in most pubs in England," said Martingale, surprising me since for some reason I'd never imagined him being in England. "You might go to Britain for the beer, but you'd never go there for the food."

We ate chicken pies with fine crisp crusts, tossed salads with a nice house dressing, and bread that tasted homemade. Not bad. John and I washed ours down with beer. Martingale drank white German wine. He saw me looking at the bottle and smiled. "You don't go to Britain for the wine, either."

He was hard to dislike, but hard to like, too. There was an elusive quality about him. He looked at John.

"You hear about Bernadette Orwell?"

John shook his head. "What about her?" He shoveled in a bite of salad.

"OD'd. Fatal. Just about the time you left for the Vineyard."

John stopped chewing and looked at Martingale. Then he swallowed and put his napkin to his lips. "No. I knew she was a little flaky, but I didn't think she was that strung out. Too damned bad. Very bright girl. She was in one of my classes year before last. I liked her."

Martingale nodded. "Rumor is that somebody dropped her. Hard. Unrequited love. Very sad, they say."

John frowned at him. "Are you telling me that Bernie Orwell OD'd because somebody left her?"

Martingale lifted his wineglass. "No. I'm just passing on gossip. I like gossip."

John dropped his eyes and stared at the table. "Well, damn," he said after a moment. "I like gossip, too. Sorry to get this piece, though."

I thought of Bernie Orwell's white powder and pills, and of her joy in Jonathan, who was beautiful and brilliant, and able to make her tremble at the very thought of his touch.

"I believe I just saw a couple of the lambs going upstairs," said Martingale. "Shall we join them in a small game of chance?"

John finished his beer. "Yes. I was having a good day until a minute ago and I'd like to get back into it."

We went upstairs to the Higher Realm. Three men and a woman were already seated at a table. There were poker chips in front of them and a few in the middle of the table. Five card stud seemed to be the game. I was feeling the drinks I'd had.

"Dealer's choice, nickel ante, two-bit limit," said John. "You don't have to lose much, but you can drop a few bucks if you want to. Let's sit in." We sat and John waved an arm around the table. "J.W., here are some of the great minds of the Western world. First names only, so you don't get confused. Tom, Mike, Dick, and Mary. This is J. W. Jackson, just up from the Vineyard and ready to have his features plucked."

A waiter arrived, took orders, and went away. A bit later he came back with drinks. I stuck with the excellent bitter drawn from the cellar. I noticed that Lute Martingale shared one habit with me. We both folded early and often. Once I caught him looking at me as I tossed them in. A little smile played on his face.

My father had taught me a few simple rules for poker. Don't stay with less than openers, don't stay if you're

beaten on the board, lose now and then when it's cheap so people will think you're a bluffer, drive people out if you've got a so-so hand that can be beaten by a lucky draw, suck them in and then stick it to them when you've got the cards, but act surprised when you win. The math of poker is easy, he'd said, but the real players go beyond the math and play the players. In games played when I was in the service, I never lost a lot in any game and made money overall. Some other people made much more and a lot of other people lost much more. On balance, I didn't consider myself a real player.

When the jazz started downstairs, I was still holding my own, but finding it harder, thanks to several additional pints of beer. Martingale, John, and Mary had made some money and the other three were losing. I found myself yawning and then almost losing money in dumb ways. I pushed back my chair and stood up.

"Folks, I'm just a sleepy country boy and you city slickers are taking me for every dime. Stay right there, John. I expect you to win back my money for me. I'll see you in the morning."

"You okay?" asked John. "You seem to be listing."

"There are worse things than listing," I said, straightening.

John looked at his cards. "Well, I must admit that these beauties make me want to stay a bit longer. We usually break up about eleven, so I'll be home then. You can find your way in the dark?"

"Eyes like a cat," I said. I made my farewells and walked carefully down into the music. A drummer was working his way through a *Caravan* solo. It took him almost ten minutes. After the other players got back into the song and wound it up to justifiable applause, I headed home. When I crossed the street I was quite wary, but no blue cars came at me out of the dark.

The warm night air cleared some of the cobwebs from my brain, but after I let myself into the house and got to

my room, I was suddenly weary again. Beer fatigue. I took two aspirin, the Jackson wisdom for helping to ward off a hangover, got out of my clothes, turned out the light, and hit the sack. I think I must have gone to sleep instantly.

I had strange dreams. I was sick. Someone was shouting in a tongue I could not understand. Great wailing noises and roaring sounds beat into my ears. Then there were slapping sounds. Slippity-slap, slippity-slap, slippity-slap. I didn't like any of it. Then someone started to whack my face. I tried to get my hands up to stop the blows. Slippity-slap! Slippity-slap! Slap! Slap! Slap!

"Stop that!" I said. "You stop that slapping! I didn't do anything to you!"

But the slapper didn't stop and the roaring didn't go away, so I tried to turn my head and get away, but I couldn't, so I tried to hit the slapper. "Get away from me!" I said.

Then the roar became words. "Wake up! Wake up! That's it, my boy! That's it!" I got my eyes open just as a hand lightly slapped my cheek. John Skye's face floated out in front of me. "That's it," he said. "Can you see me, J.W.?"

I nodded. His floating face smiled and became more three-dimensional. Then I saw that it was attached to his body, as was the hand that presumably had just slapped me.

"You're okay," said John. "Just lie there and breathe deeply."

I lay there and breathed deeply. I didn't feel well, at all. After a while I noticed that I was lying outside, looking up at stars in a black sky. I turned my head and looked around. I was on John's front lawn. There were firemen coming out of the house. John was sitting on his heels, looking at me. The lights from his front room windows touched his face.

"How are you feeling?"

"Better."

"I never should have let you come home alone. You were drunker than I thought."

"How did I get out here? I thought I went to bed." I looked down at my body. It was covered with a light blanket. I lifted the blanket. It was me, all right. I don't wear nightclothes. "I really must have been drunk," I said. "Are you telling me that I stripped and went to sleep right here?"

"No, no. You made it to bed all right. But when you were kicking off your sandals, you kicked one clear across the room and hit the valve on the fireplace. The whole house smelled of gas when I got home. It was coming out from under your door. I got in there and closed the valve and dragged you out here. Then I went in and opened up your window and every other window in the house and came out here with you. I figured the whole place might go up any second."

I looked at the house. My mind was pretty fuzzy. "Still there," I said.

He nodded. "Yeah. All aired out now, too. No damage done, after all." He stood up and went to talk to a fireman. The fireman looked at me, shook his head, and walked to the street where other firemen waited by a fire truck with a red, swirling light. They got in the truck, turned off the light, and drove away. People in other houses stood on porches and looked at us. John waved to them and came back to me. "I told them you were fine," he said. "Are you?"

I sat up. My head ached. "I owe you one," I said. "Glad your game didn't last any longer."

John smiled grimly. "I see now why they keep you chained up on that island. You're a danger to yourself up here in the real world. I'm not going to let you wander around alone after this."

"It's not been my best day," I said. I wrapped the sheet around me and put up my hand. John pulled me to

my feet and we walked into the house and down the hall to my room. The window was open, and warm night air was blowing in.

"I suppose I should get rid of that antique fireplace," said John. One of my sandals was lying by the valve. "I don't think you could hit that valve again if you tried,' he said. "And why you didn't have the window open on a warm night like this beats me. It only shows you the power of booze, I suppose. Maybe God is giving you a message about your drinking habits."

It wasn't the first time I'd had too much to drink, but it was the first time I couldn't remember what I'd done. I couldn't believe it.

"The window was open," I said. "And my sandals were right there by the bed."

John smiled. He went over to the fireplace and got the sandal and put it with its mate beside the bed. "Now they are," he said. "Get some sleep. I think you need it."

It was good advice, I thought. I looked at my watch. It was well past midnight. A new day. The previous one had been hard on me. I was glad it was gone.

The next morning I got up feeling not too bad. I went to the window and leaned out, breathing in the cool, clean air. In the soft soil of the flower garden below the window were the prints of shoes. At the time I thought they belonged to some fireman who had been checking things out the night before. I was wrong.

— 9 —

I was stiff and thickheaded, and my scratches and abrasions were sore. But I was alive, so things could have been worse. The aroma of breakfast floated down the hall from the kitchen and I followed my nose to juice, coffee, toast, sausages, and eggs. Your classic high-cholesterol American breakfast. I wolfed it down and after another couple of cups of coffee felt better.

"Some fireman squashed a few of your flowers," I said.

"Hey," said John, "I'm out of this state this afternoon on the two-thirty plane. By the time I get back, a lot of my flowers will probably be in that great greenhouse in the sky." He squinted at me. "You have any plans after you drop me off at Logan? You sticking around up here for a while, or heading right back for the Vineyard?"

"I thought I might drive up to New Hampshire, but I've changed my mind."

"Zee?"

"Yeah. She didn't go up there to be with me. I guess I'll head back for the island. With stops at various stores on the way, of course, to load up on stuff at mainland prices."

"But of course. Tell you what. I haven't exactly lied about it, mind you, but I've dropped a few hints that I'm going back down there myself. This Colorado trip is a little secret of mine. I don't want any phone calls from the college telling me I have to be back early because of some crisis or other. If they call the Vineyard, they'll get no answer." He shoved a paper across to me. "Here's my mother's address and telephone number. If you really have to get in touch with me, you can do it there. Pick

up my Vineyard mail, if you will, and forward anything that looks important."

"Your secret is safe with me. And I'll keep an eye on your place and your car."

We washed the breakfast dishes, made the beds, and closed the windows. John gave me the rest of the eggs, juice, bacon, and bread. Then we put our gear in the Wagoneer and I drove us over to 95 South and on into Logan International.

We shook hands and John got out with his bag and headed inside the terminal. I drove to Boston through the tunnel and found the hospital where Geraldine Miles was being treated. I went in only to be told that Geraldine was in the operating room having some part of her put back together again. I left a note, then got onto the Expressway South, and headed for the Cape.

By the time I got to Woods Hole and found a place in the standby line to the Vineyard, John's Wagoneer was bulging with booze, food, and other goodies I'd purchased on the way. I'd saved myself a pretty penny. A man might be able to make a living by contracting with Vineyarders to go to the mainland in a van every now and then and buy them stuff that was overpriced on the island. What island stuff wasn't overpriced, after all? He could charge a pretty good fee and the islanders would still get their stuff cheaper than they could buy it on the Vineyard. I ran this old idea through my head for a while and discarded it. I didn't like shopping that much. Besides, somebody was probably already doing it. Enough people had thought about it, certainly. People were always trying to figure out ways to live cheaply on the Vineyard, and there weren't many new ideas left.

I got on the last boat. Last car on, last car off. Perfect timing. I drove to my place through the night and unloaded my treasures, stuffing the freezer and filling shelves. I thawed some of last winter's scallops and got some rice going. Then I chopped some veggies, including plenty of

onions (since onions improve any dish except dessert), and some green peppers, stir-fried the veggies and scallops, and poured the mixture over a plate of rice. A bit of soy sauce and . . . Delish! I found a bottle of Rhine wine in the fridge and had a few glasses while I ate my late night supper. Some lingering scent of Zee was in the air and the house felt lonely, but I'd been lonely before. I went to bed and read until I got so sleepy that my eyes hurt. Then I went to sleep.

In the morning I discovered a dilemma: I wanted to leave John's Wagoneer at his house, but I didn't have a ride home. I thought of Manny Fonseca, who always went home for lunch. I phoned him at his shop.

"Hey, Red Cloud, how about swinging by John Skye's place at noon and giving me a ride home?"

"Us noble Native Americans are always willing to lend a hand to strangers in our land even though it gets us nothing but trouble. I'll be by about twelve-fifteen."

"May your tribe increase."

It was almost eighty degrees, hot by Vineyard standards, and the wind hadn't come up, so it was sticky. I weeded the garden for a while, before it got even hotter, then stripped and lay in the morning sun with the first beer of the day, perfecting my tan. If a low-flying plane filled with beautiful women flew over, would it circle before going on? Would anyone parachute out? The plane didn't show up.

At eleven-thirty I climbed into shorts, sandals, and a tee shirt that said Ban Mopeds on Martha's Vineyard, and drove the Wagoneer to John's farm. I parked the Jeep on the east side of the house, away from the prevailing southwesterlies, and checked things out. Barn and corrals were okay, so I walked around the house. The windows were locked and nobody had tried to get in the doors. I unlocked the front door and walked through the house. Everything was fine. I went back outside. The foundation of John's house was made of large granite slabs. The out-

side door to the basement was one you got to by opening wooden doors that slanted against the foundation and going down some steps made of smaller granite slabs to the basement door. I opened the outer doors and started down the steps, thinking that Manny Fonseca would be arriving at any time.

I noticed an odd red dot on the door beside me as I stepped down. It seemed to move toward me and my heart jumped and I dived down the steps.

Wood exploded over my head. I dug out my set of John's keys and frantically tried to find the one for the basement door. I tried a wrong one, then the right one, and was inside in the darkness slamming the door behind me. My heart was thumping and I was gasping. I quieted myself down, groped for the stairwell, found it, and ran upstairs. I listened. No sounds in the house. I ran silently to John's bedroom, unlocked his closet, and got out his 12 gauge Savage. Shells were on a top shelf. I stuffed the magazine full and went to a window. I stood to one side and looked out. Nothing outside. I listened. Nothing inside. I went to the library and looked outside. Nothing. I moved from room to room, looking and listening. Nothing. The outside door to the basement was under a window in the dining room. I looked out and saw that a corner had been blown off the door. I looked beyond the lawn and into the trees. Someone had been there waiting for me with a weapon with a laser scope. If I hadn't been thinking of Manny Fonseca, I wouldn't have recognized the dot of red on the door. I felt light-headed and leaned against the wall.

No time to be scared. I looked out at the trees. Maple and oak and pine, with undergrowth that made good cover for someone who knew how to use it. I looked for what seemed a long time and saw nothing. Then I heard a car coming down the driveway.

Manny Fonseca was driving right into trouble he knew nothing about. If the shootist was just potting whomever

he saw, Manny might be next. On the other hand, maybe he was only after me. If I went outside to warn Manny, I'd be a target again. Maybe if I stayed put, I could get a shot at the guy before the guy got a shot at Manny. On the other hand, maybe I couldn't.

There was no right thing to do, but Manny was an innocent party. I glanced at the trees and saw nothing. I ran to the front door and threw it open and ran to meet Manny's Bronco as it came into the yard. As I ran, I waited for the bullets to come through my ribs.

— 10 —

No bullets came. Manny saw the shotgun in my hand and was quick on the uptake. He slammed on the brakes and threw open the passenger door as I came up. I was inside while he was still moving.

"Get us out of here, Crazy Horse!"

Manny spun the Bronco, sending grass and sand flying, and we roared back up the driveway between the trees. I looked for red dots, listened for bullets coming through breaking glass or thumping through steel. I stared ahead and on either side and through the back window, but saw nothing. I heard nothing but the scream of the Bronco's engine. Then we were on the pavement and Manny spun the wheel and sent us racing toward Edgartown.

Parked under the trees on the side of the road was a blue two-door sedan. No one was in it. I caught a glimpse of the license plate. New York. I got the last three digits.

As we passed it, I looked back and saw no rifleman leaping from the trees, no movement around the car, nothing. I looked some more. Still nothing.

"Okay, Hiawatha, slow down. The bad guys are gone. Was that car there when you went in?"

"Yeah, it was there. What the hell was going on back there, J.W.?"

I told him what had happened. I was shaking.

"Damn! We'd better get the cops!"

"An excellent suggestion."

We drove to the almost new Edgartown police station beside the fire station. The chief was downtown looking after his summer cops, but after a radio call for him went out, he was in his office in five minutes. I told him my tale. I could hear a little tremble in my voice. He looked at my bandages.

"You okay? You look a little banged up."

I had been thinking. "I got these scratches up at Weststock. There may be a tie-in."

"You can tell me about it later. Right now we'll get some men up to John's place and see if we can nail this guy." He sent cars out to the farm and called the communications center. He put out a description of the blue car and asked that its driver be held for questioning. He was very efficient.

"I'm going out to John's place," he said, getting up and grabbing his hat. "You come along, J.W., so you can show me what happened. You may as well bring that shotgun so you can put it back where it belongs."

"How about me?" wailed Manny, who constantly complained that he never got to do anything really interesting. All the wars had been fought without him, and the wild West had long been tame before he'd been born, let alone before he had discovered that he was an official Wampanoag.

"He probably saved my neck," I said to the chief. "When the guy heard Manny coming, he must have taken off."

"Okay," said the chief, heading for his car. "Come on. Now what about that tie-in between this and Weststock?"

As we drove, I told him about the hit-and-run accident. "A blue car something like the one outside John Skye's driveway. I don't know if it was the same one because I didn't get much of a look at it in Weststock."

"So that's where you lost that skin. You file a report with the Weststock police?"

"I'm deeply hurt. I used to be a cop. Remember?"

"You act like a damned civilian."

"I am a damned civilian."

"I'll give them a call when we get back to the station. Maybe they know about the guy or the car . . ."

"This is probably just paranoia," I said, "but there is one other thing." I told him about the incident with the gas fireplace. As I talked, I began to calm down. Anger began to replace fear.

"You admit you were drunk," said the chief. He put on the siren.

"I've been drunker. I walked home, got undressed, and went to sleep. I didn't close the windows and I didn't kick my sandal into the fireplace and I sure didn't stand in John Skye's flower bed."

"Or so you say."

"You bet so I say."

"When we get to the house, stay in the car. We'll check the place out and then you can come in."

"The guy's long gone, Chief."

"Stay in the car."

We came to John Skye's driveway. The blue car was gone. We drove down the driveway and found two more police cars ahead of us at the house. Cops were walking around looking at things. Two of them were looking at the outer cellar door. The chief got out, talked to his men, and went into the house. After a while, he came out again and beckoned. Manny and I got out of the car and joined him and the other cops.

"Show us what happened," said the chief.

I told them what I'd done while I'd been waiting for

Manny and then took them to the cellar door and showed where I'd seen the red dot. I told them how I'd been thinking of Manny and recognized the dot and ducked, and how the wood blew up behind me. When I finished with the rest of it, the chief turned and surveyed the woods behind us. He looked at a middle-aged cop. "Morgan, you and Soames check out those woods. Any other deer hunters here? Okay, you two go, too. See what you can find."

A State Police car came down the driveway and a corporal got out and came over. The chief filled him in. The corporal went over to the door and looked at the splintered corner.

"One explosive round? A burst? How many shots did you hear Jackson?"

"I don't know," I said. "More than one, I think. Maybe just one. I wasn't counting. I know I heard the first one."

The corporal grunted and looked back at the trees where the Edgartown men were starting their search. "Came from back there, all right." He turned back and looked at the door and the granite foundation slabs. "Slugs should be about here." He walked to the foundation and knelt and peered at the stone for a while. "Yep, here's where they hit. Not much left. Looks like about 9mm. A pistol, maybe? Quite a long shot for a pistol."

"A pistol is easier to hide than a long gun," said the chief.

The corporal grunted assent. "There's a million different guns in this country. Some of the pistols you can buy have barrels ten, twelve inches long. Shoot straight at considerable distance. You know the difference between the sound of a pistol and a rifle, Jackson?"

I was feeling dumb and getting tired of it. "Somedays, maybe. Not today. I saw the red dot and ducked. All I wanted to do was get inside the house before the guy with the gun came up and tried again while I was down that

cellarway. I didn't try to figure out what kind of a gun he was using."

"Why do you think it was a guy?"

"Because I do. Maybe it was a girl. Usually it's guys who shoot."

"You got a girlfriend?"

"Yeah."

"She mad at you?"

"She's up in New Hampshire. You can ask her yourself."

"Maybe her hubby's the one who's mad at you."

I put my face closer to his. "She doesn't have a hubby."

He was beginning to enjoy himself. "Her boyfriend, then."

"Take it easy," said the chief. "I know the woman. You're barking up the wrong tree."

"Yeah? Well, maybe so, maybe not. Somebody's sure as hell mad at this guy." The corporal looked at me. "Unless, of course, you just made this up."

"You're sharp," I said. "I had everybody fooled but you."

"How'd you get yourself all banged up?"

"Protecting a state trooper from a mad Brownie scout. He was trying to give her candy outside her schoolyard and she caught on to him. Guy looked a lot like you, in fact. I made her give his gun back to him."

"You did, eh?" He bunched his shoulders. His face was red.

"Yeah."

"Hold it," said the chief, stepping between us. "Hold it right there. J.W., you take that shotgun inside and put it back where it belongs. Corporal, let's have a look back in the trees."

The corporal and I exchanged glares. I felt suddenly childish and turned away and went into the house. I unloaded the Savage and returned it and the shells to their proper places. From an upstairs window I watched the

policemen move in and out among the trees and undergrowth.

There was a telephone beside John's bed. I looked at it, then sat down and phoned the fire department in Weststock. When the phone was answered, I gave my name and said, "The night before last you sent at least one truck to a house belonging to Dr. John Skye on Academy Row. Problem with a gas fireplace. I want to talk to the fireman in charge of the operation. I'm the guy who may have caused the problem."

"Hold on. You want to talk to Scotty." I heard hollow-sounding voices speaking. A minute later a new voice came on the phone.

"Scott Wenham."

"J. W. Jackson. I'm the one John Skye hauled out of his guest room night before last. You guys came then and made sure everything was okay. I have one question. Did you or any of your men have occasion to go outside of the room where the fireplace is located? Did any of you stand outside of a window and maybe look in as part of your work?"

"No sir. Our work was all done in the house. Nobody went around back."

"You're sure."

"I'm sure. Dr. Skye had shut the valve and opened the windows and doors before we got there. We just made sure there were no leaks or fumes left. How are you feeling today?"

"Fine," I lied. "Just fine. Thanks for your help."

I rang off and thought about things. As the man said, "Once is happenstance, twice is coincidence, three times is enemy action."

I went downstairs and outside. The police were gathered around a clump of bushes. I found a space in the circle. In the center of the circle, grass was flattened where someone might have been lying down.

"If you lie down there," said the chief, glancing up at

me, "you get a clear view of the house, but they can't see you. Back there in the woods we got some footprints coming in and going out. About a size nine shoe. Maybe a boot. We'll take casts. Guy came from a car parked out there and he went back to it. He came slow and went back fast. Figure it was the blue car you and Manny saw."

The corporal opened a beefy hand. In it was a plastic bag holding three shells. "Found these," he said. "You own a 9mm weapon?"

"No."

"Maybe you borrowed one."

"Maybe I borrowed a set of size nine feet at the same time."

The corporal looked down at my twelves. "Well," he said, "if it wasn't you, it must have been somebody else. You got any enemies?"

"Just two," I said. "You and maybe a guy named Lloyd Cramer."

"Who's this Cramer?"

"He's a guy with a sore knee and a busted face."

"Cramer's the guy who beat up Dan Wiggins' niece," said the chief. "J.W.'s the guy who, ah, held Cramer until the authorities could get there."

"Oh, yeah?" said the corporal. "I think I heard that story." He almost smiled. "Maybe I just changed my mind about you, Jackson."

"To know me is to love me," I said.

"I don't know you that fucking well. This look like Cramer's work to you "

"The chief says this shooter hurried back to his car. I don't think Cramer could manage that. In fact, I don't think Cramer can bend his leg enough to drive a car."

"Maybe he hired somebody to do the job."

"Maybe. But could you find yourself a hired gun if you were a stranger on Martha's Vineyard? Cramer's from Iowa, for God's sake."

"Maybe he hired him in Boston," said the chief. "After

all, Cramer got out of the hospital several days back. He had time to make some contacts."

"Same problem," I said. "Cramer may be a turd, but he's no professional criminal. I doubt if he knows any of the Boston pistoleers. If you were Cramer, could you find a shootist to come down here and pop me off?"

"I doubt it," said the chief.

"I could," said the corporal.

"That wouldn't surprise me," I said. "But if this guy wanted to shoot me, why didn't he do it at my place? That makes more sense. If I was going to kill me, I'd scout my place when I was gone, maybe stand behind a tree until I got back and pot me at my leisure. I wouldn't have come sneaking through the woods to do it here."

"Spread out, boys," said the chief to his men. "See if you can find anything else."

"There's something else," I said to the chief, and I told him about my telephone call to the Weststock fire station.

The corporal frowned at us. "What are you two talking about?"

I told him my Weststock story.

"You mean you think this guy tried for you twice up there before he tried for you down here?"

"Somebody stomped John Skye's flowers right under the window to his guest room. It wasn't a fireman and it wasn't me."

"So you think it was this same guy. He came in through the window, saw you drunk in bed, and decided to let the gas fireplace do the job? Put your shoe over by the valve, left, and shut the window behind him. All without waking you up."

"Maybe. It almost worked."

"This guy must really want to kill you."

I'd been wondering about that. "I don't think so," I said. "I think he wants to kill John Skye."

The chief looked at me quickly. Then, just as quickly, he raised a brow. "You could be right. It makes sense out of some of this."

The corporal nodded. "Yeah. Could be. The guy's got it in for Skye, but doesn't know what he looks like. That's kind of odd, but it wouldn't be the first time a guy tried to hit somebody he'd never met. Guy finds out Skye's coming up to Weststock for a meeting and waits for him. Sees you pull up in Skye's car and go into Skye's house. Thinks you're Skye."

"Yeah. Then he sees me walk down toward the college carrying a briefcase and decides to get me right there in the street. If it works, it's just an accident. But it doesn't work, so he tries again that night. Seems to me like he must have been inside Skye's house sometime before I got there."

"Yeah," said the chief. "He could have scouted the place out while John was down here and his family was out west. That would explain how he knew about that fireplace. Thing that saved you was that he didn't expect anyone else to come home later that night."

"Maybe he was one of the people watching the firemen save the house," said the corporal. "Anyway, yesterday morning he knows he didn't get you, so he follows you down here."

"I made a lot of stops on the way," I said, "and he must have seen a lot of me here and there. But he decided to wait until we got on the island. Probably figured to get me last night while I was asleep. But when I got the last place on the last boat last night, he had to wait until this morning to come over."

The corporal grunted. "Guy knew or found out where Skye lives here on the island. Why didn't he just drive down and wait for you to show up?"

"Because he thought I was already here and would recognize his car?"

"Yeah. Maybe. So instead, he parks on the road and walks through the woods and makes himself cozy in the brush and waits for his shot. What does that tell you?"

"That he's not a city slicker," said the chief. "And that he got here after J. W. did, not before. Otherwise, he'd have shot a lot earlier."

"Yeah. Guy knows how to move in the woods. Came here and made his nest without Jackson hearing or seeing him."

"I was probably inside the house. If I'd been outside, maybe I'd have seen him."

"Maybe," said the corporal. "And if you did, he'd probably have seen you too and shot you on the spot. Sounds to me like maybe he spotted Skye's Jeep on the highway and followed you to the driveway and walked in after you. We got too many 'maybes.' We'd better call Weststock and have them take casts of the prints in the flower bed, if they're still there, and check the house for signs of B and E. If those casts match the ones we'll get here, we'll know we're doing more than guessing. I think we'd better get after that car pretty hard."

"I'll see how that's going," said the chief, moving away toward his car.

"Guy hasn't had time to get off the island," said the corporal. "We have a good chance of getting him, if he hasn't just abandoned the car."

"Which is what I'd do," I said.

He nodded. "Me too. But maybe somebody will see him do it and we'll get a description of him. One good thing: without a car, he'll be on foot. Less mobile."

"If you find his car, maybe it will tell you who he is," said Manny.

"Everybody's a cop," said the corporal. "I know that I wouldn't try a hit and run in my own car. Stolen, probably. We'll contact New York and see if they can help us out. You watch your ass, Jackson. This guy is still out there and he still thinks you're Skye."

He walked away. I looked at Manny. "Exciting times on Martha's Vineyard. You'd better call Helen and tell her where you've been. She'll think you fell into a band saw or something."

"Damn! You're right!" He headed for the house.

An hour later, I was back at the station. Manny had gone reluctantly back to work. The wheels of island justice were turning, and there were a lot of them. It is one of the absurdities of Martha's Vineyard that on an island with a permanent population of ten thousand, there are at least ten different police agencies: six town police forces, the Sheriff's Department, the State Police, the Registry of Motor Vehicles, the Environmental Police, and probably one or two I don't know about. All of these were looking for the blue car and its driver, who was presumed armed and dangerous.

"What a summer" said the chief, sucking on a cold pipe and reaching for a tape recorder. "Now, what do you remember about the guy driving the car in Weststock?"

"Not much. Youngish face, maybe thirty. I have a hard time telling how old people are these days, what with everybody trying to look younger than they are." I reached into my memory, but found very little. "A white guy. Tanned skin. Yellow hair. Shades. That's about it. The kids who saw the incident couldn't agree about much. I got the impression from what they said that the yellow hair might be a wig. Shades and a wig make a fast, easy disguise."

"You get the names of any of those people?"

"Just one. Amy Jax."

"And you think this blue car might have been that one, too."

"I think so. I couldn't swear to it."

"Okay. I'll have somebody drive you home. You think you'll be okay there? If not, I'll have an officer hang around with you for a while."

"I'll be fine. If the guy thinks I'm Skye, there's no reason he'll come looking for me at my place."

"Yeah. Now you may know John Skye better than I do, so tell me, why would somebody want to kill him?"

"I have no idea at all."

"He never mentioned anything that might give us a lead? A woman? Gambling? An argument with a neighbor?"

"Not a thing. With Mattie and the girls he's got all the women he wants or can handle. He plays a nickel-ante poker game where he couldn't win or lose much if he tried. I've never heard anyone say a bad word about him."

"A mad student he might have flunked? Some colleague who lost a committee vote somewhere along the line and blames John?"

"I don't know, but I doubt it. John's not the type to strike fire in people. He's a mild guy."

"Save me from mild guys," grumbled the chief, sucking his pipe.

I thought of Bernadette Orwell's journal entry. In the beginning, John Skye was a wonderful, wonderful person. By the following fall, Jonathan was beautiful and brilliant and she trembled at the very thought of his touch. That didn't sound too mild.

"You going to try to contact John and tell him what's going on?"

"No," he said. "Not yet. So far, we're just guessing. Besides, we may nab this guy before he gets off the island. If we do, we'll know what's really going on. You're right when you say that a guy after Skye probably wouldn't come looking for you at your place. But what if the guy really is looking for you?"

"The only guy who might be looking for me is Lloyd

Cramer, and Lloyd's not going to be in shape to do me much damage for a while. I can look after myself, so don't plan on having one of your summer kids watching over me. If it turns out that I do need to protect myself, I don't want to have to worry about protecting your guy, too."

"Famous last words," said the chief. "I'm going to have people keep an eye out for Cramer anyway. If he comes onto the island I want to know about it, and I'll let you know."

A young cop drove me home. She was very careful about her driving and very serious when she asked me if I was sure I didn't want her to stick around. She had a pistol at her belt which meant that she had taken the training and passed the tests which allowed her to carry the weapon. I thanked her and said no and she drove carefully away.

No assassin was waiting inside my house or in my shed or in my woods. I unlocked the gun case where I keep my shotguns and the rifle my father used for deer hunting in Maine. From a drawer at the bottom of the case I got out the old .38 I'd carried when everybody else in the Boston PD was opting for .357 Magnums. I'd bought the pistol cheap from a young cop who was moving up in firepower. I fired the weapon only once while on duty and it had done its job even though it was a mere .38. Like most cops, the kid who bought the Magnum never had occasion to draw his weapon. I hoped he never would.

I loaded up the revolver and went out and put it under the seat of the Land Cruiser so I'd have it in case I met the guy in the blue car while I was on the road. It struck me as a melodramatic act, but then again, people didn't try to kill me very often and I felt rather melodramatic.

I needed to think, so I got my rake and basket and headed for the quahogging grounds. Quahogs are hard-shell clams which you can eat in a lot of excellent ways: as littlenecks on the half shell (with just a touch of lemon

or seafood sauce), as clams casino (broiled with a bit of garlic butter and bacon), as stuffed quahogs (Euell Gibbons' recipe is the best—next to my own, of course), or in chowder. There's not much bad about quahogging. Preparing them is pleasant work, eating them is joy, and raking them is a time for leisurely thought.

I was after chowder makings, so I drove down to Katama, turned east over the sand, and drove all the way to Pocha Pond, on the southeast corner of Chappaquiddick, where, for reasons known only to the Great Quahog in the sky, there were no little quahogs but only big ones. How the big ones got big without being little first is a cosmic mystery whose answer I do not expect to discover until I reach that Beautiful Clam Flat with Sands of Gold.

I saw no man in a two-wheel-drive blue car trying to follow me in my four-wheel-drive Land Cruiser. Even if he had somehow prevented me from noticing him, he would have been in sand up to his hubs as soon as he left the pavement, so I felt secure.

I put on my shellfishing hat, the one with a picture of a helicopter on the front and my shellfishing license pinned to the side, and waded out into Pocha, rake in hand, basket-in-inner-tube in tow. It was an hour before low tide, so I could get a long way out, where the big ones grew. When I got there, I began to rake. I rake in circles, pivoting until I've covered the ground all around me, and then moving a few yards away and doing it over again. In an hour I can usually get a basketful and during that same hour I can think without interruption and perfect my tan. Not bad.

I ran various things through my head. None of them made sense to me. One problem was that I couldn't see John Skye as the type somebody would try so systematically to kill. On the other hand, I'd never thought of him as wonderful or beautiful, either. But then, how much do we really know about even our close friends? How much do they really know about us? We all have private, even

secret, selves which we do not share. We all have dark parts of our lives, little shames, if nothing else, which we keep to ourselves. All of us, perhaps, have given offense, some of which we may not even be aware. All of us, perhaps, have committed at least petty crimes. Dostoyevsky was not the only one to note that there is little difference between prisoners and prosecutors. Perhaps some act of Skye had provoked these assaults on his life. Perhaps I had nearly died because of Skye.

Of course, the hunter could be after me. I wondered whom I might have so offended. Cramer? Or an agent of Cramer? Who else?

A few things were fairly clear. The hunter was systematic about his work, not merely a killer on impulse, as are so many murderers who, once the moment of rage has passed, are as confused by their acts as anyone else. Skye's nemesis, or mine, as the case might be, wanted his victim dead, was willing to stay at the job, was good in the woods, and possessed the sort of weaponry most people, including most killers, don't have.

What did he do for a living? How was it that he could spend so much time hunting his victim? Most people have jobs that would prevent them from going off for a week or two to kill somebody. If they did leave, they'd be missed. Or fired. This guy apparently had both time and money.

Was he a car thief? Most people wouldn't know how to steal a car unless the keys were left in the lock. All of us have heard about jump-starting or wiring ignitions, but how many people actually know how to do it?

Not many.

If he wasn't a car thief, where did he get the blue car? Where would I get one, if I wanted one to use in a hit and run?

When my basket was full of quahogs, my brain was still pretty empty. I drove back to Edgartown and went to the police station. The chief and the corporal were there.

"Well," said the chief, "I see you're still alive, at least. Any new ideas?"

"Only two old ones," I said. "Cramer is not the guy. It's somebody after Skye, all right."

— 12 —

The corporal had a cigar in his mouth. It was unlit, but he had a match in his hand. He looked at me over the flame. "How do you figure?"

"The same way you two do. If Cramer was after me or had hired a hit man, I wouldn't have been attacked up in Weststock, because Cramer or his man wouldn't have known I was there. I didn't know I was going myself until the night before. Ergo, it was somebody after Skye."

The corporal lit his cigar. "Keen thinking," he said.

"I was really dumb before I met you," I said. "But you're so smart that it oozes out of your pores and guys like me get smart just by being near you."

The corporal blew a stream of smoke in my direction. "We called Iowa City, Iowa. They called back. Cramer is back home. His mommy is taking care of him."

"We called Weststock, too," said the chief. "They don't have anything on the hit and run, but they'll see if they can get a cast of the footprints in Skye's flower bed and get back to us."

"You'll be famous soon," said the corporal. "The *Gazette* has already called us."

"How'd they find out about this?"

The corporal feigned innocence. "Keep a shooting quiet? When you got local cops with local friends? You got to be kidding."

The local cops crack caused the chief to bite down hard

on his pipe stem. "I doubt if any of my people tipped them off, Dom."

"Somebody did."

"Yeah."

"What did you tell the reporter?" I asked.

"That shots had been reported, that nobody had been hurt, that the police are investigating. The usual. Of course, they'll be back, looking for the details."

"If they get them all, the shootist can read all about how he almost killed the wrong guy. Then he can start looking for the right guy."

"We thought of that all by ourselves," said the corporal. "Maybe you called them. Get the guy off of your ass and onto Skye's."

"You read me like a book, Dom. I figured that once he knew about me, he'd leave the island. Then you'd be off the case and some real policemen could get on it and maybe we'd have a chance of solving it."

Dom inhaled his cigar and seemed to grow larger. His face got a little red, as it tended to do when he was annoyed.

"You're a real convivial couple," said the chief. "You want to call each other names, you do it somewhere else, not in my office! I've got work to do."

"What was the reporter's name?" I asked.

The chief looked at his notes. "Patterson. New guy. Don't know him."

"Neither do I."

The phone rang. The chief picked it up and said, "Yeah." After a while, he said, "Did he, now?" Then, "What was his name?" He listened for a while longer and then said, "I guess it doesn't make any difference now. Don't worry about it, but don't talk about it anymore, either."

He hung up and looked at the corporal and me. "That was Manny Fonseca. Seems like Patterson called him at

his shop and got the details he didn't get from us. So much for official reticence."

"I never knew you used big words like 'reticence,'" I said. "I'm impressed. Why don't you call the *Gazette*? See if they've got a new reporter named Patterson."

The chief frowned, dialed, spoke, hung up, and stuck his pipe back in his mouth. "You're right," he said. "No Patterson. Damn."

"Nervy," said the corporal. "Guy wants to know what people know, calls the cops, gets nowhere, calls Fonseca, gets everything. How'd he know to phone Fonseca?"

"He saw the Bronco pick me up and take me out of there," I said. "Manny's logo and phone number are painted on the doors."

"That's probably it." The corporal looked at me. "Well, your pants can stay dry now. This guy knows that he made a mistake, so he won't be bothering you anymore. Chief, we'd better . . ."

He was interrupted by a young policemen at the door to the office. The corporal glared, but the young cop wasn't looking at him. "Chief, they found the car. Up in Vineyard Haven, parked right on Main Street. New York plates. They're running a check on them right now."

"Good. Let me know when the report comes in."

"How'd he ever find a parking place on Main Street in Vineyard Haven?" I wondered. "I can never find a parking place on Main Street."

"You can go now," said the corporal to me. "We don't need you anymore."

"I never needed you at all," I said. "By the way, cigars are bad for your health. Cancer of the mouth and throat. Give it some thought, if you can. See you, Chief."

The corporal was between me and the door. I walked up to him. Our eyes were on a level. He didn't move.

"Excuse me," I said. We stared at one another. Then he stepped back half a pace, I stepped around him, the

chief muttered, "Jesus Christ, you two!" and I went out the door.

I felt curiously alive yet empty. The shootist would no longer be after me. I hadn't realized how tense I had been. The air seemed charged with energy and the street in front of the station was mysterious and lovely. I got into the Land Cruiser and drove home. The highways and then my long driveway seemed endless.

The shootist would no longer be after me, but he would still be after John Skye. I was relieved, yet simultaneously appalled. How would Blondie now go about his hunter's quest? Would he stay on the island in hopes that John would return? That would be a dangerous course of action, but a resourceful man—and Blondie seemed very resourceful—might pull it off if he had money enough to pay Vineyard rents. Or would he go to Weststock and wait there, knowing that John would have to come back to his classes in September? One more young man in a college town would not be noticed. Just another grad student arriving early to get a good choice of quarters.

Both of those plans required a lot of money and a lot of time. Few people had both at their disposal. Even schoolteachers usually had summer jobs. So, would Blondie try to find out where John was now and go find him there? Not much chance of that, since John had not told the college where he was really going. As far as I knew, I was the only one who had John's address. Would Blondie just go home, wherever that was? Go back to his job, whatever it might be, then come back to New England in the fall to complete his work?

Why not?

I went back to the schoolteacher idea. If Blondie was a schoolteacher, it could explain why he had so much free time. Maybe he was a schoolteacher who didn't have to work summers. Not all teachers had to. Academia. Maybe the chief was right to wonder about some disgruntled student or colleague of Skye's. Skye's world was filled with

people who didn't work in the summer. Suppose John Skye's enemy was from Weststock. That made sense, since most of the people John met and therefore might anger were in Weststock, and scholars were famous for their feuds.

But how many of these academic adversaries performed assassinations? Scholars probably committed as many killings in hot blood as did any other group, but Blondie's efforts were those of an icier sort. I remembered the line "Revenge is a dish Italians prefer to eat cold." Blondie might not be Italian, but he was a cool customer.

I drove into my yard, parked, and got my .38 out from under the seat. I was glad not to need it anymore.

Something moved in the corner of my vision. I spun away behind the Land Cruiser and lifted the pistol. A man was running with uneven strides from my house toward my shed. I raised the pistol and shouted a shout I'd not shouted in years: "Stop! Police!"

The man ran on. He carried something in his left hand. I raised the pistol barrel and fired into the air. "Stop! Police!"

He ran behind my shed, where I fillet my fish and keep my smoker.

I ran around the house and looked from the far corner toward the shed. There was no cover between the house and the shed. Damn. I ran toward the shed, looking everywhere at once, pistol thrust forward. I got to the shed door, ducked low, whipped a look around back, jerked back, looked again, and saw the figure running through the trees, moving very fast with his odd, loping gait. I ran out and shouted again, then aimed well over the man's head and let go another shot. He spun around and raised his left hand. I saw flame dance from the object he held, and I dived for the ground and heard the smack of bullets hitting the shed behind me.

Jesus Christ! An automatic weapon! And me with a .38! I burrowed into the oak leaves and tried to be very small.

I heard another burst of sound from the gun and tried to get deeper into the dirt. After a while I realized I was listening to silence.

I picked my face up out of the leaves and looked where the man had been. He was gone. I rolled over and looked at the side of the shed behind me. High across the wall was a row of bullet holes. I got up and went to the wall and put my arm up. The holes were too small for my finger to fit into them. On the other hand, they looked plenty big enough.

The cops might nail him on the road. I ran to the house and got to the phone. Dead. I wasn't surprised. I ran outside to the Land Cruiser and stopped short. The left front tire was in shreds. I sighted between the house and the shed, and, sure enough, found myself looking right at the spot where the gunman had turned and fired. His second burst has been aimed at the tire.

I went back inside to the phone. My address book was beside it, open to the S's. I put the .38 back in the gun case and went outside again. I got out the jack and lug wrench and mounted my spare tire. It wasn't the world's best tire, but it beat the hell out of the one it replaced. It was three miles to the police station. To avoid some of the A & P traffic jam, I ducked right at Al's Package Store and took the back route, thus saving at least thirty seconds of travel time. I arrived at the station for the third time that day, and inside found the chief and the corporal still at work. I told my tale.

"I see why you quit the Boston PD," said the corporal. "You yell 'stop,' and he doesn't stop; you fire warning shots and he shoots real shots."

"Real shots, but not at me. He stitched my shed at least eight feet up. All he wanted to do was stop me, and his plan worked like a charm. Then he blasted my truck so he'd have time to make it away without worrying about me following him or getting to a phone to call in you

intrepid minions of the law. He could have hit me as easily as he hit the tire, but he didn't."

"A nice guy."

"I wouldn't go that far, but at least we know he doesn't like to shoot anybody he doesn't have to shoot."

"Except your friend John Skye."

"Yeah. And now he has John's Colorado address."

"How'd the guy know you had it?" asked the corporal.

"He talked to Manny Fonseca," said the chief, stuffing tobacco into the bowl of his briar. "Yeah, that's how he knew. Manny must have told him who you were and why you were out there at John's house. Guy figured since you take care of John's place, you'd know where he was, and Manny told him where you lived. Guy probably told Manny he wanted to interview you. Something like that."

"Guy moves fast," said the corporal. "Leaves the car in Vineyard Haven, makes a couple of phone calls, gets himself some new transportation, car, maybe even a moped, parks it, and walks into your place. This guy likes to walk in the woods. Snips the phone wires, gets Skye's address, and takes off just as you pull in. He cut it pretty thin, didn't he? What if you'd come in sooner, before he had a chance to find the address book? Would he have taken you out because he had no other choice? What did the guy look like?"

"He looked about average. Vineyard summer clothes. Jeans and pullover shirt. Light jacket, like golfers wear. Everything blue. Left-handed, I think. Yellow hair. Maybe that wig, again. Shades. About thirty. Runs with an odd stride, a limp. When I first saw that, I thought it was Cramer, but it wasn't."

"Cramer's in Iowa City."

"I know that. I'm just telling you what went through my mind. I knew it wasn't Cramer as soon as I thought it. It was the limp that made me think it. Smaller guy than Cramer. He had some sort of automatic weapon.

Looked like it was twelve, fifteen inches long. About .30 caliber, from the looks of the holes in my shed."

"Weapon fits," said the corporal. "Explains why you couldn't count the shots out at Skye's place. A short burst."

The chief was already sending out the description. Our man was armed and should be presumed dangerous. The corporal looked at his watch. "Maybe we'll be lucky."

"Maybe the moon is made of green cheese," I said.

He looked at me. "A Dr. David Rubinski from Newark rented the blue car on the afternoon of the twenty-ninth. Charged it on his Visa card. We talked to his wife. The real Dr. Rubinski thinks he lost his wallet at his health club on the morning of the twenty-ninth. Driver's license, credit cards, money, everything."

"Ah. And did you talk to the real Dr. Rubinski?"

"We did. At his office. Turns out he did all the right things. Called his credit card companies, his bank, everybody. But by that time our guy had rented his car and headed north."

"You talked to the car rental agency?"

"How do you think we learned all this? They rented it to a Dr. Rubinski, all right, and their Dr. Rubinski had a beard just like the Dr. Rubinski in the driver's license photo."

"Only the real Dr. Rubinski was back in New Jersey at the time. Who was at Rubinski's health club that morning?"

"We're checking that out. Which is to say that the New Jersey guys are checking it out for us. Rubinski works out early, about six every morning, before going on his rounds at the hospital. Maybe we got a break, since not too many people are usually at the club at that time. Maybe one of them was a guy with a limp. We'll see."

The chief lit his pipe. "I think we'd better get in touch with John Skye and let him know about all this."

I handed him the address and telephone number John had left with me.

"Hummph," grunted the chief. "Durango, Colorado, eh? An RFD box number on a country road. That doesn't tell us much." He dialed a 1, a 303, and a seven-digit number. He waited. Then he held the phone away from his ear and we could hear it ringing. He let it ring some more, then put it down. "Nobody home."

"It's his mother's ranch," I said. "He grew up out there. Maybe they're all out on the south forty, or something."

The corporal looked at me. "The south forty?"

"I'll try the Sheriff's Department," said the chief. "No, I won't. I don't know the county. I'll try the Durango police."

He talked to the Durango police, told them his story, got the Sheriff's Department number and called them, and told the story again. Then he listened for a while and scribbled on his notepad and hung up. He looked up at us. "Lots of Skyes out there. I got a number for one of them." He dialed, waited, and then spoke, introducing himself and asking how to get in touch with John Skye. He listened, said, "Thank you. Have him call me when he comes back," and hung up. Again, he looked up at us. "John Skye's gone camping with his family. Up in the mountains. Someplace called the Hermosa range, where his daddy used to run cattle in the summertime. Going to do some trout fishing and hiking. The twins are going to ride every day. Won't be back for a couple of weeks."

"Somebody may be waiting for him when he comes back to the home corral," said the corporal.

My very thought.

"I'll send the Sheriff's Department and the Durango police and the Colorado State Police the information we have," said the chief. "Maybe they can get somebody up to Skye's camp or cabin or whatever and let him know what's going on."

"Then what?" I asked. "Who'll they be watching for?

A guy with a beard, a blond wig, shades, and a machine gun, who runs with a limp, wears blue Martha's Vineyard vacation clothes, and goes by the name of David Rubinski?"

"Yeah," said the chief, irritated. "Something like that. By then, though, we may know more about the guy."

"You got any better ideas?" asked the corporal.

"Yeah," I said, "I do. I'm going out there myself. At least I know more or less what Blondie looks like."

"Blondie?" The corporal arched a brow.

"You better stay here, J.W.," said the chief.

"Good advice," said the corporal. "As a cop you ain't too effective."

"I'm not a cop anymore," I said. "I'm just a young man going west, like old John Soule advised."

"You ain't so young. And I thought that was Horace Greeley that said that."

"Another example that life isn't fair. Horace got the credit, but he was quoting John. Anyway, I'm taking their advice."

"Maybe that's a good idea," said the corporal. "Maybe if you get out of state, we can have some peace and quiet around here."

The chief sighed. "I'll write you a letter," he said. "You can show it to the cops out there. It won't be official and they can ignore it if they want to, but maybe it'll get you some cooperation you might need."

"Meanwhile," said the corporal, "I guess we'll all go have a look at the scene of the latest crime. You're using up a lot of taxpayers' money, Jackson. Are you worth it?"

"You're just not used to earning your salary," I said. "Real cops do this sort of thing all the time."

"Okay, okay," said the chief. "Enough of that. Jesus, what a day."

— 13 —

Sometimes your mouth is right here, but your brain is miles away. Why had I announced I was going to Colorado? Maybe I should have changed my mind. I drove home and after somebody from some police department or other sprinkled powder around and lifted a lot of prints, including, certainly, mine and Zee's, I rewired my telephone while various police officers walked through the woods, took photos and measurements, and otherwise investigated. When they left, I used the phone, in vain, to try to call John Skye. Still nobody home. Where was his mother, now that I needed her? Out on the range with the deer and the antelope?

I waited for a call from the police telling me that Blondie was in custody. No call came. Instead, some more police arrived and went into the woods to make a cast of footprints Blondie had left behind.

I waited all afternoon, then, just before five, phoned a travel agent and made airline reservations, discovering what everyone who ever tried to fly from Boston to Durango no doubt already knew: that it costs almost as much, and is twice as hard, to fly from Denver to Durango as it does to fly from Boston to Denver. Getting to Durango was apparently like getting to the Vineyard. You can fly to Boston from anywhere in the world, but you can go crazy trying to get the last hundred miles to the island. My trusty travel agent finally got me a cheaper route via Albuquerque. I drank two martinis before supper.

By the next morning, as I was packing, I had thought a lot about why I'd decided to go west. I was bored and

worried and resentful because Zee was in New Hampshire deciding what to do with the rest of her life and maybe deciding to lead one without me in it; I was deeply angry with Blondie, who, after all, had tried to kill me three times, and then had broken into my house and shot in my direction after he knew I was the wrong guy; mostly I wanted to stop Blondie before he actually killed John Skye or anyone else. I didn't like to admit this last motive, because I'd been trying hard not to get involved with problems I didn't have to get involved in. But here I was.

I decided I had plenty of reasons to go to Colorado, even though some of them might not stand too much inquiry. Hemingway once said something like moral is what you feel good about afterward, and immoral is what you feel bad about. I didn't feel good about going to Colorado, but I would have felt worse not going.

The phone rang. It was the Edgartown police. I felt excitement; maybe Blondie was in jail. He wasn't, but the cops did have some news. Yesterday Dr. David Rubinski, beardless this time because his wife had made him shave it off, had rented a car in Vineyard Haven, paying in cash, but leaving his Visa card with the dealer to assure him of his trustworthiness. The car had not been returned as scheduled, and the cops had found it in the parking lot in Oak Bluffs where the *Vineyard Queen* docks before and after its run to Falmouth. The bogus Rubinski was presumably now on the mainland.

I asked if they'd heard anything more from Newark about who he might really be. They hadn't. I phoned for a taxi. It was the first taxi I had ever ridden in on Martha's Vineyard. The driver took me to the Martha's Vineyard airport and frowned at my tip.

"You drive too fast," I said, and went to check in for my flight to Boston.

In Boston, I had almost two hours before my Albuquerque flight, so I took another taxi to the hospital and went in to see Geraldine Miles. I hate hospitals.

They're unhealthy places. Probably more people die there than anywhere else.

There was no cop outside of her door, so apparently the Boston PD had gotten the word that Lloyd Cramer was back in Iowa and that Geraldine was no longer in any danger from him. Presumably, Geraldine had gotten the same word. I walked into the room.

Geraldine looked out at me through bandages wrapped around her face. Her lips were swollen and I could see stitches in them. One of her arms was in a cast. She wore a lacy gown, not one of those backless things they give you in the hospital, so I knew that Aunt Jean Wiggins had been to see her and had made her get prettied up. There were flowers beside her bed. I sat down. Her eyes rolled to follow me.

"How's it going, kid?"

She held up her good hand and formed a little O with her thumb and forefinger.

"You don't have to talk," I said. "I just came by to see how you're doing and give you the gossip." I told her that the bluefish were pretty much gone, but that there were still plenty of shellfish and that I'd take her out and show her my capturing secrets when she got back to the island. I told her I was going out to Colorado for a while, but I imagined I'd be back on the island about the same time she was. I told her about the weather and complained about the Red Sox annual August slump, and told her the joke about the Portuguese doctor and the guy who cut off his finger. That got a little choking, muffled noise that might have been a laugh. Then I put out my hand and she put hers on it and we sat there as I babbled on. After a while, it was time for me to go.

"You're going to be okay," I said. "You're a gutsy girl. I'll see you when I get back. You'll be on the island by then."

She formed the O again and moved her fingers in a slow wave.

In the hall I met a nurse coming in. "How is she?" I asked.

"Are you family?"

"I'm her brother."

"Well, she's not brain-damaged, but it will be a long time before she's over this."

"Plastic surgery?"

"Oh, yes. But you should talk to the doctor."

"Thanks. When will she be able to leave the hospital?"

"You'll have to speak to the doctor."

"I will." I turned away. Behind me, the nurse spat out a word. I turned back. "I beg your pardon?"

The nurse looked at me with hot, tired eyes. "I said, 'Bastard.' Damn the bastard that did this and all like him!" She drew a breath, eased it out, and went into the room. I heard her voice, now gentle, say, "Hi, sweetheart."

I taxied back to Logan and later, only half an hour behind schedule, not bad for modern times, was in the air looking down at Boston as my plane banked and climbed toward the west. Airplanes do not bother me, because there are walls between me and what's Way Down There. I actually enjoy the view.

Due, perhaps, to my life on an island only twenty miles long, I was impressed by the sheer size of the United States. We flew for hours over mountains, farmlands, rivers, and lakes. I changed planes in St. Louis, home of the Cardinals who, fortunately for the Red Sox, were in the other league. I did not see the famous arch.

We flew on, over lands less green, then lands that were brown and gold, then lands that were very brown, then over mountains, then over real desert, then down into Albuquerque, where I stepped out into August heat. I tried to imagine having come all that way by covered wagon or on foot. Ye gods!

Albuquerque was, I knew, an ancient town, where people had lived long before the gentlemen of Seville had come north from Mexico to search for the seven cities of

gold. I did not, however, have time to explore it; instead, I caught Mesa Airlines north to Durango.

Mesa Airlines consisted, in my case, of one of those cigar-shaped airplanes which is so cozy that you'd better be on good terms with both the pilots and your fellow passengers. Still, it flew us north toward the rising Rockies as well as any plane might. We passed over desert, then mesa country, and almost to the high mountains themselves before the plane descended over a final mesa and landed with barely a thump. If truth be told, I actually like little airplanes better than the big ones, because I believe the little ones can fly, but I don't believe the big ones can. Look at a 747 someday, and you'll know what I mean. A thing like that will never, ever, get off the ground! Too big. Too heavy. No way!

There was a car rental place at the La Plata County airport, and I took advantage of it to rent the cheapest car they had. I had no idea where I was or where I hoped to go, but the country out there was so big that I knew I'd need a car to get there, wherever it was.

I was faintly aware of my breathing. No wonder. I was at 7,000 feet, and the mountains all around me went up from there, especially the ones to the north. I asked the way to County Road 302. Nobody at Mesa Airlines knew where it was. One of a number of men wearing wide-brimmed hats and cowboy boots said, "Damned government's put numbers on all the damned roads and now nobody Goddamn knows where to find anybody! Who you looking for, son?"

"I'm looking for a ranch owned by some people named Skye," I said. I gave him the box number.

"Hell, son," he said, "there's Skyes all over the place. A big bunch of 'em live out there on the Florida Mesa. You get yourself a phone book and start calling Skyes and you'll soon find your man." He pointed west. "Florida Mesa's right there, just the other side of the river. Highway to Durango goes right over it. Ya can't miss it." He

put a large Western hand on my shoulder, smiled, and went outside and climbed into a pickup and drove away. He'd pronounced Florida in the Spanish way, with the accent on the second syllable. I wondered why they didn't do that in Florida.

His advice seemed sensible. I found a phone and called John Skye's mother's number. The phone rang and rang. Nobody home. I had the telephone number for the Skye the chief had talked to from Edgartown, so I tried that one. A woman's voice, touched by a faint twang, said, "Hello?"

"Mrs. Wilma Skye?"

"Yes?"

"I'm J. W. Jackson. I'm a friend of John Skye, back in Massachusetts, and I'm trying to find his mother's place, but I don't know where it is. Can you help me out?"

"Oh, John's up on the Hermosa someplace. That nice wife of his and the kids are up there too. Won't be back for a couple of weeks. From Massachusetts, eh? Got a call from some policeman back there. You're a long way from home."

"Yes, I am. I understand that his mother still lives out on the ranch. I'd like to see her, but when I phoned just now, nobody answered. I thought she might be outside someplace. Can you tell me how to get there?"

"Well, I don't know if Aunt Vivian's there. Since John was going up into the mountains, she was planning to drive up to Glacier National Park, the last I heard. Ever since she got that little green Mazda, she's been batting around all over the place."

"Can you tell me how to get to her place? It's on County Road 302, but I don't know where that is."

"I suppose giving numbers to all these roads makes sense to somebody back in Washington, but it hasn't done much for the local folks, so far. Where are you?"

"Out here at the airport. Just flew in."

"Oh. Well, welcome to the San Juan Basin. First time out this way?"

"Yes."

"Sure hope you'll have time to see some of this country. We figure this is about the prettiest territory there is."

"Sure looks that way. How do I get to Vivian Skye's place from here?"

"Lots of things to do: fishing, the little train to Silverton, Mesa Verde, riding, sight-seeing, river rafting, skiing in the winter, you name it."

"Sounds good. Now, just where am I with respect to County Road 302?"

She told me and I finally got off the line. I wondered if I was going to be friendlied to death before I got out of Colorado.

There was a map in my car and on it, with the help of Wilma Skye's directions, I found County Road 302. I drove out to the highway and turned west, dropping down into a valley where the Florida River flowed over a stony bottom. The sides of the valley were rocky and covered with the sort of tough vegetation that grows in dry, desert country. I climbed the other side of the valley and found myself on a green mesa covered with farms and ranches. To the north, the blue mountains rose into the sky and ahead of me other high peaks climbed out of blue foothills. To the west, south, and east a ring of lower mountains, blue-gray and dry, fled away toward the desert country I'd flown over on my way in. It was sagebrush country, and there were cedar and piñon trees growing where there were no fields. The soil was a red clay and there were rotating irrigation devices spraying water over the fields. Fairly prosperous-looking farmhouses sat beside sometimes shakier-looking barns, sheds, and corrals. Occasionally, the barns and outbuildings looked better than the houses. The sky was bright blue, but there were thunderheads hanging over the mountains to the north.

I found County Road 302 and followed it until I found a mailbox with the right number on it. I turned in and parked in front of a large, old, well-maintained farmhouse surrounded by elm trees, a green lawn, and flower beds. Behind the house I could see a gnarled orchard. Across the road were a barn and outbuildings. Beyond them was a pond and beyond that, beside a thick grove of blue-green piñon and cedar trees, in a field of alfalfa stubble, a half-dozen horses grazed.

Barbed-wire fences lined the road and divided the land into fields. High grass marking irrigation ditches wound around the contours of the fields. I saw a few cattle in a far corner pasture and checked my directions. Yes, by God, it was the south forty! There really was a south forty!

I didn't see a green Mazda. I went to the house and knocked at the front door. Nobody home. I walked around to the orchard, then on around the house. Nobody. I peeked in through a window and saw a comfortable, old-fashioned room with furniture that had been there a long time.

I went around to the front door again and tried the knob. The door opened. So there were still people like me who didn't lock their doors. I was pleased. I shut the door and walked across the road to the barn and outbuildings. Nobody.

I crossed the road again and went into the house. There was a phone on the wall of the kitchen. I called Wilma Skye and told her where I was.

"Nobody home," I said. "No Mazda. Can you tell me how to get to the Hermosa range?"

"I sure can. We all used to run our cattle up there, before the cattle business got so bad we couldn't afford it anymore. But that's big country up there, and I don't rightly know where Cousin John is camped. Might be he's down on Clear Creek, though I doubt it. Might be there on the flats where the old Turnip Patch Cabin used to be. Might be up on Little Elk. Or he might be up at the top

of the Hermosa Cliffs, up near where the old Arnold Cabin used to be. We all used to crawl around the cliffs when we were kids. Danged near scared our parents half to death when they caught us. If I was to guess, I'd guess he's up there someplace, up toward the top of Dutch Creek. Around the Bath Tub, maybe. Good graze for the horses up there, good water, sun comes up early and goes down late, not too far from some good fishing. You get yourself a horse and somebody who knows the land, and I imagine you can find John's camp in a couple of days. Not that many places to look, if you know where you're looking."

"Where is this place?"

"Why, you just drive up the valley north of Durango and a few miles along you'll cross Hermosa Creek. You can drive up the creek for a ways, and you'll go through a drift fence. That's the lower drift fence for the range. Then you can go on up past the old sawmill for a half mile or so. But from there on, it's all trail. The Hermosa range is mostly on your right. All those little creeks come down out of it and run into the Hermosa. Range runs all the way up to the other side of Big Elk. A lot of square miles and some rough country until you get up to the meadows at the head of Dutch. The cliffs mark the east end of the range. You're going to like them! A thousand feet high, rising right out of the Animas Valley. You jump off one of them, you might starve to death before you hit the ground!" Wilma had a healthy-sounding laugh, I thought.

"So you think I'll need a horse and a guide."

"Heck, there are hikers and mountain bikers and dirt bike people who get way up there, too. And you can get yourself a Forest Service map, and try to find John's camp by yourself, if you want. But unless you know the area, you might walk around there for a week and never find squat, if you know what I mean."

"I don't have a week to spare. Where can I find a horse and a guide?"

"Where can you find a . . . ? Just a second." I heard her distant voice. "Billy? Billy Jo, come here."

Billy Jo apparently came. I heard an exchange of voices. Then Wilma Skye came back on the line. "Tell you what," she said. "I think we can take care of you right here. We've got horses and a horse trailer and Billy Jo, who knows that range better than I do. That is, if you don't mind being guided around by a genuine college graduate who doesn't have a steady job yet."

A voice protested in the background.

"I don't mind," I said. "I don't have a steady job myself. How do I get to your place?"

She told me. I went west to 550, then north, then east again at the top of the big hill. "If you go down the big hill, you've gone too far," Wilma had said. I spotted the big hill just in time and took the road to the right. A couple of miles farther along I came to a gate topped with steer horns and the name Flying Shirt-tail Ranch. There was no missing that name, and I pulled in and stopped in front of another large farmhouse. A tall, handsome, rawboned woman came out of the house as I climbed out of my little car. She put out a hard hand.

"You'd be J. W. Jackson. I'm Wilma. Mack's in town getting some part or other for that danged tractor. Pouring good money after bad, if you ask me. He should be home anytime." A dazzling girl in jeans, cowboy boots, and a checkered shirt came out into the sunlight. Her hair was dark and fell in two braids down over her shoulders. Wilma grinned and waved her forward. "Come here, sweetheart. Mr. Jackson, this is my youngest, Billy Jo. Billy Jo, this is Mr. Jackson. Mr. Jackson's come all the way from Massachusetts. He's a friend of Cousin John."

Something tingled between me and Billy Jo. She came forward and I saw that she wasn't a girl, she was a woman.

My hat, the forest green one with the Martha's Vineyard Surfcasters Association logo on the front, which I had carefully selected for the trip from my collection of hats

with other things printed on the front, was already in my hand.

"I'm the one without a steady job," she said, putting out her hand. A little smile played across her lips. Her hand was firm and lightly callused.

"My friends call me J.W.," I said. "I'm a stranger in a strange land, and I need somebody to lead me to John Skye. I gather that you can do the job."

"I can find John Skye for you, if that's what you want. When do you want to go up there?" Her eyes were dark, like her mother's, and she had the same fine bone structure in her face.

"I want to see him as soon as possible."

"That'll be tomorrow, then. Too late today. I've got to bring in the horses from the north pasture." She looked up at me. "Must be important."

I put a smile on my face. "Life or death," I said.

— 14 —

Billy Jo had wise eyes, for one so young. "Can you ride a horse? If you can't, you can either walk in, which will be tough on you because of the altitude—it's nearly ten thousand feet at the top of the cliffs—or you can give me a message to take up to John."

"I imagine I can stay on a tame horse for a while."

Her quick smile flickered across her face. "All right. Where are you staying?"

"I don't know. I just got here."

"It seems like there are a thousand motels in Durango. Find one and call me and tell me where you are, and I'll meet you there in the morning. Say, nine o'clock?"

"Nine o'clock is fine." I pulled my eyes away from her and looked at her mother. "You and John close?"

Wilma looked at me thoughtfully, then nodded. "Yes. We're kinfolk. We're friends, too."

I thought of how policemen always start looking at the kinfolk when they encounter a crime of violence and don't know who did it.

"All right," I said. "There's a man from back east who wants to meet John, but it's not in John's best interests to meet him now. The guy may come around here pretty soon looking for John. If he does, I advise you not to tell him where John is. Instead, I think you should phone the Sheriff's Department and tell them that the man is here. They should know what you're talking about. If they don't, have them call the Chief of Police in Edgartown, Massachusetts. I need to see John right away so he can decide what he wants to do." I looked at Billy Jo. "The story's too long to put in a letter. I need to talk to John."

The women looked at me.

"Of course, you could be the guy from back east that John shouldn't meet," said Wilma. "Billy Jo here might be taking you right to him."

"I can't prove I'm not."

"What's this fellow's name?"

"I don't know. He's about thirty, Caucasian, about average size, has something wrong with one leg that makes him run with a limp but may not be noticeable when he's walking. He's left-handed, and he may have blond hair, or a blond wig. That's all I know."

"No." Wilma shook her head. "That's not all you know."

"You're right. He may be dangerous. Not to you, though."

"To John."

I shrugged. "Maybe."

"Why?"

"I don't know."

A pickup truck turned in at the gate and pulled along-

side my little car. A big man got out. He was wearing the regional uniform of cowboy boots, jeans, and Western shirt. His broad-brimmed hat was stained around the sweatband. He looked cheerful and curious. When he got near, he put out a large, leather-like hand.

"Howdy. I'm Mack Skye. You ain't the guy that's been trying to sell me a new tractor, I hope, 'cause if you are, you're out of luck. I just got the part I need to keep the old Case running a while longer."

"I'm not that guy," I said. "I'm trying to talk your daughter into taking me up to find John Skye's camp." I gave him my name.

"Mr. Jackson's from back east," said Wilma, without too much expression one way or the other. "Says he's a friend of John's."

"Martha's Vineyard Surfcasters Association," read Mack Skye, squinting at the hat that was now back on my head. "That's that island where John's got a summer place. He's been trying to get us back there for years to try ocean fishing, but I'm happy with the trout we've got right here."

"We never go anywhere," said Billy Jo. "I'm a college graduate, for goodness' sake, and I've never been east of the Mississippi. And I wouldn't have gotten that far if we didn't have kin to visit in Kansas."

"Kansas!" exclaimed Mack Skye. "One trip to Kansas is enough! Nothing to see. Flatter than a punctured Texan! No mountains! Telephone poles walking in a straight line from horizon to horizon. Hell, honey, we don't have to go anywhere; we got the best of everything right here."

"Now, Mackenzie," warned Wilma, "you just stop that kind of talk. There's a world on the other side of these mountains and your daughter is going to have a look at it."

"Well, I imagine she will, but I hate to think about it. Tell me I'm right, J.W., I'm outnumbered by all these women."

"A whole lot of men can be outnumbered by just one woman," I said. "I'm staying out of this argument."

"Smart. I can just see this sweet child back east at one of them resorts, wearing one of them crotch-flossing bathing suits by the pool, and gettin' all foofed up when the sun goes down, and God knows what all . . ."

"I'm old enough to know what I'm doing, Daddy."

He wiped his broad brow. "I know you probably are, honey, but you're the last chick in the nest, and I hate to see you go. Man, it's hotter than a sheep. You like a brew, J.W.?"

"I've got to find somebody to take me up to John Skye's camp," I said. I looked at Billy Jo. "I'm not sure your daughter still wants the job."

Billy Jo opened her mouth, but her mother spoke first.

"Oh, I guess she'll take it," said Wilma. She looked at me. "If you were the man you've been talking about, you wouldn't have told us about him unless you were crazy, and you don't look crazy to me." She turned to her husband. "Mack, you take J.W. around back to the table under the big elm. J.W., you tell Mack what you've been telling us. Come with me, Billy Jo. We'll lay out some cheese and crackers and beer for all four of us. No reason why the women should work while the men loaf."

Mackenzie Skye and I walked around the house and sat in the shade of a tall elm. Once out of the sun, we were cool. I commented on it.

Skye smiled. "Air's so thin up here that your sunny side can be hot and your shadow side cold. It can be below freezing in the morning and hotter than a two-dollar pistol by noon. What is it that Wilma thinks you should be telling me?"

I told him what I'd told her. About then, the back screen door of the house swung open and Wilma and Billy Jo came out carrying a platter of cheese, crackers, and sliced ham, and four cans of Coors, made with pure Rocky

Mountain spring water. Not a great beer, but not a bad beer, either. There is no bad beer.

The Coors was just what I needed. The dry Colorado air was already sucking the moisture from my skin.

"You ain't told us much," said Mack Skye.

"He's told us enough, I reckon," said Wilma. "John's business may not be any of ours."

"John's kin," said Mack. "If he's got troubles he doesn't deserve, maybe we should know more about 'em."

"I don't know about his troubles," I said. "But I do have reason to believe that this guy doesn't have John's best interests at heart."

"Why do you think that?" asked Billy Jo.

I got some cheese and ham and put it on a cracker, took a bite and chewed, then washed the crumbs down with a slug of Coors. The Skyes munched along with me as they waited for me to decide whether to answer Billy Jo. I finished off the cracker and got myself another one. Then I told them of the incidents in Weststock and on the island. While I talked, I looked at the huge landscape to the north of the house. The green fields on the mesa flowed north to a line of willows a mile or so away. An irrigation ditch, I guessed. Miles beyond was a ridge of blue foothills topped with a jagged rimrock. Beyond that, blue-green mountains climbed into the air and beyond them, far to the north, peaks like fangs thrust toward a high bank of thunderheads. John Skye was up there somewhere. Tomorrow, with Billy Jo's help, I'd go find him.

I became conscious of a silence at the table and realized that I had stopped talking.

Mack Skye tipped up his beer and drained it. "That's a pretty good story," he said. He looked at Billy Jo. "Well, honey, I agree with your mom. You should take this man up to find John tomorrow. J.W., we'll keep an eye on Vivian's place."

Wilma nodded. "I'll get on the phone and let the other

Skyes out here know about this fellow. We've got to figure he'll phone one or another of them looking for information about John. I'll tell them to call the sheriff if this guy contacts them, and to get his name if he gives it, even though it'll probably be a fake."

"And I'll go bring in the horses right now," said Billy Jo. She looked at me with her dark eyes. "Has John got a wild side we don't know about?"

I'd wondered about that myself. "Not so far as I know. Do you know anything about him that I don't?"

"John Skye doesn't have an enemy in the world," said Wilma firmly.

"He's got one at least," said Mack. He looked at me. "Our boys are both grown up and gone, so we got room for you to put up for the night, if you'd like. Be more than welcome."

I thanked him, but declined the offer and asked him how to get to Durango. The three of them walked me out to my car. I pointed a finger at Billy Jo. "You make sure you get a nice, gentle horse."

"Sure." She grinned. "Trust me."

"Give him Mable," said her mother.

"I thought maybe I'd give him Big Red," said Billy Jo.

"No," said her father. "Don't give him Big Red."

"No," I said. "Don't give me Big Red. Give me Mable."

"I'll make sure you have a rope to tie yourself on," said Billy Jo.

"Good." I felt myself smiling at her, and thought of Ulysses. A rope had kept him from responding to the call of the sirens. Maybe it would do the same for me.

I drove back to 550 and headed down the big hill. At the bottom I took a sharp left and drove up a wide, dry valley to Durango, crossing the Animas River not once but twice before getting into town, and crossing it once again before I found a motel I could afford. As I'd crossed it the second time, a river raft full of life-jacketed passen-

gers and crew, everyone looking happy and excited, had
swept under the bridge and downriver.

Durango was a fair-sized town, with a Victorian air
about parts of it. It lay in the valley, and foothills and
the beginnings of mountains climbed away from it on both
sides. Narrow-gauge train tracks led through the town and
followed the river north, up the Animas Valley, between
rising mountainsides. Steps of white and red stone lined
the valley above town, and beyond them blue mountains
climbed into the sky.

I'd seen signs of abandoned coal mines south of town,
and knew there was farming and ranching on the Florida
Mesa, at least, but it was clear that Durango, like Martha's
Vineyard, lived off its tourists.

My first impression of Main Street was that it consisted
entirely of saloons and shops selling souvenirs and Western
arts and crafts. Once I crossed the river, heading north,
the choice seemed to be between fast food places and motels. I found a room in one of the latter, went to the
nearest liquor store (it wasn't far), bought myself a cooler,
ice, and—when in Rome—two sixes of Coors, and went
back to my room. It was hot and there seemed to be dust
in the air, although I couldn't see it. I sucked up a Coors
and opened another one and called the Edgartown police
station. I was two hours ahead of Edgartown time, so I
thought I might just catch the chief before he went home.

I didn't. He'd already gone home. I called him there.
His wife answered and I told her who I was. A moment
later, the chief's voice said, "Yeah?"

"It's me." I told him about my day.

"So you're going to see John Skye tomorrow?"

"Yeah."

"I'd pay some money to watch you try to ride a horse
up a mountain."

"Hey, you don't have to be born out here to be a cowboy, you know. Hell, Billy the Kid was born in New York
and Bill and Ben Thompson were born in England, for

God's sake. Maybe I have a natural talent for riding horses."

"Billy the Kid was just a punk who went west, and I never heard of those other two guys. I do have a name that might mean something, though: Gordon Berkeley Orwell. Ring any bells?"

"No."

"Old New Jersey money. Men mostly career military officers. This guy is the latest in the line. Family belongs to the same health club as our Dr. David Rubinski. Orwell was there the morning Rubinski says he lost his wallet. Thing is, this guy picked up a leg wound somewhere down in Central America or some such place. Some sort of a botched job. Limps sometimes. What leg did that guy at your place favor?"

"The right."

"That's the one. What hand you say he shot with?"

"The left."

"This guy's a southpaw. He's about Rubinski's size, but a lot more physical. Special Forces type. Runs, limp or no limp, works out, stays fit. Sounds like a man we'd like to talk to."

"Sure does."

"Trouble is, Orwell's up north somewhere in the Maine woods. Camping and white-water canoeing. Went in the day Rubinski's wallet went missing, and nobody knows how to get in touch with him."

"That's too bad. Anyone see him go in?"

"Yeah, he left his Jeep at some outfitting place up in the Allagash. The Orwells have done business with them before. People there saw him go off with his canoe."

"No word of him since? The family's not worried?"

"Apparently he's done this sort of thing before. Outdoorsman, like the rest of the Orwell men. His mother expects him out anytime. She's not worried."

I ran that through my head. "If he went in that day,

maybe he came out someplace else, got back into his rented car, and drove to Weststock."

"Yeah. Dom Agganis and me had the same thought. If we find him, we'll ask him about that."

"And if I find John Skye, I'll ask him about Gordon Berkeley Orwell."

"If you don't fall off that horse and break your neck, let me know what you find out. I'll try to get a picture of this Orwell guy. We'll send that and what we know about him to the police out there. If you go by the Durango police station in your travels, you might pop in and have a look at his face. See if it looks familiar."

I rang off, then phoned Wilma Skye and told her where I was.

The next morning at nine o'clock, a pickup truck towing a horse trailer stopped in front of the motel, and I got in. Billy Jo, wearing her very own cowgirl hat, smiled at me as I got in, checked the rearview mirror, and pulled out. She gestured at a paper bag on the seat beside us.

"Colon cloggers, in case you missed breakfast."

I peeked into the bag. Fresh doughnuts, a thermos bottle, and two tin cups.

"I was up with the sun, almost," I said. "Ate down the block. Sausage and eggs, hash browns, toast, juice, coffee."

"The old bloat breakfast, eh? Well then, you're probably not interested in these cloggers and coffee."

"Oh, I don't know," I said. "I think I might choke one or two down."

She grinned. "Me too. You pour."

I did and we munched our way up the Animas Valley.

— 15 —

Between rising mountains, the valley was narrow, green, and fertile. The river wound through it and the railroad tracks paralleled the highway. A black engine sending puffs of dark smoke into the air chugged along, towing a string of yellow cars filled with people. It looked like something out of the last century.

"The *Little Flier*," said Billy Jo. "Goes up to Silverton and back through the canyon. A lot of fun, and in places pretty spectacular even by local standards. Tourists love it. You should take the trip before you go home. The best way is to ride the train up to Silverton, then have somebody meet you up there in a car and bring you back down by the highway. That way, you get two good looks at the country."

"It's worth looking at," I conceded. I'd never seen such mountains. Their lower slopes were covered by oak brush and pines. Farther up the slopes, quaking aspen grew, mixed with more pine and spruce. Great rimrocks broke the slopes into steps, and red sandstone escarpments climbed up from the valley floor. Along the edges of the valley, houses, old and new, could be seen.

"Old ranch houses and new places built by folks who've retired or who just love the country," said Billy Jo. "Lots of Texas and California money. Otherwise, this hunk of country is what you might call economically deprived. It used to live off of mining and ranching, but now it lives off of tourists."

"Let me guess," I said. "Wages are low, unions are rare, prices are high, houses are expensive, and work that really pays anything is hard to find."

She nodded. "You've got it. How did you guess?"

"Places that live off of tourists are all like that. I live on an island that's like that. College kids who want to vacation come in the summer and take what jobs there are, and then leave in time to go back to school . . ."

"Right again."

We crossed a small, clear river running from the mouth of a narrow valley off to the left. A promontory topped by red cliffs split this valley from the Animas Valley.

"Hermosa Creek," said Billy Jo. "We could go up there and ride in from the end of the road, but we're not going to. We're going around to the foot of the Hermosa Cliffs and taking the Goulding Trail up to the top. I think John will be up there somewhere. He likes the meadows and the cliffs more than he likes being down in the canyons."

We left the flat green valley floor behind us and drove into wilder, rockier country. Farms gave way to pasturelands scattered between granite cliffs and forests of pine, spruce, aspen, and oak brush. Rivulets of clear water flowed in and out of marshes and between rocks. To our left, quite suddenly, a row of gigantic cliffs broken only by a few narrow rimrocked cuts rose into the sky. The farther we drove, the higher they got. Ahead of us, huge ragged mountains touched the clouds with their peaks.

"Engineer Mountain," said Billy Jo, nodding toward it. "Spud Mountain yonder. Those are the Needles off there. Lots of peaks around here over fourteen thousand feet. We won't be going quite that high today."

She slowed and turned off the highway. We rattled along a dirt road between pines and oak brush, pulled off it, and stopped.

"Here we are," said Billy Jo, setting the hand brake.

I got out and looked up. The cliffs seemed to hang over me. I could see hawks wheeling in the air way up there. It was a long way to the top.

"Would it make any difference," I asked, "if I told you I have a mild sort of acrophobia? When I stand on cliffs, I'm always sure they're going to choose that very moment

to crumble. When I lean on balcony railings, I'm sure they're going to break right then. When I'm on the edge of something high, I always feel like the wind is going to blow me over."

"A fine time to tell me," said Billy Jo, putting shapely hands on her shapely hips. "If you want to see John, you have to go up there. Or you can stay here and I'll go up alone. I can tell John what you told us. What do you want to do?"

"We manly men actually know no fear," I said. "We just claim to so lesser mortals won't feel so jealous."

"It's worked with me," said Billy Jo. "I'm not a bit jealous. Shall I unload the horses or not?"

I eyed the horses. It had been a long time since I'd been on a horse. "These guys don't bite, do they? Which one is Big Red?"

"Neither one." Billy Jo laughed. "And they aren't guys, they're mares. Maude here is for you. We use her for a packhorse, usually. Not too smart, but not a mean bone in her. I'll ride Matilda. Maude's her mother, but Matilda's got some Thoroughbred in her from her sire. Good spirit. They're both good in the mountains. Shall we get them unloaded, or do you want to go home?"

She was about half my size and obviously not afraid of mountains or big animals. I looked at her, at the horses, and up at the cliffs. On the Vineyard, fishermen say, when speculating about future possibilities of success, "If you don't go, you won't know."

"Let's do it," I said.

"Good. I think you'll be okay."

The mares were already saddled. Billy Jo backed them out of the trailer, tightened cinches, eyed my legs and adjusted the length of my stirrups, put bridles over the halters, and lashed on saddlebags.

"Food," she said. "We'll be up there about lunchtime." She handed me a yellow slicker. "Tie this on behind your

saddle. Weather changes fast up here, and we could get a shower."

Except for the clouds over Engineer Mountain and the Needles, the sky was brilliant blue. Nevertheless, I tied the slicker on. Local knowledge should never be ignored. When I finished admiring my work, I saw Billy Jo slide a rifle into a scabbard on her saddle. I must have raised an eyebrow.

"My 30–30," she said. "Just in case."

"Just in case of what?"

She waved toward the mountains across the valley. "You never know. Fellow over toward Emerald Lake swears he saw a grizzly earlier in the summer."

"What do you usually shoot?"

"Deer. Got an elk last year, too."

"I don't think it's deer or elk season."

"I don't plan on shooting any deer or anything else. But, you never know. Like they say, it's better to have a gun and not need it than to need it and not have it." She swung up onto her mare with an effortless grace. "Time to move out. Let's see you climb aboard."

Billy Jo and Manny Fonseca would probably hit it right off, I thought. They could sit around and swap quotations about the benefits of shooting irons. I looked Maude in the eye and told her to stand still while I got on. She did, and we started up the trail.

The trail zigzagged up through a break in the cliffs. Maude was a wide-backed, comfortable old mare, and did her best to make my ride an easy one. Ahead of me, Billy Jo rode easily, looking back at me now and then to make sure I was still there.

We climbed steadily, stopping now and then to let the horses blow. Maude began to sweat early and kept it up, but rolled along without complaint. Behind us, the valley began to fall away, and across it more distant mountains began to rise into view. We passed through a break in a

rimrock and later climbed through another. The oak brush disappeared and we climbed through evergreens and white-barked aspen, whose trunks were marked in black lines by the initials and dates of previous travelers. The aspen leaves danced in the light breeze and sunlight shimmered on them.

A tiny stream had, over millennia, cut through the thousand feet of stone that formed the cliffs and had created the crevice through which we now climbed. It still flowed through the gorge, falling over rock faces, winding through tiny marshes, and then plunging on down the slope. We rose beside it and later crossed it as the gorge began to open into a more gentle vale.

Suddenly Maude's ears were up. Ahead, Billy Jo was pointing. Three deer, heads high, were looking at us from the trail in front of us. They flicked their white tails and bounded away out of sight.

"They don't let you get that close in deer season," said Billy Jo, with a grin.

We came to a cabin and passed it by. Billy turned in her saddle and gestured.

"Used to be a cabin here they called Flagstaff. Old cattle camp in my grandfather's day. Rotted down long ago. They call this new one Craig Cabin, after a local guy who loved to hunt up here. Could be that he and his friends used up more decks of cards and whiskey bottles than they did bullets, but they always had a fine time one way or another. The top is right ahead."

We rode through an open meadow and up a ridge and hit a trail and a log drift fence. Beyond the fence, the land fell away to the west.

"They fence across these breaks in the cliffs to keep the cattle west of here," said Billy Jo, while our horses blew. "Between the breaks, the cliffs do the job. The creeks that run down into the Hermosa start up here behind the cliffs and run off yonder." She pointed toward a

distant cluster of mountain peaks. "Those are the La Pla-
tas. They're the ones just west of Durango."

There were mountains flowing away in every direction. I
had never seen so far except from airplanes. We rode to the
right, and passed through a gate in the drift fence. My rump
and legs were getting sore in spite of Maude's easy gait.
Billy Jo rode as if she and her mare were one being.

We came out into a green meadow and Billy Jo reined
her mare off the trail and into the dappled shadows of a
grove of aspen. She swung down, removed Matilda's bridle,
and tied her to a tree. Matilda immediately began to graze.

"Lunchtime," smiled Billy Jo, digging into her saddlebags and bringing out sandwiches and a thermos. "I'm
hungrier than a timber wolf with tentacles."

Maude was ready for food, and so was I. I swung down
and immediately felt a number of pains in places I didn't
remember hurting before. My legs did not want to hold
me up. I forced them to do their job, took off Maude's
bridle, and tied her so she, too, could graze.

"Nifty knot," observed Billy Jo.

"Bowline," I said. "You can put a lot of strain on it
and it'll still untie easily. Sailor's kind of knot." I minced
over to the log where she was sitting and eased myself
down.

"I've never seen the ocean," said Billy Jo.

Lunch was meat loaf sandwiches and iced tea. I got
right into mine.

"Mighty fine," I said after a while.

"You do seem to have worked up an appetite." Over
her sandwich, Billy Jo was watching me with curious eyes.
I realized that though I was just old enough to be her
father, I didn't see her as my daughter. The air was thin
and I was a bit light-headed. Billy Jo, on the other hand,
didn't seem light-headed at all. "I've never been on an
island, either," she said.

"I've never been on top of a mountain.

"After you left yesterday, I remembered the twins talking about you," she said. "I got the idea from them that you were a lot older than you are."

"I'll have to talk to Jen and Jill about that when we get to their camp."

"You don't look old at all," said Billy Jo. "Tell me about your island."

I told her some things about Martha's Vineyard. "The highest point on the island is about a mile and a half lower than we are right now," I said, finally, "but that's high enough."

"Tell me about the ocean. I've only seen it in the movies."

I looked at the mountains sweeping away from us in all directions. "It's like this. It's huge and beautiful and peaceful sometimes, and wild and dangerous other times. And it doesn't care about you one way or the other. I like it and I like this." I gestured."

"That's how the desert is, too," she said. "It doesn't care, either. Men work it for its treasures, and sometimes they do okay. Other times they don't."

"See," I said. "You know more about the ocean than you thought." I gestured with my hand and it touched hers. A spark jumped. She looked at me. Her eyes were deep and dark. In the corner of my eye I saw something move in the meadow below us. I looked and saw a small wolf trotting along. Billy Jo followed my gaze.

"Coyote. They're beginning to come back. They were nearly wiped out years ago, but now they're back. Maybe he'll sing to us tonight."

Our hands were no longer touching. We watched the coyote trot out of sight. Billy Jo looked at the sun and then at me. "We'd better get going if we want to get back down to the valley before night."

She flowed to her feet and I climbed gingerly to mine. "I may not *be* old," I said, "but I damned well am a lot older than I was before I got on old Maude."

She laughed. We bridled the mares and climbed aboard and rode on. At a place no different than any other to my eyes, Billy Jo led us off the trail and through a forest where I realized we were on a small trail. She pointed at the ground.

"Shod hoofs. A day old."

I looked and saw hoofprints for the first time. We went through a dark spruce forest and came out into another grassy clearing. The ruins of a cabin lay fallen against the far hillside. Beside it were three tents fronted by a grill mounted on stones over a fire bed. Smoke lifted lazily from the fire bed. There were saddles over a log beyond the tent and horses were tethered on the hillside. A spring had been dug out and fenced in so that cattle could not tramp it down.

Maude whinnied and a horse on the far slope lifted its head. Two lookalike heads poked out a tent. The twins, Jill and Jen. They squinted at us, then ran out and waved.

"John Skye's camp," said Billy Jo. "Right where it was supposed to be."

— 16 —

"Gosh," said Jill or Jen, "what are you doing here, J.W.? Hi, Billy Jo."

"We never would have guessed in a billion years!" said the other twin. "Hi, Billy Jo."

"Hi," said Billy Jo, hooking a nice-looking leg over her saddle horn, and smiling.

"Mom and John will really be surprised," said one twin.

"Or did they know you were coming?" asked her sister.

"No, they didn't," I said. "Now, which one of you is which?"

"I'm Jill," they both said.

"They do this to me," I said to Billy Jo.

"No, we don't," said one of the twins. "My sister does, but I never do."

"You do, too," said the other one. "I'm the one who doesn't. Mom says it's not nice to confuse J.W., so I'm very careful never to do it. Do I, J.W.?"

"I've always liked you best, Jill. Unlike your sister, you have an honest face."

"I'm Jen. I'm the one with an honest face."

"That's what I just said. Where are your folks?"

They waved toward the east. "Out there on the top of the cliffs. Probably just looking out across the valley. You want to see them? Come on! We'll take you there!"

They didn't bother with saddles or bridles, but ran out into the meadow, untied two horses, and swung aboard them bareback.

"Those two can ride like the wind," said Billy Jo approvingly as she unwound her leg from the saddle horn.

"What is it with girls and horses, anyway?"

"Freud probably thought he knew," she replied. "Control of something big and fast and powerful, maybe. Maybe having something strong between your legs and being swept away by it."

"Aren't controlling and being swept away opposites?"

"We're not talking logic here," said Billy Jo, her dark eyes looking at me from under the wide brim of her hat.

"Come on, you guys!" came the shout of a twin.

I caught myself actually running my tongue along my lips as I met Billy Jo's eyes. It made me smile. I looked at the twins riding their dancing horses in the meadow. "We'd better go," I said.

"Yes."

"Come on!" said a twin, and she and her sister galloped off.

"Let's trot along," said Billy Jo, kicking Matilda out of her walk.

We trotted. I bounced. Pain.

"Take your weight on your legs," said Billy Jo, looking back. "It would be a shame if you ruined yourself so early in life!"

I used my legs and tried to adapt myself to Maude's pace. More pain, but not as much. We trotted along after the twins, who in time came galloping back to see where we were and finally trotted along ahead of us.

We passed over rolling green meadows and through patches of forest and back into meadowlands. A rounded grassy hillside rose gently in front of us. On top of it I could see two horses tied to a lonesome tree.

"Come on, J.W., gallop!"

The twins and Billy Jo kicked their heels and their mounts broke into gallops. Maude, not to be outdone or left behind, broke into one of her own. I grabbed the saddle horn and hung on and we galloped up the slope.

At the top, suddenly, there was nothing in front of us. Instead, as though some giant knife had sliced straight down through the mountain and cut away its other half, we were at the rim of an incredible cliff that fell a thousand feet to the valley floor.

I yanked on the reins and Maude slid to a stop. I felt ethereal and barely heard the laughter of my companions as they swung to the ground. Maude danced a bit and I could feel both of us staggering toward the cliff.

Then Billy Jo was at Maude's head, patting the mare's nose, holding her halter rope, grinning at me.

"You've just had the official introduction to our favorite part of the cliffs." She laughed. "My dad brought me up here on a run, and his dad did it to him, and John's dad did it to him, and he did it to the twins. It's great. This little rise looks like every other one you've ridden over, but there's no other side!"

I dismounted in a rush and again felt my legs almost collapse. Some invisible force seemed to be drawing me over the cliffs, and I fought against it.

"Hey," said Billy Jo. "Relax. The rim's twenty feet away from you. You couldn't fall over it from here if you wanted to."

She was right, of course. There were several yards of grass between me and the empty air that marked the edge of the cliffs. I put my will against my fear and forced a bit of it away. I made my weak legs walk me toward the rim.

In front of me a stunning panorama revealed itself. Beyond the yawning valley below, the jagged Needle Mountains rose like shark's teeth into the sky. To their right, wave on wave of ragged mountains flowed into the distance. A thousand feet below my feet, the valley floor revealed a long lake and tiny dots that I recognized as houses. The highway was a narrow line along which moved smaller dots that I knew were cars. Hawks soared between me and the valley floor, riding the winds, gashing gold vermilion. It was an awesome view whose grandeur and wild beauty were so astonishing that for moments I even forgot my fright at being where I was.

Billy Jo walked to my side and looked out over the precipice at our feet. "When I think of Colorado, this is what I see in my mind. I can't imagine a more magnificent sight."

"I can't either." A soft wind was blowing at our backs and I felt it pushing me toward the rim. I felt lightheaded. The limb of a small spruce was near me. I closed a hand around it.

"Everybody's afraid of something," said Billy Jo gently. "Personally, I can't stand spiders. If I was a secret agent, and you captured me, all you'd have to do would be to put me in a room with spiderwebs and I'd tell you anything you wanted to know. Why don't you sit down?"

I sat. It was good to feel the ground under my rump. I was immediately more secure. I looked at the cliffs flowing away on either side of us and dropping out of sight into the valley. I felt giddy. I looked at the horses. They were grazing within feet of the cliff top, totally ignoring

it. I reached inside myself and found some more willpower and pushed against my fear. Billy Jo sat beside me and pointed here and there.

"Electra Lake. Good fishing there. Some really big trout. The smaller lake is Haviland. That's Animas Canyon, where the train goes on its way to Silverton. Silverton's right over behind those mountains. Old mining town. You really should go up there before you go back east. Just north of here is the Purgatory ski area. They have lifts that bring you up about this high, and then you ski down again. Do you ski?"

"No."

"You probably water-ski, instead."

"No. I sail, but I don't water-ski. I don't like fast boats. I prefer sailing."

"I like all three: skiing, waterskiing, and sailing. Fast boats, too." She made a gesture that took in half the world. "Navaho Lake is just over south of Ignacio. They've got all kinds of boats over there. I've been on a sailboat there. I don't really know how to sail, but I liked it."

A twin came along the cliff top to us. "Hi. Mom and John are down on the ledge that goes to the cave. They said I could bring you there. Come on."

"The cave?" If there was a cave, it had to be in the cliffs. I didn't want to get any closer to the cliffs than I already was.

"John's cave," explained Billy Jo. "It's just down there." She pointed toward a grove of trees growing precariously at the top of the cliff. "He says he found it when he was a kid up here with his father. There's a ledge below those trees there that leads down and back this way. About three feet wide. It gets thin and bends around a corner, and then there's this cave that cuts back into the cliff. John's showed us all where it is. He's very proud of it. I think he actually crawled over to it when he was a kid."

"Great. The ledge is three feet wide and then it gets

thin. Three feet is thin enough! Aren't any of you people afraid that you'll fall off?"

"We never go on the really thin part," said a twin. "John and Mom made us promise. We go on the ledge as far as the corner and look around, though. That's not dangerous!"

I looked at Billy Jo. "Not dangerous?"

She shrugged. "Well . . ."

"You can go on your hands and knees," said the twin. "I did that the first time myself, but I don't anymore."

"I'll tell you what," I said to her. "I'll go with you to where the ledge starts and have a look. But I'm pretty sure that's as far as I'm going. I don't like it up here. I mean, it's beautiful, but I'd rather have a big thick glass wall between me and out there, so I can look, but can't go over the edge!"

"Oh, you won't go over the edge, J.W.," said the twin, unsympathetically. "Come on."

I got a grip on my spruce limb and arranged my legs under me, then noticed Billy Jo's hand reaching down. I took it and she tugged and up I came. In hospitals little nurses toss big patients around like they're made of feathers, so I wasn't surprised at her strength. Our hands lingered a moment longer than required, then parted. I felt a bit breathless.

"This air is thin," I said, looking down at her.

"Come on, you guys," said the twin. "Mom and John want to see you!"

"You have to let go of that tree before we can go," said Billy Jo.

I let go of the spruce and Billy Jo put out a hand as if to catch me should I fall. I didn't fall. After a moment, she smiled, turned, and followed the impatient twin. I trailed gingerly after her, feeling the cliff sucking at me, enticing me over its edge.

We entered a tangle of spruce and aspen trees and fallen logs. The roots of some of the trees were exposed,

thrusting out into the air beyond the lip of the cliff. Why the trees had chosen such a place to grow, I could not imagine. It was another of Nature's myriad mysteries.

Suddenly, the twin grinned at us and was gone.

"Careful now," said Billy Jo. She put out a hand and I took it, and she led me around the stump of a lightning-blasted spruce and over a rotting log. She stopped and pointed with her free hand. "There."

Where? I looked and saw nothing, then looked some more and saw bent grasses at what appeared to be the very edge of the cliff. I inched forward and abruptly saw the beginning of the ledge slanting down on my left. The twin appeared around a corner of rock, grinning and beckoning. "Come on, come on! Mom and John are right here!"

But I had gone far enough. I raised my free hand. "No way. You go and tell John and Mattie that I'll be waiting up here whenever they decide to return to solid ground. Be careful now." The twin made a face and disappeared. I pulled on Billy Jo's hand, and she turned into me, tipping back her head so she could look up at me from beneath her hat brim. "Lead me to the promised land," I said. "I don't know where it is, but it's at least fifty feet away from this cliff. A nice log to sit on would be nice. One looking out over the trail we followed to get here. You know what I mean?"

"Trust me," she said. She led me through the grove of trees to its far side, where we could look west over the rolling meadowlands through the dancing shade of aspen trees. "See? There's even a log for you."

I sat down. She sat beside me. I looked at her hand, which was still in mine. I took a deep breath, then another.

"Thin air." I looked at our hands again and then into her eyes. "I'm a little old to be holding your hand."

"I think it feels pretty good," said Billy Jo. "I haven't done this since my boyfriend and I split up this spring . . ."

It did feel pretty good. Billy Jo's hair and eyes were dark and Celtic, her hand was small and strong.

"Do you have a girlfriend?" she asked.

I thought of Zee. "I have a woman friend. She's not a girl."

"I'm not a girl, either."

"But you had a boyfriend."

"That's why we split up. He's still a boy. I was a girl when we met, but now I'm twenty-one, and I'm not a girl anymore. She's left you, hasn't she?"

They say there's a little bit of woman in every girl and quite a bit of boy in every man. I was considering this old saw when I heard voices behind us. "This will have to wait," I said. I pressed her hand and let it go, and got up to meet John and Mattie and the twins.

I kissed Mattie and took John's hand.

"What a nice surprise," said Mattie. "What in the world brings you out here?"

"I need the love of a good woman," I said. "So I came straight to you."

"You're a smooth-talking city slicker, J.W. So you took John's advice and came out, eh? Good! The girls will have you riding like the Lone Ranger before you go home."

"Yeah!" chorused the twins, who could imagine nothing better than riding horses every day.

I looked at John. "Show me your cliffs," I said. He looked surprised. I smiled at the women and girls. "Ladies, if you'll excuse us. This is manly business. You understand."

Mattie looked at me with curious eyes, then nodded. "Of course. When manly men get together, they must do manly things. Come along, girls. You too, Billy Jo. Let's go find some wildflowers for a bouquet for camp."

"Very womanly of you," I said.

"Don't be long."

"We won't," I said. "Come on, John." I started back toward the cliffs. After a moment, he followed me. I made my legs carry me through the grove of spruce, right to

the edge of the cliff. The air tried to suck me over, but I put my back against a tree trunk and stabilized myself.

John came up to me, a thoughtful look on his face. "Why are you here, J.W.? Why did you want me away from Mattie and the girls? Something's wrong. What is it?"

I decided to get right to it. "Did you ever hear of a man named Gordon Berkeley Orwell?"

"Gordon Berkeley Orwell?" He stared at me and then at the ground, and then at me again. "No. Who's Gordon Berkeley Orwell?"

"How well did you know Bernadette Orwell?"

"She was a student of mine. Medieval Literature. Year before last. Smart girl. Pretty emotional at times. I know she was into campus activities. Student government, marches for women, gay rights, that sort of thing. The idealistic type. This Gordon Orwell a relative of hers?"

"You were never anything more than just her teacher?"

His face was suddenly expressionless. He cocked his head slightly to one side. "What do you mean?"

"Were you her lover? Were you her confidant? Were you her special friend? Anything like that?"

He studied me. "This isn't like you," he said. "I've never known you to ask people such questions."

"I'm asking them now."

"My private life is none of your business."

"I know."

He looked at me through professorial eyes. "You talk to me and then I may talk to you."

"All right." I told him about the shootings on Martha's Vineyard and about Gordon Berkeley Orwell. "I think Gordon Orwell is after your ass," I said finally. "All I can think of is that it has something to do with Bernadette Orwell. Maybe he's mad at you because of her."

All of the blandness had disappeared from his face. "You mean that he tried to kill you, because he thought you were me? Good God!"

"That's why I need to know if there was anything between you and Bernadette. I need to know why he's after
you. You need to know that even more than I do."

He looked at me, then turned and stared out over the
valley. Then he shrugged his shoulders and looked at me
again.

"Bernie Orwell was one of my better students. From
the first time she started attending my class, though, it
seemed like she wanted something more from me. You
wouldn't know, because you've never been a teacher, but
now and then every teacher has had a student who has
what we used to call a crush. I don't know what the
current slang word would be. It's always awkward for the
teacher at the time, and it's generally embarrassing for
the student after the crush runs its course. Anyway, Bernie
liked to stay after class and walk with me to my office.
She began to make appointments with me, and then
would come by without them. At first I thought she was
just an eager student.

"Then I learned that her father had died that summer,
and I guessed that I was a substitute. A father-lover figure, if you will. She was at a fragile time in her life. You
know: emotional, quick to change mood. I felt sympathy
for her, but I figured that before very long she'd see that
I wasn't what she thought I was. That's usually how these
crushes work out. But it wasn't until the end of the term
that she stopped coming around. I figured she'd probably
found somebody else, maybe somebody more her age. I
didn't see much of her after she finished that one class,
though we were friendly enough when we happened to
meet. If Gordon Orwell thinks I was romantically involved with Bernadette, he's dead wrong."

"He may be wrong," I said. "But you're the one who
may be dead."

17

John looked out over the gigantic cliffs, frowning. I looked too, and felt a wave of nausea and weakness. I forced myself to keep looking.

"I don't care about your private life one way or another," I said. "I hope you understand that."

"Yes," he said. "I understand."

"I wanted to ask you when Mattie wasn't around . . ."

"You don't have to explain. You thought that if Bernadette and I did have something going, you didn't want Mattie to hear about it from you."

"Something like that."

"Is this Gordon Orwell related to Bernadette?"

"I don't know. They both live in New Jersey. It would be a funny coincidence if they weren't related. I expect to find out more when I talk with the local cops. The chief, back in Edgartown, is checking Orwell out and sending what he knows on to them."

John was looking out into the vast space that hung between us and the mountains across the valley, but he wasn't seeing it: he was blind to all but his thoughts.

"The chief thinks Orwell may be coming out here. Is that it?"

"That's a possibility. Orwell got your mailing address from my desk. I found your mother's ranch by using the phone. Orwell could do the same."

"But I'm not there."

"I found out where you are."

"You think Orwell can do that, too? Find me up here?"

"I don't know."

An ironic little smile flitted across his face. "If I stay

up here, he may come; if I go to the ranch, he may be waiting; if I go back to Weststock or the Vineyard, he can find me at his leisure. I think I have a problem."

"Maybe not. A lot of cops are aware of him. Maybe they'll find him."

"And what if they do? What charge can they bring against him?"

A good question. "Using a stolen credit card to rent a car?"

"How long will that keep him in jail?"

"Not long, if at all."

He turned away from the cliff. "We have to tell all of this to Mattie. She and I don't keep things from each other."

The wind pushed me toward the cliffs as I stood away from the tree I'd been leaning on. I thought of *The Book of Five Rings* and the wisdom that advised warriors to hold themselves already dead so fear of death would leave them. But the wind still pushed at me and my belly felt awash with acid and I had to force my legs to carry me after John, away from the cliff and into the trees where the ground beneath me felt more solid.

The women and the twins were leading the horses down from the edge of the cliff and across a meadow as we emerged from the trees. They carried wildflowers.

"Are you through with the manly stuff?" asked Jill or Jen.

"There's not enough time in one life to do all the manly stuff that needs doing," I said. "But we got some of it done."

"Good. Let's race back to camp!"

Billy Jo laughed. "I don't think that J.W. is up to a race back to camp!"

"Sure he is! Sure you are, J.W.! Come on! We'll give you a head start!"

"Forget it, Jill," I said. "Race with your sister, if you have to race with somebody."

"I'm Jen," she said.

"No, you're not," said Mattie. "You're just giving poor J.W. a hard time. You and Jen go on ahead, if you want to, but J.W. probably wants a very slow trip back to camp."

"Very slow," I agreed.

"Gee whiz," said Jill. "Well, okay. Come on, Jen!"

The two of them swung up onto their horses and were away at the gallop.

"Youth," sighed Mattie, looking after them. "I hope they don't break their necks!"

"We have to talk," said John.

"I thought as much," said Mattie.

John looked at Billy Jo.

"She knows about most of it," I said.

"Tell the whole thing then," said John.

I repeated what I'd told John. When I was through, Mattie asked the key question.

"What are we going to do?"

"I think that you and the girls should go to your mother's house for a while," said John.

"Forget that idea," said Mattie firmly. "We're a family. We do things together."

"Just until we get this misunderstanding straightened out."

"No." Mattie looked at me. "It is a mistake, isn't it? Isn't that what you said? Well, if it's a mistake, and this Orwell knows it, then he'll stop this, won't he?"

"I don't know," I said. "He apparently doesn't think it's a mistake." I looked at John. "You're sure you never heard of this guy?"

John's face looked like an honest one. Of course the same can be said for the face of any good con man. "Not that I remember," he said. "But I'm not the world's champion name rememberer."

"He's good at names before 1500 A.D.," said Mattie. "It's the ones since then that he forgets. What if we can get ahold of this Orwell and tell him he's after the wrong man? Can't we do that somehow? Can't the police get

him and hold him at least long enough to tell him he's after the wrong man?" She put her hand in John's.

"If they get their hands on him, they can try to tell him that. It can't hurt."

"If we're going to get to the truck and trailer before dark, we've got to get started," said Billy Jo, glancing at the afternoon sun.

"Look," I said to John and Mattie. "Even though I knew you were up here somewhere, I'd have been a long time finding you if Billy Jo hadn't brought me to your camp. This guy's in the same boat. Why don't you all just stay up here for a few more days, and give me a chance to find out what's going on. I'll talk to the local cops and phone east, and then I'll come back up here and you can decide what to do."

They looked at one another. There was an appearance of innocence about them that I thought might be mis- leading. Some unspoken agreement was reached and they turned back to me and nodded.

"All right," said Mattie. "We'll stay here for a while longer."

"I'll be back in two or three days. Maybe sooner." I put a smile on my face. "I may come back with good news."

"Do you think so?"

"Sure," I said.

"We'd better get back to camp," said John. "And you two had better head on down the trail while you still have some light."

Billy Jo had been working on her saddle and now ducked under her mare's neck and handed her scabbarded 30–30 to John.

"Here. Just in case."

He looked down at the rifle in his hands. "Just in case of what?"

"You never know. The magazine is full, but the firing chamber isn't, so you'll have to jack a shell in before you shoot. You know how to use one of these things?"

Mattie frowned skeptically at the rifle, but said nothing. John slid the rifle partway out of the saddle scabbard, looked at it, and slid it back in. "My father had one of these when I was a kid. Model 94 Winchester. I think I can still remember how it works."

Billy Jo grinned. "Good. I never met a Skye who didn't know about rifles, but I wasn't sure an East Coast English professor would remember such things."

"I wasn't always an English professor," said John, with a crooked smile. He lifted the rifle. "Thanks."

Billy Jo nodded and mounted her mare. "We'd better be moving, J.W."

I climbed up on Maude and we rode down through the meadows and woods to the camp, where the twins had long since been waiting. Their parents dismounted.

"Hey," said a twin, "I thought you were going to stay, J.W."

"Not tonight. No sleeping bag . . ."

"We've got extra blankets."

"No change of clothes . . ."

"You can borrow some of John's!"

"No beer!"

"Oh, so that's it! We should have known. Are you coming back?"

"In a couple of days."

"Well, bring your sleeping bag and clothes and a pack-horse loaded with booze, so you can stay awhile! We want to teach you how to ride!"

Oh, wretched thought. "Thanks," I said. Behind them, I saw John carry the rifle into his tent. Then I followed Billy Jo out of camp.

Going down the Goulding Trail was worse than going up. My legs were rubbery and sorer than ever when we finally reached the pickup and trailer, parked now in the long shadow of the cliffs. I got off Maude and almost fell down, but managed to lead her into the trailer and tie her halter rope to the front rack. Then I crawled into the

cab and admired Billy Jo as she smoothly turned us around and headed us down to the highway. There, she turned right, and we started for Durango. I looked up out of my window at the darkened cliffs and the bright sky that topped them. I liked them better from down here.

"Beautiful day for a ride," said Billy Jo. "You'll be stiff tomorrow, but you'll survive. Riding takes muscles you don't use doing other things."

I gave an experimental moan and she smiled.

"I know a fake groan when I hear one. You have a couple of shots of red-eye and a good night's sleep and you'll feel a lot better."

"Have one with me," I said. "I'll treat. The bar of your choice."

She thought awhile. "Okay. But just one. I've got to get these horses home. Let me see . . . I've got it. Just the place for a man who likes his barley pops. A joint that makes its own beer!"

I brightened. "Sounds just right!"

We drove down into the Animas Valley. Long shadows reached across the valley floor from the west, but the eastern cliffs were ablaze with sunset light. In Durango Billy Jo parked the pickup and trailer west of the railroad tracks and gimpy me walked with her up to Main Street. There, right beside Radio Shack, was Carvers bakery, cafe, and— yes!—brewery! We took a booth, declined the waitress' offer of food, and ordered two Animas City Amber Ales. They arrived and we touched mugs.

"Cheers. And thanks."

I drank. Delish! Durango found increased favor in my eyes.

"What are you going to do about this man Orwell?" asked Billy Jo.

"I don't know if I can do anything, but now, at least, John knows what's going on. I'll talk to some cops. You know, a town with its own brewery can't be a really bad town."

"Then you'll love this one. It's got two."

"No!"

"Yes. Down toward the end of Main, Father Murphy serves his own brews."

"Well, when we're done here, we can go there."

"Sorry. The horses. Remember? Next time."

"I owe you more than a beer," I said. "I owe you dinner, at least. I'd like to take you someplace. Maybe some good Mexican food. We don't get much of that on the island."

She smiled. "You get Mexican food and I'll have seafood."

"Can we do that in one restaurant?"

"Maybe we'll have to go out twice."

"Maybe we will."

"Why don't we start tomorrow night? You can talk to your people during the daylight."

"All right. Shall I pick you up?"

"I'll pick you up, since I'm the one who knows where we'll be going. Seven?"

"Seven it is."

She finished her beer and flowed up onto her feet. It seemed a shame to leave before trying the Purgatory Pilsner or the Iron Horse Stout, but she had the wheels, so I floundered up in turn.

Back at the motel, I was very conscious of her body next to mine.

"I'll see you tomorrow night, then," she said. "If I can help you out before then, give me a call. You have my number."

I got out and she drove away. I thought of her sleek body and dark eyes, and her dark hair sweeping down from her broad-brimmed hat.

I went inside and went to the phone on the bedside table. The chief, in Edgartown, would be at home. I figured he'd had time to finish supper so I put through a call.

"I thought it might be you." He sighed. "I've had a nice day. I knew it couldn't last."

— 18 —

"I'm doing your wife a favor by calling you," I said. "Everybody knows you can't talk and smoke at the same time, so she'll thank me for temporarily saving your house from another fumigation from your pipe."

"Annie likes my pipe," he said, probably truthfully. They had been married for over thirty years and he'd been puffing his briar all that time and probably longer. I had once smoked a pipe myself, and still missed it.

I told him that I'd found John Skye and that tomorrow I was going to see the local cops.

"They'll have the latest information by then," he said. "You can have it now.

"Early this morning Gordon Berkeley Orwell came out of the Maine woods, made sure he was seen by several people at the outfitting station, got into his Jeep, and drove off. We figure he had time after he left the island to ride up near there by bus, get out someplace not too far from where he was supposed to be hiking, walk into the hills, and come back out again where people could see him. On the other hand, maybe he really was up there in the woods all along, and we've had our eye on the wrong guy."

"Do you think you've had your eye on the wrong guy?"

"No."

"Did Gordon Berkeley Orwell have a sister named Bernadette?"

"Yeah. A student up there at Weststock College. Died this summer. Drugs. Weststock, that's where this Orwell guy, if it was him, tried to hit Skye the first time. Drugs, Skye, Orwell's sister. If there's a tie-in, that seems to be it. How'd you know about Bernadette Orwell?"

"I met her last spring when a bunch of Weststock students stayed at John's place doing some sort of sociology study. Skye says she was a student of his a year ago, but that he's barely seen her since."

"Does Skye do drugs?"

"He does booze."

"Did he ever do other drugs?"

"Is there anybody under sixty who hasn't at least tried grass?"

"I don't know. Some, probably. Do you believe him about not seeing the girl since the class she took?"

I'd been running that through my head. "Yeah, I think I do. Of course, I'm also the guy who predicted the Sox would go all the way last year. Where's Orwell now?"

"He went home. Back to New Jersey. He's had a bad couple of years. His father died summer before last, and his sister OD'd this summer. His mother's the only one left. Orwell was stationed down south of the border somewhere. Central America or maybe farther south. Adviser to some army or government or other, or maybe he was something more than that. Home on extended leave."

"Career man?"

"Captain. Assigned to some kind of special outfit. Too young for Nam, but he's been a few other places as near as I can tell. The Pentagon is being pretty cagey about just what it is he does."

"How'd he get the limp?"

"In the line of duty, we're told."

"How?"

"We're not told."

"Where is he now?"

"How should I know? He was home earlier today."

"Can you give me his home phone number?"

"No. Police business."

"Weststock College will have Bernadette's home address and phone. I can get it from them. It'll just take longer."

"Wait." He put me on hold. After a while, he came

back. "I had to call the station on the car radio." He gave me the number. "What are you up to?"

"I want to find out if Orwell's still there. If he is, I want to talk to him. If he's the guy who's after John Skye, I want to know it. If he isn't, I want to know that, so I can tell John to watch out for somebody else."

"His mother is at their home. She's lost a husband and a daughter, so don't be too tough."

"I'm not tough."

I hung up and called the New Jersey number he'd given me. A thin female voice answered.

"Hi," I said, putting a bit of aped Colorado twang into my voice. "This is J. W. Jackson. I heard ol' Gordy is back stateside and I thought I'd give him a call and talk some old times. Is this Miz Orwell?"

"Yes. You're a friend of my son, Mr. . . ."

"Jackson. J. W. Jackson. Pleasure to talk to you, ma'am. Yes, ma'am, Gordy and me have been a couple of places together. You know. Sure hope he's there. Like to talk to him while he's up here."

"I'm sure he'd like to see you too, Mr. Jackson, but I'm afraid Gordon isn't here right now. He's gone out to Jackson, Wyoming, to do some hiking in the Grand Tetons. You just missed him."

"Durn! Wyoming, eh? He leave you an address or any such thing, Miz Orwell? Sure like to say hello . . ."

"I'm afraid he didn't. Where are you now, Mr. Jackson? Perhaps you'd like to come by for some tea. It's always a pleasure to meet my son's friends . . ."

"Ma'am I'm in a phone booth in Atlanta, so I'm afraid I can't accept your invitation. Sure do thank you for it, though. Gordy just now headed out, eh?"

"Yes. He flew west just this afternoon. He'd been up in Maine, you know. Why, I barely saw him before he was off again. Oh, dear. He'll be so disappointed to miss your call. Perhaps he can contact you later . . ."

Then I did a cruel thing. I said, "That'd be terrific.

Say, how's that sweet sister of his doin'? I tell you, old Gordy sure dotes on that girl."

There was a silence. Then the thin voice spoke. "Oh, I'm so sorry. Of course you couldn't know. Bernadette died earlier this summer. It was . . . very sudden . . ."

I made myself go on. "Oh, damn! Pardon, ma'am. I sure am sorry to hear that. That's about as bad a thing as can happen to you. Yes, I sure am sorry. How are you and Gordy doin'?"

"It will take us time, Mr. Jackson. Right now everything is . . . You must have heard how Gordon hates those Eastern colleges. Just like his father in that respect . . . Then to have this happen . . . It's been a difficult time for us. First the colonel and now Bernadette . . . To be straightforward, it's almost driven Gordon mad. I'm half mad myself at times . . . But I must ask your pardon. These are family matters . . . Still, I do wish Gordon had a friend to talk to . . ."

"Yes, ma'am. Gordon can find me if he wants me. Just tell him J. W. Jackson called. Well, I got to go. Nice talking to you, ma'am. Awfully sorry about your daughter. You have a nice day, now."

"Yes. A nice day. Thank you."

I hung up and opened another beer. I felt like lead. Was it worth it to hurt a mother to learn only that her son was almost mad with grief? I didn't know. What I did know was that Gordon Berkeley Orwell could be showing up anytime now. I wondered if I should go out to the airport and just sit there. Sooner or later, he should step off some plane, if he was coming. Then I thought some more. I was wrong. He could fly to some other town and then drive to Durango. I thought of his mother's voice. It was the voice of a woman who hadn't had many nice days lately.

I finished my beer, got into my car, and drove downtown. Durango was alive with automobiles, brightly lit stores, bars, and restaurants. I found a parking place and walked along Main Street. There were souvenir shops

with Japanese-made Indian headbands, bows with rubber-tipped arrows, rubber-tipped lances, all apparently furnished by the same oriental wholesaler who provided the goods displayed at the Indian shops at Gay Head. There were stores with windows heavy with silver and turquoise necklaces, rings, and watch bands. There were stores with windows full of cowboy hats, boots, and belts. There were lots of restaurants and bars.

I went into the Diamond Belle Saloon and found myself in a re-created Gay Nineties bar, complete with mustachioed bartender and barmaids in tiny dresses and net stockings. I wondered if the barmaids felt exploited. The bar was noisy. Under a balcony at the back of the room was a sign I appreciated: Work is the curse of the drinking classes. True. There was a rail at the foot of the bar. I put my Teva on it and ordered a Sam Adams. No luck. I ordered a Bass Ale and did better. The Bass was smooth and good.

Half of the men in the bar were wearing cowboy hats, and the other half were wearing baseball caps. I wondered if I should buy myself a Stetson. Maybe some boots, too. Then I thought again. Where would I wear cowboy clothes on Martha's Vineyard? I listened to the noise. Western accents and tourist accents. People seemed pretty happy. I had another Bass and felt it. The altitude, maybe.

I went out and down the street to the train station. No trains this time of night. I turned and walked back up Main Street. I came to Father Murphy's Pub. I went in and discovered that Father Murphy served not one but two locally brewed beers! I drank a glass of each while I devoured a sandwich. Durango seemed to be an excellent town. Two breweries. Who'd have thunk it?

I thought some more about buying cowboy clothes. Nah. Then I thought awhile about Gordon Berkeley Orwell. After a while I went to find my car. It took a while, but I managed it, and then managed to find my motel, too. On the way I saw a lot of churches. I wondered if there were more bars, churches, or motels in Durango. I

thought it would be a close contest. I wondered what Zee was doing, and then remembered Billy Jo Skye's hand in mine. I took two aspirin and went to bed.

In the morning I had a bloat breakfast at the diner and went downtown to find the police station, which turned out to be on Second Avenue across Tenth Street from the county courthouse. Arrest 'em, jail 'em, try 'em, hang 'em. All in one city block. Western justice. I was impressed. I parked and went into the station.

Police stations are a lot alike. This one was newer than others I'd seen, but otherwise pretty familiar-looking. I gave my name to the cop at the front desk and asked for the chief. The desk cop raised an eyebrow and I handed him the letter the chief in Edgartown had written for me. He read it, looked at me, then handed the letter back and gestured toward a door. "Back there, Mr. Jackson."

I went through the door and found myself across a desk from the chief. I gave him my letter, which he read and handed back.

"Sit down," he said. I sat. "Well, Mr. Jackson, what can I do for you?"

"You've heard about this man Orwell."

"Yes. So far, of course, there are no real charges against him."

I told him about my experience in Weststock and on the Vineyard. "I talked to his mother last night," I concluded. "She said Gordon Orwell flew west yesterday afternoon. To go hiking in the Grand Tetons."

"Maybe that's what he's doing."

"Maybe." I told him what I'd been doing for the past two days. He listened patiently. I said, "If Orwell really is after John Skye, he may be showing up here pretty soon."

"We'll keep our eyes open, but you have to remember that we have thousands of tourists coming in here all summer long. We might miss him. Easy enough to do. We don't know what he looks like."

Neither did I. "The chief is trying to get a picture of

him. He said he'd wire it to you." I got up. "Maybe
I'll talk with the sheriff, too."

"Good idea." He put out his hand and I took it. "Don't
be rash, Mr. Jackson. Remember that you don't really know
whether this man Orwell has actually done anything."

"Somebody really did something."

"Yes, but let the police handle it. Thanks for coming by.
Stay in touch. If you learn anything more, let us know."

I went across the street to the courthouse and told my story
to a deputy sheriff. He also shook my hand, thanked me, and
told me to leave the matter in the hands of the professionals.

I found a phone booth and called Billy Jo Skye's house.
Her mother answered. She said she was glad I'd called.

"A man phoned this morning, wondering if I knew how
he could get in touch with John Skye. Said he was a friend
of his."

"Did he give his name?"

"Yes. He said his name was J. W. Jackson. I did what
you said. I called the Sheriff's Department and told them
about it."

The deputy I'd talked to hadn't mentioned it to me.
Maybe he didn't know about it. Or maybe he just didn't
think it was any of my business. Some cops are like that.

— 19 —

"Funny man," I said to Wilma Skye.

"Of course, if John and his family hadn't recognized
you, there was no way we'd know this guy wasn't you,"
she observed. "Or, for that matter, that you were who
you said you were."

True. "What did you tell him?"

"I told him to call back this afternoon. That maybe I'd

know then. Then I phoned your motel, but you were out. Then I got a call from Alison, that's Mack's brother's wife, and she said she'd gotten a call, too. J. W. Jackson looking for John Skye. She called the Sheriff's Department, too."

"What did she tell the guy who said he was me?"

"Told him she didn't know where John was. Fellow asked her how he could find the farm. She told him because she couldn't figure out how not to. Figured he'd find it anyway. They've got these maps with all the road numbers marked on them, you know. You can get them in town."

"No damage done."

"What should I tell him when he calls back?"

A good question. I didn't know a good answer. "I'll call you back," I said.

I went back to the Sheriff's Department. The deputy was gone. I told another deputy my story and my thoughts and what Wilma Skye had just told me.

The deputy raised a restraining hand and glanced at a page of scribbles in front of him. "Wilma Skye says that a guy calling himself J. W. Jackson phoned and said he was looking for John Skye. Later Alison Skye told us the guy talked to her, too."

"Right. And Wilma told the guy to call back this afternoon."

"Right. But the guy really wasn't J. W. Jackson, because you're J. W. Jackson, and you think the guy might really be . . ." He looked down at the scribbles, "Gordon Orwell. Is that right?"

"Right."

"Is this going to make more sense to somebody else than it does to me? I sure hope so."

I hoped so too. I went back out to the phone and rang Wilma Skye. "When this guy calls back," I said, "tell him that someone will meet him at Vivian Skye's place with a map so he can show him exactly where John is. I'll be the someone."

"That doesn't sound like the world's best idea."

"I'll have the edge. I'll expect him, but he won't expect me."

"Didn't you say this guy took a couple of shots at you?"

"Yeah, but he didn't really mean it the second time."

There was a silence at the far end of the line. Then Wilma asked, "You have a gun?"

"No."

"You swing by here on your way. Matter of fact, come for lunch. I understand that you and my little girl have a date tonight, by the way."

"There are no secrets between a daughter and her mother."

"I wouldn't be so sure about that. Come out about noon. Mack will be home thereabouts. Might want some words with you."

"About me and Billy Jo?" Good grief!

"No. Well, maybe. I had in mind this idea you have about meeting this Orwell fella. I think we might talk a bit before you go off to confront the lion."

"See you at noon then." I knew where the power was. If I didn't show up, she wouldn't give Orwell my message.

I found a window and looked at myself in the reflection. Martha's Vineyard Surfcasters' cap, thrift shop shorts, Teva sandals, and a shirt that said Al's Package Store. No weirder than the threads a lot of tourists were wearing on the street, but not very native Durangoish. I'd been wearing almost the same clothes when Orwell had shot at me on the island, and if I showed up like this at the ranch, he might recognize me and either shoot or take off before I could get close to him.

I went into one of the stores with cowboy clothes in the window and bought myself a wide-brimmed straw hat with a wire around the brim so you could bend it into any shape you liked. I also got a Denver Broncos tee shirt. Then I drove back to the motel and spent some time punching and bending my new hat and rubbing it in the

dirt to make it look old. I soaked the shirt in the sink, wrung it out and tied it in a knot, and put it in a sunny window. By the time I had changed into jeans and my old army boots and it was time to leave for the Skyes' place, the hot, dry air had done its job. The tee shirt looked wrinkled and used. I put it on and drove back to the sheriff's office. I thought I looked quite local.

The first deputy was back. He and the second deputy were together. The first deputy looked at my get-up and shook his head. "Maybe we ought to throw you in jail before somebody else does. If we don't have any laws against vagrants, I think we can make one up pretty fast. We just got some news that might interest you. Come in here."

I followed him into a room and he handed me two sheets of paper.

"Faxed about an hour ago," said the deputy.

One was a picture of a man in army uniform looking intently at the camera. His hair was trim and his gaze was level. There was a slight scar on his left cheek.

"Gordon Berkeley Orwell," said the deputy. "Taken about three years ago, apparently. Now we know what he looks like, at least. I figure we'll tell the guy to come to the ranch, then put a couple of men out there in the ranch house and wait for him to show up. Ask him a couple of questions and maybe get to the bottom of this."

My first thought was that the deputies were horning in on my plan. My second was that it made sense for them to do it. My third was the first one all over again, and my fourth was the second again. I put my foot on my fifth, and told them what I'd planned to do myself.

The first deputy frowned. "Okay, but now you just stay out of it and leave things to us."

The second piece of paper said that Captain Gordon Berkeley Orwell had a private gun collection and was said to favor a Beretta 125 nine-millimeter parabellum Italian machine gun with a blowback action offering a choice of burst or single shots out of a thirty-two-round magazine.

With the butt folded, the Beretta was 16.46 inches long. Corporal Dominic Agganis of the Massachusetts State Police was of the opinion that the Beretta had been fired at one J.W. Jackson on Martha's Vineyard.

"What do you think?" asked the deputy.

"The right size gun and the right caliber. Could be. Tell your men to be careful. This guy is a tough cookie and pretty slick."

"We're not too bad ourselves," said the deputy.

"I'm going out to Mack Skye's place," I said. "When the guy phones in, we'll tell him to go to the ranch. Then I'll call you."

"Call us at Vivian Skye's ranch," said the deputy, "because that's where we'll be. Jake and I will go out there right now, so we'll be able to check the place out before Orwell shows up."

"The front door of the house is unlocked," I said, "and you can put your car in the barn so it'll be out of sight. I mean it about being careful."

"Mr. Orwell is the one who needs to be careful," said the deputy.

I drove, via a liquor store, out to the Florida Mesa. I wished I had a pickup. Then I'd look perfect.

Billy Jo raised both eyebrows.

"I want you to feel I'm just like the guys you grew up with," I said.

"I'm not interested in the guys I grew up with. I'm interested in some other kinds of guys." She gave a crooked smile. "You do look the part, I must admit."

"Mine was a great loss to the stage."

"Come on around back. Mom and Dad are already into the iced tea." She nodded. "If you add a shot of whiskey to that, you'll have a seven-course meal."

I lifted the six-pack of Coors. "I'll be glad to share."

We walked around the house. The wind was gentle in the trees and the lawn was thick and green. It was cool

in the shade. Mack and Wilma Skye were at the table covered with food. Mack got up and put out his large hand, which I took.

"Hey, you must have really made an impression on my little girl. Went to town this morning and got herself some new diggers for the big date."

Billy Jo blushed. "I did not! I needed them anyway."

Diggers? What were diggers? "What are diggers?" I asked.

Billy Jo gritted her teeth. "Underwear, if you must know. But I didn't get them for our date! Daddy, how could you say such a thing!?"

"Well, sweetheart, I . . ."

Wilma clicked her tongue. "Never mind, Mackenzie. Your jokes aren't always as funny as you think they are. Sit down, J.W. You too, Billy Jo. You know better than to take your daddy seriously when he's only trying to be funny. Try some of those muffins, J.W. And there's some roast beef there, or some ham if you'd rather have that. That cheese is good, too. Don't just sit there, Billy Jo, put some food on your plate. You're getting too skinny. It's not healthy."

"I'm just fine. And I'm not skinny."

"What do you think, J.W.?" asked her father. "Is she about to blow away, or not?"

"She looks fine to me." I reached for the roast beef.

"Thank you," said Billy Jo. "Now that that's settled. I think I will have something to eat." She started stacking her plate. A twenty-one-year-old woman can eat a lot, I discovered.

After a while, Mack popped one of my beers and took a long slug. "Well, son, what's this about you going over to Vivian's to meet with this fella who says he's you? Doesn't sound too smart to me."

"As it turns out," I said, "I don't have to go through with the master plan. The Law is going to attend to it." I told them about my talk with the deputies.

Wilma and Mack looked at each other. Billy Jo looked at me. "I'm glad," she said, and reached her hand toward mine.

Just then I heard the ringing of the phone in the house. Billy Jo's hand stopped. We all looked toward the sound. Wilma rose and waved the rest of us down. "I talked to him before, I'll talk to him now." She looked down at me. "I'll tell him to go to the ranch. That someone will meet him there in an hour . . . Who?. . ."

"Your nephew," I said.

"My nephew." She nodded. The phone rang. She trotted toward the house.

"The world's getting mighty strange," said Mack. With one hand, he squeezed his beer can flat. I opened another can.

Wilma went into the house and the phone stopped ringing. After a while she came out again.

"Done," she said. "I gave him the message, then called the deputies at the house, but nobody answered. They must be outside. I'll try again in a few minutes."

"How'd he seem?" I asked.

"Soft voice. Cheerful."

"I guess now we wait."

"Well, I'm going to wait up in the north quarter section," said Mack. "Still got half a field to plow. I'll see you all later. Wilma, you stick close to the house. Billy Jo, you might show J.W. around a bit."

He went off.

"Finish your beer," said Billy Jo, easing back in her chair. "Nothing's going to happen for an hour."

Once you got out of the shade, it was a thirsty day. I took the remains of my six-pack with me and we finished it while Billy Jo led me down to the corrals and through the barn and outbuildings. It was a well-maintained place. There were horses in a pasture behind the barn and there was a pond beyond them and a grove of piñon and cedar trees beyond that.

"All sagebrush once," said Billy Jo, sweeping her hand across a panorama of green fields. "My grandfather ran

cattle here, but now we mostly farm and only keep enough beef for our own table."

We circled back to the house.

"Pit stop," said Billy Jo.

"You can't buy beer," I said, quoting the ancient wisdom. "You can only rent it."

Wilma was coming out of the house as we went in. She was carrying a basket, wearing cotton gloves, and headed for the garden.

"Those deputies must be hunkered down in the chicken coops or somewhere. Called them half a dozen times, but never got hold of them. Damnation, people should stick to their plans. Too late to call them again. I'm going to do some weeding." She went past us and I looked after her. I didn't like what I'd heard her say.

Billy Jo was first in line for the bathroom, and thus it was that when the phone rang I was the only one there to answer it. I did.

A gentle, ironic voice asked for Mrs. Skye.

"She's outside. Can I take a message?"

"Who's this?"

"Just a friend. Who's this?" I thought I knew.

"Another friend. Yes, you can give her a message. Tell her that her nephew never showed up and the two guys that came instead didn't know a thing about where John Skye is. Tell her I'm really disappointed with her."

"Orwell, is that you?"

There was a silence. Then, "Who's this?"

"J. W. Jackson. Don't hang up. You're after the wrong man. Call me at . . ."

The phone clicked in my ear.

Billy Jo came out of the bathroom and saw me with the phone in my hand. She also must have seen something in my face.

"What happened? What's the matter?"

"I think there's trouble at Vivian's place. Do you have another gun in the house? I prefer a rifle or shotgun."

She nodded.

"Get it, please. And some shells."

She went away without a word and I phoned the Sheriff's Department and told them to get some people out to Vivian Skye's ranch. As I hung up, Billy Jo came back with both a deer rifle and a shotgun. I took the shotgun and punched shells into the magazine. "I'm going to Vivian Skye's house. Stay here by the phone."

"No. I'm coming with you. I can shoot."

A rifle had better range than the shotgun. "All right. Let's go." We went out and got into my car. I saw Wilma coming out of the garden as we drove out. She dropped her basket and started running toward us, but I didn't stop.

— **20** —

There was a low ridge west of Vivian Skye's place. A large irrigation ditch ran along it, and there were willows and cottonwood trees growing there. When I got there, I stopped the car and looked at the farmhouse and then at the corrals and outbuildings on the other side of the road. The gates on cither end of the corrals were open. No one was in sight. Beside me, Billy Jo punched shells into the magazine of the 30-06 she held, muzzle down, between her legs.

"When we get there," I said, "I'm going to stop the car on the road and leave the engine running. I want you to stay by the car with the rifle and cover me while I go into the house. If you see somebody laying for me, shoot him. If I get inside and you hear shooting, but don't see me come out afterward, I want you to get away. You understand?"

"Yes."

"And watch your back. Maybe Orwell isn't in the house at all. He might be on the other side of the road in the outbuildings."

"Yes."

There were beads of sweat above her upper lip, and her eyes were bright.

I drove up to the gate to the driveway and stopped and looked at the house, then at the outbuildings. No movement. I felt as I'd felt when I'd gone out on patrol in Vietnam. Hollow, fatalistic, jumpy, frightened. I got out of the car, pumped a shell into the firing chamber of the shotgun, and ran toward the house, trying to see everywhere at once.

Nothing moved.

I slanted toward the front door, stood to one side of it, and pushed it open. I heard muffled sounds from somewhere inside. If I'd had a grenade. I could have tossed it in and then ducked in after the explosion; but I didn't have a grenade. I listened some more, flattened against the wall of the house. I heard the sound again. A voice somewhere deep inside the house. I heard nothing in the room beyond the door. I took a deep breath and ducked through the door, shotgun level.

An empty room. Doorways leading out of it. I went silently to the first one. An empty kitchen with a door leading outside and another into a hall. I went to the hall. The muffled voice seemed louder.

It took me ten minutes to go through the ground floor and second floor of the house.

Nobody.

The only place left was the basement. I stood to one side and pushed open the door to the basement stairs. The muffled voice was suddenly silent. There was a light switch on the wall beside the stairs. I reached across with the barrel of the shotgun and flicked it on. Light flared up from below.

I waited, listening. I didn't want to go down the stairs.

I popped my head out and tried to see down there. No good. I went down the stairs fast, shotgun thrust in front of me, waiting for the bullets. I saw a wall and spun, putting my back to it, swinging the shotgun across the room as I looked for Orwell and his Beretta machine gun.

The two deputy sheriffs I had talked to were staring at me with white faces and wide eyes. Their hands were cuffed to water pipes. Their pistol holsters were empty. One had a bloody head.

"If he's here, say so quick!" My voice sounded flat and small.

"No. No, he's gone! We're mighty glad to see you!" The deputy I'd first spoken to nodded toward a table across the room. "Our guns and the keys to the cuffs are over there."

I got the keys and gave them to the deputies and went upstairs and outside. Billy Jo stood behind the car, looking at me over the sights of her 30–06. I walked out to her and told her about the deputies. "Now we'll do the out-buildings," I said. "Cover me again. You're good at it."

She looked over my shoulder. "Wait a minute. Here comes some help."

The deputies came up. They looked happier than they had looked in the basement. I told them I was going to search the outbuildings.

The first deputy looked at Billy Jo. "You better stay out of this, miss."

"Nobody's taken her gun away from her," I said. "You two ever in the service?" They both nodded. "Okay, let's sweep these outbuildings. Billy Jo'll cover our asses."

With three men, the job was faster. In the barn we found the deputies' truck parked right where they'd left it, but we didn't find Orwell. We went back to the road.

I heard sirens to the west, and soon two Sheriff's Department cars and a State Police car topped the hill to the west and came toward us, lights flashing. The deputies looked embarrassed.

"I'll listen in while you explain to everybody what happened," I said, as Billy Jo and I unloaded our weapons and put them back into my car.

Soon we were surrounded by more policemen than had probably ever been in one spot on the Florida Mesa. One was the sheriff of La Plata County. He did not look pleased.

"The guy was here when we got here," explained the first deputy. "We put the truck in the barn and went up to the house and he was waiting for us. Must have been watching us all the time. Covered us when we came through the door. Jake tried for him and got his head broke. Took our guns and cuffed us to the pipes in the basement. Asked us why we were there. I told him we'd gotten an anonymous tip. He didn't push it. Then he went upstairs and made a telephone call and came down again."

"Asked us who'd given us the tip," said Jake, as a colleague tended to his bloody head. "Ted said we didn't know. Seemed to just be making talk to pass the time. Got nervous when the phone rang, but we never told him it must be for us. Scary bastard. Asked where John Skye was, but didn't act like he really expected us to know. Finally he said somebody would be along by and by. Told us to be sure to keep working in the country where we'd be safe. Then he left. That's all there is to tell. Guy's dangerous."

"More than can be said for you two," growled the sheriff. "What'd this fella look like?"

Jake looked at his partner. "Average-sized guy. Levi's, denim shirt, blue baseball cap, army boots. Hairy, hippie-looking guy. Brown hair, stringy, down to his shoulders almost. Big moustache, beard. Tanned, blue eyes, wire glasses. Favored one leg a little. That about it, Ted?"

"Left-handed," said Ted. Jake nodded.

The sheriff grunted. "Sounds like a makeup artist. Grant, put that description out."

Grant, who was young and clean-cut and staring at Billy Jo, jerked to attention and went to a radio.

The sheriff looked around. "You obviously didn't see his car when you came in. How do you figure he got here and then got away?"

"If I was going to do it," said Billy Jo, "I'd have parked my car in the woods behind the barn. He had the same idea. Look for yourself. The corral gates are still open and there are fresh car tracks under and on top of the ones the deputies' truck made when they put it in the barn."

All of the policemen looked at her, then all of them looked at the gates and tracks.

"Young lady," said the sheriff, "if you ever want a job, come and see me. All right, a couple of you men follow those tracks down into the woods and see if you can find anything useful. I doubt if there'll be much there. We got anything to make a cast of these tire prints? I didn't think so. Well, trooper, let's have a look at the house. Maybe this guy left his name and address and telephone number behind. We need a couple of clues like that to make up for my deputies' police work."

Ted and Jake looked unhappy.

I drove Billy Jo home. Orwell was apparently a man who was good at disguises. A blond grad student, a bearded doctor, a hippie with long hair and wire glasses. Who would he be next?

Wilma met us with a frown, and we told her what had happened. She looked at the ground and then at me. There was fire in her eye.

"Billy Jo's a grown-up woman, so I've got no say about what she does with herself, but I don't take kindly to you putting her in harm's way like that."

"Yes, ma'am."

"Mom, I made him take me," said Billy Jo.

Wilma sighed. "Yes, I imagine you did." Then she swept us both with hard, worried eyes. "I still don't like it."

"It's okay, Mom."

"Spilt milk," said Wilma. "Well, put those guns away where they belong before your father gets back to the house. No use to get him worked up for no good reason." She turned away.

"Mrs. Skye," I said. "I need some help."

She stopped, her back still turned. Then, slowly, she faced me and stood silent.

"I need to talk to Orwell. When I told the police about his phone call, I made a mistake. I should have met him myself. If I'd done that, I could have talked to him. I might have been able to convince him that he's after the wrong person . . ."

"And you might have gotten yourself handled worse than he handled the deputies," said Billy Jo fiercely. "They didn't know where John was, but you do. He might have made you tell him."

"Maybe." I looked at Wilma. "I need to talk to him."

"So?"

"So if he contacts you, will you tell him where I am, and give him my telephone number? Will you do that, at least, and tell him I want to talk to him?" I had a thought. "Tell him that he owes me that much, at least, since he almost killed me three times."

"He won't call."

"If he does . . ."

She frowned at me, then said, "Hmmph. All right. Billy Jo, you'd best get those guns back where they belong." She turned away.

Billy Jo flashed me a look. "I'll see you tonight," she said.

I blinked, then remembered. "Yes. Tonight."

I drove to my motel and got ready for the date I'd almost forgotten. My cowboy clothes were all pretty grungy, so I wore clean jeans, an almost-as-good-as-new thrift shop polo shirt with a little animal over the pocket, and my Tevas. Casual, but not too far from tourist chic. When Billy Jo knocked on my door, I was ready to go.

Billy Jo was also ready to go. A crisp blouse, a dark skirt that fell below her knees, low-heeled shoes, and a ribbon holding her long dark hair. She wore golden earrings and a bracelet in the shape of a snake on her wrist. Her perfume was elusive and tantalizing. Her bronzed skin glowed. I felt underdressed.

"Where are we going?"

"Francisco's."

"Mexican food?"

"You bet."

"Seafood?"

"You got it."

We drove downtown and parked and walked into the restaurant. When we got to our booth, Billy Jo said, "I'll have a cocktail."

"What will it be?"

"You order it. I'll drink it."

The waiter looked at me. I looked back.

"Tell your bartender to rinse two glasses with dry vermouth and then put a double shot of Stoli and two olives in each glass. I want the Stoli ice-cold."

"Yes sir."

"Sounds just right," said Billy Jo.

"Do I get to order your meal, too?"

"No, I'll take care of that. You can tend to the wine, though."

The drinks came. We touched glasses and drank. Smooth as new ice.

"You're a gutsy girl," I said. "I'm glad you were out there today."

Her face was young and her eyes were shining. "I liked it. I never had a feeling like it before. Standing there with the rifle, wondering what was going to happen. It was a rush."

It hadn't been a rush for me.

"You did well," I said, but I wasn't happy about her feelings.

"I've read about soldiers being afraid and excited all at the same time," she said. "Now I know what they mean."

"I'm just glad he'd pulled out."

"What do you think happened out there? I mean, nobody expected him to be there first, did they?"

"I think he went there early for the same reason the deputies did: to scout the place and get the drop, if need be, on whoever came out to meet him. He's an old pro, and an old pro always gets the edge if he can."

"Why did he call Mom after he'd already locked up the deputies? He must have known they were trying to set a trap. Why did he still wait for somebody to show up and tell him where John is? That doesn't make any sense."

"He didn't know whether the deputies were there instead of the messenger or whether they were there for some other reason. They told him that they'd gotten an anonymous tip, remember. Maybe he figured the messenger was still going to come. When he'd called your mother, she told him that her nephew was going to be there. It was only when the nephew didn't show up that Orwell knew it had been a trap. He must have been pretty annoyed. The interesting thing to me is that he didn't take it out on the deputies. He could have killed them both, but he didn't."

"Why didn't he?"

"I don't know. He could have killed me at my house, but he didn't. Maybe he just wants to kill John Skye. A professional killer doesn't like to kill people for no reason."

She was leaning back in her chair, looking at me with her bright, dark eyes. "I never met anybody like you. Somebody who knows about these things, somebody who gets involved in these things."

There is a C and W song that says ladies love outlaws.

"I don't know about these things and I don't get involved in these things," I said, thinking that it was time to deflect such talk. "I'm just here because I don't want John to get killed."

"I watched you out at Vivian's ranch. How you moved, what you did. I don't know anybody who knows what you know." She touched her tongue to her upper lip.

"All you saw was a guy who was in the army once. Anybody who ever had any service experience knows how to do what I did. The two deputies knew."

"But you told them what to do." She leaned forward on her elbows. "You've been shot at, haven't you?"

I have a bullet lodged near my spine. Put there one night by a frightened would-be thief I'd trapped in an alley when I was on the Boston PD. Sometimes I wonder what will happen if it moves a little bit.

I said, "I have some shrapnel in my legs from a Viet Cong artillery round. Or maybe it was a mortar round. Anyway, the guys who fired it didn't even know I was there. We never saw each other. War isn't very romantic."

"Have you ever shot at somebody?"

I had shot at the woman in the alley six times as she had been trying to shoot me some more. After all of the shots, my partner had been afraid to come into the alley because he thought the person I'd been chasing might be waiting for him. Finally he'd come on in anyway and found first the dead woman and then me, lying in my own blood in a pile of trash. I considered him a very brave man.

I put a smile on my face. "Thousands. I shoot at one or two before breakfast every day." I beckoned to a waiter. "Let's eat."

She ordered lobster, I ordered chicken enchiladas. There was a Freixenet Cordon Negro Brut on the wine list, so I ordered that to wash things down. Spanish champagne with enchiladas? Why not?

When the waiter went away, she put her hand on my arm. "You're dangerous," she said. "I like the way I feel with you."

She had youth's fascination with Eros and Thanatos. A heady and dangerous mixture whose glamour had probably once lured me as it now lured her. She was a very

beautiful young woman, and I liked the feeling of her hand on my arm and the way she looked at me. I understood why some men can't stop trying to be attractive to such women.

Just then a voice said, "Mr. Jackson? Miss Skye? I hope I'm not interrupting."

— 21 —

I looked up and saw the normal Western uniform of boots, jeans, and checkered shirt, topped by a clean-cut face that was vaguely familiar. I ran it through my memory and came up with the young deputy sheriff who had been eyeing Billy Jo out at the ranch before being sent off to make a radio call. I felt Billy Jo's hand slip off my arm.

"Sir, ma'am. Sure don't mean to intrude, but I'd like to speak to you, sir."

"No problem," I said, "Grant, isn't it?"

"Yes sir. Grant Taylor."

"Grant Taylor," said Billy Jo.

"Yes ma'am," said Grant Taylor, with a smile.

"You were out on the mesa this afternoon."

"Yes ma'am."

"This is Billy Jo Skye," I said.

"Yes sir. I know who she is. How do you do, ma'am?"

"Hello."

"Yes ma'am. Hello. You're looking mighty pretty tonight, if I may say so, ma'am."

"Thank you. Aren't you a little young to be calling me ma'am? You don't look any older than I am myself."

"I'm two years older, ma'am . . ."

"How do you know that?"

"Because I know your big brother, ma'am. We were in

school together up at Boulder and he told me all about you."

She sat up straighter. "Why haven't I met you before this, then? Josh must have brought a dozen of his pals home for one holiday or other."

He ducked his head, "Well, ma'am, I was usually working on holidays, trying to stretch the money I got for being in the army after I got out of high school. Shucks, I wish now I had come down home with him!" He grinned a boyish grin. She smiled.

"You're from someplace else, then?"

"Yes ma'am. Up Gunnison way. Came down here to go to work for the sheriff. I was military police in the service, and studied criminology in college, and I like the work."

"That where they taught you to call women 'ma'am'?"

"No ma'am. I think my daddy taught me that. He said if it was the right way to address the Queen of England, it was probably good enough for most other women, too. I hope you don't mind."

The smile was still on her face. She put out her hand. "I don't mind, but my name is Billy Jo."

He stared at the hand for the blink of an eye, then shook it with his own. "Grant."

"Grant." She sat back.

"Billy Jo." He straightened.

My eyes had been moving back and forth between them. I touched his arm. "You wanted to say something to me?"

"Oh. Oh, yes sir. Sure do." He flicked his eyes at Billy Jo, then back at me. "It's about this Orwell fellow. You want to step up to the bar for a minute . . . ?"

"No. Sit down. Billy Jo knows as much as I do. You can talk to her, too."

Billy Jo nodded approvingly, slid over, and tucked her long skirt under her thigh. Grant Taylor slid in beside her, bumped against her, got red, and slid back a few inches.

"Sorry, ma'am," he said. She smiled at him.

"Well?" I asked.

"What? Oh. Yes sir." He put his elbows on the table, got his face straight, and dropped his voice. "We've been in touch with people back east, as you know, and some new information has come in. We were going to try to get in touch with you tomorrow, but when I noticed you in here, I thought I'd just get it done now. This Orwell fellow is scheduled to go back on duty in ten days. That means that he'll be out of our hair before too much longer."

"Unless he goes AWOL."

"Yes sir. But apparently he's a career officer in a family of career officers, so I doubt if he'll go AWOL. You never know, of course."

Of course. "Anything else?"

"Well, Jake and Ted have been working with our artist and the photos we have of Orwell, trying to figure if he was the guy who ambushed them. You know, adding a moustache and beard and long hair to the photo, that sort of thing . . ."

"And they think that it could be, but they can't be sure, right?"

"Right, sir. The sheriff and the Durango and State police all have Orwell's picture, so we think we might pick him up. If we do . . ."

If you do, I thought, you don't have anything to hold him on unless Jake and Ted can identify him, which they probably can't.

"If you get him," I said, "I want a chance to convince him that he's after the wrong guy."

He nodded. "If we get him, you'll get your chance," he said.

Our waiter appeared, bearing a tray of steaming dishes. Grant Taylor slid out of the booth, smiled at Billy Jo, shook my hand, and moved away toward a table of young people his age, all of whom seemed to be looking at Billy

Jo and me. I turned back to her as the waiter put down our food and drink.

"I think this merits our undivided attention," I said, as I inhaled the aromas floating into my nostrils.

"You sound like you have functioning taste buds. Dare I hope that you're not just another man who'd eat a bale of hay if somebody poured some whiskey on it?"

"I'm not a logger, lover." I tried the wine and found it cold and otherwise satisfactory. "When you live alone, it's easy to get in the habit of just tossing together whatever's easiest to cook. I make a point of not doing that. I like good food and I feed myself as well as I can. Right now I plan to tear into these enchiladas, and I advise you to do the same with that lobster."

"Yes sir!"

She did, and I did.

After a while she drank some wine. "So you live alone."

I thought of the times Zee had been in my house with me. Then I thought of the times she hadn't been, and wondered if she would come back to the island after her conferences in New Hampshire.

"Most of the time," I said.

"Not all of the time?"

"Sometimes a friend stays with me."

"A friend." She popped some lobster into her mouth.

"Yes." I mopped up the last of my enchiladas. I was still hungry. There must be some appetite stimulant in thin air. We had ice cream for dessert, then came coffee and cognac and the bill. I presented my plastic.

Billy Jo looked across at me. She had a comfortable, not-yet-sated expression on her face like the one I thought must be on my own. "Now what do you have in mind?"

"I've been thinking of several possibilities," I said. "First I thought you and I might go back to my place."

"Ah." Her eyes were dark beneath half-lowered lids.

"But then I remembered that I have to go up through the cliffs and see John Skye tomorrow, and tell him what's

going on. So I'm going to ask you to do something else instead. I'd like you to take me up there again in the morning. That means . . ."

She rolled her eyes. "I know what that means. That means you want me to go home so I can get up early and get the horses and gear and the trailer and the truck and meet you here . . . when?"

"Actually, I want you to go home so I can get up early. Nine?"

"Nine. You . . . ! All right, all right!" She slid out of the booth. "I'm sure you need to get right at your beauty sleep, so let's go."

As we walked by the table where Grant Taylor sat, he stood up and smiled. "Good night," he said.

Billy Jo glanced first at me and then at him. "Good night, Grant," she said. He got a friendlier look than she gave me.

At my motel, she sat stiffly behind the steering wheel as I got out.

"I appreciate your help, Billy Jo."

"My pleasure. Good night." She spun gravel pulling out. I had to smile, but another part of me hated to see her go, and I wondered if I was a fool to send her away.

There was a message waiting for me at the desk. A Mr. Malone had called. He'd call again later.

I drove to a liquor store and bought ice and a six of Coors. Back in my room, I was halfway through the first Coors when the phone rang.

"Mr. Jackson?"

"Mr. Malone?"

"That name will do. I understand you want to talk with me."

— 22 —

It was a very ordinary-sounding voice, but it sent a little shiver up and down my spine.

"First, you should know that this line isn't tapped," I said. "Nobody's going to try to trace your call."

"Very reassuring. I can trust you, of course." A tone of almost amused irony.

"Actually, you can. I want to talk to you. I take it that you got this number from Wilma Skye."

"Yes. I told her that I was calling from the Durango Police Department and that we had some news that we wanted to get to John Skye. She said that you were trying to get in touch with this fellow they think is named Orwell and that we should give the information to you. I take it that Mrs. Skye is not a fool, that she realized that I am no policeman, and that she gave me a message you wished to give the man you call Orwell. What is it that you want to tell him?"

I didn't think I had much time to make my case. "It's simple enough. I've known John Skye for many years. I will swear to you on the sacred book of your choice that he had nothing to do with either the life or the death of Bernadette Orwell. He was one of her professors for one semester and nothing more. He was never her lover or anything like it. If she killed herself out of love, it was not out of love for John Skye."

There was a silence before the voice spoke. When it did, it was cool and detached. "Your friend has deceived you. The girl's diary tells a different tale. It says that she loved him and that John Skye used her and abandoned her and she could not bear it. In the modern liberal world, perhaps the idea of professors seducing their students is

meaningless, the notion of abandonment hopelessly gauche, the idea of the girl afterward committing suicide laughable. Perhaps at Weststock College a professor so exploiting a young woman student is such a commonplace event that it means nothing to either the woman or the man. But in the world where some others live, it means a great deal. Those others believe that men such as Skye owe a debt, and they mean to collect it."

"Someone may owe you a debt, but it's not John Skye. John has been married to a woman he loves since before Bernadette was his student. He doesn't seduce students. You're after the wrong man."

"No sir, you are wrong. And now I fear I have no more time for this conversation. I only telephoned you in the first place because someone nearly killed you by mistake. For that he apologizes. He thought that you were Skye. You should count yourself lucky that he was thrice careless. He usually is not."

"You were wrong about me, and you're still wrong about Skye."

"You haven't seen the girl's journal. It's very clear." A note of fury entered his voice. "These Eastern colleges, these leftist dilettantes! So sophisticated, so liberal! They corrupt whatever they touch." Then the fury was gone as fast as it had come. The voice was cool once more. "Orwell women traditionally have gone south to college, Mr. Jackson, but Bernadette would have none of it. Weststock, only Weststock would do. Such irony. See what came of her attending that school. Drugs, loveless sex, betrayal!"

I wondered about the almost instantaneous changes in vocal tone. Did the anger come from conviction or from some other, deeper malaise? I was aware of an anger inside myself.

"I did see the journal," I said. "I found it on Martha's Vineyard and mailed it to New Jersey."

"And being an honorable man, you apparently did not read it first." I could see the twist in his lip. His voice

rose. "John Skye was first her professor. A year later, he was her lover! 'Dear Jonathan,' 'sweet Jonathan.' Names of endearment. She was so happy . . . so trusting! Then . . . abandonment! Some other woman . . . !"

I had a growing certainty of my own. "I don't believe it. I've known John for years . . ." My voice sounded different to me.

His ear was sharp. "You're not telling me what you really believe."

True. "That's not so," I said.

"You know where he is. Someone wants to find him."

I thought of tomorrow. "John Skye is innocent. Besides, his wife and children are with him!"

"He has betrayed them just as he betrayed Bernadette Orwell. How many other women has he seduced and abandoned? How many more will there be? Where is he?"

"I'm his friend . . ."

"He does not merit your friendship. Where is he?"

"He's in the mountains."

"Take a certain person to him."

"I won't do that."

The voice became gentle. "Don't be afraid. The person only wants to talk. Perhaps John Skye can persuade him. Perhaps there is some explanation for the writings in the journal. If John Skye is indeed innocent, as he claims to be and you think he is, the person will walk away and that will be the end of it."

"He is innocent."

"Someone will listen to him," said the voice. "If you are concerned about his family, you need not be. His family is of no interest to this person."

There was a silence. My mind was racing. As long as Orwell was after him, John could know no peace. He could never know when the moment would come. If not here, then back in Weststock, or on the island, or abroad, should John travel there. Orwell would find him.

"I'll talk to him," I said. "I'll tell him you want to

speak to him, to listen to him. I want this matter settled without any more trouble."

"Good. You're his friend. Arrange a meeting, if you can."

"No. No meeting. Walkie-talkies. There's a Radio Shack downtown. I can get them there. You can be in one place, and John will be in another. You won't see each other."

"You're a careful fellow."

"I don't want any violence."

"You don't want violence. What of the violence that Weststock professors impose upon the minds and bodies of the young women who are their students? Pah!" He paused. "Very well. Make the arrangements. Shall we say for the day after tomorrow? I'll be in touch."

The phone clicked and buzzed in my ear. I put it down. The half can of Coors was warming in my hand. I drank it. I did not like my anticipation of what was to come and tried to come up with alternatives. None of them seemed any better. I sat on the bed and thought about everything I knew having to do with the case. Then I called the desk and told them when to wake me up in the morning, brushed my teeth, and went to an uneasy bed. I was awake a long time and up early.

In the morning I shaved. Why? I wondered. It was a curious habit. If hair grew on your face, why not leave it there? Why did we shave some hair and not other? Women shaved armpits and legs; men shaved faces. Why not chests? Why not crotches? Certain exotic dancers did shave crotches, I knew. Why?

My level of intellectual activity was obviously not too high. I went out for a Colorado breakfast, then drove downtown to the Sheriff's Department. The sheriff wasn't in. I left him a message: call the Jackson, Wyoming, police and have them check automobile rental agencies to see if Gordon Orwell had rented a car, probably a four-by-four. If he had, get its make and number and put out a local APB for it.

Then I went to Radio Shack and bought two walkie-talkies and put them in my small backpack. I was waiting for Billy Jo when she stopped her pickup and horse trailer. She looked a little puffy around the eyes. My glands did a little dance anyway. I decided not to comment upon either eyes or glands. She had doughnuts and coffee, so she didn't intend for us to starve, however put out she might be about last night. I told her about my visit to the Sheriff's Department.

"Why did you ask them to do that?"

"Orwell set up an alibi for himself back east when he pretended to go into the Maine woods. He made sure there were plenty of witnesses to say he'd gone there, but he was actually down in Massachusetts having a couple of whacks at me. Last week, when he found out John Skye was out here, he told his mother he was going to hike in the Tetons. So I figure he did it for the same reason—to prove he was somewhere else when he was actually going to be down here. I think he probably went to Jackson, right where he told her he was going, and rented a car using his own credit card, probably a Jeep or some such machine, and told a lot of people that he was going to hike in the Tetons, and bought some camping gear and paid for it with the same credit card, then didn't go to the Tetons, but drove as fast as he could down here to Durango. He could have gotten here in less than a day."

"I never thought of that," she said.

There were rearview mirrors on both sides of the truck. I leaned forward and looked in mine. There were cars coming up behind us. I said, "Neither did I until last night, which may explain why I'm not head of the FBI." The cars passed us and went on ahead. I looked in the mirror again. More cars.

After a while, Billy Jo said, "What are you going to tell John? He can't stay up there forever. Sooner or later he has to come down, and this Orwell will be waiting for him."

"Maybe the cops will have Orwell by then."

"Or maybe Orwell will be back on duty. But even if he is, he'll get leave sometime, or retire. He can wait."

True. Revenge was not always an impetuous act. I thought of the old Beacon Hill political ethic: don't get mad, get even. It was a code that required action, but not immediate action.

"I'll tell John that Orwell wants to talk to him," I said. "He'll have to decide what to do. You and I can't solve his problem for him."

"I hate this!" she said in sudden anger. "I hate not being able to do anything!"

The sages have observed that to live is to suffer. Still, it is a bitter discovery when we make it ourselves, as most of us do sooner or later.

"Don't worry," I said. "It's going to work out. The bad guys don't always win these things, you know."

She thought about that for a while, then flashed me a wan smile. "I guess you're right."

All the way up the valley, I looked in the rearview mirror, wondering if any of the cars behind us were following us. When we turned off the highway at the foot of the cliffs, all of the cars drove right on toward the north. That was encouraging. On the other hand, if I'd been following us, I'd have gone right past too. And come back later.

Before noon we had topped the towering cliffs and were riding north toward John Skye's camp. Our horses had made a trail that only a blind man could miss, so I'd spent a good deal of time looking over my shoulder. I had seen nothing. That meant that Orwell either wasn't there or was there and was very good at his work.

— 23 —

There were a half-dozen white-faced cows grazing on the first meadow we came to. Two healthy spring calves were with them.

"You're a cowgirl," I said to Billy Jo. "Can you round up these cattle, or whatever it is you do, and drive them back down the trail we just rode up?"

"Sure. Why?" Then her eyebrows lifted. "Oh, I see. Wipe out our trail." She frowned. "Do you really think we might have been followed up here?"

"No, but I'd like to be sure."

"I'll take care of it. You stay right there and don't try to help."

I stayed put, and she swiftly had the bunch of cows and calves headed back along the trail. She and her mount seemed a single creature, graceful and lovely, sensual and efficient. I watched her and her little herd go out of sight into the trees.

After a while I saw her coming through the trees a considerable distance from the trail. She had ridden back where her horse's hoofprints wouldn't be easily spotted.

"No problem," she said, as she came up to me. "I booed them back to the drift fence gate. This Orwell guy would need a crystal ball to know where we went from there." She smiled. There was a glow in her face that made her look wildly beautiful. She liked the idea of danger. She would give some man fits, I thought. More than one man, probably. Me, maybe.

"Good work," I said. "I've been thinking. Too many

people know that John's up here on the cliffs somewhere. I'd like to talk him into moving somewhere else. Not down out of the mountains yet; that's too dangerous. Somewhere else up here. Where?"

The games we were playing interested her, and her mind was quick. "Clear Creek. It's down on the other side of the Hermosa. You have to ford the river to get to it. Good camping ground, good water, good grass, good fishing. That's the place."

She rode ahead of me, her annoyance of last night washed away by her sense of adventure. My rump and legs hurt, but the sight of Billy Jo's graceful body swaying so easily atop her mare took my thoughts away from my discomfort.

When we rode into John Skye's camp, we found no one home.

"Fishing," said Billy Jo, after dismounting and having a quick look around. "Rods and creels are gone." She looked at the sun, then at her watch. "Probably down Dutch Creek. Be back in a couple of hours, most likely. Loosen the saddles and take off the bridles, and I'll get the fire going." She looked inside the black gallon coffee-pot that sat on the grill. "Camp coffee. Best in the West. You never empty the grounds; just add more now and then. Eggshells to keep them down. More water when you need it."

"Terrific."

It was, too. Black as a politician's soul, but with a lot more character. I tasted it all the way down.

Billy Jo sat on her heels and looked at me sitting on mine. She had excited eyes. They flicked toward the big tent, then back at me.

"Is the rifle there?" I asked. I didn't really care, but I needed a distraction.

"What?"

"Is the rifle there? Your 30–30?"

"Oh. No. I guess he took it with him."

"Good. That means he took us seriously. I want him to take us seriously." She looked impossibly attractive. I seemed to be staring at her.

She flowed up onto her feet. "Let's go for a walk. It's too nice to just sit here." She put out her hands and I put up mine and she pulled me up. Pain. I gave a mighty, only partially feigned, groan.

"You just need some exercise," she said. "Come on." Hand in hand we walked out of camp onto the nearest meadow. The afternoon wind made waves in the meadow grass. It looked like a green sea. The sun was warm. Around the meadow, the spruce and quaking aspen moved in the wind. I felt about fifteen years old. I was excited and uneasy. Her hand in mine felt electric.

We reached the edge of the trees, and came to a fallen log. Suddenly she stepped onto the log, turned, and looked down at me with a hungry smile, her hands on my shoulders, pulling me close. My head came to her chin. Her breasts touched my face. I thought of how the Vineyard would be without Zee, and felt my will dwindle and fade and my passions rise. My arms went around Billy Jo's waist and I felt hers go around my neck and head, and then I lifted her off the log and let her body slip down until her lips found mine. I held her there, her feet not touching the ground, her body hard against me, her mouth searching, her breath short.

We were both gasping when I eased her to the ground. I saw a bit of blood on her lips, and touched it with my finger. She put up her own hand, touched the blood, and looked at her hand.

I tried to will my hunger for her away. It didn't want to go. My arms pulled her against me. I saw acquiescence in her eyes, felt it in her flesh. I put my hand to the nape of her neck and brought her face up to mine. When I let her go again, her eyes were wide and vague.

Some sound intruded upon us. I first brushed it away, then grasped at it. A voice, distant and high. I tied my

tiny will to that voice, bound myself to it like Ulysses had himself bound to the mast while the sirens sang. Billy Jo looked dazedly at me.

"It's one of the twins," I said, my voice sounding strange to my ears. "Listen."

And indeed it was one of the twins, or perhaps both of the twins. And the voices were getting louder.

"They're back," I said. "They've found our horses in camp, and they're looking for us."

"Ah." Billy Jo, confusion on her face, stepped away. Her hands went to her hair, to her clothes, to her face. I handed her my handkerchief and she put it to her lips. I found her hat, which had fallen to the ground, and she put it on.

My heart was pumping and my breath was short. If desire at ten thousand was this exhausting, what would sex do to me? I remembered hearing that most people used up the same number of calories having sex as they got from eating one brownie. That was at sea level, of course.

I looked out into the meadow and saw a rider coming in the distance. I felt a surge of gratitude not unmixed with regret.

I took Billy Jo by the shoulders and sat us down on the log. "Look," I said. "This won't make any sense to you and it doesn't make much to me either. There is a woman back in Massachusetts who means more to me than I can tell you. She's gone away and she may not be coming back, but I am, by God, not going to fuck around with you or anybody else until I know for sure. Do you understand me? You are the loveliest thing I've seen since she went away. Worse yet, you have allure. You attract, you have the power to entice. If I were in any situation other than the one I'm in with this woman, I would be in your pants right now, twin or no twin. But I'm not going to get in them, so just keep them on while I'm around!"

I gave her a shake and she looked at me with aston-

ished eyes. Then, unexpectedly, I heard myself laughing. I felt totally absurd.

"Jesus," said Billy Jo. "What's so funny?"

"Me. Not you."

"Hi," said the twin, galloping up. "So, here you are. We saw your horses and Mom said you'd probably gone for a walk and she was right, as usual. What's so funny, J.W.? Are you telling her the Pig with the Wooden Leg joke again?" She looked at Billy Jo. "He always laughs when he tells that joke. He thinks it's great. Shall I bring you your horses, so you can ride back?"

Billy Jo adjusted her hat. "No. No, we'll walk back. Go tell your mom that we're coming."

"Catch any fish?" I asked, still smiling.

"We got enough for a good supper. Are you staying?"

"I'm afraid not. Next time."

"You never stay! Well, my sister is over the hill somewhere, looking for you, so I've got to go find her and tell her you're not lost anymore. See you in camp!"

The twin was off at a gallop.

"Here," said Billy Jo, handing me my bloody handkerchief. She looked at me. "You're a strange guy. I don't think I know anybody like you."

"And you're a woman and a half, and it's a good thing for me that I don't know many like you. Let's go find John and Mattie."

We walked across the meadows and down to the camp and on the way I knew something had genuinely changed between us. We talked like friends. I have had occasion to observe that in the absence of love, lust will do. Now it seemed that maybe the reverse was also true.

"What happened to your lip?" Mattie immediately asked Billy Jo.

"Branch hit me. It didn't even hurt."

"It's swollen."

"It'll be all right."

Mattie looked at me and then back at Billy Jo and said, "Hmmmph."

John, oblivious to this small drama, said, "Well, what's going on down in the real world?"

I told him what had happened out at the ranch, what I'd learned about Orwell from the police, and about the phone call I'd received. "Orwell thinks John is responsible for Bernadette's death," I said. "Suicide after love betrayed."

"He's insane!" Mattie took John's arm in her own. She looked like a goddess protecting a mortal lover.

"He's wrong, at least," said John.

"He doesn't think he's wrong," I said, "but he wants to talk with you. Says he'll listen to your side. Whatever you decide about that idea, I think you two and the girls ought to break camp and go down to Clear Creek tonight." I got out the radio and told them about the walkie-talkie plan. "He wants it to happen tomorrow."

"Excellent. I think I will talk to him," said John, turning the radio in his hands. His tone was thoughtfully professorial.

"You will not!" said Mattie, astonished.

"I'm sure I can convince him that he's wrong."

"And what if you can't? What then?" Her tone was that of a mother speaking to a child proposing some wild idea.

John maintained his tone of academic detachment. "I'm sure I can. His idea is so completely absurd that only a madman could believe it once given the facts."

"That's exactly the point," said Mattie. "This guy is crazy!"

"Mattie could be right," I said.

"There! J.W. thinks I'm right. The twins will think I'm right. You agree, don't you, Billy Jo?"

Billy Jo hesitated. "Well, you'll be safer if you all go down to Clear Creek . . ."

"You see? Everybody agrees. This man Orwell is obvi-

ously disturbed. You can't reason with a disturbed man, and you know it. We'll break camp right now." Mattie squeezed her husband's arm. "Please, John, be reasonable."

He looked down at her in mild surprise. "Why, I usually think of myself as a reasonable man, Mattie."

"I'd be careful with this guy," I said. "He's pretty slick."

"He's dangerous, no doubt," nodded John. "But if we use these radios when he and I talk, he'll have no opportunity to do anything foolish before I have my say. Afterward, he'll have no reason to pursue this vendetta."

Mattie snorted. "This man is a trained professional in the Special Forces or whatever, and you're a college professor! No contest! Be sensible!"

"Now, now, my dear, please be calm . . ."

"Calm!"

"Yes, calm."

"And what if he doesn't believe you? We have to go back to Weststock. What then?" Mattie naturally asked the right question.

John answered it. "We'll be no worse off than we are now."

"I want us to be better off!"

He patted her arm in that way men have of trying to calm the fears of the ones they love. "All I want is an opportunity to speak with him. I'm sure I can convince him of his error."

I was not so sure. "Where do you want to do it? Up here somewhere or down in town? Or somewhere else?"

He squinted at the sky, then swept his eyes over the surrounding meadows and trees. "Up here, I think. He may be younger and better trained at this sort of hunting game than I am, but I know this country and have acclimatized myself to this altitude, and that will be to my advantage. It will balance things out. Yes, we'll meet up here."

I looked at Billy Jo. She shrugged and looked at Mattie.

"We should leave this to the police," said Mattie.

"The police have had their try," said John gently. "If this plan fails, they can have another go. But with luck, we'll settle the matter before they need to."

"All right, then," I said. "You break camp and move down to Clear Creek. Tomorrow I'll bring Orwell here. I imagine he'll have that machine gun of his, just in case you and I are planning a double cross of some sort. Where will you be? Where do you want Orwell?"

John thought, and then pointed to the east. "I want him yonder, on the cliff where the twins brought you the other day. The meadow runs right up to the cliffs there beside that grove of woods where the ledge goes down to the cave. I'll be watching from that ridge between here and the cliff."

"You'd better be hunkered down pretty good. I'll have to take him over the ridge, and this guy has good eyes."

John gave me a small smile. "He won't see me. Neither will you, even though you know I'll be there. Nobody's born a professor, remember. I was a kid playing cowboys and Indians up here, then I was a real cowboy, and then I was a hunter, and then I was in the army, all long before I became the effete East Coast pointy-headed intellectual I am today. I want Orwell in the meadow, in plain sight on top of the cliffs, before I'll talk to him. That way I'll know where he is, and he won't have any chance at monkey business, if he decides to try any. He'll have to come across a half mile of open meadow to get to where I am, and by that time I can either shoot him or be long gone."

Though I knew that people do things you'd never guess they'd do, I wondered if John could actually shoot somebody. I didn't want him to have to make that decision.

"I think being long gone is the best idea," I said. "After you talk, we'll wait on the cliffs for half an hour, so you can pull out. Then I'll take him back down the trail, and that will be that."

"And what if he doesn't buy John's story?" asked Mattie hotly. "What about that?"

"Why, I'll be gone," said John. "I'll make my way down to Clear Creek. I'll be quite safe, my dear. And if worse comes to worst, I'll have Billy Jo's rifle, after all."

"Wonderful." Mattie shook her head. "A middle-aged literature professor with a deer rifle against a trained soldier with a machine gun!" She obviously hadn't bought the macho image of John in his pre-professor days.

There were shouts from the meadow, and the twins came galloping over the waving green grass.

"What channel shall we use?"

"Thirteen," said John. "One of my many lucky numbers."

I looked at my watch. "About this time? That'll give Orwell and me time to walk up here and get out to the cliffs. I don't want him to have a horse, because that would let him move too fast. In fact, I want him to be tired when he gets here. I don't want him frisky at all."

John looked at his watch and nodded. "All right. When I see him out on the cliffs, I'll call him."

The twins rode in just in time to see Billy Jo and me climb into our saddles. They looked disappointed, which, compared to how Mattie looked, was not too bad.

"See you at Clear Creek," said Billy Jo.

We rode out as Mattie and John were extolling the virtues of Clear Creek to their questioning children. I didn't seem to be getting any better at riding. Everything from my hips down seemed to hurt. I imagined that meant that any hopes I had of becoming a rodeo rider had best be set aside. I was glad to let them go.

All the way down the trail I looked for signs that someone had come up after we had, but I saw nothing. There was no one waiting for us at the truck and trailer and there were no car tracks or footprints on top of those we'd made coming in that morning.

"You're the keen-eyed Westerner," I said to Billy Jo. "See any sign that we've had a guest?"

"Not a one, Kemo Sabe."

I had her drop me off at the north end of Durango, just in case Orwell was watching the motel. I didn't want him to know that she was involved in this matter. She raised a hand to her bruised lip. "If you ever change your mind about this other woman . . ."

"I don't plan to."

"But if you do . . ."

"Half the men in Durango will hyperventilate if you just bat your eyes at them. Believe me."

"I'm not interested in half the men in Durango. She must be some kind of woman."

"She is."

I shut the door and she drove away. I walked south along Main Street thinking about Zee and worrying about tomorrow.

— 24 —

By the time I got to my motel, I'd worked a lot of the kinks out of my bones. It was beer time, so I had a couple out of my cooler while I thought things over.

Both John and Orwell had said they wanted to talk. If they were telling the truth, John's plan might work. Of course, people with vested interests in issues didn't always tell the truth. I ran four scenarios through my mind: John and Orwell were both telling the truth about wanting to talk; John and Orwell were both lying about wanting to talk; John was telling the truth and Orwell was lying; Orwell was telling the truth and John was lying.

I thought some more. After a while, I decided to give up thinking, and went out for some food. I had stiffened up again and knew now why cowboys walk funny. I drove downtown past sidewalks full of tourists and had a steak

at the Ore House. When in Steakland, eat steaks. I washed mine down with more Coors. Not bad.

I was home brushing my teeth and still thinking when the phone rang. I recognized the voice.

"I really don't think you're set up to trace this," said my caller. "But just in case you are, I don't plan to stay on the line. You want to talk to me, you go down to the Main Mall and go to the public phones there. When one of them rings, you answer it. Ten minutes." The phone clicked in my ear.

Ten minutes. I finished brushing my teeth, put on my straw hat, and went out into the neon night. I was in the Main Mall wondering if the guy wearing cowboy clothes and chatting on one of the telephones there was chatting on the one Orwell planned to use to call me when the man on the phone hung up and turned to me.

"Hello, Mr. Jackson," he said. "You're right on time." He gestured. "I thought this would be a good place for us to meet. Very public, no police that I can see, but a lot of civilians who might get hurt if either one of us tries to damage the other. Let's take a walk along the street, shall we?" He ran his eyes over me. "I don't see any sign that you're armed. Are you?"

I was looking at a young man with a drooping black moustache and the over-the-ears hairstyle seemingly favored by many young men in Colorado. He wore the hat, the boots, the denim jeans and jacket, and the plaid shirt that constituted the unofficial Durango uniform. I looked through the moustache and saw the face of Gordon Berkeley Orwell that I'd seen taken from the fax machine. If I were Max Carrados, could I have smelled spirit gum? Did people still use spirit gum to stick on false moustaches and the like?

"I have a pocketknife and fingernail clippers," I said.

"Ah. I, on the other hand, have a pistol tucked away, so I imagine that gives me an edge, should I need it. Will I?"

We walked out onto Main Street and turned right. The train depot was down that way a few blocks. "I don't think you'll need any firepower," I said.

"You must forgive me for telling you that I'd be calling on the mall phone. Tactics. Never let the enemy know your real plans. You understand."

"Yes. I talked to John Skye today. He's willing to speak with you tomorrow. He thinks he can persuade you that you're after the wrong guy. He thinks that once you are persuaded, you'll go away."

"If he persuades me, you may be sure that I will do exactly that. What scenario does your friend have in mind?"

I told him.

We walked down the street, two men in Western hats glancing briefly into windows filled with turquoise and silver jewelry as we walked and talked.

"So you plan to take me up there, eh?"

"I know where Skye wants you to be before he'll talk to you. I don't think you can find the place by yourself."

"I don't like going into places I haven't scouted. I'm never sure about what might be waiting for me."

"You have that Beretta machine gun. You can keep that in my back while we're hiking, if it will make you feel any safer."

He smiled. "So you know about the Beretta. Do you think your friend Skye will attempt to ambush us?"

"No, I don't think so."

"How about someone else? You, for instance. Or will the police be waiting for me?"

"I haven't told the police about this. They botched things pretty badly out at the ranch."

"I should believe you, of course." Two pretty girls came walking toward us. He stepped aside and they went between us. He never looked at them. "However, I make it a practice not to believe people too often. Tomorrow, you say?"

"Yes. We should start up the trail no later than nine or so in the morning, if we're to be out at the cliff in time."

"Where is this trail?"

"You can get a map of the San Juan National Forest from the Forest Service. You'll find the Goulding Trail going up the cliffs about halfway between Rockwood and Haviland Lake. They tell me that there are other trails going up, but that's the only one I know, so that's the one we'll use."

"I have one of those maps. Describe the trail to me."

I did.

"There's a cabin near the top?"

"Yes."

We walked. I thought that if I were Orwell, I wouldn't like the idea of coming up the trail toward a cabin where someone I couldn't see could see me and could be waiting. I remembered walking into villages in Vietnam and hating that very thought.

"And up on top there's another trail? Which way do we go?"

"I'll tell you that when we get there."

"Again, I must trust you, eh?"

I was suddenly angry. "Who are you to be talking about trust? You're the guy who almost killed me three times. I haven't done a damned thing to you. Do you want to do this thing, or not?"

"I don't plan to get my ass blown off by some wacko professor or his friends, I'll tell you that!" We came to the depot and pretended to look at advertisements for the Silverton train. After a while, he said, "Here's what I'll do. I'll meet you at the top. We can go the rest of the way together. You're going to start up about nine?"

I thought he would probably go up very early tomorrow morning, so he could scout the area before I got there. But I couldn't be sure, and because I couldn't be sure, he

would be safe. He might even meet me at the bottom of the cliffs and go up with me, instead of going up earlier. He didn't like to let the enemy know his real plans, after all.

"I figure it will take me a couple of hours to hike up to the top. I'm not acclimatized to these altitudes."

"Nothing personal, but I'll expect to search you when we meet, so don't bring a weapon."

"Pocketknife and fingernail clippers. You, of course, will be dressed."

"Dressed," he said. "I haven't heard that expression since Jacksonville. The first time a guy told me he was dressed I didn't know what he was talking about. Yes, I'll be dressed. I will be a stranger in a strange land, after all, and if I'm going to have trouble, you're going to have more. Please wait here for a few minutes. I will see you tomorrow at the top of the Goulding Trail."

I watched him walk away up the street. After he disappeared beyond the nearest crowd of tourists, I went to my car and drove to my motel, brooding all the way.

— 25 —

Early the next morning, I got into my car and drove to the Sheriff's Department.

A deputy said the sheriff was in his office, spoke into a phone, and waved me through to the inner sanctum. The sheriff was chewing a matchstick. He pointed me to a seat. I asked him if they'd contacted the Jackson, Wyoming, police about Orwell renting a car there. The sheriff rolled his cigar to a corner of his mouth.

"As a matter of fact, we did. That was a good idea of yours. Orwell rented a Chevy Blazer. Blue. We've got the

license plate number, but we haven't seen the car. Never knew there were so many blue Blazers in La Plata County until we started looking for this one."

"He might have changed the plates."

"We thought of that."

"You can't stop them all."

"That's right. Somebody back east said you were a cop once."

"A long time ago. Any other news from the east?"

"Some. Orwell was an actor in high school and college. Liked to play roles where he could try to look like somebody else. No surprise there, is there? He looks different every time anybody reports seeing him. Hell, we don't even know if all these sightings really are Orwell."

I had seen him close up. I knew.

"For all we know," said the sheriff, "the real Orwell may be up there in the Tetons, camping out."

"Yeah, that could be," I said. "But if it's not Orwell, I don't know who it could be. Anything else?"

"Yeah. This Orwell fellow is on special leave of some sort. Seems he got hurt on some job—down south of the border someplace, nobody's saying exactly where. His old man died a while back. The two of them were close, I guess. Then this summer, his sister pulls the plug on herself. Tough times for Orwell. Things seem to have piled up on him. His special leave seems to be for mental R and R. Could mean he's slipped a cog. Could also mean nothing." The sheriff shrugged his big shoulders, and a crooked smile played around his matchstick. "Ten-cent psychology. Worth a dime less than you pay for it."

I thought of Orwell's mother, who had suffered losses as great, but, as is often the case with women, had not decided to kill someone because of them. I got up. "Thanks for your help. I'll keep in touch. If I get any smarter, I'll let you know."

Out on the streets of Durango, the tourists were enjoying themselves. Beyond the buildings, the rimrocked

hills rose in wild purity toward a bird's-egg-blue sky. The tourists did not know that a killer was perhaps walking among them, and the innocent earth did not care.

Back at the motel there was a message to call Billy Jo. I decided against it, but as I did, the phone rang. It was Billy Jo.

"My grandfather's old .45 Colt Peacemaker is out here," she said. "It must be a hundred years old, and it hasn't been fired in years, but it still works. I could bring it in to you."

"No, thanks. I don't want a gun."

"It's better to have one and . . ."

"No. There's not going to be any shooting."

"You're sure."

"I'm sure. I want us all to get out of this without anyone getting hurt."

"Be careful."

"Yes."

At eight o'clock, I parked at the foot of the Goulding Trail. There were car tracks leading farther ahead. I followed them on foot and came to a blue Chevy Blazer with New Jersey plates. It was tucked out of sight behind a clump of oak brush. I tried the doors. Locked. I tried an experimental call: "Orwell, come out, come out, wherever you are, and let's get going!"

No answer. Of course, the man I had decided was Orwell had never actually admitted that he was that person. If any of this ever came to trial, I could never testify that anyone calling himself Orwell had actually admitted to anything. Clever Orwell.

I looked up at the cliffs. Hawks were riding the winds like dots in the sky. I was wearing my very best hiking gear: shorts, a tee shirt advertising Papa's Pizza, my old combat boots, and my forest green Martha's Vineyard Surfcasters Association cap. I had a small knapsack containing the second walkie-talkie, a light jacket, a plastic canteen of water, and a ham and cheese sandwich. I de-

layed long enough to cut myself a walking stick, then, having no more excuses, and feeling empty and fatalistic, I started up the trail.

A bit after eleven, puffing like the little engine that could, I passed the Craig Cabin. There was a padlock on the door. I went on up toward the ridge, taking slow steps with many pauses, like the climbers you see in those movies of Everest. I got to the trail at the top of the ridge and sat down, sweating and breathless, my legs weak as Billy Beer.

To the east, between promontories covered with spruce and quaking aspen, I could see the mountains beyond the Animas Valley rolling away toward infinity in giant blue waves. Around me the wind sighed in the trees. At my feet the green meadow I had just ascended fell away to the tiny log cabin and on down to the stream that had, over a million years, cut the gap in the cliffs that made the Goulding Trail possible. It was all shining, it was Adam and maiden. The innocence of the wilderness. I stared at it with fascination.

"You came," said Orwell's voice from behind me.

I nodded.

"If you'll slip off that knapsack, I'll just have a peek. That's it. Ah. Lunch. Very good. Stand, please."

I stood.

"You will allow me," said his voice, and I felt his hands pat me down. "Thank you," The hands went away.

The knapsack landed lightly beside me. I picked it up, and turned. Orwell, wearing green fatigue pants and a green tee shirt and cap, was putting the walkie-talkie into a backpack. There was a pistol in a camouflaged cloth holster on his belt. There was a flap snapped over the butt of the gun. Orwell got his arms through the straps and hoisted the backpack up onto his shoulders. He noticed me noticing the pistol.

"No machine gun. I hope you're not disappointed, but they're hard to get through metal detectors at the airports.

This pistol, on the other hand, goes through more easily. It's a Glock. A lot of it's plastic."

"I fired one once."

"Did you? An excellent weapon, I'm sure you'll agree." He gestured toward my scarred legs. "You are a veteran, I note. I recognize shrapnel scars when I see them. Asia?"

"The recent unpleasantness in Vietnam."

"I was too young, but my father was there. I was at Grenada and Panama. The men of my family attend all of the wars."

"I was an amateur soldier, not a professional."

"That is an important difference between us. Shall we go?"

I pointed north.

"After you," he said, with smiling mouth and icy eyes.

We walked north alongside the rail drift fence until we passed through the gate and came, a bit later, to the first of the great, rolling meadows that gave such fine graze to the cattle which summered there. Off to the southwest, the peaks of the La Plata Mountains pointed into the sky. On the far side of the first meadow, a few white-faced cattle grazed. It was a quietly pastoral scene, and I was struck by the irony of our tense intrusion upon it. The cattle lifted their heads and looked at us, then returned to their feeding.

Orwell seemed unaffected by the altitude that was making me pant. We came to the dark spruce woods that grew on the north slope of the vale where Skye's camp had been, and I found the trail leading through the trees. When we emerged on the campsite, Orwell said, "Stop."

I stopped and looked at him. He was standing half hidden by a tree, sweeping the terrain with field glasses. He took his time, then returned the glasses to his pack, and gestured to me to go ahead. I walked down into the campsite.

Orwell approved of it. "Water, graze for the horses,

early sunlight, flat spots for tents. Good place for a hunting camp. Where's the nearest fishing stream?"

I didn't know. I pointed to the east. "We go that way."

We walked across the meadow Billy Jo and I had
crossed only yesterday, found the trail leading out to the
cliffs, and walked through groves of trees and over meadows under the warm nooning sun. We came to the ridge
where Skye had said he'd be hiding. I'd seen no hoof-
or footprints on the trail, and wondered if he was there.
I didn't look to see if I could spot him. We passed out
onto the last green meadow that led up to the cliffs and
walked on.

We crossed the meadow, climbed the last rise, and were
suddenly there, atop the cliffs. I felt the old familiar ver-
tigo as I puffed for breath and looked across that horrible
void to the magnificent mountains on the far side of the
valley.

"This is the place," I said, tasting bile in my throat.

"Magnificent!" Orwell smiled and stared at the scene.
"I've not seen anything like this since the Andes."

Now I knew why these heights were not affecting him.
The Andes were even loftier than the Rockies. Seeing him
smiling at the magnificent scene before him, I was acutely
aware of the paradoxical truth that a sensitivity to beauty
and the desire to kill can exist in the same person.

"It is amazing," I said, feeling the wind trying to push
me over the edge, feeling the earth beneath my feet preparing to break off and plunge into the valley.

"An excellent spot for lunch," said Orwell. "You look
a little green around the gills, Mr. Jackson."

"I am a little green. Acrophobia."

His eyes were sweeping the cliff top. "But before we
eat, a little scouting, eh? Those trees off to the north will
wait, but I think I'd like a look at this grove just south
of us. Naturally, I want you to come along. Just in case
you have someone in there waiting for me, you
understand."

"Yes."

We went into the grove, Orwell behind me somewhere. I stayed away from the edge of the cliff and felt pretty good when I couldn't see it. We came to the far edge of the grove and turned back. We swept the place twice before Orwell was content that no one was there, and we returned to the spot where the meadows reached the cliff.

"I take it that we are being watched from some place out there," said Orwell, pointing to the ridge where Skye had said he'd be, then sweeping his hand north toward the trees on that side of the meadow. "A long shot with a rifle, so we're fairly secure. Still, I am putting a great deal of trust in you, Mr. Jackson."

"I want you to decide that you're after the wrong man, and then I want you to go back to the Andes, or wherever it is that you'll be going. I'm not interested in harming you, and I don't want you to harm anyone else."

"A romantic humanist, eh? How nice." Orwell had dug a can of rations out of his pack, opened it, and begun eating. I had no appetite. "I may not be going back to the Andes," continued Orwell. "This leg of mine. Infuriating, but not surprising! I may end up stateside, sitting at some damned desk!"

There were anger and despair in his voice, which surprised me. When I had gotten my million-dollar wounds, I'd felt only gratitude that I was still alive and might not have to go back into action. But then I was no career military man.

"For every man on the lines, there have to be a dozen supporting him," I said carefully. "You know that."

"The Orwells do not sit at desks!" He glanced at his watch, and got out the walkie-talkie. He switched it on and looked at me.

"Channel thirteen," I said. It was the first time he had admitted to being Orwell.

He put the walkie-talkie beside him on the grass.

"It's more than the leg," he said conversationally. "I'm

home on special leave. Stress. My father's death, my sister's death this summer." He flicked his eyes at me. "I believe they think I've lost control. What do you think?"

"You're terrific," I said. "You're sitting there with a pistol at the top of the cliff, you've come two thousand miles to kill a man because you think maybe he seduced your sister, you already tried to kack me three times, and now you want me to tell you whether I think you're out of control? Forget it."

His laugh surprised me. "Don't contribute to the unbalance of the patient, eh? Very sensible. I withdraw the question. I apologize, as well."

Just then the walkie-talkie crackled. Orwell's smile went away. He picked up the radio.

"Dr. Skye? Yes, this is he. I'm listening. Make your statement."

He flicked his eyes toward me. They reminded me of the eyes of a snake. I made myself sit still.

— 26 —

I knew that my anger was a manifestation of fear, but the realization did not bring me calm. I listened irritably and watchfully while Orwell held the walkie-talkie to his ear. He said nothing. John Skye, as many academic types tend to do, was apparently making what he considered a reasonable argument. Intellectuals are inclined to believe that people are, ultimately, rational and that given certain facts they will arrive at proper conclusions. I was not so sure. I watched Orwell's face, trying to read something there that I could not read in his silence.

After a time, he suddenly looked at me. His eyes were without expression. He held up a hand, palm toward me,

in that way people do when they are listening to something important. Then he spoke into the radio.

"Yes. Yes, you have. I am immensely grateful to you,
sir . . . Yes, I understand. I will tell him . . . Yes. Would
you like to talk to him? Yes, here he is . . ."

He held the walkie-talkie toward me, and I took it.

"Yes, John?"

"I told him everything, and he's agreed that he's been
wrong. Thank God! I told him that I'm going back down
to my family, but that it would be best if he doesn't meet
them, since Mattie is pretty worked up about this whole
affair. He understands that. He's agreed to stay with you
for a half hour or so, so I can assure Mattie that I haven't
been fooled and followed back to camp."

"Ah."

"It's all over then. I can't thank you enough, my
friend."

"I'll take it out in beer. Best to Mattie. You'd better
get going."

"Yes."

I thumbed the radio off and retracted the antennae. I
turned to Orwell. He was staring at the ground and had
a curious look about him.

"So John convinced you, eh?"

He raised his eyes. They were hollow-looking, devoid
of feeling. His lips tightened, then one corner of his mouth
flicked up. He nodded toward the west. "He's been out
there watching us with field glasses. Now he'll slide away
and go wherever he's going."

He rose and walked to the edge of the cliff. "This is
unbelievable country! Look at those mountains. The hunting must be good here, too. Elk, deer . . . Do they hunt
bear? They do in Maine. I hear that cougars and grizzlies
are coming back to this country. That would be something, wouldn't it? To meet a grizzly up here." He turned
back to me.

"Your friend Skye spins a fine web of words. The

kind he spun to catch an innocent girl. He thinks he's caught me, too, but I listened to his silence as well as his words. He talked long of my poor sister's early affection for him, and longer still of his own innocence. But he said nothing of taking her to his Vineyard house this summer, or of abandoning her there and taking up with another girl! What a liar sweet Jonathan is! And what a fool."

"No!" I said, getting up. "John didn't take her to the Vineyard . . ." My voice trailed off, since if I insisted that John had not done it, I might be obliged to say who did, and thus put another life in harm's way.

But Orwell was not listening. He was carried away by his own convictions. "He'll go back to his wife and kiddies now, thinking that I'm going to go away forever and he'll never see me again.

"And he's right about that. He won't ever see me again. But I will see him. Sometime when he least expects it! Damn him!"

This last was shouted, for I was already running into the grove of trees.

"You can't get away!" he called after me. "I know that grove from end to end! You can't hide! And if you try to escape across the meadow, I'll just run you down. You're not accustomed to these altitudes, but I am. Give it up! Make it easy on yourself!"

But I was into the trees by then, running, zigzagging, waiting for the thump of bullets. None came. I looked back. I didn't see him. I ran toward the cliff and came to it suddenly. My head swirled and I staggered away. I seized my fear and pushed it from me. I walked along the edge of the cliff. I heard Orwell's voice somewhere behind me, to the north.

"It's no use, Jackson. I babbled too much just now, so you've got to go. Nothing personal, I assure you. We sometimes have to do this sort of thing in my work. Today's friend is tomorrow's foe, or becomes a danger

too costly to keep alive. Come out. I'll make it painless."

I worked my way along the edge of the cliff and came finally to the log that marked the entrance to the ledge leading to Skye's cave. I climbed over the log and found the ledge. I crept out onto it and lay flat, feeling the tug of the void, the suck of the vacuum, drawing me over. I clung facedown to the stone. I was condemned by my silence. I could not trade Jack Scarlotti's life for John Skye's. I tried to dig my fingers into the ledge.

Orwell's voice went away. I heard nothing. Then the voice came again, this time from the south.

"You're very good, Mr. Jackson. I was sure I'd have found you by now. Please step out and save us this trouble. I assure you that I'm better at this sort of thing than you are. The end of this game is certain."

The afternoon sun was slanting shadows toward the east. Below me, the shadows of the great cliffs were already stretching across the valley floor. In not too many hours, it would be night, and not even Orwell could see in the dark.

The thought occurred to him as well. I heard his laughter. "I hope you aren't depending on the night to protect you. I have night glasses, as you should have expected from an old soldier like me. You won't see me, but I will certainly see you. Besides, you won't really last that long. Do come out, so I can shoot you cleanly. Otherwise you may suffer considerable pain before I can dispatch you." Then he said a strange thing: "Oh, God, I'm tired, I'm tired."

A half hour later I heard the brush of leaves and the sound of a snapping branch. He was moving just on the other side of the log.

I stopped breathing. To see me he had to come over the log and look to his left. There was no apparent reason to do so, and he did not. I heard him move on.

The next time, he *would* cross the log, because by then

he'd have searched out all of the logical spots and would be doing the illogical ones.

I got up on my hands and knees, closed my eyes, and crawled down the ledge, brushing my left shoulder against the cliff face as I kept as far as possible from the abyss on my right. I came to a spot where there was no stone for my guiding shoulder to touch, and I opened my eyes. My stomach turned and my head whirled. I was looking a thousand feet straight down over the edge of the ledge, which narrowed sharply and cut back to the left around a corner of stone.

I brought my eyes up and around and saw the cave. It was a wide, hallowed space under a rimrock that made it invisible from above. The nearer corner went back out of my sight. Twenty feet of narrow, rotten ledge linked me to it. The ledge looked too narrow for me to negotiate on my hands and knees. I got up and plastered myself to the rock face and moved ahead.

A flat stone under my feet tipped. I cried out and tried to become part of the cliff. Small stones fell away into the void.

I shifted my feet and moved on, my boots uncertain on the ragged surface of the ledge. I stared at the cave and took coward's steps, feeling rather than seeing. Stones tumbled into the silence beneath my feet. And then I was there, scrambling with undignified haste back under the overhanging rimrock. I felt sweat on my brow and saw that my hands were trembling.

I heard a voice from above.

"Mr. Jackson, I do believe I heard your voice. Thank you. I knew you had to be somewhere near the cliff, but I didn't know where. If you'd like to jump, that will be even better. Please do! Meanwhile, I thank you again for that shout."

I didn't have much time or much to work with. I unlaced my boots and, with my pocketknife, cut a four-inch length of the tongue from one of them. I felt quite doomed

and, curiously, quite detached. I punched a hole in either end of the portion of tongue and knotted a shoelace to it.

I now had a crude but serviceable sling. I was no David, and I was long out of practice, but there was nothing else. I tied a loop in one end of the shoelaces and hooked my middle finger through it. I held the other string between thumb and forefinger.

"Well, well," said Orwell's voice from beyond the bend in the ledge. "What have we here? Where does this lead? I believe I'll find out."

I would probably get only one try, but there were plenty of rocks for ammunition, so I took my time in selecting two: both squared-off pieces of sandstone an inch and a half by an inch and a half that fit pretty nicely into the sling. I said goodbye to Zee and wished her happiness in her new life, and stood up, the sling hanging by my side.

A hand appeared around the corner of the ledge. A moment later Orwell's face peeked around, jerked back, and peeked around again. He was a careful man.

"Ah," he said, "there you are." He swung up the Glock.

I stepped out of sight into the nearer corner of the cave. It was a shallow depression that barely hid me from him.

"You're making a mistake," I called. "Skye wasn't with your sister on the Vineyard."

"Such loyalty. Very commendable, I'm sure," said his voice. "But it's too late for such argument. Don't you agree? Won't you step out and make this easy for us both? No? Well, I should have known you'd not cooperate. I harbor no hard feelings, though, and I hope you feel the same."

I waited thirty seconds, then popped my head out. He was just rounding the corner. I ducked back, counted to ten, stepped out, and whirled the sling.

He heard the whir, looked toward me and swung the Glock up as the rock flew from the sling toward him. The stone did not hit him, but instead hit the cliff beside his

face and shattered. Pieces of the sandstone hit his face and, as he involuntarily turned from the pain, he shifted his weight and the flat stone beneath his feet slipped.

As I fed the second stone into my sling, he teetered and swayed and the hand holding the Glock swung wildly. He groped in vain at the cliff, but found no hold for his hand. Then, quite slowly, it seemed, he leaned outward, and, even more slowly, fell. His eyes were wide and feral, but I thought he had a look of relief on his face. He did not cry out as he disappeared. I listened for a long minute and heard nothing of his passing.

— 27 —

As I crept back along the ledge to the safety of the cliff top, and felt the power of gravity tugging at mc, I thought odd thoughts. Where had Orwell fallen? Into some black hole? Into some heaven or hell? I knew his body was somewhere beneath the ledge, on some outcropping of rock, perhaps, or at the foot of the cliffs, where it might be found or it might not. No matter. Orwell no longer needed that broken husk of what had once been a man. If he still had needs, they were of a different kind. As I climbed over the log hiding the entrance to Skye's cave, I realized that although I'd been careful coming along the ledge, I had not really been afraid of falling. It was as though such falling had no significance just then.

I walked down from the cliffs through the darkening night, and knew that I had had enough of violence, of revenge, of retribution. I found no place for it in my soul. I located my car and drove to my motel. I was tired. I had a Coors and thought about the bother which would ensue when I told the sheriff what had happened. I real-

ized that the law had no more significance to me in this matter than the thought of falling had when I left the cave. What could the law do for Orwell or for me? Time enough to deal with that issue when the police learned, as sometime soon they surely would, of the blue Blazer at the foot of the Goulding Trail. I phoned the airport and, it being mid-week, got a space on the next morning's early flight to Albuquerque. Then I phoned Wilma Skye.

"It's all over," I said. "John convinced the guy that he was after the wrong man."

"Did he? Well, that's good. Where is the man now?"

"The last time I saw him, he was near the top of the cliffs," I said. "He told me he hoped I had no hard feelings about things."

"And do you?"

"None I can't live with. I'm heading home tomorrow morning. Please tell everyone goodbye for me. And when John comes down out of the hills, tell him I'll have a bluefish waiting for him when he gets to the island."

"If you go down to Francisco's you can tell Billy Jo goodbye yourself."

"Billy Jo and I are just friends, nothing more."

She sighed. "So she tells me. Well, I can't say I'm sorry about that. She's just a girl . . ."

"No," I said, "she's not just a girl. She's a beautiful young woman who makes my glands jump up and down. It just happens that I have a commitment to another woman who does the same things to my hormones and takes up all my thoughts too. Say goodbye to Mack. Thanks for everything."

But I couldn't let it go at that, so I drove down to Francisco's. Inside, I saw Billy Jo. She was smiling across a table at Grant Taylor. They looked like a pair. Maybe his boss would give her a job, as he'd said he would, and she would have a chance to compare her fantasies of adventure with the realities of law enforcement. And while she did that, she could search out the realities of Grant

Taylor. She was at the right age for such explorations. I backed out the door.

In Albuquerque there was a seat available on a TWA flight to Boston via St. Louis. I landed in Boston a bit after five, and telephoned the hospital which told me that Geraldine Miles had checked out. After I identified myself as a policeman interested in her case, I was told that she had gone to Martha's Vineyard with her aunt and uncle. I ran to catch the bus to Woods Hole.

The bus and ferry people have an infamous schedule that seems deliberately designed to keep passengers from making connections. A lot of buses to Boston leave Woods Hole just before the ferries from the island arrive there, and a lot of buses to Woods Hole arrive just after the ferries have departed for the island. No one knows who sets up these schedules, or why, but there is no islander who has not, at one time or another, been victimized by them.

I was lucky. I caught the last boat to the island. I stood on the deck and felt the soft air soothe me. It was a far cry from the high, dry air of Colorado. I was glad to be breathing it. I was glad to be breathing any air at all.

I got into one of the taxis at the dock in Vineyard Haven. The driver stared at me.

"J.W. What are you doing in a cab? You never ride in cabs."

"I'll have you know I've ridden in several this very year. Take me home, Jeeves. I'm a weary traveler. Any bonito around yet?"

"I'm just a taxi driver. I don't have time to go traveling or fishing like you rich, retired types. How should I know?"

"Well, are there?"

"There are a lot of boats around the Oak Bluffs dock."

"Excellent news."

I had him drop me off at the top of my driveway. I got a week's worth of mail out of my box and walked through the Vineyard night down the long, sandy drive to my

house. I never lock my door, so I never need to find a house key. So far, nobody has stolen the place. I was glad to see it again, and went inside and turned on the lights.

There was no message on the answering machine, because I don't have an answering machine. The only sounds were of the wind in the trees and a night bird I could not identify. I went to the freezer and got out some scallops I'd frozen the winter before and put them, Baggie and all, into some hot water to thaw. I found a Sam Adams beer in the fridge, and had some of that. Coors could not compare. I got a flashlight and went out to the garden and came back with some carrots and broccoli. I cut the carrots and broccoli into pieces and parboiled them while I got some rice started. I put the carrots and broc into my big wok with some olive oil. I had another Sam Adams and wokked the veggies for a while with just a bit of Szechuan stir-fry sauce, then added the thawed scallops. When the wok stuff was ready, so was the rice, so I loaded up a plate of both, laced it with soy sauce, and had at it. Delish! It was good to be home.

The next day, I was early to Collins Beach, where I keep my dinghy. I rowed out to the *Shirley J.* and found her well. There was only a breath of wind, so I motored out of the harbor and headed north across the shallows toward Oak Bluffs. One of the joys of a catboat is that she'll sail on water so thin you could make it into windowpanes. For the shoally Martha's Vineyard waters, no better boat has ever been designed.

There were already boats anchored around the ferry dock when I got there, but there was plenty of room for me. I dropped the hook and got out my gear. The water was like undulating glass in the morning light, and the sun was a giant grapefruit low in the eastern sky. It was going to be a hot one.

By noon, I was stripped to my daring bikini bathing suit and sweating. I had two nice five-pound bonito in my fishbox and was feeling pretty good. The wind was coming

up from the southwest and the tide had turned so that the *Shirley J.* now swung in the opposite direction on her anchor line. It was time to go home.

In those light airs, it was a two-hour trip under sail, but I was in no hurry. I was, after all, one of those people out there in the sound in a boat about whom people on shore often said enviously, "Boy. Wouldn't it be nice to be out there on a day like this?"

I tacked in past a crowd of people on the Edgartown town dock, waved at some waves I received, slid past the yacht club, and fetched my stake with an eggshell landing. I looked around. No one was watching. There are hundreds of observers when I come in too fast or too slow or otherwise screw up my landings, but never anyone there to see me do it right. It's a law of the sea.

I rowed ashore and took one of my fish to the market. Bonito is a cousin of tuna, and is oily enough to be good for seviche, so I took the other one home just for that purpose. Bluefish is about the best fish there is for seviche, but I didn't have a bluefish, so bonito would do. The secret of a great seviche is using fresh, oily fish and adding hot peppers to the other veggies. The lime juice cuts the oil, and peppers give the dish a nice bounce. I have been known to make a meal out of my seviche alone.

Seviche was not the only thing on my mind. I needed to double-check something. I dialed Weststock College, told the switchboard lady that I had been told that a Dr. Jonathan Scarlotti was on the faculty and that I wanted to find out if he really was so I could interview him for an article I was writing. Yes, she said, Dr. Scarlotti was indeed a member of the faculty, and would I like to talk to him? I said no, that I was between planes, but would catch him later, thanks very much.

I hung up and had a beer. Jack Kennedy, Jack Scarlotti, Jack be nimble, Jack be quick, Jack of all trades. Jack of hearts.

I decided to think about something else, and got to work on the batch of seviche: cutting a couple of cups of half-inch bonito cubes; peeling and chopping a big tomato; chopping up a medium-sized onion, about a quarter of a big red pepper, and a couple of little chili peppers; crunching two small garlic cloves; adding about a half cup of tomato juice and not quite as much lime juice and olive oil; then tossing in some chopped parsley, a bit of thyme, and some salt and pepper. I put all this together and stuck it in the fridge to stand overnight.

Salivating in expectation, I then went out and weeded the remains of my garden, which was only a shadow of its earlier self, but still had plenty to offer. By the time I had reached my psychological weeding barrier, the sun was well to the west and it was martini time. I collected crackers and cheese, a pitcher of ice, a cold bottle of Stoli, and a glass, and went up to the balcony. The tempo of my island life, so interrupted by Orwell, was reestablishing itself.

There were still tyro surf sailors learning their game on the tranquil waters of Sengekontacket Pond. Beyond the pond, the highway on the spit of sand linking Edgartown to Oak Bluffs was busy with cars headed home from the beach. Beyond them, sailboats stood white against the dark sea and evening sky. I made myself a drink and cut some cheese and sat and ate as I gazed out over the serene beauty before me. I could not imagine a place I'd rather be.

If Zee were here.

I wished she were beside me. We'd been apart for two weeks, but a world of time had passed. If she left the island for good, could I bear to stay without her?

Could I bear to leave with her?

I had another icy martini and watched the night come down. The Cape Pogue Light began to shine. Across the dark waters of Nantucket Sound, lights on distant Cape

Cod flickered into view. Stars began to appear. After a long time, I went downstairs, stirred the seviche, and went to bed.

The next afternoon I drove to Iowa's house to take his family some seviche and to see how Geraldine Miles was doing. Iowa was fishing with Geraldine, but Jean was home. She thanked me for the seviche. I thought she looked rather grim.

"Don't tell Iowa that it's raw fish, and maybe he'll eat it," I said. "How's your niece?"

Women are realists. "The bandages are off of her face, but she'll never look the same. She has more plastic surgery ahead of her. She may be pretty, but she won't be beautiful again. I could kill that man."

"How's the rest of her? How does she feel?"

"She's walking well. She has some trouble with one of her arms. It doesn't work just right, but she says it's getting better. She's in good spirits, but she's . . . fragile. I don't know what she'll do if she ever meets him again. And I don't know if she'll ever be able to trust any man again. It's a hateful thing he did to her."

Yes, it was. Instead of making Cramer whole, love had torn him apart. His center could not hold. His anarchical side had been loosed upon Geraldine.

"He's here, you know," Jean said. "Here on the island."

I felt a coldness in my soul.

"You've been gone," she said, "so you wouldn't know. He came four days ago. He phoned her. Can you imagine that? Said he was sorry. Begged her to forgive him. He got his car from the police and came out here to the house and just parked outside. We called the police and they came and he went away. We went to the judge and got a court order for him to stay away, and the police gave it to him. But I don't have much faith in court orders, if you want to know the truth."

Trouble in paradise. I'd had enough of it in Weststock

and Colorado. "I'll be glad to bring over a sleeping bag and hang around," I said. "He probably won't do anything if someone's here. I don't have anything better to do for a couple of weeks, and by then he'll probably have run out of money or time or both, and be gone back to Iowa."

"We don't ever leave her alone," said Jean. "We're afraid he'll . . . I don't know." She put her hand up and tucked in some imaginary strand of loose hair. "The police are being very good about it. If we call, they'll come immediately. Still . . ."

"Do you have an extra bedroom? If you don't, I can sleep in my truck."

"I only worry when Dan's gone and Gerry is here with me. Look at what we've come to." She opened a closet door and showed me a shotgun. "It's loaded. Dan took us to the Rod and Gun Club and made Gerry and me shoot it. I can't believe I have to have a shotgun in my closet just to live in my own house!"

She was right. It was a sorry way to have to live. "Dan just wants you and Geraldine to be safe," I said.

"Safe." The word was short and brutal, like a gunshot. Then she looked up at me and gave me a small smile. "No, dear, you don't need to stay with us. Dan isn't going to leave us alone anymore. We talked it over at breakfast. The three of us are going to stay together until that man leaves the island."

"Good." I tried to make light of it. "In that case, don't tell Dan that I got two bonito yesterday. If he hears that, he may change his mind about staying home."

"More likely, he'll make Gerry and me go fishing with him, and leave the house with nobody in it! That'd be just like him, bless his soul!"

"I'll come by now and then," I said.

"You'll be welcome."

As things turned out, the first time I showed up was nearly the last.

— 28 —

At dawn the next morning, on Dogfish Bar, where I was casting for bluefish, something very large took my Ballistic Missile. Almost certainly a large female bass. There is a thrill to catching a bass which is different than the one you get catching anything else, and I felt it then. The strength of the fish, the rising light, the loneliness of the beach, all combined to create a wonderful half hour.

The water is shallow at Dogfish Bar, and there are rocks on the bottom to snag your line if you're not lucky. My fish did not want to come in. It chugged away with my line, then reluctantly let me haul it back toward the beach. It swam up toward Gay Head and took me with it, over the rocky beach. I slowed it and led it in closer to shore. It turned and swam back toward Menemsha. I followed over the rocks and hauled it in even closer. I could almost see it. It was a major-league fish.

Then it was gone, and I was reeling in a parted line. I had no regrets except for the loss of the leader and lure since, after all, I was after bluefish and would have let the bass go if I had landed it. Now Nature would have to remove the hook and in time would do so, rusting it in two and allowing the lure to fall from the lip of the great fish so that no harm would, in the end, be done.

I re-rigged and fished some more. A dozen casts later I had my bluefish, a little guy who, as fish will, had mistaken my popper for something more tasty. He looked exactly the right size to fit into my frying pan, so I gave up fishing for the nonce, walked back to the Toyota, and

drove out of Indian Country back down island for breakfast.

Juice, fried fresh baby bluefish, eggs over light, toast made from homemade bread, black coffee. The gods never had it so good.

It was a prince of a day. A new sun in a clear sky. Just enough wind to move sailboats over the water. A day for beaching and kite flying. Already the cars were lining up along the road across the pond, and young parents were hauling children, blankets, cribs, umbrellas, beach balls, and kites down close to the warm and gentle water.

I then mowed the lawn with my almost-as-good-as-new lawn mower, salvaged long ago from the Edgartown dump during the golden age of dump picking, before the environmental fundamentalists seized control of that once best of island secondhand stores and changed it into a neat, antiseptic place which soon, no doubt, will demand passports from its users. I am not one to mow my lawn any more often than it absolutely needs it, but it was getting hairy enough for me to begin to lose things in it, so a clipping was in order. I clipped it wearing sandals and nothing else, as is my occasional wont.

By the time I was through, I was sweating all over and in need of some beer and a swim. I got into my dinky bikini, put a couple of Sam Adams in a cooler, and drove to South Beach. A few hundred people were there ahead of me, but I got into four-wheel drive and turned east and got away from most of them. A half mile down the beach, I laid out my old bedspread on the sand, nailed it down with the cooler and my big beach towel, and plunged into the briny.

Perfect. I swam out and back in, floating on my back amid the mild breakers, wondered if there really were sharks just off shore, as some fishermen had told me there were, and finally came in over the thin strand of pebbles that hung on the sand just where the waves broke. I tow-

eled off my head and hands and lay down on the bedspread with a beer. I felt good. If Zee had been there, I
would have felt perfect.

In mid-August, the sun is in the same place in the sky
as it is in mid-April, so tans are hard to maintain. I gave
mine two hours, then packed up. There were many kites
still in the air, indicating that those who were vacationing
on the island were not about to abandon the golden sands
so soon in the day. I didn't blame them. If I had been
paying as much to be here as they were, I wouldn't have
left either.

At home, I showered off the salt in the outdoor shower,
slid into more modest clothes, and went to Iowa's house
to see how things were and to do some bragging about
my bluefish. As I drove up, I saw a car with Iowa plates
parked in front. Between the car and the house were Iowa,
Jean, Geraldine Miles, and Lloyd Cramer.

Lloyd Cramer's arms were moving up and down in
gestures of appeal and he was leaning forward. Geraldine
Miles had Iowa's shotgun in her hands and was pointing
it at Cramer. I stopped the Toyota, flicked my CB to
channel nine, and sent out an SOS to anyone whose ears
were up to get the police to Iowa's house. I repeated the
message, but didn't wait for an answer. I got out and
walked toward Lloyd Cramer through air thick with the
sound of his voice. That voice was a droning plea, a series
of promises. I thought the shotgun muzzle swung a bit
toward me.

"Hold it, J.W.," said Iowa in a strained voice that
spoke through Cramer's babble. "Gerry's not used to
guns."

"It's me, Geraldine," I said. "Nobody's going to get
hurt."

The gun muzzle wavered away. I walked slowly up to
Cramer, my ears filled with the mad sound of his voice.
He was begging to be taken back, swearing love eternal,

promising to reform, admitting guilt, pleading for one more chance.

I looked at Geraldine. The shotgun was none too steady. "Point the gun at the ground," I said over the sound of Cramer's voice. I put what I hoped was a friendly smile on my face. "I don't think you want to hit me, but that's what might happen if you shoot. Please, Gerry, point the gun at the ground."

I was beside Cramer now, but he didn't notice me. He saw only Geraldine. He was pouring out his convoluted soul in a steady stream of words, asking her to forgive him and take him back. I saw the shotgun barrel drop and Iowa move carefully toward his niece.

"I think he's got a gun," said Iowa's flat voice.

"Mr. Cramer," I said, and touched his shoulder. He swung an arm as though to brush away a fly and his voice continued to fill the yard with pleas. "It's time to leave, Mr. Cramer," I said. "Geraldine doesn't want to talk to you now. Come along." I stepped around in front of him, beneath him and Geraldine.

He was a big man. His eyes were wild and full of tears and focused behind me on Geraldine. There was indeed something thrust inside his shirt that didn't belong there. I said, "Mr. Cramer," and the eyes found mine. "I know you love her," I said, "but she needs more time. Let's get you back to your car. You need some rest. I know you don't want to hurt anybody, so it's best that we leave."

He was crying. "I don't want to hurt anybody! I never did! I love Gerry!"

"I know you do," I said. "Come on. Let's go to the car. I'll go with you. We can talk. I'm sick of trouble and I know you are, too."

I put a hand on his arm and he blinked at me and we stepped back toward his car. For a moment I allowed myself to think that the situation was going to work out. Then he suddenly said, "I know you!" He pushed me

away with a big hand and with his other groped inside his shirt. "You were there in her room! You're the one! You want to take her away from me! I won't let you! I'll kill you both!"

The hand came out of his shirt with a pistol in it. He swung it toward the people behind me. I got hold of his wrist with both hands and twisted it to one side as he squeezed off the first shot. Then his other hand was a fist as big and hard as a brick, beating at me, pounding me down. Another shot went off between our bodies. I got a knee into him, but that great thundering fist was making the world fade. Then I lost the wrist and he jerked away and swung the pistol toward me. I went for him again as the pistol swung into line and a shot boomed.

Cramer's face disappeared in a flower of blood and bone, and he went backward onto the ground. I turned to see Geraldine Miles with the shotgun in her hands. Her face was white as whey, but she was struggling to pump another round into the firing chamber and coming forward, her eyes fixed on Cramer. I turned back. The pistol had fallen from Cramer's hand. He wasn't going to use it anymore. In the distance I heard sirens coming. I put out a hand toward Geraldine as she stepped toward Cramer's body and raised the shotgun again.

"It's okay, Geraldine," I said. "It's all over. He's as dead as he's ever going to get."

Geraldine said a word which at one time would have been called unprintable, and shot Cramer again. I took the shotgun away before she could give him another round and thumbed on the safety. Behind us, Jean and Iowa stared at us, then came forward. Jean took Geraldine in her arms.

"It's all right, dear," said Iowa gently. "All of us are all right now."

Geraldine looked at her uncle. Her battered face was red and contorted. Her voice was like a knife. "He's dead! He's dead! The turd is dead!"

I had rarely seen such hatred on so young a face. I wondered if it would ever go completely away.

"I thank you," I said to her. "If it wasn't for you, I'd be lying there instead of him."

Geraldine stared at me and said nothing.

"And if it wasn't for you, J.W.," said Iowa in a shaky voice, "we might be lying there. What a world we live in."

The first police car came into the yard. The driver took one look at things and called for a lot of backup. Then he went to Cramer's body, felt for a pulse, stood up, and looked around in a confused way. We all waited in the yard for the rest of the police to come. It was a soft August afternoon. Overhead, the pale blue sky held a few gentle-looking clouds. At South Beach, the kites were no doubt still flying. On the green grass of Iowa's front yard, Cramer's blood soaked slowly into the ground.

— 29 —

"You're always where the trouble is," said Corporal Dominic Agganis.

"I'm just not lucky, I guess."

"You'd better get out of the trouble business," said Agganis. "You've already used up eight of your lives."

"You've talked me into it. From now on, you can have all the trouble. "If you're done with me, I'm going home."

"Oh, I'm done with you, but other people aren't." He nodded across the yard toward the house where Iowa, Jean, and Geraldine were talking with the Edgartown police, the sheriff of The County of Dukes County, another state cop, and some other cops I didn't recognize. The yard was full of them, too. "The girl will be charged. We got a hotshot DA with political ambitions, and you can

be sure he'll bring her to trial if he can. There'll be a grand jury, at least, and you, my friend, will be on the witness list."

"Good. Self-defense. She saved my life and her own."

"So you say." He yawned. "We'll see what the grand jury says. I got to go talk to the lady in question. See you in court." He walked toward the house.

I drove home and poured myself a double vodka on the rocks and went up to the balcony. The view was as lovely as ever, but it meant nothing to me. I had felt this way before, and knew that in time I would feel better, that I would stop feeling empty and angry just because justice was rare and love elusive.

I drank my vodka and tried to let the beauty of the world flow into me. I had read that when the Navaho poets walk across the great, dry, brutal desert which is their home, they are not aliens to it. "Beauty before me," they say. "Beauty behind me. Beauty all around me." Martha's Vineyard, green and golden, surrounded by the eternal sea, was no desert, but rather a small Eden. Still I felt remote from it. I tried to let its gentle splendor enter my eyes and the sounds of its gulls and songbirds enter my ears and find my soul.

When it was dark, I went downstairs, still moody, knowing that I would have a bad night. Of all the earth's life-forms, only man wishes things were different. It is his bane, his absurdity.

But bad nights end, and the sea is a great restorer. It is indifferent to our fears and joys, merciless, beautiful, terrible, and nurturing. In the morning I went down to the harbor and rowed out to the *Mattie*, John Skye's lovely old catboat. She was beginning to collect some hair around her waterline, but was otherwise fine. Because he had chosen to spend so much time in Colorado, John had barely used her this summer. As I checked her bilge and bowline, I thought of Dr. Jonathan Scarlotti and his little

band of graduate students, who had not had time to go sailing in the *Mattie*. I wondered if Dr. Scarlotti would ever know that he had perhaps indirectly been the cause of the deaths of Bernie Orwell and her brother, and what effect it would have upon him if he knew. I wondered if I should drive up to Weststock and make sure he at least knew his role in those deaths. The prospect appealed to part of me. I thought Dr. Scarlotti was exactly the sort of exploiter of women that Orwell had hated.

I rowed to the *Shirley J.*, put a bag of clothes and a cooler of food and drink aboard, and put to sea. I needed to sort things out.

I sailed on a broad reach all the way to Woods Hole, caught a fair tide through the narrows, and beat into Hadley's. I wound up the centerboard, found a shallow spot far from the other boats anchored there, and dropped the hook. I didn't want company. I took a swim, then sat in the wide cockpit and watched the yachts come in for the night. I was still there when the stars came out.

The next day I had a fair wind all the way to Newport, and the day after that to Block Island, where I anchored for two days while I walked that lovely little island from end to end, and ate my lunches on a long veranda overlooking the old harbor. On the third day, the rains came, so I stayed in the cuddy cabin and read again Childers' wonderful *Riddle of the Sands*, a required item in any ship's library. In the middle of the afternoon, it began to rain even harder. I put on my daring bathing suit, so no water-soaked sailors who might be looking would be shocked, got some soap, and went out into the cockpit and had a shower. The rain was hard and cold and felt good. It kept raining, so that night I cooked inside.

The following morning was gray and cool, with spats of rain blowing in on a southwest wind. I hauled anchor and beat out to sea, taking a bit of a pounding as I cleared the harbor entrance, but then having a better time when

I headed north to clear Sandy Point, and finally having a fine following wind as I swung up toward Martha's Vineyard.

I sailed all day and into the night, because the *Shirley J.*, for all her many virtues, is not too swift. In the last of the light, I dropped the hook outside the entrance to Cuttyhunk, that tiny, westernmost member of the Elizabeth Islands. The people on Cuttyhunk live there partly because they like to be alone. I understood that desire, and did not go ashore.

At first light, I pulled anchor. In light morning breezes, I loafed along on the Buzzards Bay side of Nashawena and Pasque, then cut through Robinson's Hole, and caught the east tide past Tarpaulin Cove toward West Chop. The late morning wind came up and I had a fine sail. I rounded West Chop, crossed to East Chop, noted that the bonito fishermen were still at work around the Oak Bluffs ferry dock, and headed for home close-hauled.

I was back on the stake by mid-afternoon, and ashore a half hour later. I put my gear in the Toyota and walked down to the Navigator Room for a beer. When I came out, the chief was drinking coffee across the street in front of the Dock Street Coffee Shop. I walked across.

"Home is the sailor, home from the sea," he said.

"As the general said, 'I have returned.' "

"Your millions of fans will be greatly relieved," said the chief. "Your boat's been gone for eight days."

"My, Grandma, what big eyes you have."

"The Law never sleeps. I've been trying to get hold of you for a couple of days. The harbormaster told me the *Shirley J.* was gone. Where you been?"

"Sailing, sailing, over the bounding main. Block Island and points between here and there. Why do you want to see me?"

"The DA is going to convene a grand jury."

"I figured as much. I guess I would, too, if I was the DA. A man's been shot to death, after all."

"I imagine he's going to make as much as he can about that second shot after Cramer was down."

"I'll testify that Cramer seemed alive to me and that I was in fear of my life."

"The doctors will testify that he was probably dead."

"I'm no doctor and neither is Geraldine Miles. I thought he was still alive."

"Geraldine told us that you said he was dead."

"She was confused. She only wanted to save my life. His pistol was still in his hand."

"When we got there, it wasn't."

"I kicked it out after she shot at him the second time. I was in fear of my life. I'll testify to that."

"You spent a lot of that time in fear of your life. You got a lawyer?"

"No. I don't trust lawyers."

"Maybe you'd better get one. Perjury is a bad rap."

I spread my arms. "Perjury? Me, commit perjury? What are you talking about? I'm a fisherman! Would a fisherman lie?!"

The chief stared up the street. His mouth was kinking, almost as if he wanted to laugh. Instead, he drank some coffee.

"I don't think a grand jury will bring an indictment against her," he said, "but you never know."

"They won't, if I have anything to say about it."

"So I gather. There's another thing. The Sheriff's Department in La Plata County, Colorado, say they've found a car rented in Jackson, Wyoming, by one Gordon Berkeley Orwell, but carrying the New Jersey plates that are supposed to be on Orwell's New Jersey Jeep Cherokee. They wonder if you know anything about that."

"I'm the one who told them to look for that car. Where'd they find it?"

"How should I know? At the foot of a trail that goes up some cliffs or other. They want to know if you know where Orwell is. Seems that they talked to John Skye and

he said he saw you and Orwell at the top of those cliffs. The sheriff hasn't talked to anybody who's seen Orwell since. Wonders if you know where he is."

Where was Orwell? Was he smiling down at me from heaven? Frowning up at me from hell? Floating disembodied in the primal fluids of the universe? Had he been reabsorbed into the World Soul? Had he seen the white light of Truth? Were the energies that once had taken the form of his earthly life been recycled into some new shape? A flower? A fish? A cancerous cell in some smoker's lung?

I told the chief about how I'd taken Orwell up to the top of the cliffs so he could talk with John. Then I said, "After he and John talked, I talked to John on the walkie-talkie. John told me that he had convinced Orwell that he was after the wrong man. I stayed there on the cliffs for a while, then came down. The last time I saw Orwell, he was near the top of the cliffs. The last thing he said to me was that he hoped I had no hard feelings."

"You didn't toss him off the cliff, then?"

"I have acrophobia," I said. "I get sick if I get too close to the edge of high places. Ask John Skye. Ask Mattie. Ask the twins. Ask John's niece. They'll all tell you."

"He was scheduled to return to duty, but he didn't show up. Apparently very unlike him. Do you think he was suicidal?"

"I think you have to be a little off center to do some of the things he did. I don't know if he was suicidal."

"They say he was on special leave. Stress syndrome, or some such thing. Do you think he might have jumped?"

"I don't read minds."

He finished his coffee and dropped the paper cup into a refuse disposal container. Edgartown is a neat town, and the chief would never drop his cup in the gutter.

"I don't read minds either," he said. "Glad I don't. I wouldn't want to know what a lot of people are thinking."

"How's Geraldine Miles?"

"Women are tough. I just hope this doesn't make her

too tough. It's not good to be too tough." He walked up Main Street.

I went home, showered, shaved, brushed my teeth, and dressed up in my fancy clothes—Vineyard Red slacks, a blue shirt with a red anchor over the pocket, boat shoes without socks, my belt with little sailboats on it, and called Iowa's house. Jean answered.

"I want to take your niece out on a date," I said. "Do you think she'll go?"

"I don't know, J.W. Why don't you ask her?"

"Put her on the line."

Geraldine's voice said, "Hello?"

"J. W. Jackson here," I said. "I want to take you to dinner. I just got back from a week at sea, and I need to look across the table at a real, live girl and talk to her instead of to myself. Can I pick you up at six?"

"I don't know. I'm not sure . . ."

"Great! I'll see you at six. You have a white dress?"

"Well . . ."

"A white blouse will do. You look terrific in white. See you at six. Wear your dancing shoes."

I rang off and made myself a martini, wondering if I knew what I was doing.

At six, I picked up Geraldine. She was wearing low heels, a dark skirt, and a white blouse. Her hair was combed so that it partially covered the side of her face that was most hurt.

"Very nice," I said. "The Veronica Lake look."

"Who's Veronica Lake?"

"A woman in my father's world. Let's go." I gave her my arm.

We ate at the Navigator Room, which not only has excellent food, but also has the best view of any Edgartown restaurant. She ate with little bites and had white wine. Afterward I talked her into having coffee and a cognac. Everything went on my plastic card. I had so much on there already that a bit more didn't hurt at all.

When we were through with our cognac, I walked with her down to the town wharf and we went up to the balcony and looked at the boats. The stars were just beginning to come out. There was a soft wind from the south.

After that I took her to Oak Bluffs.

"What are we doing here?" she asked, with a small smile.

"We're going to dance," I said.

"Oh, I don't know. I . . ."

"Anytime before last year, you'd have been taking a chance if you danced with me," I said, "because I was terrible. I never knew where my feet were, or what I was supposed to do. But Zee Madieras has made me into a new man. She showed me how to dance any kind of dance, and now I'm going to show off with you. Come on."

We went into the Atlantic Connection. It was crowded and the music hurt my ears, but the dance floor had space for two more, and I led her there. I put my arm around her waist, took her right hand in my left one, and stood there, holding her gently against me.

After a while she looked up at me. "This is it? This is the way you dance?"

I smiled down at her. "Great, isn't is? As long as I don't move my feet, I can dance any kind of dance."

"And this is what your friend Zee taught you?"

"A terrific teacher. She changed my life. Isn't this fun? God, when I think of the years I was ashamed to step out onto the floor!"

Geraldine put her head against my chest and began to laugh.

We danced until pretty late, and then I took her home. That week I took her fishing and clamming and quahogging. I took her out dancing two more times. We danced at the Hot Tin Roof and again at the Connection. Toward the end, I began to shuffle around a little, just to show I was willing to experiment. When I took her home that night, she pulled my head down and kissed me.

"Thanks," she said. "Uncle Dan says that Zee Madieras is due home tomorrow. I guess that means you won't be taking me out anymore."

"There are a lot of nice guys who'll want to take you out," I said. "Just give them a chance."

That night I didn't sleep too well.

Zee's ferry came in mid-afternoon. I had spent the day doing things that needed doing around the house. I was under the Toyota trying to find an irksome little oil leak when I heard a car coming down my driveway. I suspected that I needed a new gasket for my oil pan. On the other hand, maybe I could get away with just tightening a couple of bolts that had loosened up. The car stopped and a door opened. I slid out from under the Toyota and looked up at Zee.

My heart turned over.

I brushed at some grease on my shirt, then looked up again. Zee was walking toward me. She was wearing a pale blouse and skirt that emphasized her dark loveliness. She walked in beauty, like the night, right up to me.

"Well," I said. "You've come back."

"Yes."

"Were your conferences enlightening?"

"Yes."

"Have you made any decisions?"

"Yes."

"Do you have a lot to talk about?"

"Yes."

"With me?"

"Yes."

"I have a lot to talk about with you, too," I said, "but first things first. Will you marry me?"

"Yes," she said. "Yes, I will."